HERITAGE OF POWER BOOK 3

LINDSAY BUROKER

Origins

Heritage of Power, Book 3
by Lindsay Buroker
Copyright © 2018 Lindsay Buroker

No part of this book may be reproduced, scanned, or distributed in any printed or electronic form without permission. Please do not participate in or encourage piracy of copyrighted materials in violation of the author's rights. Thank you for respecting the hard work of this author.

This is a work of fiction. Names, characters, places, and incidents either are the product of the author's imagination or are used fictitiously, and any resemblance to locales, events, business establishments, or actual persons—living or dead—is entirely coincidental.

CHAPTER 1

SWEAT DRIPPED DOWN THE SIDES of Lieutenant Rysha Ravenwood's face, but she dared not take her hands from the hilt of her sword to wipe it away. Her spectacles fogged in the cool evening air, leaving her opponent a blur.

A barrage of blows came her way. High, high, low, followed by a swipe from the side. Mud squished under her boots as she danced about, doing her best to anticipate those attacks and block in time. Only quick reflexes and a good sense of balance kept her on her feet, her opponent's sword clashing off the edge of her own rather than slicing into her.

Her spectacles fogged further, and frustration welled inside of her. She could barely *see,* damn it.

She wouldn't yield, wasn't even sure her ferocious opponent would *let* her yield, but she longed to ask for a three-second break so she could wipe her lenses. This wasn't fair. But she knew a real enemy—whether airship pirate, Cofah soldier, or dragon—wouldn't give her a break.

Rysha felt a modicum of pride that she was doing as well as she was. She hadn't been able to shift the momentum and take the offensive, but at least she had so far blocked everything the big, muscular man threw at her. Then she leaned her weight into her front foot in an attempt to counter a parry, and a boot that she hadn't noticed swept in, hooking her behind the knee.

Before she could compensate, it pulled her leg out from under her. She lurched backward, trying to regain her balance, but her opponent surged in to take advantage. He slashed toward her face with his sword. While she was busy jerking her blade up to defend, he slammed his weight into her chest.

Rysha fell backward, her shoulders hitting the mud with a squish. She tried to turn the fall into a roll, as she'd been taught, both to save her back and to put distance between her and her foe, but he was too fast. Weight settled on her chest—it was either his knee or a steam carriage—and the edge of his sword came to rest against her cheek.

She opened her hand and let the *chapaharii* blade, Dorfindral, fall from her fingers. A sense of disgruntlement emanated from the sword. Had she been battling a sorcerer or dragon instead of a normal man, she knew the blade would have objected even more, maybe taking over her body and guiding her to defend herself more competently. She was tempted to whisper the Old Iskandian words that told the sword to "take over," just in case it could do something to get the weight off her chest so she could breathe, but that might escalate this encounter from a sparring match to a blood bath. One that would mostly involve *her* blood, she wagered.

"You don't just watch the *blade*, Lieutenant," her foe—and instructor—Colonel Therrik growled. "You need to be aware of everything your enemy is doing. The whole body is a threat. And don't forget to watch what's going on around you too. Enemies don't always stand back and attack you one at a time."

"I don't think she can watch much of anything with her spectacles all fogged up and spattered with mud," came Captain Kaika's dry observation from the side.

Therrik finally removed his blade and his knee, grumbling as he stood up. Rysha didn't catch all the words, but it sounded like, "…can't believe they let some blind kid into the elite troops."

Her cheeks heated from more than the exertion of the sword fight. Technically, she was only in the elite troops *training* program. The aches and pains afflicting her entire body reminded her that she'd endured a sixteen-mile run with a full pack and all her gear that morning, followed by hand-to-hand combat with the other recruits. This sword work was an after-hours extracurricular activity for her and the other three *chapaharii* sword wielders, preparation for the inevitable return of hostile dragons to Iskandian skies.

"Maybe she can get a dragon to fix her eyesight," Colonel Grady, another elite troops officer who'd been selected to wield one of the blades, observed as Rysha pushed herself to her feet and wiped her spectacles. "I understand the one with the temple is back in town and offering his services as a magical medic. Magical medic, I like that." He grinned, a boyish grin that seemed odd on a man who'd probably killed hundreds of people during his career. Then he fished a worn journal out of his pocket and pulled a pencil nub out of the spirals. It looked like the notebooks the pilots kept for making flight-related calculations in the air, but his was full of words written in a tiny script. He found an open spot and scribbled in it. "Magical medic. For when you've got a headache." He grinned again. "Not a true rhyme, but I can make it work with the right inflection."

Perhaps seeing Rysha's curious expression, Kaika explained, "Colonel Grady fancies himself a bard."

"More of a songwriter," the colonel explained, ignoring a groan from Therrik. "But I do perform with my brother and his troupe in between missions."

"All those language schools the army sent you to, and *that's* what you do with your education?" Therrik demanded.

"'Tis a poor brain that can only figure out one thing to do with a language." Grady put his notebook away, still grinning. "Who said that? That's a quote."

"Trudusky," Rysha supplied.

"Hah, I knew it."

"Let's get back to work," Therrik said. "No *dragon* is going to be defeated by someone singing at him."

"Are you sure?" Grady asked. "I seem to remember a fairy tale about a maiden winning a dragon's love by singing to him."

"You're *not* a maiden."

"But I'm a handsome and virile soldier. I might attract a female dragon with my words." Grady looked at Rysha, as if she might know something about the subject.

Rysha grimaced. The new female dragon, Shulina Arya, had appeared earlier in the week when she'd been in the middle of running the obstacle course. While soldiers all over the field had shouted in alarm and run for their weapons, the dragon had alighted atop the wall and asked Rysha if she needed assistance going over it. Rysha had refused with a polite, "No, thank you." A few seconds later, as she clawed her way through the low crawl, Shulina Arya had requested more stories. Finally, after Rysha made it through the course, and the whole fort had been alerted to the dragon's presence, Shulina Arya had flown down to stand next to her, then asked if she should have appeared in ferret form, so as not to alarm the humans. As if it hadn't already been too late for that.

Fortunately, the soldiers had realized she was one of the friendly dragons before doing anything stupid, such as shooting at her, but everyone was now referring to Shulina Arya as Rysha's dragon. This wasn't the first time a male soldier had asked her if female dragons shape-shifted and enjoyed spending time with virile men. At least Colonel Grady's speculation was more subtle, and possibly only a joke.

"Who told you that you were handsome, sir?" Kaika asked, saving Rysha from having to respond. "You've got a nose like a tomahawk, eyes the color of mud, and only half an ear on the left side."

"Really, Captain. It's at least three-quarters of an ear. And I can still use it to hear a woman's mellifluous tones."

"Seven gods, he reminds me of Zirkander," Therrik grumbled.

"Ah, General Zirkander!" Grady grinned again. "I wrote a ballad about him and the exploits of Wolf Squadron a couple of years ago."

Therrik growled. "I knew there was a reason we'd never been on any missions together."

"Yes, because I get sent out to gather intel. You get sent out to shoot people."

"Shoot? I usually use my bare hands."

"Charming," Kaika murmured.

Grady tapped his chin thoughtfully, pulled out his notebook again, and wrote something else.

Therrik scowled at him, but only for a second. He pointed at their muddy practice field. "You two women pair up. Run through the eights drill while we've still got some daylight left. Minstrel, you and I will—"

"Company coming," Kaika said, nodding toward the walkway overlooking the exercise field. "*Royal* company."

King Angulus strode toward the stairway leading down to the field, six guards in dark blue uniforms trailing closely behind him. A familiar officer wearing a leather flight jacket strolled at the king's side, the light from the gas lamps glinting off the polished gold rank pins on his collar and cap. General Zirkander.

Startled by the king's appearance—what was he doing out *here*?—Rysha sheathed Dorfindral and hurried to wipe as much mud off her uniform as possible. Which yielded less than optimal results.

The start of summer was only a month away, but it had rained every day this week. As she'd observed while attending school here, the capital shared the predominantly cloud-covered and damp climate of her family's valley to the south.

Angulus stopped at the top of the stairs and eyed the field below. Someone had spread wood chips to create a path to the various training stations, but they were as soggy as the surrounding mud.

Zirkander made a megaphone with his hands and called to them. "Kaika and Ravenwood, report!"

"Yes, sir," Kaika called back and ran toward the stairs, her boots squishing in the mud.

Startled to have been included, Rysha paused a few seconds before taking off.

"Why are they getting singled out and not us?" Grady asked.

"Jealous you won't be able to sing your ballad for Zirkander?" Therrik asked.

"Oh, he's already heard it," Grady said as Rysha sprinted after Kaika. "My brothers and I shared it with him at a tavern one night. He was impressed. Bought us beers."

"Probably to shut you up."

Rysha didn't hear the rest. She hurried, trying to catch up with Kaika.

At six feet, they were both tall women, but Kaika seemed to have longer legs, legs that propelled her along like an antelope bounding across a meadow. Rysha, her sword scabbard banging against her leg and mud flying up to spatter her spectacles, didn't feel nearly as agile, not at that moment. She had won all manner of sports contests as a girl, but that had rarely involved slogging through mud while wearing combat boots.

They ran up, stopping at the bottom of the stairs, and saluted both men. Fortunately, genuflections to the king weren't required from soldiers in uniform.

Zirkander propped an elbow on the railing as he casually returned the salutes with his free hand. Angulus inclined his head in a nod.

"That sprint must have been for you, Sire," Zirkander said. "Women don't usually run that fast when I call them over."

"That's not what the stories say." Angulus slanted him a look Rysha couldn't quite read.

Zirkander shrugged easily. "You can't believe everything in those stories."

Rysha wondered if the king had heard Grady's ballad. Or perhaps there were other ballads. The pilots did get a lot of coverage in the newspapers, and even the king was on record as calling the members of Wolf Squadron national heroes. As far as Rysha knew, few of the elite troops received that distinction, even though they trained assiduously—if not obsessively—and went on missions every bit as dangerous as those the pilots went on. She'd been aware of Captain Kaika's career for years, but only because she'd been fascinated by her—the only woman who'd passed the rigorous physical tests and qualified for the elite troops—and wanted to emulate her.

"You're wearing mud," Angulus told Kaika quietly, meeting her eyes.

"Yes, it's terribly fashionable this year. And it's good for the skin. Helps me keep a healthy glow."

"Is that your secret?"

"One of them. I can't share them all." Kaika winked.

They shared a smile, reminding Rysha that they reputedly had a relationship rather different from the kind most soldiers had with the king.

Angulus's face grew more serious as he turned to address Rysha. "Lieutenant Ravenwood, what's your progress on the *chapaharii* research?"

"It's only been a week since we returned from the Antarctic," Kaika said before Rysha could open her mouth. "And she went to her grandmother's funeral for a couple of those days. The rest, she's been training from before dawn until dusk, including extra training with the swords."

"I've found references to seven weapons, Sire," Rysha said. "Three spears, two swords, a shield, and a bow—I'd be quite fascinated to see how a bow works. Does it require special *chapaharii* arrows or is the bow itself sufficient when using regular arrows? That one is a question mark, so it may not be worth investigating. However, it *is* believed to be in some ruins in Dakrovia, rather than on Cofah soil, so it might be easier to get to. One spear is also in Dakrovia, in a wealthy plantation owner's personal collection. It would likely have to be bartered for, and possibly only granted on a loan. There aren't many known weapons out there that aren't in personal collections or museums. I believe Prince Varlok ordered all the Cofah museum pieces extracted and put into the hands of his troops. The empire is even more inundated by dragons than we are right now. Oh, I also found evidence that a little over three thousand years ago, there was a high concentration of the swords on Rakgorath. It's unknown whether any remain, as the criminals running the place might have found them and sold them, but it might be worth sending an expedition."

Rysha trailed off because Kaika was staring at her with her mouth dangling open.

"When did you have time to do research?" Kaika asked.

"I stayed up late a few nights. I also had some time while I was waiting for my turn on the rifle range yesterday."

"I thought you were reading a comic book."

"I just told Corporal Oakridge that so he wouldn't make fun of my academic tendencies," Rysha said.

"If that corporal makes fun of you again, you punch him in the nose."

"We were told we're not allowed to hit the other rookies outside of combat practice."

"Then it's a good thing you have permission from a superior officer."

Rysha looked up at Zirkander and Angulus, doubting they should be discussing rule-breaking openly in front of authority figures. Not that Zirkander, still leaning against the railing, one boot crossed over the other, was a particularly daunting authority figure. Angulus, on the other hand, always appeared stern and forbidding in photographs, and that sternness also came through when he addressed his subjects for speeches.

But now, he only shook his head and told Rysha, "You're lucky she didn't recommend blowing up this corporal. She has a fondness for explosives."

"Yes, Sire. I look forward to learning about demolitions from her once I pass my training and officially become one of the elite troops."

Even though the odds were against her succeeding at that, Rysha refused to say *if*.

"Good." Angulus turned toward Zirkander and opened his mouth, but paused before speaking and frowned at his officer's relaxed stance.

Zirkander pushed off the railing and straightened, clasping his hands behind his back in a parade-rest stance. Even so, he couldn't quite manage the blank-faced, serious-soldier expression most privates mastered after being yelled at a few times. His lips looked like they might crook into a smirk at any second.

"Has anybody ever told you that you look insolent even when you're not doing anything, Zirkander?" Angulus asked.

"On a daily basis, Sire." His lips lost the battle and formed a full smirk.

Angulus grunted. "Get the non-Cofah locations from Ravenwood. The empire hasn't been at our throats since their emperor mysteriously disappeared, so let's not start anything by stealing from them."

"Mysteriously." This time, Kaika smirked.

"Pick some pilots and form a couple of teams," Angulus continued to Zirkander. "They'll take the two-man craft and each fly one of our elite troops. Therrik will choose likely candidates from his people."

Zirkander's smirk disappeared. "He's not *going*, is he? He gets airsick, you know."

"Many people do when their pilot flies them upside down through Crazy Canyon." Angulus lifted a hand to forestall whatever retort Zirkander planned to make. "He can pick himself if he wants. I don't care who goes, so long as they're reliable people who can take care of themselves in a fight. And find Sardelle or someone to help you ensure none of them have dragon blood." Angulus issued an exasperated grunt. "I had Colonel Quataldo picked out to wield one of the dragon-slaying swords." He waved at the blades sheathed at Kaika's and Rysha's waists. "Imagine my surprise when the sword zapped him."

"Uh, yes, Sire. I could have told you about that. Apparently, his amazing egg-carving skill isn't purely a result of natural artistic ability."

Rysha wrinkled her brow. Egg carving? She'd seen the elite troops colonel around the fort a couple of times but had never spoken to him and had no idea what they were talking about. Nobody else appeared surprised by the comment, so she kept her mouth shut.

ORIGINS

"Make sure you've got people along who can actually wield the weapons if you're able to recover them," Angulus said.

"Are *we* going?" Kaika cocked her head toward Rysha. "Our lieutenant has already had her training interrupted once. While she's quite qualified to do research, she hasn't passed the tests yet, so she's not ready for missions."

Rysha wanted to object, but how could she? She'd been sent on the mission to destroy the dragon portal because of her academic knowledge, not her four months of experience as an artillery officer, nor the three weeks of elite-troops training she'd endured before going.

"Sometimes, officers have to take on responsibility beyond their rank," Angulus said, opening an apologetic hand toward Rysha. "Kaika, you two are going on another mission, one General Zirkander has convinced me will be worth the time and resources." Angulus's lips thinned as he eyed Zirkander again. "Including sending two *chapaharii* blades off to who knows where."

"I didn't request the swords, Sire. Just officers who Captain Trip knows and trusts."

Trip? A tiny knife twisted in Rysha's heart.

She hadn't seen him since their team reported to Angulus in Zirkander's office in the citadel. Since then, she had been extremely busy, as Kaika had pointed out, but there had been a few nights when she'd thought about heading to the men's barracks to look for him, to see if he wanted to talk. But she'd reminded herself of her vow that she wouldn't spend time with him until she found a way to ensure that she, and nobody else, could control Dorfindral.

As with the other *chapaharii* weapons, it wanted to kill those with dragon blood flowing through their veins, those whose ancestry gave them the power to perform magic. And Trip was such a person. *More* than such a person. Two thousand years ago, during the First Dragon Era, there must have been numerous people walking around who were half human and half dragon, but right now, Trip was possibly the only person in the world with that much dragon blood.

"If he's going to look for a dragon," Angulus said, "he had better have along people who have the power to hurt it. By their reports—" he waved to Kaika and Rysha, "—we have no way to know in advance if this dragon will look favorably upon him or be interested in allying itself with Iskandia."

"This is true, Sire," Zirkander said. "It might try to flambé them for a snack."

"I just love it when Zirkander recommends me for a special mission," Kaika muttered to Rysha.

Despite the words, her eyes gleamed. Kaika probably *did* love it, the potential to become a snack notwithstanding.

"I'll pick the pilots and tell them to pack, Sire," Zirkander said. "Kaika, Ravenwood, you better pack too. You're going to help Trip find his papa dragon. We're assuming it's alive somewhere, since his mother found it. And did interesting things with it. I guess that makes it a *him*." Zirkander's lips twisted. As comfortable as he was around magic, even he seemed to find the idea of dragons having sex with humans a little startling. "Pack your weapons and whatever research material you might need, and meet at the hangar two hours after morning formation. Trip and the rest of the team will meet you there."

"After morning formation?" Kaika asked. "That's so late, General. You usually send us off at dawn. Or earlier."

"First formation of the month tomorrow morning." Zirkander winked. "I hear there will be a few promotions. And I suspect Trip will be pleased to have his recent one to captain recognized in front of the new squadron he's finally gotten a chance—a brief chance—to work with."

"Ah. Yes, sir."

"Did he choose us for the mission, sir?" Rysha wasn't sure how she felt about that. A part of her danced inside at the idea of seeing him again, and once again putting to use the fancy rifle mount he'd built her to use in the flier, but she vividly remembered Dorfindral taking over and forcing her to attack him.

Her archaeology and history degrees meant she was a good person to take along on a search for a dragon, but she wouldn't have expected him to request her after that incident. Though he clearly didn't hold it against her. That knife twisted in her heart again at the memory of Trip asking her to walk along the harbor with him at sunset some evening, and her having to tell him that she couldn't, not until she had control of that sword.

Rysha had been meaning to go out to see Sardelle, to see if she had any suggestions about how to gain that control, since her own research hadn't turned up anything besides the original command words.

Command words that only worked until an enemy came along who *also* knew them. Unfortunately, she hadn't had time yet for that visit.

"Actually," Zirkander said, "I chose you. Trip hasn't shown much interest in announcing his unique heritage to the world, so I thought it would be best to pick people who already knew about it."

"Did he mention…" Rysha grimaced. "Well, I guess it would have been in the report."

"The part where you and your sword attacked him?" Zirkander asked.

"Yes, sir."

"He didn't, but I've seen it happen before." Zirkander's affable face lost all of its humor. "Unfortunately, that's the tradeoff—the risk—that comes with those swords, that they can be used on magical friends as well as foes."

"I'm hoping to find a way to ensure they'll obey only their wielders."

"Oh? That would be research worth doing." Zirkander looked at Angulus, who nodded gravely back. Rysha thought that might mean she would be removed from the mission in order to stay here to do that research, but then Zirkander added, "Take some books. You can study up on the flight to wherever Trip says you're going."

"Trip's in charge?" Kaika asked dubiously.

"Nah, he won't be the ranking officer. But since it's *his* papa dragon, he'll have to be a consultant."

Papa dragon. Such an innocuous name for Agarrenon Shivar, the elder gold dragon that, according to Bhrava Saruth, had sired Trip.

Despite her busy week, Rysha had managed time to look up the ancient dragon—he'd been around back when humans were first mastering agriculture—and he sounded anything but innocuous. She feared Trip would be disappointed if they did find him. She'd already warned him not to expect fondness or even an acknowledgment from the dragon. And she suspected Zirkander's joke about flambéing might be closer to the truth than he realized.

Rysha touched the hilt of Dorfindral, suspecting she would need the sword on this mission.

CHAPTER 2

TRIP KNOCKED ON THE DOOR of the two-story cottage outside of town that Sardelle and General Zirkander shared with Sardelle's magic-wielding students and occasional dragon house guests. He'd yet to see a neighbor out in any of the yards on the dead-end street, or even a sign that anyone occupied the handful of houses. Maybe the unorthodox visitors had driven others away.

He felt bemused—or was chagrined the word?—to know that he qualified as one of those visitors.

The door opened, revealing Sardelle standing inside, her black hair down and her newborn baby swaddled in a wrap in her arms. She must have been in the middle of doing motherly things.

Trip winced, feeling guilty for interrupting her. He shouldn't have come out this evening. Oh, Sardelle had insisted—she'd only taken two days off from tutoring him since she'd given birth earlier in the week—but he still felt guilty.

"Here, ma'am," Trip blurted and thrust out a tool he'd made. "It's for you and the general. It's a wine opener. With some special features. See here? This grips the bottle, so you can open it one-handedly. That'll come in handy for, uh…" He waved at the baby, though he didn't mean to suggest she would be, or should be, swilling wine while mothering.

"It's very nice. Thank you. And I look forward to trying it, just as I do the apple corer and slicer." Sardelle smiled. "But you don't need to bring a gift every time you show up for lessons, Trip."

"I know, ma'am." He bit his lip. "But you won't let me pay you."

"I know what officers make. The military isn't overly generous, considering you risk your lives daily."

"I could still pay you. I don't have many expenses."

"There's no need for payment, I assure you." Sardelle backed away from the door, nodding for him to come inside. "I enjoy teaching, and it's an honor for me to instruct a student of your caliber."

"Are you sure? Because no teacher has ever said that to me before. I distinctly remember the words 'trying' and 'easily distracted' on a lot of my report cards."

The baby's eyes were closed, but he made faint cooing noises, and a tiny hand lifted in the air, fingers opening and closing. Sardelle plucked something off a table behind her—a ring toy with little disks that clacked together. Trip eyed it as she placed it in the baby's grip. Would toys make better gifts than housewares? He might be able to come up with something suitable.

"Among the Referatu," Sardelle said, "it was always considered an honor to teach. A part of myself is passed along in what I teach, just as my instructors shared a part of themselves when teaching me. It's a legacy of a sort. One day, you'll teach others."

Trip decided he shouldn't admit that he would prefer to teach someone how to make a wine opener than how to use magic. Everything he'd learned in the last couple of weeks continued to daunt him, and he was far more alarmed at the idea of having a dragon for a father than he was intrigued.

Oh, she knows you'd rather play with tools than magic, Jaxi, Sardelle's sentient soulblade, spoke into his mind from wherever she was in the house. *Nobody here is obtuse. Or unobservant.*

Just nettlesome, answered Trip's new soulblade, Azarwrath.

The sword hung in a scabbard from his belt. Even though Trip felt self-conscious attempting to learn magic under the "eye" of a fifteen-hundred-year-old sorcerer, Azarwrath hadn't been amenable to being left back in the barracks.

You had better not be referring to Sardelle, Jaxi growled.

I was not. She is a healer and knows the proper place for a woman in society. She is also not nosy or intrusive.

Insult me again, and I'll smite you into a puddle of molten ore.

You haven't the power to do so.

"Trip?" Sardelle had moved through the living area and into the doorway of a room that did double duty as Zirkander's home office and her meditation and instruction salon.

"Sorry, ma'am." Trip hurried to follow her, moving around the massive couch custom-made from shot-up flier parts. "Our swords were arguing again."

"Yes, I know."

No, she definitely wasn't obtuse or unobservant.

"Do you want me to take the baby, Sardelle?" Tylie asked, flouncing out of the kitchen with another child snugged against her hip, Ridge and Sardelle's toddler. What was her name? Marinka.

"Maybe in a little while. I think he's about to settle down for a nap. Thank you for watching Marinka."

"I *love* babysitting," Tylie said.

Thank the gods someone does, Jaxi said. *I was glad to be here to help Sardelle with the birth, but there's been so much squalling in the house.*

Trip scratched his head, perplexed as to how a magical sword that specialized in fireballs could "help" with a birth.

By being supportive, genius.

One imagines that her fireballs might be less alarming than her notion of support, Azarwrath murmured.

Trip followed Sardelle into the office and sat across from her on a floor cushion. It looked like it would just be the two of them this evening. Maybe his ego would have a chance to recover. It had been squashed by having an eleven-year-old boy and twelve-year-old girl outperform him in joint lessons. Even though he told himself they'd had much more practice, having been training with Sardelle for the last year, it was hard to be outshone by children.

How are you doing with your bank vault? Sardelle asked telepathically, her eyes closing.

She referenced the exercise Jaxi had first introduced him to where he imagined his mind inside of a vault so other sorcerers—and dragons—couldn't read his thoughts. At least that was the goal.

Working on it, ma'am. And also on trying to expand the vault to keep those around me from having their thoughts read. But I haven't had a dragon to practice on to see if it's working.

If you want a dragon, we would be happy to send one with you to the barracks, Sardelle thought.

I don't think the CQ sergeant would appreciate that.

We'll warm up with mind-protecting exercises today, then move on to your specialty, creating and manipulating fire. Later, Tylie will bring her soulblade Wreltad in. He's agreed to work with you on mind control, one of his specialties.

A shiver went down Trip's spine. *Mind control, ma'am? I don't want to control anyone.*

That's heartening to hear, but it will help with all the mental arts. I understand you had some luck dealing with dragons and forcing their barriers down by attacking their minds.

Oh, right. Yes.

Trip forced aside his squeamishness, telling himself this was for the greater good. It would be useful if he could protect his fellow pilots from dragon attacks, as well as assist those who wielded the *chapaharii* blades.

An image of Rysha flashed into his mind, smiling as she shared her research findings, then standing up for him back in that tavern when others had singled him out for having un-Iskandian bronze skin and dark green eyes. Or maybe just because he was odd. Funny how many people had picked up on that even before he'd realized he had more than a well-developed sixth sense.

A clunk sounded as the front door opened.

"We're in here, Ridge," Sardelle called, her eyes still closed as she sat cross-legged with the baby in her arms.

"I have company," came the general's response. "Is everybody decent?"

"Olek is naked inside of his wrap, but I believe everyone else is fully clothed."

Trip scrambled to his feet and saluted as Zirkander walked in while removing his cap and scraping his fingers through his short brown hair. He flicked a lazy return salute toward Trip as he headed for Sardelle.

"Naked inside his wrap?" Zirkander asked. "Sounds scandalous." He bent to kiss the top of her head.

The baby's eyes opened, and he lifted both hands. Zirkander lowered a finger, and tiny ones wrapped around his.

"Can I borrow your student for a few minutes?" Zirkander waved his free hand toward the living area.

From his position, Trip couldn't see through the doorway, but he let his senses drift outward. His heart lifted when he recognized Rysha's aura.

Had she come to see him? Or Sardelle? Probably Sardelle, he decided, not without disappointment. Trip hadn't been telling people he was coming out here in the evenings. As futile as it surely was, he was trying to pretend to the rest of his new squadron mates that he was simply Captain "Sidetrip," a perfectly normal pilot with a penchant toward disobeying orders and following hunches that begged him to investigate. Maybe that wasn't entirely normal.

"I don't know about that," Sardelle said, taking Ridge's arm and letting him help her to her feet. "He hasn't yet mastered mental power forging."

"I'm still working on that too." Zirkander winked.

Sardelle swatted his arm.

"Trip, you ready for your mission?" Zirkander tilted his head toward the living room.

Trip also sensed Captain Kaika out there, strolling into the kitchen where Tylie, the dragon-in-human-form Phelistoth, and the toddler were talking and preparing food. Presumably, Tylie was doing most of the work.

With a surge of anticipation—and alarm—Trip realized this had to be about the mission *he* had suggested. The one that had seemed like a good idea at the time, but that terrified him now that he'd had more time to think about it.

"Yes, sir," he made himself say and followed Zirkander to the doorway. "Thank you for your help, ma'am," he told Sardelle before stepping out of the office.

"You're welcome. I can send along some workbooks if you're going to be gone long."

"Workbooks?" Trip imagined sheets urging him to identify nouns and verbs and prove he could count the number of fish in a pond.

"I made them for my younger students." Her lips curved upward. "You may be ready for them."

"*May.*"

"May. We haven't worked on everything they touch upon, so you'll find challenges."

For your information, Jaxi thought, *you have to move the fish around in the pond on the page. Without cutting the paper and using glue.*

Does your commentary mean I'm not being successful in keeping my bank vault door closed? Trip asked.

It means that Iskandian soulblades are nosy, Azarwrath said.

Don't make me have Sardelle take me outside so we can have a showdown, Jaxi told him.

"Good evening, Captain Trip," Rysha said, heading toward the office as Trip stepped out of it. She smiled at him, but she also looked like she wanted to hurry past without a longer encounter.

He stepped aside so he wouldn't be in her way, but his heart broke a little. He still wasn't entirely certain her distance was because of the problem with controlling the sword. Their first kiss had been before the revelation about his heritage had come out. Of course, there had been a kiss *after* that too. A quick one before they went into battle together. She'd spoken of them spending a weekend together in a quaint rural cottage in her family's valley, something he'd fantasized about more than once since then.

Sardelle appeared in the doorway, and Rysha stopped short.

"Ma'am, General Zirkander brought me here so I could ask you a couple of questions about the *chapaharii* weapons."

Sardelle nodded. "I know."

"Oh. Uhm, right." Rysha hesitated, appearing disconcerted at this demonstration of telepathic communications happening around her, but she pushed her spectacles up on her nose and recovered. She still wore her army uniform, a rumpled and mud-spattered one with a knife gash in one sleeve. They must have come straight from the fort. She didn't appear to have brought Dorfindral with her. Probably wise considering all the magic in this house. "It's about the command words. And… power." Rysha glanced at Trip.

"Do you want me to leave?" He couldn't tell if that glance meant she was uncomfortable talking about this in front of him. He looked for Zirkander. Hadn't the general wanted to talk to him?

But Zirkander was involved in a conversation with a silver-haired man Trip recognized as Phelistoth in shape-shifted form. He didn't notice Trip's glance. The words "coffee maker" came up, and Zirkander frowned at the dragon.

"No," Rysha said. "I'm trying to figure out a solution for my problem with Dorfindral, which is also your problem with Dorfindral."

"The problem where he wants me dead?" Trip asked.

"Yes, and has been allowed to—ordered to—use me to try to make that happen. Despite me using the command words." Rysha winced and faced Sardelle again. "Ma'am, I've heard from you and Captain Kaika that the *chapaharii* swords have turned against their wielders before."

"Multiple times, yes."

The baby cooed and waved a hand. Rysha smiled briefly and wriggled her fingers back, but she was clearly too distracted to admire a newborn. "When it happened to me with Trip, I was saying the control words, but so was a Cofah sorceress on the other side of the chamber."

Sardelle nodded without surprise.

"The times you witnessed it, was it something similar? And did the words of the new speaker override the words the wielder used?"

"The first time it happened," Sardelle said, "we'd just acquired Kasandral, and nobody knew about the words. The queen spoke them, and the sword took over Cas—its wielder at the time—and used her to attack me. After that, we were able to find an old book with the command words in it. Cas memorized them, and they worked to quell the blade in normal situations, but the dragon we soon battled knew them somehow. He might have plucked them out of her mind, or he might have learned them long ago in his lifetime. He uttered them, and even though Cas kept saying the words, the sword chose to listen to the dragon."

"Good."

Sardelle arched her eyebrows. "Good?"

"I have a hypothesis, and your experiences support it."

"That the swords take any opportunity to do as they wish?"

"No. I mean, that's possible, but my hypothesis is that those with dragon blood have more power to control the *chapaharii* weapons than we do—than *I* do—even though they cannot themselves touch them."

Trip remembered the battle in the ice chamber and Kiadarsa shouting those nonsensical words. Was it possible that if *he'd* known them, he could have spoken the "stand down" command, and the sword would have obeyed? If so, he needn't have traded all those blows with Rysha and broken her spectacles to finally get her to stop.

The baby squirmed, and Sardelle shifted him to her other arm. "I don't believe that makes sense since the weapons were specifically made to destroy those with dragon blood. Why would they be more likely to accept orders from their enemies?"

"Not their enemies," Rysha said. "Their *allies*. During the Rider Wars, the magical battled the magical, dragons against dragons and sorcerers against sorcerers, right?"

"So history tells us."

"The *chapaharii* weapons were made for battling enemy magic-users, but as you've seen, they were a threat to friendly magic-users. Those who forged them and imbued them with their power would have known this. They may have made the command words, not just for the wielders themselves, but for their dragon-blooded allies."

"But if their enemies knew them—"

"Most likely, they didn't *intend* for their enemies to ever know them. Originally, they were made in Iskandia, and that's why the command words are in Old Iskandian, right? Eventually, the Cofah stole some of the weapons and also, if the texts I've read are accurate, the knowledge of how to make them. After a while, the words probably weren't a secret, but originally, they may have been designed to be spoken by people with power. Think about it. The sorcerers wouldn't have wanted their allies who were wielding the weapons to be able to turn on them. This could have been a failsafe, giving more weight to words uttered by someone with dragon blood."

"Hm, you're persuading me of the possibility. I suppose the thing to do would be to set up an experiment." Sardelle looked at Trip, and he wondered if he should have sneaked over to join the coffee-maker conversation. Tylie had come out and was standing beside Phelistoth now. But, no. If Trip could help Rysha, he had to do so. Especially if Dorfindral was truly the only thing keeping them from a date.

"What can I do?" he asked.

"I didn't expect to find you here, but this is fortuitous." Rysha pulled a folded piece of paper out of a mud-spattered pocket. "Can you memorize these? I'll see you tomorrow for the mission, and I'll have Dorfindral. We can see if you're able to override me. I'll tell the sword to stand down, and you tell it to attack. Or vice versa."

"What if it doesn't work, and you end up attacking me, and we can't stop it?"

"I'll bring all my extra pairs of spectacles with me on the mission, just in case." Rysha smiled, but the gesture didn't reach her eyes.

"You could simply try it with the commands for *stand down* and *stand ready*," Sardelle said.

"Yes, good. We'll try that." Rysha's smile warmed.

Trip liked that smile, and his stomach flipped in nervous anticipation as it turned fully onto him, but he also worried this experiment might not be as easy as they made it sound. The last thing he wanted was for Rysha to end up attacking him again, and him having to break her spectacles—or worse—to stop her.

Further, there was the possibility that a day would come when he *couldn't* stop her. Last time, he'd had both Azarwrath and Jaxi to aid in his defense, but Jaxi was back with Sardelle now. And from what he'd heard, Rysha and the other new blade wielders were training under Colonel Therrik, improving their skills with the weapons.

"Captain Trip," a shy voice came from the side. Tylie walked over and smiled tentatively. "If you make another gift for Sardelle, we could use a new coffee maker. Phelistoth tried to make coffee by himself this morning."

"It didn't go well?"

The silver-haired man strode back into the kitchen, an arrogant and defiant tilt to his chin.

"Phel is a scholar, not an engineer," Tylie said. "He hasn't mastered appliances."

Zirkander shook his head, his expression one of exasperation as he looked at Trip. "I can't believe one of the most powerful beings in the world, one capable of razing enemy airships, controlling the minds of armies, and eating a cheese wheel whole can't work a coffee maker."

"Human contraptions sometimes mystify dragons," Sardelle said mildly.

"I feel like we should be able to use that to our advantage somehow," Zirkander said. "By hurling legions of coffee makers at Cofah-sympathizing dragons."

"They would just incinerate them," Trip said.

"Apparently, that's what happened to *my* coffee maker. When someone got cranky and frustrated." Zirkander scowled at the kitchen, then pointed at the front door. "Let me steal you from the ladies for a minute, Trip. It's about your new assignment."

"Yes, sir."

Trip trotted around the couch to join him on the front stoop, though his mind was already contemplating the various coffee makers he'd seen and what might be done to enhance one. He would have to keep the design simple, thus not to thwart dragon users, but surely, he could add a few useful features.

"You'll leave after first formation," Zirkander said without preamble. "It took me a while to finagle permission to send fliers—and those swords—on an adventure that will presumably take you out of the country, but the king has personally approved it now. Your team will meet you in the hangar, and you can tell them where you're heading first."

"Am I in command, sir?" The notion daunted Trip, even if the mission had been his idea, and the entire purpose was to find the dragon who had sired him.

"You're in subcommand."

"What does that mean?"

"That if three people are sleeping or otherwise unavailable, then you're in command."

Trip snorted.

"But you'll be directing people where to go. You have some ideas of where to start?"

"I thought I'd see if my grandparents know any more than what they told me as a kid, sir. At the least, they should know the continent my mother was exploring before she came back pregnant."

Trip's mind boggled at the idea of his mother having slept with some strange dragon in a far-off place. He remembered her as a strong, adventurous woman, but also a soft-spoken and kindly potion maker. What had possessed her to seek out a gold dragon? Could it have been an accident? Or could the dragon have... coerced her? Thinking of that made him shudder, but he couldn't dismiss the notion, not when he'd sensed dragon power firsthand, and there were many stories of dragons controlling people. Forcing them to act against their wishes. He prayed that Agarrenon Shivar would have a noble streak and wouldn't have done any such thing.

"Let's hope that with Lieutenant Ravenwood's researching acumen, you'll be able to narrow it down further than a continent," Zirkander said. "We'd like to see you back sometime this year."

"Is there a deadline, sir? A date you expect us back?" Trip couldn't imagine the king wanted those swords out of the country for long.

Zirkander nodded. "You've got a month."

"Yes, sir."

"If you hear of any trouble going on back here in Iskandia earlier than that, we'd appreciate it if you come back sooner to help."

From the grim set to Zirkander's face, Trip worried he had a reason to expect there would be trouble.

"Have there already been dragon attacks?" he asked.

"Several in Cofahre, and we've had reports of sightings in Iskandia. A few of our officers have suggested that some of the dragons are working together and that these look like scouting missions. Humans have spread out across the world since the dragons first left. Now that they've returned, the dragons may have noticed that there aren't many areas left for them to claim. Unless they conquer an existing nation or nations."

Trip nodded, not surprised at the intelligence reports coming in. Few of the dragons he'd met seemed interested in simply blending in and living in peace with humans. Even Iskandia's greatest ally and the most amenable dragon he'd met, Bhrava Saruth, had insisted on a temple and wanted people to worship him as a god.

"I'll try to find Agarrenon Shivar and get back as quickly as possible, sir. *With* him."

That was, after all, why he'd come up with this mission to start with. He hoped to secure his sire's assistance as an ally to Iskandia. Since Agarrenon Shivar had, according to multiple sources, been respected among the dragons at one point in time, Trip hoped that would still be true, that his sire might be able to convince other dragons to leave Iskandia alone. Trip just had to convince Agarrenon Shivar that he wanted to help.

Zirkander gripped his shoulder. "Good luck."

CHAPTER 3

AS THE FLIER SQUADRON SOARED over the Ice Blades, cold wind whipped at Rysha's face, making her wish she'd brought a scarf. They were part of the uniform for the pilots, as much so they could wipe engine grease spatters off their goggles as for warmth, but their passengers were left to their own devices. Since it was late spring back home, and there'd been no mention of arctic visits, Rysha hadn't thought to pack winter gear, but they were flying even higher than the fifteen-thousand-foot peaks, and the frigid air knifed through her jacket.

Another flier swooped past overhead, startling her. It spun in a languid roll while it sashayed back and forth in the sky. The pilot—was that Trip?—spiraled downward in a dive, then pulled up after his craft nearly kissed a glacier smothering the side of one of the mountains.

Rysha hadn't considered it before, but now realized Trip's dragon heritage might contribute to his love of flying.

"What are you doing, *Sidetrip*?" Major Blazer asked from the cockpit in front of Rysha, the words just audible over the wind and the cigar clamped between her teeth.

"Enjoying myself, ma'am," came Trip's voice over Blazer's communication crystal. He guided his flier into a few more spirals as he swooped up to rejoin the formation.

"This is the army. We don't allow soldiers to enjoy themselves in public."

"That's a rule?" Trip didn't sound that abashed. Maybe because he was used to Blazer's grouchy streak by now.

Rysha had been surprised when everybody from the portal mission had shown up at the hangar, having been assigned to accompany Trip on this new mission. Zirkander must have thought Agarrenon Shivar would make trouble and that Trip would need numerous allies to convince the dragon to join them. Even so, Rysha had expected a smaller team. She'd also expected Lieutenant Leftie to be excluded, since he'd been glaring daggers at Trip and his dragonness ever since they left the Antarctic. Had Zirkander not known about that? Or had he known but hoped Leftie would get over his problem if he and Trip went on a mission together? Since both men had been transferred into Wolf Squadron, Zirkander wouldn't want any strife between them.

"Absolutely," Blazer said.

"Aw, Major," Duck drawled over the crystal. "Sometimes, a pilot just gets an urge and has to satisfy it. You know that."

"No satisfying urges in public, either," Blazer said. "You can do that in your room alone at night."

"That's disgusting, ma'am."

"I certainly think so."

"I thought Captain Kaika was the only one who made immature sex jokes," Leftie spoke from his flier's cockpit. Kaika lounged behind him while polishing her *chapaharii* sword, Eryndral. Alas, since Leftie had no dragon blood, the sword wouldn't convince her to crack him over the head. "Though she seems old for it."

"That's *Major* Kaika now," Blazer said. "Didn't you see her shiny new pins?"

"*Finally*," Kaika said. "I was beginning to think I'd die a captain. Who knew that blowing up enemy warships and airships wasn't worth a promotion? That you had to scrag a dragon portal?"

"You didn't see that in the army handbook?" Blazer asked. "Should have read the fine print."

"Ha ha. And to answer Little Leftie's question, you can make immature sex jokes at any age. I fully intend to be a lewd octogenarian, teaching younglings how to blow things up from my rocking chair."

"Did you call me *Little*, ma'am?" Leftie asked. "I assure you, I'm anything but."

"Just on the one side?"

Leftie groaned and glared over at Trip, the one who'd originally shared the story of how Leftie had received his nickname. Rysha thought he might engage Trip in some banter, as he would have done a few weeks ago, but he looked back toward the route ahead without commenting. Trip gazed toward him for a long moment, but didn't say anything, merely turning his own focus back to the route ahead, the last of the mountains before they flew down toward the grassy foothills at the base of the Ice Blades.

Though Trip was too far away from Rysha for her to make out his expression, especially when he wore his goggles and scarf, she felt certain she would have read hurt in his eyes if they'd been closer. It made her want to hug him as soon as they landed.

Dorfindral, his scabbard stuck between the seat and the side of the seat well, oozed discontent into her mind. An image of chasing after Trip with the bared blade popped into her thoughts.

Rysha growled and muttered, "*meyusha*," the term for "stand down." She refused to let the sword influence how she felt about Trip or anyone else. She looked forward to trying her experiment, seeing if Trip could control the blade now that she'd given him the command words. Then she could hug him without worrying about repercussions.

She was surprised he hadn't seemed more excited at the prospect. That morning, she had arrived at the hangar early, hoping they might perform the experiment before everyone loaded up. But he'd arrived later and had granted her only a brief smile before engaging in a conversation with Blazer and Zirkander. It had almost seemed as if he was avoiding Rysha.

"There's the ocean," Duck said brightly as they flew out of the Ice Blades. "*My* ocean. Provalia is just to the south of Charkolt Province, my home. I grew up in the woods down there. It's real rural out there still. I was mostly raised by wolves."

"That explains a lot," Leftie said.

"Like my cunning wilderness wiles?"

"Not exactly."

"We have company," Trip said, after having been relatively quiet for most of the flight over, presuming he hadn't been chatting with his seat mate.

The surly Cofah warrior Dreyak rode in his flier once again, something that had perplexed Rysha. Supposedly, he'd been along on their last mission to assist them in destroying the portal. But that was done, so why was he with them again? Supposedly, he was only getting a ride as far as Charkolt, but that didn't make sense to her, either. What could be in Eastern Iskandia that would interest a Cofah?

Blazer had asked that exact thing, and Zirkander had only shrugged and said, "The king said he could go with you if he wants. Apparently, you charmed him, Blazer, and he couldn't stay away."

To which she'd responded, "I'm about as known for charming men as you are, General."

"Please tell me it's not *hostile* company," Blazer said in response to Trip's comment.

"It's Bhrava Saruth and Shulina Arya," Trip said.

"Shit, I'd rather have hostile company."

"I like Bhrava Saruth," Duck said. "And the new female seems friendly too. They're like hounds ready to join their people for a hunt."

"I suggest you don't call the dragons hounds when they're close enough to hear it," Blazer said.

"Actually, dragons can't hear," Rysha said, leaning forward so everyone would hear her over Blazer's crystal. "At least, not in the way humans do. They feel vibrations, both in the ground and in the air, and it's believed their physical senses are augmented with magic."

"So we can or *can't* call them hounds?" Blazer asked.

"They'll sense you calling them that, rather than hearing it."

Greetings, humans! Shulina Arya's voice rang in Rysha's skull so strongly that it made her head ache. Speaking of vibrations… Could raw mental power vibrate? *Are you going on an adventure? Will it be fun? You did not invite us along.*

As the fliers dropped out of the foothills and headed across farmland and toward the coastal city of Charkolt, the two gold dragons appeared in the distance behind them, just coming down out of the mountains.

You're welcome to come along, Rysha thought, mostly because telling a dragon she couldn't do something didn't seem wise. Would Shulina Arya be monitoring her thoughts and catch her words? *We were sent on this mission by the king. It's possible he didn't think you would be interested in accompanying us.*

Angulus also would likely prefer that Bhrava Saruth and his allies be close to the capital, so they could defend the city or other parts of the country if trouble came to Iskandia.

I love adventures! Shulina Arya cried, the words even stronger than before, and Rysha winced. She doubted the dragon had any idea how loud her voice sounded in a human's mind or that it hurt. What would it be like to have such power and not even grasp how damaging it could be? *And stories. Will you tell me more stories tonight? I want to hear more about the dragon riders.*

Tonight? Rysha thought. *Tonight, I may need to help Trip research his heritage, but I should have time for a few.*

I would like to hear the one about the first dragon rider again.

That is a favorite of mine.

"Cougar Squadron Headquarters," Blazer spoke into her crystal. "This is Major Blazer from Wolf Squadron. We've got four fliers coming in for the night. Do you have somewhere to put us up?"

"That depends, Major," came a prompt and concerned reply. "Will it *just* be your fliers? Or are you looking for lodgings for those two dragons too?"

Rysha understood the reason for the man's concern. He hadn't said as much, but he had to be wondering if the squadron was fleeing from those dragons.

"The dragons can find their *own* lodgings," Blazer said.

"I promised to tell stories to one of them," Rysha felt compelled to add.

"Correction," Blazer said. "Our lieutenant has offered to share her bunk with them."

"Sounds crowded." The man sounded less concerned, but still wary.

"Those dragons are friendly to Iskandia, Captain Vapors," Trip said. "Bhrava Saruth and Shulina Arya."

"That you, Trip?"

"Yes, sir."

"Thought you were bringing your western trouble out east to us for a second. All right, we'll make room in the hangar for your fliers. Vapors, out."

"Vapors?" Kaika asked. "One wonders how that name came about."

"Let's just say that you wouldn't want to be in *his* back seat, ma'am," Leftie said.

"Ah."

The dragons soared closer as the pilots steered their fliers toward the base on the north end of the city. The tang of salt air teased Rysha's nostrils. She marveled that they'd made the entire trip before dark. It would have taken three days in a steam carriage, thanks to the steep, treacherous road over the Ice Blades.

Thrusters activated, and the fliers settled onto pavement outside a large hangar similar to the one back in the capital. Blazer came down right next to Trip's craft, and Rysha caught his gaze as he tugged off his cap and goggles. She hurried to unfasten her harness, grab her pack, rifle, and sword, and swing to the ground. Since Blazer was in charge, she ought to be able to handle greeting the locals. This could be Rysha's chance for her experiment. Better here than outside of some barracks room—or in front of Trip's grandparents' house. He'd mentioned starting his search with them.

"Trip," she called, ducking under the tail of his flier and catching him before he could hustle off. To her surprise, he carried Jaxi as well as Azarwrath. Had Sardelle believed he would need the extra help of two soulblades again?

With them hanging in scabbards attached to his belt, he, even in his army uniform, looked more like some mighty sorcerer of old than a soldier.

"Hi, Rysha." He smiled, but a hint of concern lurked in his eyes. He glanced at the scabbard on *her* belt.

Since it was still daylight, she couldn't tell if a green glow oozed from it, but she did sense the sword's growing agitation, more for the approaching dragons than because of Trip, she thought. This might be the perfect time for a test. The dragons could step in if things got out of hand.

"Do you have the words? This is a big open place." Rysha gestured to the pavement around them. "It would be a good place to test the sword. Hopefully, we won't *need* an open place, because you'll tell Dorfindral to stand down, and it will. But just in case."

"I have them." Trip looked like he would say more, but unbuttoned a pocket and withdrew and unfolded the paper she'd given him. "We can try."

"Good." Rysha slung her pack off her shoulder, stepped back several paces, and drew Dorfindral.

Not only did the sword's blade glow, but it was like a pale green sun emitting light. The hilt throbbed in her hand.

Hunt! it seemed to cry in her mind. Images of attacking Trip and then whirling to slay the two gold dragons sprang into her thoughts. Those images were so intense that she had to catch her breath, mentally straining to keep from carrying out the actions. The dragons hadn't even arrived yet, so there was only one person she could have acted upon.

Trip watched her, sadness replacing the concern in his eyes. He kept his hands at his sides, open and not touching the hilts of the soulblades.

Rysha started to whisper the word for stand down, but caught herself. "You do it," she told Trip. "The second term on the list."

"*Meyusha*," he said without looking.

Dorfindral's hilt stopped throbbing, and did its glow lessen slightly?

"*Meyusha*," Trip said again, stretching a palm toward the blade, as if to calm a snarling dog.

This time, Rysha felt power pouring off Trip, his dark green eyes blazing with some inner strength, a greater-than-*human* strength, and her breath caught. Dorfindral's glow disappeared entirely, the blade going dark in her hand, but she barely noticed. She couldn't look away from Trip.

He lifted his gaze from the sword to her, and a fierce tingle of energy surged through her veins as their eyes met. She felt so drawn to him that the thought of staying away repulsed her. She took a step, thoughts of touching him, *kissing* him, flooding her mind.

Trip turned his gaze from her, looking to the pavement and lowering his hand. It took a moment for Rysha to recover, for her brain to start working again. She looked down at the *chapaharii* sword, its blade still dark. No thoughts of hunting and slaying dragon-blooded individuals pushed into her mind.

"Trip," she blurted. "It worked."

He looked back at her, and he was his normal self, that alien—dragonly—aura she'd glimpsed a few times before once again tamped down.

Rysha leaned the sword against the side of the flier and rushed to Trip. "It worked," she repeated. "Do you know what this means?"

She flung her arms around him before thinking of military decorum and whether it was appropriate to hug him here. She grinned and kissed him on the cheek.

Trip's eyebrows rose, and he lifted his hands, resting them on her waist. "I..."

He didn't know what to say? He ought to be elated, just as she was. Now, they could walk side by side together and face their enemies without worrying about those enemies forcing them to turn on each other. And she could sit behind him in his flier. Maybe leaning forward now and then to play with his short hair, pushing her fingers through it and rubbing his warm scalp.

"We could go on that walk along the harbor now," she added, lowering her voice to a whisper. The words came out a little tentatively.

Even though his hands were on her waist, he seemed wary. Rysha almost wished she'd kissed him when he'd been Confident Trip, power crackling in the air around him. She felt certain he would have kissed her back then, would have pulled her against him without hesitation. But, she reminded herself, it was the quiet, awkward Trip that her mind had always been drawn to, and that deep down, she worried might disappear one day.

"I'd like that," Trip said, smiling. "You could leave your pointy friend at home, and we wouldn't have to worry about it."

"That seems reasonable. You don't take guard swords on dates, right?"

"I wouldn't think so. I haven't seen the instructions that came with it."

"There were no instructions. Hence my ongoing problems. Maybe I should make a pamphlet for future wielders. A nice meaty set of directions and useful information. With a glossary of Old Iskandian terms. A table of contents to make it easy to search. Oh, and I could put all manner of relevant material in the appendices. I *love* appendices. By the time I'm done, it could be just like the technical manual for your flier."

"The technical manual that's five hundred pages thick?"

"Exactly."

"Your eyes are gleaming."

Rysha grinned and leaned into him. "Observant of you to notice."

Trip lowered his mouth toward hers, and anticipation thrummed through her body. But before their lips touched, someone cleared her throat behind him.

"I was wrong," Blazer called over her shoulder to someone. "Ravenwood will be sharing her bunk with two dragons *and* a pilot."

Trip's cheeks reddened, and he dropped his hands and stepped back.

"I'm not sure we have rooms large enough for all that in Charkolt," Captain Vapors said. A freckled officer about Rysha's age, he now stood next to Blazer. And Kaika. And Leftie. Seven gods, when had they all sneaked around the fliers? And how long ago had they done it? "We're not the huge metropolis the capital is," Vapors added.

"You don't cater to freakish sexual practices?" Blazer asked.

"Sleeping with dragons isn't that freakish," Kaika murmured. "Assuming they shape-shift into humans."

"This conversation has gotten far too strange for my simple mind. This way, officers." Vapors waved and led the way toward the hangar.

Trip hung back, so Rysha picked up Dorfindral and waited for him to start walking before falling in at his side. Aware of the snickers and backward glances, she didn't walk *closely* at his side. His cheeks were still red; she felt chagrined too. What had she been thinking? She was a professional, not some horny girl who couldn't keep her paws off a man in public places.

"Sorry," she whispered.

"That we didn't get to finish?"

She snorted. Yes. "That I didn't wait for a less public place to fling my arms around you. I was just delighted that it worked. I wish I'd figured that out earlier."

"Hm." His features grew guarded.

"Why aren't you as delighted as I am?"

"I just… I don't want any power over you, Rysha. Or your sword. And I suspect that when you have time to consider it, you'll realize you don't want that, either. You want to control your own destiny, I'm certain."

"I wouldn't have joined the army if I expected to have any control over my destiny," she said, though she had to admit that his words rang true. She'd resented it when he'd stopped her by breaking her spectacles with his mind, by knowing her weakness and exploiting it. It wasn't as if it was a hidden weakness, but it had still felt like a betrayal. Was this so different? She'd be the hand wielding the sword, but would she come to resent it if she knew that he was the one with the ultimate power to control it? "As far as Dorfindral goes, I'd rather *you* be able to control it than some Cofah enemy."

"So, I'd be the lesser of two evils?"

"That's not what I mean."

"What happens when a dragon knows the words and uses them? Sardelle said that happened. A dragon's power would override mine, and then you'd still be in the same situation."

Rysha's shoulders slumped. "You're stealing my delight, Trip."

"I'm sorry." He lifted an arm, as if he might wrap it around her shoulders, but they were entering the hangar, and there were even more officers inside. He lowered his hand. "You can still write a technical manual, if it'll make you happy."

She snorted. "Would you read it if I did?"

"Every word."

"Did you read the flier technical manual?"

"Every word."

She squinted at him, trying to decide if he was pulling her leg. But he appeared earnest. Well, he *was* an engineer. Maybe manuals excited him as much as glossaries and appendices excited her.

Trip stopped so abruptly Rysha thought he'd forgotten something in his flier. But he looked down at Dorfindral, not back out the door. His fingers twitched, as if he wanted to reach for it, and she almost stepped away so he wouldn't succeed. The *chapaharii* weapons zapped those dragon-blooded souls who attempted to touch them.

Trip must have remembered on his own because he closed his fist and brought it to his mouth. "I'm having an idea."

"Is it an interesting one?"

"I hope so. Look, those weapons are thousands of years old, and I know we've lost a lot of the lore from the time period."

"Such as technical manuals," Rysha said.

"Precisely. If they existed, they're gone, right?"

"As far as I've been able to determine. A book the Referatu had is the best resource I've heard of, and that was just a list of command words and a bit on the history."

"Someone created those swords at one time, and someone programmed the weapons so that those particular words affected them."

"Programmed?"

"Like a loom or a mechanical construct being given a punch card full of operational instructions," Trip said.

"Right, I understand, but I imagined there being some kind of magical... imbuing."

"Oh, I'm sure it was all magical, but what I'm saying is that someone had to do it. Why couldn't someone today change the control words to something specific to that sword?" Trip pointed at Dorfindral, then lowered his voice. "To something only you know. Or at least to something written down and stuck in the sword's storage box so that only the current wielder knows them."

"That's quite an appealing scenario," Rysha said, warming to the idea right away. If she alone knew the words that Dorfindral responded to, she wouldn't have to worry about a mage or dragon using them. Assuming she could keep from thinking about them if someone was telepathically reading her mind. Even then, it was better than using commands that had been in books for thousands of years, books that any number of people had doubtless read over the centuries. "I don't suppose you know how to do it?"

Trip smiled lopsidedly. "You'd be surprised at how little I know about magic right now. Sardelle gave me a workbook so I'd have a way to practice while I'm away. It's a copy of one she originally made for ten-year-old students. I looked at the first sheet, where you're supposed to move these fish inked on the page to the other side of the page, and I have no idea how to do it."

"You have to start somewhere."

"So I'm told. I'll consult with Jaxi and Azarwrath on my punch-card programming idea."

"When do we leave, Trip?" Duck called from a group of Wolf Squadron and Cougar Squadron officers standing around the desk by the hangar door.

"What?" Trip had been gazing thoughtfully at Dorfindral.

"To visit your grandparents. Didn't you mention that your grammy is a good cook?" Duck rubbed his belly. "After flying all day, I'm hungrier than a bear after winter hibernation."

Blazer and Kaika nodded and smiled agreeably. Even Leftie's expression grew wistful. Only Dreyak seemed indifferent to dinner. He said something to Blazer, then walked toward the exit. Maybe this was as far as he would travel with their group. Rysha couldn't imagine what he wanted in Charkolt.

"I didn't warn my grandparents that I was coming," Trip said. "Or that was I showing up with a bunch of soldiers to feed."

"That was rude of you," Kaika said. "You better apologize when we arrive." She pointed to the door, making it clear he should lead the way.

"Somehow," Trip said, heading for the door, "I don't feel like my lot in the army has changed much since I got promoted from lieutenant to captain."

Rysha walked at his side. "Given all the other things that have happened since then, aren't you glad about that?"

Trip chewed on the inside of his cheek. "Actually, maybe so. Things have seemed more normal today than last week." He waved vaguely in the direction of the south pole. "Maybe Leftie will start talking to me again," he added, a sad smile tugging at his lips.

His morose expression made Rysha want to wrap an arm around his shoulders. But with the others trotting to catch up with them, she refrained.

CHAPTER 4

"*A*LL OF THEM?" GRAMMY ASKED after she and Grampy hugged Trip, exclaimed their delight at seeing him, and heard him apologetically say he'd invited his teammates to dinner.

Technically, he hadn't *invited* them, but he well remembered the quality of the mess hall food on Charkolt Base, so he couldn't blame them for wanting to avoid it. There were eating houses in town, of course, but he was encouraged that they'd wanted to dine with him. Maybe, as Jaxi had suggested, he'd been overly sensitive about feeling like an outcast. Maybe they just needed time to get used to the revelations about him.

My words are wise and usually correct, Jaxi said.

Also modest.

False modesty is insincere and irritating. When you're fabulous, there's nothing wrong with letting the world know you're fabulous.

"We don't mind waiting," Trip said. "I can help you cut vegetables if you want."

"No, no, Lamby. I've seen you in the kitchen. It's a wonder the army gives you a utility knife. Here, come in, all of you." Grammy stepped back and waved everyone into the house.

Grampy watched silently, nibbling on the stem of his corncob pipe as he eyed the invaders, probably wondering how long social propriety required he stay before he disappeared into his workshop.

Grammy's white hair was twisted up in her usual bun, her blue eyes sparkling as Trip introduced everyone to her. Plump, aproned, and welcoming, she was exactly how he remembered. Not that it had been long since he'd seen them, only a month since he'd been ordered to his new post. It just seemed like that had been ages ago. So much had happened since then.

"Did she call you *Lamby*?" Duck whispered, coming up to Trip's side.

"What did the wolves call you?"

"Dragon-hearted."

"I don't believe you."

"I was upset I couldn't get Wolf Squadron to let me keep the name."

"I'll bet."

Leftie hung back as the others tramped into the living room, looking around before choosing spots on the perky floral furniture. They looked out of place in their gray and blue uniforms. Blazer plucked at one of the afghans Grammy had knitted and draped across the back of the couch. Cat fur stuck to the afghans, though the owners of it, Jangles and Tricks, were in hiding. Trip sensed them under the bed in the back room.

He marveled that sensing things around him had so quickly become second nature, but then realized he'd never had trouble finding the cats when he was looking for them. He'd never had trouble finding much of anything.

After offering to get drinks for everyone, Grammy disappeared into the kitchen, whistling cheerfully though she had to feel some stress at this unexpected task of feeding eight people instead of two. Grampy hung back in the doorway, not looking like he knew if he was supposed to make conversation with these strangers or not. He'd never served in the army, nor had he been enthused when Trip proclaimed his desire to join.

Leftie, too, hung back, glancing toward the front door often.

"You don't have to stay," Trip told him quietly, still standing in the hallway himself.

Leftie jumped.

"I'm sure you have lady friends that have been pining in your absence," Trip added, wishing they could go back to trading jokes instead of sharing this ongoing awkward silence. At least, *he* found it awkward. Maybe Leftie preferred it.

"That is undoubtedly true." Leftie watched Grampy walk into the living room and take the remaining seat, Jangles' rocking chair. Technically, it was Grammy's rocker, but she rarely sat still for more than ten minutes, and the cat always claimed it for himself, in its entirety, whenever she got up. Leftie's eyes narrowed. "Did they know?"

"That I'm a charming and gentle soul?"

"Please, I've seen you mow down pirates. They find you as charming as a toenail fungus. And far more deadly." Leftie turned the squint on him.

"They knew I was… different."

Leftie snorted so hard that Trip was surprised his tonsils didn't fly out his nostrils.

"I'm here tonight to see how *much* they knew." Trip shrugged. "I'm actually hoping they know more than I think they do. Otherwise, I don't know where to start looking for *him*."

"Be better if we don't find another dragon. We've got plenty."

Trip wondered if Wolf Squadron would field a suggestion that they change Leftie's nickname to Grumpy.

"Why did you come along then?" Trip asked.

Had Zirkander not given Leftie a choice? He supposed that was the most likely explanation.

Leftie didn't meet his gaze. He studied a framed watercolor of a tulip on the wall. "I figured you'd get yourself killed without someone looking out for you," he finally said, the words coming out grudgingly, as if a tugboat had to drag them through a silt-filled channel far too narrow for them.

It wasn't exactly a smile and a heartfelt clap on the shoulder, but the admission that Leftie still cared made Trip feel better. Or *did* he care? Maybe he simply felt obligated for some reason. Though Trip couldn't imagine what that would be. Over the years, Leftie had stood up for him far more times than the other way around.

"It does seem inevitable that one of my side trips could lead to death," Trip said, aware of Rysha occasionally glancing in their direction.

Grampy had asked the others what brought them out here, and nobody seemed certain about whether they were supposed to mention dragons or Trip's sire, so a range of different stories was coming out.

Trip supposed he should go in there and explain the truth. Or maybe he would draw his grandparents aside for that.

"Blazer says I should be polite to you," Leftie said, glancing at his face for the first time. "Since you could incinerate my balls now."

"Even if I had that kind of precision, I wouldn't touch another man's balls." Trip looked at the soulblades hanging from his waist. "Jaxi might burn your buckle off and leave your trousers around your ankles. She has a mischievous streak."

Leftie's lip curled, making Trip wish he hadn't reminded him of the soulblades' magical presence. They'd finally been talking for the first time in over a week.

"What about the other one?" Leftie asked.

"He's less mischievous and more..."

Majestic and stately, Azarwrath supplied silently. Fortunately, he didn't share the words with Leftie, who was definitely not ready for telepathic communication from swords.

"Old," Trip said.

Really.

Jaxi giggled.

"And majestic and stately," Trip added, having no wish to alienate his new friend. Though he wasn't sure yet that the adjectives applied to someone who kept insisting a woman's place was in the healing tent.

Or the kitchen, Azarwrath informed him. *Your grandmother knows her place. I do hope she cooks excellent food. You haven't yet gone to a restaurant with fine cuisine so that I could experience something other than military rations or pirate fare. It's been so long.* A deep sigh resonated in Trip's mind.

The kitchen? Jaxi asked. *How can you have such primitive notions when we found you in the hands of a female pirate throwing power like Therrik hurls privates around in the training arena?*

Berasa and I disagreed often.

I bet a lot of women disagree with you often.

"Trip?" Leftie prodded him in the arm.

"Sorry, did you ask a question?"

"No, but you had this weird distant look in your eyes. Is that your doing-magic face?"

"It's my listening-to-two-soulblades-arguing face."

"Huh, I wouldn't have guessed that had a dedicated expression. You looked a bit like Colonel Anchor before he drops his morning cannonballs."

"That's concerning."

"I'll say."

Grammy entered the living area with a tray of drinks, and Trip decided to take the opportunity to draw Grampy aside. As much as he would like to stay here and enjoy a pleasant evening with his family, Zirkander had given him a deadline, and he felt it looming over him. He needed to learn what he could and hope he had a route to give the other pilots in the morning.

If not, he would have to direct Rysha to the local library and hope for the best. It was too bad he hadn't grown up in this house, because there would more likely have been clues lying around. But he well remembered why his grandparents had moved often… whenever some neighbor or teacher had noticed Trip's oddness.

Trip stepped into the room and touched his shoulder. "Grampy? Can I talk to you for a moment?"

"Certainly." Grampy pushed himself out of the chair with alacrity. "Do you want to go to the workshop where there are fewer—" he looked around at the people filling the seats, "—interruptions?"

"I'd love to see what you're working on this week."

"And suggest frilly improvements for it, no doubt."

"My improvements are useful, not frilly. Frilly is those doilies spread all over the living room tables. There are more here every time I visit."

"Your grandmother retired too early, I fear. Her hands don't know how to be idle."

Trip waved a parting to Rysha, who was the only one watching him. Blazer was leading an argument about whether Cougar Squadron and the other more remote units were as well trained and experienced as Wolf and Tiger squadrons. Trip was glad Vapors hadn't come along, or the discussion would have ended in blows. It might still, with Leftie defending their old unit.

"What's truly brought you back to Charkolt, Telryn?" Grampy asked, opening the door to the detached workshop in the backyard. He stepped inside and groped for the lantern and the matches underneath it.

Trip resisted the urge to light it with his mind, something he'd done about five thousand times one evening, under Sardelle's observant eye, as he'd perfected the size and shape of the flame that appeared. For a typically serene woman, she had a tyrannical streak when it came to teaching. Trip could also conjure an intangible lightbulb that would float in the air at his shoulder, so long as he didn't lose his concentration. Thus far, that was something he'd only managed for three minutes.

"We're looking for my father," Trip said, figuring there was no point in dawdling.

The flame came to life, revealing Grampy's raised eyebrows as he touched the match to the wick. "We?"

"We. My superiors think he might be able to help defend Iskandia from dragons."

Interestingly, Grampy didn't question that. "Do you know who he is, and if he's alive?"

He walked around, lighting a few more lanterns. The spacious workshop had a couple of large stationary tools that could be powered with a steam engine in the back, but he rarely used them. He preferred hand tools for almost everything, the hammers, saws, planes, and snips lovingly cleaned and arranged on peg boards and shelves. A few sawhorses and clamps supported his current project, a large dining table with the legs not yet attached. It wouldn't likely end up with cup holders.

"I was hoping you knew more than you or Mother ever told me. I have a name, but that's it."

"Then you have more than I have." Grampy picked up a piece of sandpaper and rubbed it over the table top.

"Did Mother at least say which continent she met him on? You must have known where she was traveling to some extent. Didn't she ever send back letters?"

"Oh, a few here and there. Your grandmother might have them in her sewing desk still, though…" He shook his head. "That's not an old sewing desk. We had to leave her first one and all of the furnishings the last time we moved."

Grampy didn't look at Trip as he spoke, and there was no hint of blame in his words, but Trip winced, nevertheless. In his youth, he hadn't understood that all the moves had been to escape people suspicious of him. His grandmother had finally explained it once when he'd been insistent, whining at her because they were leaving his best friend behind. His grandfather might not even know that Trip knew why they'd moved.

"What are some of the places she traveled to often?" Trip sensed someone in the yard outside. Rysha. She seemed hesitant. Wondering if she should leave them to their privacy? "I know she used to look for new ingredients for her tinctures and formulas."

Trip had early memories of her creating stinky salves in the kitchen, and knew she'd always been trying to concoct new and useful formulas with the dried ingredients she'd collected during her travels. By the time he came along, she'd been done with those travels.

"Dakrovia, the Cnat Islands, a *lot* of islands all over. For a while, she had a steady fellow with his own schooner, and we thought he might have been your father, but he was very blond, pale, freckled, and usually sunburned." Grampy looked over at Trip, at his un-freckled and un-pale skin. "Rakgorath and the Desert Isles I remember were places she visited in those last years of her travels," Grampy added. "She went through a phase of incorporating cactus flowers into things. I believe she also spent a few months in Cofahre, learning from a renowned herbalist there."

Trip stepped into the doorway and waved for Rysha to join them. So far, he hadn't narrowed things down at all. He could probably cross the north and south poles off his list, since they weren't likely to have much foliage to excite an herbalist, but that was about it.

Rysha poked her head into the workshop. Grampy had returned to sandpapering and didn't notice her. Trip didn't know what his grandparents—especially Grampy—would think about a woman in uniform. They'd mentioned once when he'd brought a few squadron mates for dinner that women hadn't been allowed to serve when they had been young. Grampy would probably agree with Azarwrath on some matters.

"Has a list of her recipes survived?" Rysha asked.

"Recipes?" Grampy looked at her.

"Grandfather, this is Lieutenant Rysha Ravenwood. She has an academic background in addition to being an artillery officer. Rysha, this is Leamm."

"It's good to meet you, sir. If I could see the ingredients lists for formulas she was creating around the time Trip was born, and there happen to be a lot of herbs from one continent, or even a particular area of a continent, I might be able to make some guesses."

Trip nodded warmly toward her. He wouldn't have thought of that.

"Hm." Grampy scratched the gray stubble on his jaw. "Might be something like a recipe book in the sewing desk. I know Trip's grandmother did manage to keep some things that belonged to Zherie."

"Good. We'll check. Trip, what town were you born in? If it's small enough, people might remember your mother there—and maybe someone was a friend of hers and might know where she'd been. Or were you—" Rysha nodded to Grampy, "—there in those days too? Were you with Trip's mother when he was born, or did you become more of a part of his life after she passed?"

It amused Trip that she'd taken over the questioning right away—and was doing a better job of it.

"Oh, we were all in the same part of the province at the time. Had property at the edge of Ramshead, and Zherie had a cottage right on our land. But Telryn wasn't born there. Zherie came back the summer of 851, I believe it was, and said Telryn was three months old then, though his grammy thought he looked a little older than that. Either way, we don't know where he was born. Zherie said it was at sea."

Trip fell against the doorjamb. "You mean I wasn't—I mean, I thought Mother was pregnant with me when she returned, not that I'd already been born." He frowned, wondering if the birth date he'd been given was truly his birthday. "She told me that. I'm sure of it."

"She had a few different tales related to you."

"That's interesting," Rysha said.

"Or alarming," Trip murmured.

"What story did she tell *you*?" Rysha asked. "Or did it also change? It's possible she had a number of lies going and forgot the details of them. That happens regularly to people, especially if they have to remember a lie over several years."

Trip scowled at the idea that his mother would have lied to him.

Grampy went back to sanding, the same spot over and over again. "In the little town we lived near, it was considered scandalous for a woman to have a baby out of wedlock. I'm sure she felt the pressure to make up stories to explain it. I'm not sure why she never told us more about the man—your father—but Grammy didn't pry. I've always suspected Grammy believed it happened against Zherie's wishes."

ORIGINS

Trip gripped the doorjamb. That possibility would have been appalling no matter what, but now that he knew a dragon had been involved, it seemed horrifically feasible. Dragons could control people's minds, right? If Agarrenon Shivar was the kind of being who would force a woman to have sex with him… Seven gods, did Trip truly want an ally like that? Even if the dragon could help Iskandia?

"I prefer to believe the story she told us, of meeting a handsome man while she was exploring and falling in love with him. But then things didn't work out in the end, and they parted ways and she lost track of him by the time she learned she was pregnant." Grampy scrubbed harder at the table. "Maybe I'm a romantic."

"I don't think Grammy would agree with that," Trip said, though he would prefer to believe that version of the tale too.

"I buy her doily-making materials when I go to the market." Grampy looked at Rysha. "Isn't that romantic?"

"Yes, sir. Trip fixed a table in a tavern for me." She bit her lip, as if she wasn't sure she should have mentioned that.

Had she considered that romantic? If so, Trip vowed to repair every wobbly table, cracked flagstone, and potential splinter that stood in her path.

"Did he?" For the first time, Grampy smiled. He gave her a closer look too.

"We should check that sewing desk." Trip pointed toward the house, hoping to forestall further discussions of romance.

"Of course. Come back if you want to interrogate me further, young lady."

Rysha blushed.

"That was hardly an interrogation, Grampy," Trip said. "She didn't pull any of your fingernails out."

Grampy looked at his cracked and battered nails, kept short so they wouldn't interfere with his work. "I do appreciate that. Grammy's lotion already has to work hard to keep them from bleeding. That's one of your mother's recipes, you know. It's too bad she never put more effort into packaging and selling her tinctures. She only wanted to invent new ones."

When Trip and Rysha walked in the back door, the scents of Grammy's "coconut crunch" fish filets baking in the oven alongside cheesy potatoes filled the house. They almost made Trip detour to the kitchen, but voices still came from the living area, so dinner hadn't been called yet.

He led the way to what had once been his bedroom but had been converted to a crafts room with bolts of fabric and baskets of yarn fencing in the only original piece of furniture that remained, the bed. Potpourri flakes that hadn't been entirely cleaned up after a spill dusted the quilt. A sack of dried flower petals slouched in one corner. The last time Trip had spent the night, he'd dreamed he was trapped in a greenhouse, a gardener with a pitchfork stabbing him every time he tried to escape.

Your imagination is quirky, Jaxi observed.

Clearly, his subconscious constantly worries he'll be discovered and hanged for being a sorcerer, Azarwrath said.

Hanged or poked? By a pitchfork.

I've dreamed of my death at the hands of mobs armed with all different manner of weapons on numerous occasions, Trip admitted. There wasn't much point in hiding things from soulblades that could read his mind. Once, after a captain in his squadron had remarked on how odd it was that his hunches were always right, he'd experienced nightmares of his comrades pushing him against a wall and unleashing a firing squad.

Telryn, Azarwrath said sternly, *while it's understandable that you've grown up with these fears, there is no reason for you to continue suffering them. You have the power to stop any of these scenarios from happening. Once you are more experienced, you will gain confidence in your abilities and understand this.*

Most of the people who were truly hanged or drowned for being witches, Jaxi added, *had little to no actual power. If they had, they would have been able to escape those who persecuted them.*

Trip thought of his mother's awful death and didn't find the statement that comforting. Why did people have to be so damn superstitious about magic to start with? Did they ever later realize they'd killed innocent people? Or gotten the wrong person? He wasn't sure, but he'd always suspected his mother had been hanged because of something *he* had done.

"Trip?" Rysha had navigated around the bed to the sewing desk, the floor around the chair the only place completely cleared of baskets, tools, and pieces of snipped fabric. "Do you think it's all right to snoop, or should we ask your grandmother for permission first?"

Trip hesitated. He didn't want to interrupt her while she was preparing dinner. Besides, she might not be as open as Grampy had been. Trip had always sensed that she'd known more than she'd told him. Perhaps she'd been hiding the secret that Grampy had alluded to, that his mother hadn't been a willing participant in his creation.

His eyes stung as he thought about that again, and he hurried to blink away the tears that threatened. What had he expected? That his mother had convinced some dragon to fall in love with her? Could dragons even do that?

"Go ahead and snoop," he said.

Trip sat on the end of the bed, deciding she might be better than he at inspecting old letters and recipe books. Besides, he now worried he might find proof of events that would distress him. If his mother had been… injured, he didn't want the details. It was bad enough that he'd been there when she'd been hanged, forced to watch by the callous villagers that should have been friends, not enemies.

Noticing Rysha gazing at him with concern, he added, "This used to be my bedroom, so I could argue that anything in it is fair to look through, right?"

"This is your bedroom?" Rysha crinkled her nose.

"*Was.* When I was here, it didn't smell like dead roses. It had strong, masculine scents."

"Like what? Dirty sweat socks?"

"Uhm." Trip didn't know how to recover from that claim, especially since her guess was close to the truth. "Like woodworking tools. Sawdust. Paint and wood glue. Anvils." Not entirely untrue. He'd spent a summer working for the smith down the street and had enjoyed pounding the malleable alloys into shapes.

"If you kept all those things in your room, it's no wonder your grandmother felt the urge to redecorate." Rysha investigated nooks and crannies in and around the sewing desk as she spoke. "Though I'm surprised—well, doesn't it seem weird to come back, and your room is basically gone?"

"Did your parents leave your bedroom intact when you left for school?"

"Yes, it's the same as it always was." Rysha extracted a clump of old, opened letters. "There are still stuffed dragons on the bed. I told Shulina Arya about them, and she wants to see the place someday."

"I suppose, since you grew up in a castle, there are plenty of rooms, so space wasn't a concern."

"It's a manor."

"How many rooms does it have?"

"Rooms or bedrooms?" Rysha set the letters on the bed, then pulled a couple of logbooks out of a drawer stuffed with crafts magazines.

"What's the matter?" he teased. "It would take too long to count all the rooms?"

"My brain is occupied with other matters."

"That sounded like a yes."

"There are thirteen bedrooms and nine bathrooms."

"Indoor bathrooms?"

"Of *course* indoor. The manor was renovated and brought into the modern age before I was born."

"This was the first house I lived in that didn't have an outhouse." Trip smirked and waved toward the hall and the single small indoor bathroom.

"I refuse to feel bad about your simple upbringing now that we know you're half *dragon*. That is way more amazing than the fact that my family has a manor. I bet you could wave a hand and magic a manor into existence."

"I probably have to master the first page in Sardelle's workbook first."

"Fine, after a year of training, you'll be able to magic manors into existence." She gathered the books and letters and sat cross-legged on the bed with them, but she looked at him instead of immediately investigating her finds. "Trip, don't you understand how much power you'll have? That you *do* have? Once you learn how to use it. Those mages of old, especially the ones that were direct offspring of dragons, ruled *cities*. If people sent armies against them, they simply used mind control to turn the armies around. Or they could conjure up a hurricane to knock the entire army into the ocean. If there hadn't been multiple people like that back then, along with dragons who were even more powerful than the mages, they could have easily controlled entire nations by sheer magical strength."

"Did anybody like them? Because they sound like assholes."

Rysha snorted. "*Trip.*"

"I don't want to be an asshole, Rysha," he said softly. "I'm afraid that having all that, being able to do all that… How could it not change you?"

"I'll let you know if you start changing, Trip." She patted the back of his hand, then dug into the letters.

ORIGINS

As smart as Rysha was, Trip didn't know if she truly comprehended his fears of becoming someone evil. Or even someone who did evil by accident by being oblivious. He hoped he never gave her a reason to understand fully.

"Some of these letters are from your grandmother's sister, but here are some from Zherie. Your mother is the only Zherie in the family, right?"

"Yes."

"You're twenty-five now?"

"Almost twenty-five, yes."

"Most of these aren't dated, but a few are." Rysha started opening envelopes and reading, skimming through the loopy cursive writing.

Trip's gut tightened. He'd forgotten what his mother's handwriting looked like, but he recognized it as soon as he saw it. Even though he'd vowed to let Rysha do the researching, he found himself leaning closer to peek over her shoulder.

"This one got a ride on a steamer out of Rakgorath," Rysha said. "It's the right year. Your birth may have coincided with her interest in cactuses. No wonder you're so prickly."

"I'm not prickly. I'm appealingly smooth."

"Remarkable considering how much of your youth you apparently spent rubbing sawdust and wood glue all over yourself." She smirked at him, but looked back at the letter in her hands before Trip could decide if he wanted to swat her. It seemed a crime to swat someone who wasn't looking. "Nothing about lovers in this one." Rysha flipped through a few more letters from the same time period. "Hm, this is interesting. She talks about how she was buying herbs at the Lagresh market—how odd to think of a city run by criminals as having a farmers' market—and someone mentioned an intriguing mold growing deep in the dark recesses of the dragon-rider ruins in the cliffs to the north of the city."

"Intriguing mold?"

"That's what it says. She was quite excited about it." Rysha pointed to a line. "It seems your mother was as odd as you are, even without having dragon blood."

"If you keep teasing me, some of my adoration for you may wane."

She leaned her shoulder against his. "What if I kiss you after I tease you? Will that keep things from waning?"

"Things should start to swell in that case."

"How intriguing." She rested her forehead on his shoulder and swatted his chest. Good, he'd been certain swatting should be involved in this exchange at some point.

"Like mold?"

"I certainly hope not."

Trip expected her to pull away and return to the letters, but she held the position, even though her spectacles had to be mashing into the bridge of her nose. She left her forehead on his shoulder, and her hand settled on his chest. He looped an arm around her and rested his temple against the top of her head, enjoying the softness of her hair. He hadn't seen her often without her army cap on and promptly decided her red-blonde locks were lovely. And also that he wanted to tug them free of that bun so they would fall about her shoulders.

Laughter drifted down the hall, reminding them that there were others in the house, and Rysha pulled away. She shuffled through the envelopes. Some had postage stamps with dates. Others simply had his grandparents' address, perhaps given to some merchant heading this way to hand-deliver.

"It looks like she was in the Desert Isles before Rakgorath, but that would have been too late for her to have been impregnated and to have made it back by the summer of 851. Or spring of 851 if your grandmother was right, and you were older than three months. How odd that she just took off for more than a year at a time."

"There you go, calling my mother odd again," Trip said, though the joke was half-hearted. He was dwelling again on the surprising revelation that he'd already been born when his mother returned home. It seemed strange to imagine her choosing to give birth in some foreign country, especially one full of criminals, like Rakgorath. Having a baby at sea didn't sound any better. Why wouldn't she have hurried home to be with her parents for the delivery? Had she been kept away against her will? Would a dragon have *done* that? What if she'd been forced to escape and tramp pregnant across some desert?

Trip pushed his hand through his hair, not caring that he shoved it all out of place.

"It's more your story that's odd," Rysha said. "I'm going to try to draw your grandmother aside tonight and ask her some questions. Can you tell when either of them is lying to you?"

"I've always had the sense that Grammy was withholding a few things."

"Can you read her mind and check?"

"No."

She arched her eyebrows.

"I mean, I guess I could try, now that I know a few things about that, but…" He grimaced, feeling such tactics should be for enemies, not relatives. And did he truly want to *know* all the details? "We came looking for a lead to Agarrenon Shivar. That's all. We just need to know where my mother was when she was… when I was conceived."

"I think it has to be Rakgorath." Rysha held up the letter. "Going by postage dates and these three letters, she was there for at least six months. Even allowing that you might be older than you originally thought, Rakgorath still matches up."

"I can't believe I might already be twenty-five."

"A doddering old age, to be sure."

Trip snorted. "How old are you?"

He hadn't wondered before, and it occurred to him that she might be older, since she'd gotten all those degrees before going to the military academy for officer training.

"Twenty-seven."

"Damn, I should be making you canes instead of gun mounts."

She shoved him in the shoulder. "*Now* who's teasing who?"

"Is your interest in me waning or swelling?"

"I don't have anything that swells. You should be glad." She smirked and nudged her spectacles upward on her nose, a gesture that he was growing to love.

"Yes," he said agreeably, gazing into her eyes and wondering if anyone would notice if they didn't show up for dinner.

He'd no sooner had the thought than footfalls sounded in the hall, the house's old floorboards creaking.

Rysha shifted away from him and opened the logbooks that she hadn't yet investigated. Or maybe those were recipe books.

"Ah, there you two are," Blazer said, peering into the room. "I was sent to make sure you weren't sullying your grandmother's crafts room with sexual acts."

Rysha's cheeks reddened, and she bent even lower over the books—the pages were covered in Mother's handwriting—as she murmured, "No, ma'am."

"You were sent?" Trip asked. "By whom? I'm positive my grandmother wouldn't have said such a thing."

"Then you don't know your grandmother well." Blazer smirked. "Kaika has drawn out her ribald streak."

"That's alarming." Trip scooted off the bed. "Rysha? Are you coming to dinner?"

"I'll be there soon. If nobody objects, I want to go over these books. I assume we can't take them with us?"

"Uh, I could ask, but Grammy probably doesn't want to let them go. Those items may be all she has left of her daughter."

"They're wonderful. Look at these sketches. And how tidily everything is listed." Rysha flipped to the back, then looked up at him, her eyes bright. "Trip, there's an *appendix*."

Blazer, still standing in the doorway, said, "I've never heard anyone say that word so lovingly."

"Yes, it's strange that Rysha thinks I'm the only odd person in this room."

"Definitely strange." Blazer peered about, her gaze catching on the bookshelf. "Are those sewing magazines from the Maddingtorn Pattern Company?" She stepped inside to look closer. "They *are*. The magazine went out of print decades ago, but they have all these great patterns for work clothing for women. Not like those stupid fashion pattern magazines that come out of the capital today with dresses that no woman could possibly want to wear. Dresses that don't even have *pockets*. What the hells?" Blazer pulled out one of the dusty old magazines to flip through.

"Why would you need to sew work clothing when you predominantly wear army uniforms?" Trip asked.

"I do occasionally get days off and wear other things. But clothing isn't all I sew." Blazer stopped to admire a pattern for an outfit that looked like it was designed for climbing mountains. Distractedly, she added, "One of my recent projects was a set of placemats with fliers on them."

"I'm definitely not the only odd person in this room," Trip said.

The women, engrossed in their reading material, didn't acknowledge him. Or hear him, most likely.

He walked out to the living room and found Grammy ushering people into the dining area.

"You make sure no sexual acts were going on in that room, Captain?" Kaika asked as he fell in at the back of the group.

"Only Rysha and Blazer are in there now."

Kaika smirked. "That doesn't preclude anything."

"I think they're too busy reading to contemplate more vigorous activities."

"How boring. You two figure out where we're going next?"

"Lagresh in Rakgorath, I believe," Trip said.

His grandmother was adjusting place settings at the far side of the table, but she looked up, her blue eyes widening with concern. Trip hadn't intended to delve into her thoughts—it was bad enough he'd delved into her sewing desk without permission—but something reared forward in her mind, and he glimpsed it without trying. His mother standing in an old farmhouse, not one Trip recognized. She cradled a baby in her arms while tears ran from her eyes.

"I can't let them find him," Mother said in the vision. "He's mine, and he deserves to grow up as a normal boy, not as some pawn to maniacs. But we can't stay here. An ocean may not stop them. They know my name. They'll figure out where to look. We have to move. I'm sorry I brought this trouble here, Mama, but I had to warn you. I knew they'd come here to look. We have to move."

"Are you sure you aren't overblowing this? He's just a baby." Grammy came forward and pulled down the baby's blanket to see his face. She didn't believe Zherie's story about a dragon. "He looks like a normal baby." Deep green eyes opened, peering around curiously. Grammy lifted her gaze to meet Zherie's eyes. "Your baby? You didn't say…"

"My baby," Mother said firmly. "They're not taking him from me. Ever."

No, they'd taken Mother from *him*.

A lump formed in Trip's throat.

Grammy dropped her gaze to the table, adjusting a fork again, and the vision—the memory—dissipated.

Trip could have pried further, but he'd seen enough. Enough to be concerned. Had some person or organization—criminals?—wanted him because they'd figured out Mother had given birth to a half-dragon boy? And was that part of why the family had moved so often when he'd been little? Maybe it hadn't *always* been about someone noticing his oddness. How long had the person or organization hunted for him? At some point, they must have given up. Maybe after Mother had been killed, they'd lost track of the family.

He shivered at the idea that someone might have wanted to raise him like some animal bred to fight. To use the power he barely knew he had now, at twenty-five. What if he'd grown up being trained like the kids at Sardelle's house? But trained by someone a lot less noble and caring than Sardelle. Someone who wanted to use a powerful sorcerer to some nefarious end?

It hadn't happened, he told himself, and nobody was going to turn him into a tool at age twenty-five. He had nothing to fear from visiting Rakgorath as a grown man.

His gaze shifted toward the dark window, night having long since fallen. Even though his thoughts were logical, he couldn't help but dread what they might find when they reached the continent.

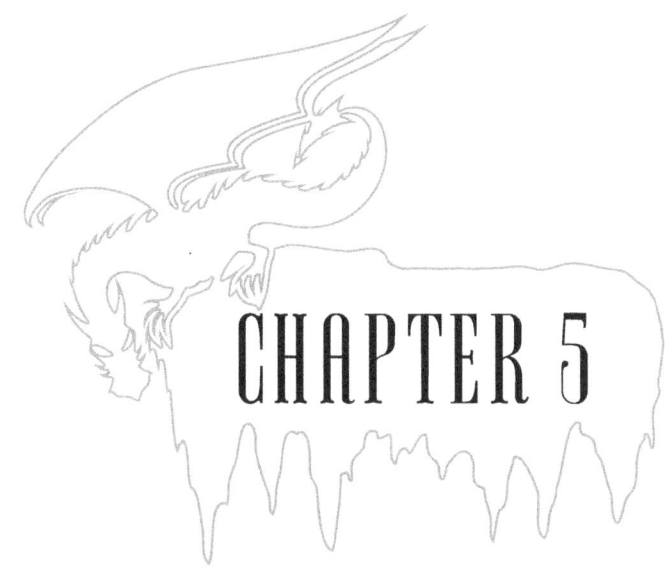

CHAPTER 5

*G*REETINGS, STORY TELLER! SHULINA ARYA'S words burst into Rysha's head with alarming cheer.

Good morning, Shulina Arya.

Even though she had spent an hour regaling the dragon with stories the night before, while Shulina Arya perched unnoticed on the roof of Trip's grandparents' house, Rysha still felt strange thinking words of a conversation in her mind. But, as with the previous night, the dragon didn't have any trouble understanding her.

Rysha peered at the rooftops of the buildings the squadron passed as they strode through Charkolt, wondering where the dragon was now. And if Bhrava Saruth was with her. He hadn't come for story hour, nor did she know what Shulina Arya had done after she dozed off.

We played in the ocean, Shulina Arya thought brightly. *We shape-shifted into dolphins and frolicked with several real ones. They thought us odd, but they were very welcoming. We didn't have dolphins in the other world. Or oceans. It is so beautiful here.*

I'm glad you're enjoying yourself. And Rysha was. She hadn't noticed that any other dragons did. Oh, she'd witnessed Bhrava Saruth enjoying belly rubs while in ferret form, but Shulina Arya seemed to enjoy every aspect of exploring the world. *This* world.

Where will your team go next? Do you need the assistance of dragons? Will you tell me stories along the way? Such as about dolphins? Where did dolphins come from? I tried to ask them, but they insisted on showing me their favorite places to fish. I do not think they fully understood me. Or they were distracted by Bhrava Saruth. He was being a pest. He tried to convince them to worship him. He's so self-centered.

Rysha thought about pointing out that Shulina Arya had accompanied Bhrava Saruth out here, despite his self-centeredness. But instead, she answered the question. *I took a marine biology class in school. I could probably tell you a few things about dolphins. Would you like to hear about the other species on their phylogenic tree?*

Indeed, yes. On our journey. Where do we travel to next?

A continent to the east of this ocean. We call it Rakgorath.

What? rang Bhrava Saruth's voice in her head for the first time.

Good morning, Bhrava Saruth, Rysha replied, not certain if that question applied to Rakgorath or had something to do with acquiring dolphin worshippers.

Dragons do not go to Rakgorath-ilthin, Bhrava Saruth said.

Any dragons? Why not? Rysha slowed down, again glancing to the rooftops, wondering if the dragons were nearby.

The magic dead zone.

What is that? Shulina Ayra asked.

Rysha felt too stunned to ask any questions, at least for now. She'd never come across information on a "dead zone" in any of the historical texts discussing dragons. Nor had she seen anything on atlases or read anything regarding such a zone in the histories discussing the continent. Was Bhrava Saruth truly a reliable source for this? If he was... would it be a waste of time to visit the continent? If dragons never went there, that could mean Trip's sire wasn't there and never had been.

But that didn't make sense. There had been a dragon-rider outpost there once.

It is a vast desert expanse where we cannot sense things around us, Bhrava Saruth said, *and many of our magical abilities do not work or are unreliable. It is a miserable place for other reasons too. There is little water, little palatable game. I don't believe there are sheep anywhere on the continent. There are certainly not humans who will bake mango tarts for dragons. I highly doubt mango trees can live there.*

ORIGINS

The open gate to the army installation came into sight. Realizing she'd fallen behind, Rysha hurried to catch up with the others.

The entire continent is inhospitable to dragons? she asked, wanting to make sure she understood correctly.

Extremely inhospitable. The dead zone does not exist along the coast or in the mountains, but that does not make it friendly. The humans there shoot at you if you come close. They are very surly. Completely unacceptable as worshippers.

Has it been that way a long time?

Oh, yes. Thousands of years, I believe, though my grasp of time may not be as divine as the rest of me. I lost track of how long I was locked in my imprisonment. There was once a dragon-rider outpost there that protected one of the cities, but the inhabitants were, as I said, surly. And unappreciative. Eventually they drove the dragons and sorcerers away from their shores. I believe the outpost has been abandoned for a long time. We will not go with you to that continent. No sane dragon would.

We? Shulina Arya asked. *You believe you can speak for me?*

Of course I can. You are new to this world. I am old and wise, and therefore, a suitable guide for you. We shall stay here, where the humans are less bristly. Would you not like to swim with the dolphins again?

Are you asking that because it would be enjoyable or because you want me to help you convince them to worship you?

Yes. Bhrava Saruth shined a mental smile into Rysha's mind—and likely Shulina Arya's too. *I have never had an underwater temple.*

Rysha did her best to ignore the rest of Bhrava Saruth's speculation, though he did continue to share it with her. She was mulling over what he'd said—the more pertinent tidbits—and considering if she should warn the others. She didn't know how reliable Bhrava Saruth was, but maybe she should ask Trip's opinion.

As they passed through the gates, it occurred to her that a continent known to be repulsive to those who relied upon magic might make the perfect hiding place for a dragon that didn't want to be noticed. Where better for a dragon to live in anonymity than somewhere no sane dragons would visit?

"I heard you're going to Rakgorath," a familiar voice said from behind Trip.

He was outside the hangar, packing his flier for the journey across the ocean. Most of the squadron had opted for sleeping on the floors or sofas at his grandparents' house rather than returning to the guest quarters in the barracks. Trip hadn't slept much at all, reliving his grandmother's memories about him, so he felt cranky and out-of-sorts this morning.

"What do you want, Dreyak?" he asked, turning to face the Cofah warrior.

Dreyak's head was freshly shaven, his pack on his back and his weapons at his belt.

Somehow, in his irritation, Trip pried with more than words, and he glimpsed thoughts—memories—of Dreyak at the docks early that morning. He'd been looking for ships bound for Rakgorath and been frustrated that nobody was heading that way. As everyone told him, it was a loathsome, desolate desert land with the only population centers run by criminals. It wasn't a safe place to dock, and only the captains that were criminals themselves—or extremely desperate for work—took their ships there for trade and cargo deliveries. The only person who'd been willing to take Dreyak had quoted an exorbitant rate, more money than he had on him. He'd decided to come up to the airbase with the thought that he could bribe one of the local pilots. He'd been shocked to learn that Trip's group had plans to head there.

"You're reading my thoughts," Dreyak stated.

Trip almost flinched, alarmed at having been caught—he hadn't even meant to pry. Damn it, what was happening to him? He'd thought he would learn to control his power better with training, but it only seemed to be rearing its head more frequently.

Once a swordsman has been trained to block, it's impossible for him to allow a blow to land, Azarwrath told him.

It sounded like some old Cofah quotation—Dreyak would probably know it—but Trip wasn't sure how it applied to him.

He means it's tempting to use your abilities once you know how, Jaxi said. *It's especially exciting when you're first learning.*

I'm not excited about much right now, Trip promised.

Maybe your subconscious is.

I doubt it.

"Because you weren't answering my question," Trip said.

"I thought I was better at hiding my thoughts from prying telepaths." Dreyak sighed. "But I suppose you're more than the average telepath."

"What are you looking for in Rakgorath?"

"Don't you know?"

"Emperor Salatak?" Trip had seen that in Dreyak's thoughts when they'd been in the Antarctic, that his reason for being in Iskandia and joining the squadron hadn't *solely* been to close the dragon portal. He'd hoped to find the three-years-missing emperor, the Cofah believing that Salatak had been captured by Iskandians and perhaps exiled by King Angulus himself. As long as there was doubt, Prince Varlok remained a prince only. Trip imagined that limited his power somewhat, but he didn't know why it mattered to Dreyak. Unless Dreyak had been sent by the prince, and his presence on the portal team had been designed to allow Dreyak an opportunity to snoop around the Iskandian capital.

"Emperor Salatak," Dreyak agreed.

"What makes you think he's in Rakgorath?"

"Since I was one of those who helped your team close the dragon portal, I was granted some trust in your capital. Some leeway."

"From the king?"

"From everyone." Dreyak drew a folded letter out of his pocket with a broken seal on it. He didn't open it to show it, but Trip assumed it was written proof of permission. "I investigated and found a few people to question. Not those who were a part of the original mission, unfortunately, but there was a soldier who was among those who transported a bound and hooded man to a desert island off the coast of Rakgorath."

"Huh." Trip was surprised the king would have squirreled away a political prisoner in such a distant location. It was hardly convenient to the capital. But maybe he'd feared people, people just like Dreyak, would have thought to look for Salatak close to Iskandia. "If you're trying to find a man that my king exiled—and I have no idea if that's what happened, because I was still finishing school then—I can't help you."

"Take me to Rakgorath," Dreyak said. "That's all I ask."

He locked gazes with Trip, and Trip sensed Dreyak trying to use the small amount of power he had to manipulate him. A few weeks ago, he probably wouldn't have known Dreyak was doing anything, or he only would have known something felt weird, but now, it was blatantly obvious.

"I may not have figured out how to move the fish pictures from one side of the pond to the other, but I can tell when someone's trying to manipulate me," Trip said.

Dreyak's forehead furrowed.

Trip hadn't shown him the workbook, so that wasn't surprising.

"I need to get there," Dreyak said. "I'm not trying to free my— Salatak. Even though it's true that I've had to be stealthy and was here as part of a ruse to throw off your king, I don't truly believe we want different things. I want Varlok to be crowned Emperor of Cofahre, and I already know your king believes he's a much more reasonable man to deal with than Salatak was. Varlok wants to solidify what Cofahre has, not conquer more enemies."

"Then why are you looking for Salatak?"

"To find some evidence to prove he's dead. My people won't crown Varlok until they know for certain."

"But he shouldn't be dead, right? Not if he's in exile. How can I believe you want to do anything but free him? What else makes sense?"

Dreyak shrugged. "Read my thoughts if you wish. I don't truly believe he's still alive. Maybe your king kept him in exile for a while, but would he truly have done it indefinitely? Paid for guards to stay with him, for food and water to be brought in?"

"I have no idea. If Angulus had wanted him dead, why would he have exiled him in the first place?"

"Because killing the leaders of other nations sets a bad precedent if you yourself are a leader of a nation." Dreyak shrugged. "And it's possible your king only wanted him exiled indefinitely, but..." Another shrug. "I knew Salatak. And for the last year, I've sensed—I believe he's gone."

"You *knew* him?" Trip squinted. "Who are you, Dreyak?"

Dreyak gazed blandly back at him.

"You ready, Trip?" Blazer asked, coming around the nose of the flier. She twitched when she saw Dreyak. "What are you doing here? Again?"

"Trying to talk Captain Trip into giving me a ride."

"Did you notice these at any point in your journey?" Blazer touched the rank pins on her collar. "I'm in charge of this little mission. You want a ride, you come see me."

Dreyak snorted in dismissal. "You would do as he wished if he wished it. Trust me."

Blazer scowled at Trip.

Trip lifted his hands, not appreciating Dreyak reminding his teammates that he wasn't the same as they were. "I'm not wishing anything right now, I assure you."

"You better not be." Blazer pointed a finger at Dreyak's nose. "If we take you to Rakgorath, we're leaving you there."

"That's acceptable," Dreyak said calmly.

After holding his gaze for a long second, Blazer stalked back the way she had come. Belatedly, Trip realized that Dreyak might have influenced her.

He's not particularly powerful or that well trained, Azarwrath said, *but he does have dragon blood. He's likely used to getting what he wants when dealing with mundanes.*

I shouldn't have allowed that. But Trip didn't know what he could have done. Grabbed Blazer's arm and shaken her?

Typically, a sorcerer working with or protecting mundanes in my time would have challenged an enemy sorcerer attempting something like that. Or, if the sorcerer was the more powerful of the two, he would have simply punished the enemy for his presumptuousness.

An image flashed into Trip's mind of two men in colorful silk clothing with furs draping their shoulders, standing off against each other. One raised his hand, and the other dropped to his knees, gripping his head and crying out in pain.

Trip stepped back, his head bumping against the lower wing of his flier. The image disappeared from his mind.

He waited, hoping Jaxi would comment, calling it savage and letting him know that few sorcerers had been like that by the time she'd lived.

His was a more savage era, Jaxi said, *perhaps because more people with more power were about and had to vie against each other, but it wasn't uncommon for people to enforce the law by inflicting pain on others, even in my time. However, you can simply learn to extend your* bank vault around your friends' minds to stop others from manipulating them. Admittedly, the inflicting-pain method tends to be more effective and teaches enemies not to try again.

I'll work on my bank vault, Trip thought firmly.

Make sure to throw some sewing pattern magazines in there to keep Blazer entertained while you're protecting her.

Was that a joke? Trip remembered thinking of decorating his mental bank vault with metalworking magazines the first time he'd created it.

Naturally. Did you not automatically recognize my wit?

Dreyak tossed his gear into the back of the flier. He eyed Trip warily out of the corner of his eye, but that didn't keep him from clambering up after the pack.

Trip sighed. *If we take him, will we regret it?*

You're the one who can pierce his veil, Azarwrath said. *What did you see?*

Trip hadn't gotten the sense that Dreyak was lying, but he also hadn't been trying to scrape every thought from the man's mind. Had that been a mistake?

It's a long flight over the ocean, Jaxi said. *You can scrape his thoughts while he's a prisoner in your back seat.*

And flip over and dump him out if you don't like what you discover there, Azarwrath added.

You two aren't quite the mentors I imagined soulblades being.

An odd thing to say, Azarwrath said. *I'm in quite an agreeable mood. I enjoyed your grandmother's excellent cooking last night. We must visit her more often, Telryn.*

What would you recommend I do to my enemies if you weren't *in an agreeable mood?*

Perhaps we should wait to have that discussion another time, since you grew squeamish at my first suggestion.

"Can't wait," Trip grumbled and climbed into the cockpit.

Just don't be afraid of your power to such an extent, Jaxi warned, *that you let it keep you from helping friends. You're sensitive, which is better than being an egomaniac hurling power around without thought, but you won't forgive yourself if someone is hurt, or worse, when you could have done something.*

CHAPTER 6

A HOT SUN BLAZED DOWN FROM a clear blue sky, and for the first time, Rysha felt that summer was on its way. She enjoyed it for the first hour, and then tugged her jacket over her head for the rest of the flight in an attempt to keep her freckled skin from turning lobster red.

The continent that came into view late in the afternoon was entirely tan, the color of dust. If there was a single tree along the shoreline, Rysha couldn't see it. Farther inland, a chain of mountains stretched from north to south, but they were the same color as the surrounding desert.

The fliers were still miles from land, but Rysha could already see why rulers from previous eras had turned this into a continent of penal colonies. Iskandia had marooned criminals on its western side, while Cofahre had often used the eastern, the side closest to its own western edge. Not many scholars had studied Rakgorath in recent decades, nor did the newspapers ever report on the goings on here, so Rysha knew little of the current state of affairs.

"Think there's anywhere down there to land fliers?" Duck asked.

He was her pilot for the day, but Rysha doubted the question was for her. He did look back occasionally and ask her how she was doing, often while providing some insight into the workings of the animal kingdom, but most of his chitchat was directed at his fellow pilots.

"I don't know," Blazer responded, her voice faint to Rysha's backseat ears. "I've never been here. I'm not sure any Iskandian pilots have been. Trip? Leftie? Cougar Squadron ever get sent across the ocean?"

"Not this ocean, ma'am," Leftie said.

"No, ma'am," was all Trip said.

Rysha peered toward his flier. It was ahead and to the left of Duck's. Trip hadn't spoken much during the long flight across the water, and he hadn't explained, at least not to her, why Dreyak was once again riding behind him.

"I see some docks," Blazer said. "Small ones. Nothing elevated for airships, as far as I can tell. No runways, but that isn't surprising. Until recently, only Iskandia had fliers."

"There are artillery weapons on either end of that harbor," Trip said. "On those elevated hills. See them? The hills are man-made."

"Are you using magic to discern that?" Blazer asked. "Or are your eyes a lot better than we thought?"

"Which answer would make you the least uncomfortable?" Trip asked.

Rysha would have smiled, but his tone didn't sound dry or amused. It sounded like a genuine question.

"I liked it when we all pretended those swords were giving you the answers," Leftie grumbled.

If Rysha had been flying behind him, she would have smacked him. She'd spotted Trip and Leftie talking at Trip's grandparents' house and had thought that encouraging, but Leftie still sounded dour. What would it take for him to get over that?

"Jaxi informs me that there are men manning those artillery weapons currently," Trip said, "and that they're rubbing their weapons while looking at us." He paused. "They may also have orders to—"

A boom came from the northern end of the harbor. A cannonball arched up and toward the fliers.

Rysha gripped the sides of the seat well, but neither Duck nor the others altered their course.

The cannonball sailed past to the left and well above their heads before reaching its apex, then plummeted toward the ocean. It disappeared into the deep blue water with an infinitesimal splash. At least it appeared infinitesimal from their altitude. The fliers were still a couple thousand feet in the air.

"Shoot at us?" Blazer suggested.

"Possibly," Trip said, his tone dry, a hint of his humor showing for the first time that day.

Rysha thought of the night before, of how much his humor had come out when they'd been alone together. He was far more reserved with the others around.

Another cannonball shot out, this time from the southern artillery platform. It sailed past a good fifty yards to the right of the closest flier.

"Hard to be alarmed by that," Duck said, "after having dragon fire spewed at you and getting clubbed by their wings."

"True," Blazer said, "but they'll find their range soon if we keep flying straight."

"Maybe this is like the pirate outpost," Leftie said, "and we're supposed to pay a toll in order to land."

"Hard to pay the toll *before* landing."

"We could fly over the city and drop nucro coins."

The cannons fired two more balls, the projectiles sailing closer this time.

"*Nucros* aren't what I'm in the mood to drop on those people right now," Blazer said. "We'll head south and find a quiet beach to land on. Trip, you sure you want to start your search in Lagresh? If there was a dragon living down there, they wouldn't need to fire cannons."

"This city was mentioned in my mother's letters. There's supposed to be a dragon-rider outpost to the north."

"Then let's find a quiet beach to the north. Maybe we can bypass the city altogether."

Rysha touched the rifle mounted to the side of the seat well and also Dorfindral's hilt. To her surprise, the sword emanated warmth, and a little warning buzz ran up her hand.

"That's not from Trip, is it?" she asked, though she knew the sword wouldn't respond.

"What's that, Ravenwood?" Duck called back.

"My sword is buzzing."

"It thinks there's magic around? More than the usual stuff that comes from the flier crystals?"

"It seems to." Rysha leaned forward to yell toward the crystal. "Trip, can you tell if there's any magic in the city?" She didn't see anything else up in the sky with them as they turned north along the coastline.

As cloudless and clear as it was, she could see for miles, if not dozens of miles.

"We don't sense anything coming from the city," Trip said after a moment.

"Anyone else get concerned when Trip talks about himself like he's multiple people?" Leftie asked.

"No," Blazer said. "He is multiple people right now. What do the swords say, Trip?"

"They know little about this continent and less about the city. They're not sure if there was a purge in the past or if sorcerers or shamans survived and magic will be typical here. Jaxi says she was here once, before Sardelle's time, and that it looks about the same now as it did then." After a short pause, he added, "Azarwrath says something similar."

"So, this is the continent that time forgot?" Blazer asked. "Those cannons do look to be about a thousand years old. Let's hope that means that's all they've got to throw at visitors."

"I believe the magic Dorfindral is sensing is coming from the dragon-rider outpost. It's not that far up the coast."

The city fell out of sight behind them as the fliers soared north along dusty cliffs that matched the rest of the continent. Below, whitecaps surged, and waves crashed against the rocks.

Rysha bounced in her seat at the idea of exploring an old dragon-rider outpost, and she scoured the cliffs with her gaze. Nothing in the letters she'd read had led her to believe they would find answers in it, and she didn't even know if Trip's mother had ended up visiting it—none of the recipes in those journals had mentioned intriguing mold as an ingredient—but they ought to be able to spend a few hours exploring it. Maybe, if all the chambers hadn't been looted, they could find a mention of Agarrenon Shivar. Even if they *had* been looted—given the reputation of the continent and the outpost's proximity to a large city, that seemed likely—wall carvings or statues of dragons might remain within.

"There are some caves in those cliffs," Duck said. "What's a dragon-rider outpost look like?"

"They were often built into mountain tops and cliffs just like this," Rysha said, pleased to have the opportunity to share her knowledge. "It allowed the dragons to take off from an elevated position and offered some natural defense from invaders, beyond whatever magical booby traps were installed. There are typically only one or two ways in, sometimes *no* ways for those who don't come on dragon back. Did you know—"

"Are those just caves then?" Blazer asked, waving toward the cliff. "Or was this outpost overly endowed with entrances?"

"I suspect Trip could more accurately tell you than I if there's a large system of chambers and tunnels hollowed out in the rocks over there," Rysha said, a little miffed at being cut off, "which is what you would expect from an outpost. They generally housed up to a hundred people and as many as a dozen dragons. If the dragons weren't shape-shifted, they took up a lot of space."

"That was a yes or no question, Ravenwood," Blazer said.

"Stop picking on my lieutenant," came Kaika's voice over the crystal, distant since she was in the back seat of her flier.

"I'm not picking on her; I'm trying to get her to be succinct."

"Which she takes as a personal affront, I'm certain. She's trying very hard to educate you."

Rysha blinked at this unexpected—and unorthodox—defense. She wasn't positive Kaika wasn't teasing her, too, though her teasing was always good-natured. She looked toward Trip's flier, thinking of the much more appealing teasing that they had shared the night before. But his focus was toward the cliffs, and he seemed unaware of the group's banter.

"Are you affronted, Lieutenant?" Blazer asked.

"No, ma'am. Just mildly miffed."

"See?" Kaika said. "You miffed the only one here who knows about these outposts."

"Are we closer to the magic you sensed, Trip?" Rysha asked. "Bhrava Saruth mentioned a magic dead zone on the continent. I'm not sure how reliable a source he is."

"A magic dead what?" Blazer asked.

"Dead zone. It's supposed to be farther inland, though. An area where dragons aren't comfortable flying because their magic is affected."

"The rider outpost is in the cliffs farther up ahead," Trip said. "Hollowed-out chambers and tunnels, and some residual magic. That's likely what the *chapaharii* swords are sensing."

His flier dipped lower to soar along near the cliffs, about two-thirds of the way up their wind-scoured faces. A waterfall poured out of an orifice in the rock, surprising Rysha. Judging by the barren look of the land so far, she wouldn't have expected rivers anywhere, but she supposed rain had to fall once in a while, or people wouldn't have been able to live on the continent at all.

"Will there be a place where we can land the fliers?" Blazer asked.

A few seconds passed before Trip answered. "I sense that the main cavern where the dragons took off and landed has collapsed and is filled with rubble. That would have been the most likely landing spot. Those other caves Duck noticed are small and don't connect. There's a beach up ahead. We might be able to land there and find a path up to the cliffs. I sense an entrance on the bluff up above, but the terrain is very rocky up there and for miles around. It would make landing above the outpost difficult.

"So we're landing on a beach instead?" Duck asked. "Nothing like having to clean sand out of flier parts—and human parts."

"It shouldn't be a problem unless you and your flier are going to roll around in it," Blazer said.

"I don't know about that, ma'am. Sand has a tendency to get into nooks and crannies."

"Nobody wants to hear about your nooks and crannies, Captain," Leftie said.

"There's the collapsed cavern," Trip said, pointing to his right.

Rysha could make out a slight ledge protruding from the cliff and could tell there had indeed been a large opening there once, but rubble filled it, completely blocking what would have been the landing area. She couldn't tell if it had been collapsed by natural or man-made—or dragon-made—means, but suspected the latter. The cave-in had likely happened long ago, during the Rider Wars.

"That ledge is too narrow for us to land," Blazer said, "and there'd be nowhere to go even if we did. All right, where's this beach?"

"We're almost there, ma'am," Trip said, "but I sense… hm."

"Ravenwood talks too much, and he talks too little. How did I end up in charge of this crew again?"

"Are you saying you don't adore us, ma'am?" Duck asked. "I'm moderately wounded."

"I'm surprised you can think about wounds when you're busy imagining sand in your nooks and crannies."

"There's some magic on the beach," Trip said, as the sandy swath came into view ahead, a mile-long gap in the cliffs before they continued northward. It was as if some giant had come along and torn a massive piece out of them. "The soulblades believe there could be booby traps."

"Booby traps?" Blazer asked. "Who booby-traps a beach?"

"A city full of criminals more bristly than porcupines?" Duck suggested.

"Also, there are people inside the outpost," Trip added.

Blazer frowned over at Duck's flier—at Rysha.

She lifted her hands. She hadn't promised there wouldn't be.

"The outpost isn't far from the city," Rysha said. "It's probably a popular spot for looting or just exploring."

"Wonderful," Blazer said. "Can you tell what the people are doing, Trip? Are they all over the place or in a group?" Blazer tilted her wings and banked toward the coast. "Follow me, gents. Let's see if we can find a non-booby-trapped landing spot."

"We can't read their thoughts or tell what they're doing," Trip said. "Azarwrath believes some of the lingering magic about the place is designed to protect the inhabitants from spies."

"So, we don't know if that's an army lying in wait or a passel of school children on a field trip?" Duck asked.

"Let's find a spot to land first and worry about the field trip later." Blazer flew up and skimmed over the rocky bluff.

Duck soared over it, too, and Rysha peered over the side of the flier. As Trip had warned, the rugged terrain appeared unsuitable for landing fliers. Walking upon it wouldn't be easy, either, though she spotted a narrow path winding between boulders.

"I'm sensing magic up here too," Trip said as the squadron sailed over the rocky bluffs. "More booby traps, perhaps."

"What?" Blazer asked, starting to sound cranky.

"Sorry, I didn't notice it before. The exterior magic mingles with the interior magic. I'm surprised the outpost still has defenses around it after all these years."

"How did a group of people get inside if everything is booby-trapped?"

"Maybe that path isn't booby-trapped," Leftie said. "It looks like it heads back toward town. Maybe foot traffic is allowed, and they just don't want people landing airships or fliers here."

"As in, the locals are allowed in, but not visitors from other nations? I need a smoke, damn it."

"At least nobody is firing on us now, ma'am."

"Give it time," Blazer grumbled. "How far north are we going to have to fly to find a spot to land? And will we be able to find a way back to the outpost?"

"There is a path that looks like it comes up from that beach," Leftie said.

He had to have eagle-eyes. Rysha could barely make it out.

"Let's head to the beach," Trip said. "I think I can direct us to land between the traps. They're less frequent down there than right above the outpost. If they were planted in the sand, it's possible some have washed away."

"Lead the way," Blazer said, then lowered her voice to mutter, "Something I never thought I'd say to a young officer known for wandering off on side trips."

"We'll land one flier at a time," Trip said. "I'll go first."

Grumbled curses sounded, more muffled and distant than his words. Dreyak speaking from his back seat? Maybe he didn't want to be the test subject.

Trip's flier sailed toward the beach while Duck, Leftie, and Blazer flew in large circles overhead.

"Is that a boat back there?" Leftie pulled out his ball charm and brought it to his lips. "To the south? Toward the city?"

"You mean that speck of gray in the water?" Blazer asked.

"Yes, ma'am."

"It could be someone was sent out to make sure we didn't find a hospitable landing spot," Duck said.

"Or it could be someone going fishing," Blazer said. "Though I suppose we better not bet on it. At least these people seem primitive when it comes to weapons. Mundane weapons."

Trip's flier settled onto the beach, high up above the waterline. His right wingtips almost brushed the cliff that rose at the back of the sandy stretch.

"Next," Trip said. "Set down approximately seven feet behind my tail."

"Approximately?" Blazer dipped the nose of her flier downward.

"Precisely would be better."

"I thought so."

As Rysha watched the fliers descend, carefully choosing their landing spots with Trip's guidance, she wondered if they should have flown inland and tried to find a better place in that direction. But the dead zone Bhrava Saruth had mentioned worried her since magical energy crystals powered the fliers. Did it start up a few miles from the coast? Or dozens of miles? Would Trip be able to sense the area before they reached it? She wished the dragon hadn't been distracted by the lack of sheep on the continent and had given more details.

The third flier landed, and Rysha gripped the sides of hers as Duck took them down. The others already rested in the sand in a precise line, everyone looking at the ground around them.

Duck landed without trouble, Trip pointing him to a spot near the cliff. Rysha spotted the trail Leftie had mentioned. It led up the cliff in switchbacks in an area that wasn't as sheer as others.

Rysha climbed gingerly down from the flier and eyed the beach. It appeared entirely normal, a little hard to walk on where they were, with flatter, wetter sand closer to the water. Waves rolled in and battered that lower half of the beach.

"What does a magical booby trap act like?" Kaika asked. "Explosives?"

"Wander around on the sand, and maybe you'll find out." Blazer was chomping on a cigar instead of smoking it. That one might not survive long enough to be enjoyed. "We're going to need a couple of people to stay here and guard the fliers. Trip, fish the comm crystal out of yours, will you? We'll take it along so we can talk to each other."

Trip opened his mouth, and Rysha thought he might point out that he and the swords could telepathically communicate with those left on the beach, but after a pause, he simply said, "Yes, ma'am," and climbed up to comply.

"I need to go to the city," Dreyak said.

"Nope, you got a free ride, and in exchange, you can stay here and guard the fliers with Leftie." Blazer pointed a finger at him when his mouth opened. "You use your damn magic on me again, and I'll cut your flesh pole off. Don't think I didn't realize three seconds later what you did."

Dreyak's chin lifted, and his eyes blazed with indignation. "You'll never get anywhere close to my *pole*, woman. I am a supreme warrior, trained by Cofah masters at armed and unarmed combat."

"Notice he didn't deny manipulating me," Blazer told Rysha.

Rysha had no idea when this had happened, so she only lifted her hands. She was far more interested in the outpost than in arguing on the beach.

Trip hopped down, the glow of the crystal visible through his curled fingers. "I suggest we save pole-removal discussions for later. That boat

Leftie saw is coming this way. Along with three others. Possibly *five* others. Two more are pulling away from their docks right now. They are all of a similar make."

"What kind of boats are they?" Blazer faced the ocean. Since the beach was set back from the cliff, they couldn't see far to the north or south.

"Not Cofah or Iskandian models that I'm familiar with," Trip said.

"Local specialties," Kaika said. "Let's hope they're only armed with cannons if they truly are after us."

"They're fast," Trip said. "They'll be here soon."

CHAPTER 7

"WE CAN'T ABANDON THE FLIERS if there are boats full of hostiles coming. Mount back up." Blazer ran for her cockpit. "If we have to fight them, better to do it from the air."

Rysha rushed to return to her spot behind Duck, but the roar of engines made her pause.

A gray metal craft sped into view, moving so quickly it bounced over the waves like a rock skipped on a pond. Designed like a dart, it couldn't have been more than fifteen feet long, but it was almost entirely enclosed, its metal sides appearing to be armored. The two weapons mounted in the prow looked like the latest technology, something similar to the shell guns Rysha had practiced on at the academy.

"So much for being the city that time forgot," she muttered.

Two more boats sped into view as the twin weapons of the first rotated toward the beach.

Blazer's thrusters fired, and she flew into the air, Kaika already loaded in the seat behind her.

"Ravenwood," Duck yelled from his cockpit. "Get in!"

Rysha intended to obey, but she spotted Trip. He left his flier behind and strode down the beach toward the water, the two soulblades held in his hands.

"Go without me," Rysha ordered, grabbing her rifle and stepping away. Her instincts told her to stay down here and protect Trip in case he got himself in trouble.

Bhrava Saruth's words about the magic dead zone popped into her head. What if the soulblades' magic didn't work here?

Duck's flier lifted off, leaving her alone and exposed in the sand. Leftie's craft had also roared into the air.

The lead boat fired, two shells blasting in Trip's direction. One hit an invisible barrier well in front of him and exploded. The second flew high over his head, the aim wild. It slammed into the cliff above Rysha, blowing up with eardrum-pounding intensity. Shards rained down upon her, and she yelped and jumped to the side before a boulder slammed onto her head.

She gulped. This might have been a stupid idea.

The fliers soared over the boats, noses dipping so the pilots could rain down bullets. The boats fired back, some of their shells sailing skyward now.

The craft were mostly armored, but not entirely. When one motored by, showing its side to Rysha, she spotted a single man in an open cockpit. The sides and top partially protected him, but there was a clear glass windshield, and his back area was open. The fliers might be able to hit him with bullets. Kaika's explosives would be better. Rysha hoped she had some prepared.

She had nothing prepared and felt useless standing at the back of the beach with her rifle. She might be able to get a shot off now and then, since the boats were circling close to shore, alternating firing at Trip and at the fliers. But right now, she was too vulnerable to relax and shoot.

A couple of large boulders marked the base of that trail up the cliff. Maybe she could use them for cover. She started in that direction, but halted, her foot in the air. The booby traps. She'd forgotten.

Go, Trip spoke into her mind. *I'll guide your steps so you're not in danger.*

He wasn't even looking at her. He faced the battle with the swords raised, and a fireball blasted from Jaxi's blade. Azarwrath hurled lightning toward one of the boats as it sped by. It blasted into the armored side, arcing in three directions, one branch hitting the pilot in the back. The man's scream was audible even over the roar of the waves and the pounding of the fliers' machine guns. The pilot crumpled to the deck, his entire back blackened. The boat sped into one of the cliff walls, and blew up with a fiery orange explosion.

Trip watched grimly, nothing triumphant about his gaze.

Rysha picked a careful path toward the boulders. For the most part, she chose her steps, but once, an invisible force guided her to the left, closer to the cliff. Trip. He still wasn't looking at her, and she found it unnerving that he could guide her like that. His words about her possibly resenting him if he was the one to control her sword—and *her*—popped into her mind.

Something to consider later.

One of the boats roared close to the beach again, hardly disturbed by the waves rising and crashing to the shore. She paused and lifted her rifle. The boat's side was to her, the open part of the cockpit in sight, so maybe she could get off a useful shot.

But Azarwrath's red lightning sprang out first. Once again, it curled around the armored vessel, reaching the pilot even in the steering compartment. An instant later, one of Jaxi's fireballs swallowed the entire boat.

An explosion blew farther out over the water—Kaika had dropped a bomb from her flier. It must have missed, because the boat sped away from the smoke and flames, turning and angling its guns upward to return fire.

The boat the soulblades had attacked didn't turn, its pilot presumably dead. It ran up onto shore, making it almost all the way up the beach before its momentum stopped. What had been gray metal was black now, and nothing stirred inside the craft.

Rysha reached the boulders and hid most of her body behind them, leaning out only far enough to fire. If she got the chance. The battle had moved farther away from the beach. She counted at least four more of those boats. She didn't know if the fliers had taken any down, or if Trip's soulblades had been responsible for all the crashes. As quickly as the boats moved, she could understand why the fliers would struggle to target them, especially when the armor protected ninety-five percent of them.

Trip and the soulblades hurled more attacks, this time at targets she couldn't see but that she was sure he sensed. There was nothing wrong with their magic, and she felt silly for having stayed down here. He didn't need her to defend him, and she would have had a better angle for sniping from the air.

She looked up the trail, thinking of climbing higher so she could see the battle better. But someone was up there, near the top of the cliff. Two someones. They wore loose white clothing and hoods that hid their faces, so she couldn't tell if they were men or women. Not that it mattered. What mattered was that one was waving a spyglass and pointing at the beach, at *Trip*, while the other pointed a rifle at him. At his back.

Did the soulblades know? She had no idea if Trip's barrier was merely protecting him from the front or if it wrapped all the way around. She *did* know he had to be lowering it every time the soulblades attacked.

Rysha jerked her rifle to her shoulder and aimed. The angle was horrible, with the rock half-hiding the sniper's body, but if she hit any part of him, that would make him think twice.

The figure leaned over the edge, and she imagined his finger tightening on the trigger, even if she couldn't see that far. Rysha fired first.

Her bullet skipped off the rock at the man's feet with a blast of dust. Damn it. She fired again as he jerked his rifle down to point at her. His buddy dove out of her sight, but she had a good look at the first man. Her bullet slammed into his forehead as he fired.

She threw herself sideways into the sand, knowing the boulders did nothing to cover her from above. Her enemy's bullet slammed into one of them, and shards of rock flew. Rysha scrambled around to the other side of the boulder, glancing toward the water to make sure a boat wasn't in view, one that might shoot her in the back as she hid from the threat above.

Twin chimneys of dark gray smoke wafted up over the waves, and one of the fliers buzzed past overhead, but that was all she saw. Good.

Rysha leaned out, rifle pointed at the clifftop. She was positive she'd hit the sniper in the forehead, but she hadn't done anything to the second man. She waited, her heart banging against her ribcage, with her finger on the trigger. But the second man didn't stick his head out again.

He might run along the cliff to find another spot, another place from which to attack Trip. Trip, who may or may not be aware of the threat from behind and above him.

Though she risked being caught in the open, Rysha ran up the path, legs pumping as she headed for the first switchback. She kept her rifle pointing upward, her head tilted back, watching the clifftops.

A couple of times, she risked glancing toward Trip. She happened to be looking down as the water receded alarmingly, revealing all manner of seaweed-covered rocks and kelp beds on the sandy bottom. Trip waved his hands, and a huge wave appeared in the distance. A tidal wave. Seven gods, was he creating that? It might smash the boats to shore, but it might bury him and his flier too.

Movement caught her eye up above. The figure in white.

Glimpsing a rifle in the man's hands, Rysha fired before she had a chance to aim fully. The figure leaped back out of sight again. She didn't know if she'd hit him. Assuming not, she ran faster, her thighs burning. The climb would have been steep and arduous under any circumstances.

Finally, she neared the top. She forced herself to slow down. For all she knew, a hundred more snipers might be crouched up there.

She poked her head around a rock outcropping and spotted the first figure she'd shot right away. The form lay crumpled and unmoving among boulders near the edge of the cliff. But where was the other person?

The lumpy, rocky terrain, with clumps of cactus pads thrusting up from soil pockets, offered numerous hiding spots.

Rysha climbed off the trail and risked pulling herself up onto a boulder so she could see over the terrain.

A tremendous splash came from the beach below, and she gasped as that tidal wave swept in, towering over Trip's head. He hadn't moved. It swept over him, and he disappeared from sight as the wave crashed in, swallowing the entire beach. Water slammed high against the cliff behind it.

Horrified and captivated, Rysha almost missed the movement to her left. She whirled and spotted white behind a clump of cactus.

She fired an instant before she rolled off her boulder perch. The crack of a firearm sounded as she dropped to the ground.

Rysha had no idea where the shot went, or if she had hit her target, and cursed herself for being distracted. She scrambled behind the boulder and checked her bullets before sticking her head out again. She knew precisely how many shots she had left before needing to reload, but she needed a few seconds to gather herself. Sweat dripped down the side of her face, and her hands shook from the near misses.

Knowing she couldn't risk delaying long—her enemy might already be creeping toward her—she took a deep breath and peeked around the far side of the boulder. She jerked her head back, expecting the man to fire right away.

But she didn't hear the crack of a rifle. Nor did she hear the booms of explosions from below. Wind swept across the clifftop, the roar of the ocean diminished from her lofty perch. As much as she wanted to peek below and see if Trip had survived his own tidal wave, she had to deal with the immediate threat first.

Rysha poked her head out again, this time for long enough to give that cactus a good look. A myriad of thorny pads grew out in all directions, but they didn't entirely hide the white of the man's clothing behind it. He appeared to be curled up on the ground. Injured?

She thought about waiting him out, but remembered Trip's warning about more people inside the outpost. There could be reinforcements already on the way.

Keeping her rifle trained on the man behind the cactus, Rysha crept out from behind cover. She advanced in a low crouch, her finger on the trigger. If the man so much as moved, she would fire again. She doubted the cactus pads would stop a bullet.

The breeze whipped at his loose white clothing, and she almost mistook it for movement from the man, but she kept from firing. If he was already dead, there was no point in wasting bullets. If he was only injured, it would be good to question him. She wanted to know if all this was because the inhabitants didn't welcome visitors, or if someone had known Iskandians looking for a dragon were coming—and if that someone objected to that. It was hard to imagine that news of this mission had leaked or would interest many people besides Trip, but Rysha wouldn't rule anything out.

As she stepped around the cactus, the man finally moved. His hood had fallen back, revealing bronze skin and short black hair. Blood dripped from his mouth, and pain furrowed his brow, but he looked at her with clear, cogent eyes. The hand pointing a pistol at her chest was steady.

Rysha smoothed her expression, trying not to let him know she was worried—terrified. Her rifle pointed at *his* chest, so he did not have the advantage over her. Except perhaps in knowing that he was already dying and that he had nothing to lose.

"We have a healer," Rysha said. "You needn't sacrifice yourself. Tell me why you attacked, and I'll ask him to come up and take that bullet out of your chest."

And the one out of his shoulder. Judging by the red stains to his dusty white clothing, she'd hit him twice. The one to his chest looked to have hit a lung, and his wheezing breaths lent credence to that.

"It is… my oath," he rasped, more blood dripping from his mouth, spilling onto the dry parched earth under his head. "Sacrifice."

His accent was like nothing Rysha had heard, neither Cofah nor Iskandian, though he spoke the language that, thanks to the empire's millennia of conquering, was common in most of the world.

"You feel you have to sacrifice yourself? Why?"

Her shoulder blades itched, and she wanted to take a moment to look around, to ensure nobody was creeping up on her, but she dared not break eye contact. She sensed that if she did, he would shoot her.

"Sworn… to serve. Brother… Brotherhood of… Dragon."

"The Brotherhood of the Dragon? I've never heard of them. Why do they want me and my friends dead?"

"Just… the infidel. The usurper. He will not… not usurp. We… not follow… unworthy one."

"The infidel? Is that Trip?" Rysha couldn't understand how these people knew anything about Trip, but they had definitely been aiming at him. "I think you have the wrong man. We're from Iskandia. We're not here to usurp anything."

The man's eyes widened. "He comes."

The finger tightened on the trigger, and Rysha's instincts kicked in. She fired and flung herself out of the way.

The rocky earth pummeled her when she struck it, but she sprang to her feet and whirled back. Blood spilled from a new hole in the man's chest.

He should have cried out in pain—or died outright—but he seemed too far gone to feel pain or be fully aware. He held his pistol, staring at it in confusion. He pulled the trigger, but nothing happened. Bleakly, she realized his gun must have jammed when he fired at her. That might have been all that had saved her from taking a bullet to her own chest.

A shadow appeared, and Dorfindral thrummed at her hip, wanting to be taken out of its scabbard. She turned, her rifle ready, but she was almost positive she knew who approached. The sword hadn't been complaining about the snipers.

"Trip," she said in acknowledgment, lowering the rifle.

He stopped at the man's head and looked down. The man moaned, trying to pull his trigger one last time, though he wasn't aiming at anything now. Once again, the pistol failed to fire.

His arm finally slumped to the ground. His fingers opened, and the firearm fell free of them. As the man stared up at Trip, his eyes glazed over. A few seconds passed before Rysha realized he'd stopped breathing.

"Did you..." She stopped herself from asking if Trip had killed the man with his mind. He wouldn't do that. Besides, with the injuries the man had received, it was surprising that he hadn't died earlier. "How did you survive that tidal wave?" she asked instead.

Trip's gaze shifted toward her, and there seemed a hint of sadness in it. She worried he was reading her thoughts, that he knew she had, only for a second, wondered if he would use his powers to kill a defenseless man.

"You're not even wet," she observed.

"The swords shielded me, then lifted me over it and to safety as the water receded. *I* had to shield my flier myself since they were less concerned about it. Good thing I figured out how." He smiled, though it was quick and faint. He looked tired.

"You've figured out how to create tidal waves?"

"Apparently. I realized..." Trip gazed out toward the edge of the cliff and the ocean beyond. "Jaxi said something earlier, that I would regret it if my hesitation to use my power got friends hurt. I started thinking about ways I could quickly end the fight instead of standing there trading blows with them."

"Makes sense."

"The tidal wave destroyed the boats when the water threw them against the cliff. All the pilots were killed instantly or quickly drowned." He continued to stare into the distance, his face bleak, his eyes haunted.

"It is a great power to wield," she said, "and I can see why you want to be careful with it—I'm *glad* you want to be careful with it—but I think that was going to be the end result no matter what. Kaika was dropping bombs on their heads, and I watched your soulblades turn two of the pilots into charcoal."

"True. But I wish I'd found a way to simply dissuade them from attacking us. I've hesitated to study mind manipulation, but what if I could have convinced them to forget they saw us and go back to the harbor? They might have been reprimanded by their superiors, but it would have saved their lives."

"Maybe. Or maybe they would have simply come after us again, by land if not by sea. This Brotherhood of the Dragon seems to think you're here to usurp something. Also that you're an infidel."

Trip's brow creased, and he looked back at her. "What?"

"That's what this fellow said." Rysha waved at the dead man, then stepped back. It didn't seem right to stand around and have a chat over a fallen warrior, or whatever he'd fancied himself.

"The men in the boats were the harbor's equivalent of police officers. They were sent to make sure we didn't land within a hundred miles of their city. They believed we—Iskandians—were here to scout on behalf of our government and that we had hostile intentions. One was convinced we'd come to try to take over the city and that we would turn it into an Iskandian territory."

"As if King Angulus would want anything here." As Rysha gazed inland at the barren rocks, dusty flats, and the lifeless mountains in the distance, she couldn't imagine anything except the hardy cactuses growing here. Had there been any ore in those mountains, Iskandia, or more likely the Cofah, would have taken over the continent long ago. The fact that they hadn't suggested there wasn't much there. "Regardless, I don't think this fellow was part of the local enforcers. He was targeting you specifically."

"I saw. Thank you for protecting my back."

Their eyes met, and a warm tingle went through her. It shouldn't have mattered, but she felt inordinately pleased that he had noticed.

Trip crouched, his gaze drawn back to the man and the tip of something just visible on his bare, bloody chest. A tattoo? Or a brand?

Trip pushed the loose wrap aside to reveal a brand in the shape of a dragon, its maw thrust upward, its tail curled toward the back of its head. Rysha hadn't seen the symbol before.

"Brotherhood of the Dragon," she assumed.

"You're familiar with it?"

"Not even vaguely."

"He said they want me dead?" Trip touched his own chest.

"He did."

"This mission is turning out to be far different from what I imagined."

"That's an understatement."

CHAPTER 8

TRIP KEPT HIS SENSES STRETCHED outward as he followed Rysha, Blazer, Duck, and Kaika across the uneven rocks at the top of the cliffs. The trail they had followed up from the beach had seen so much use over the years—centuries?—that the stone was worn smooth. Even so, it wasn't always easy to follow, as it blended into the surrounding rock in places. They realized that stacks of flat stones had been placed to mark the way and that they could find the trail again if they spotted a stack in the distance.

Dreyak and Leftie were back with the fliers. Dreyak hadn't been pleased about the assignment, making it clear that he had come to investigate the city, but he had agreed to stay until the others returned.

"Are we sure this is the way to an outpost entrance?" Blazer asked. "And not just the trail to the city? Because I don't particularly want to visit there. I'm feeling rather unwelcome at this point."

Trip had shared with the others what he'd learned—Jaxi had pried into some of the boatmen's thoughts as they battled—that the attack vessels had been sent to keep Iskandians from scouting their city for possible takeover.

"Up ahead, a trail branches off, a route that leads toward an entrance hole," Trip said. "This trail does lead back to the city eventually, so we don't want to miss that stub."

"I'm glad we brought plenty of provisions," Blazer said, "but after about two days, we'll need to find a water source."

Trip nodded. Since water weighed so much, it was rarely packed into the fliers in great quantities. "I'm sure we can sneak into the city at night if we have to."

"Just send Dreyak," Duck said. "He's oddly eager to visit the place."

"His mission is different from ours." Trip thought about sharing what he'd learned of Dreyak's mission, but didn't think it would change anything for them.

"Tell me about it," Blazer grumbled.

Rysha fell back to walk at Trip's side. "Do you sense anyone else out here?" She nodded toward the rocks to either side of their trail. There were plenty of places that people could hide. "I've worried that other members of this brotherhood might be in the area. And angling for you." She gave him a worried frown.

Her concern touched him, as did the fact that she'd stayed on the beach, wanting to watch his back. He was relieved she'd been up on the clifftop by the time he'd considered creating a tidal wave—he still wasn't sure how he'd done that, other than through sheer will—or he would have had to worry about protecting her. Was it odd to worry about protecting the person who was worrying about protecting him? Or was that how relationships went? He'd had so few that he had little experience.

"I'm puzzled by that," Trip admitted.

"Puzzled by people wanting to kill you?" Blazer asked. "Doesn't that happen often?"

"It didn't until I joined Wolf Squadron."

"Everyone in Cougar Squadron adored you?"

Trip thought of Colonel Anchor. Definitely not. "No, they didn't adore me, but they didn't want to kill me. There's a place in between those two extremes, I've observed."

"Yes, it's called indifference," Kaika said. "It sounds like your old squadron was indifferent to you."

"Is it wrong to miss those days?" Trip murmured to Rysha.

She grinned at him and lifted a hand, as if to swat him, or maybe give him a reassuring pat. But out of nowhere, she frowned, her hand freezing. She glared at the sword on her hip, sighed at it, and lowered her hand.

ORIGINS

Trip thought about ordering the sword to stand down, but decided he should only override it in emergencies. Hand pats weren't emergencies.

"What I don't understand," Duck said, "is how someone knew Trip was coming. Or did they just sense those swords on him and know he was an enemy? Oh, there's the trail." He waved toward a cairn of rocks marking the turn.

"I'll keep my ears, eyes, and other senses open and hope for answers." Trip thought of his grandmother's memory and considered mentioning it, but he would prefer not to sound like a kook for implying he was some important being that people had been after for twenty-five years. Besides, it had sounded like whoever his mother had been worried about had wanted to steal him to raise, not to kill. Whatever she'd experienced probably had nothing to do with this brotherhood.

Duck stopped when they reached the side trail. "Who's going first?"

"Trip and his senses," Blazer said.

Rysha frowned, as if she didn't like him being volunteered to walk into danger, but Trip nodded. Even if he wasn't in command, this was his mission.

He slipped past the rest of the group and headed down the trail. The opening he had sensed was in the ground rather than in some raised mound of rock, as he had expected. It looked more like a well than a doorway. But the people he'd sensed before were in chambers under them—far under them—so going down made sense.

There are a lot of people down there, Jaxi observed. *Seventy-five? A hundred? I can't get any hints as to what they're thinking, but they all seem to be congregated in the same area.*

Maybe we can avoid it.

Trip crouched at the edge of the hole. It was only four or five feet in diameter. An iron stake had been driven into the rock beside it, and a frayed rope descended into the darkness. It looked like it had been there for years. Or decades.

He gripped it and lowered himself into the hole. He walked down the stone wall until he reached places where it curved inward, and he was forced to hang fully from the rope. Now and then, his pack bumped against the far side of the shaft. The sword scabbards threatened to tangle up in his legs, and he imagined them being pushed outward by condensed air. He felt sheepish for using magical power for that, but better than getting his legs caught and losing his grip.

It's good to practice exercises where you use small amounts of power with precision, Azarwrath told him.

You only need to feel sheepish for using it to float your drink across the room and into your hand because you were too lazy to get up, Jaxi added.

A sorcerer has no need to physically get his own beverage. Maybe Azarwrath had regularly floated beverages about.

Other than to keep his leg muscles from atrophying.

Could we discuss this later? Trip peered over his shoulder, expecting to see some light soon. If there were people down here, wouldn't they have lit lanterns? *Or never,* he added.

Spoken like a man whose leg muscles will atrophy by the time he's thirty, Jaxi said.

Form a light of your own, Telryn, Azarwrath suggested. *There are none lit in the immediate area.*

Trip thought about asking him to do it for him since he was concentrating on not falling, but he would feel puny making such a request after the tidal wave he'd created.

He paused, willing a small bulb-shaped light into existence. He floated it down the shaft underneath him until it illuminated a pale yellow-tiled floor twenty feet below. The thick rope ended in a coil.

Well done, Jaxi thought. *Soon, you'll be able to master the first page of the workbook.*

A flush warmed Trip's cheeks. He wished the soulblades couldn't witness him doing—struggling with—his homework. He'd figured out how to create an illusion of those fish appearing to have moved, but as soon as he stopped concentrating, the illusion disappeared, and the fish returned to their original position.

The rope shivered as someone followed him down. Kaika.

Trip hopped to the ground and moved out of the way. He floated his lightbulb up the shaft to help the others, focusing to keep it from disappearing as he gazed up and down the tunnel he found himself in. Hallway, he decided, not tunnel.

When he'd been descending, he had imagined a cave system akin to something carved out by miners. However, in addition to the tiled floor, tiles covered the walls, each one holding a yellow and blue pattern faded by time. It was as if this had been the inside of an ancient palace rather than some remote outpost. Here and there, tiles had fallen—or been removed—but the pattern remained mostly intact. The ceiling wasn't tiled, but it was as smooth as a table his grandfather had sanded numerous times. Occasional dark, square marks dotted the center, as if objects had once been mounted along the ceiling.

I believe there used to be light fixtures there, Jaxi said. *Similar to what we had in the Referatu stronghold in Galmok Mountain. And that are now used as your fliers' power sources. I wonder what these people use them—or used them—for. They may have been removed centuries ago. I also wonder if this implies that this was an Iskandian dragon-rider outpost. As far as I know, the Cofah sorcerers never made anything quite like our lamps.*

"You've got an abstracted expression on your face, Captain," Kaika said. She'd dropped down beside him and had spent less time studying the hallway.

"Jaxi and I are discussing lamps."

"I always wondered what powerful sorcerers spent their days pondering."

Rysha joined them on the ground and promptly walked to the wall, rested a hand on a tile, and grinned. "These are Iskandian. Early Dinya Era. That marks this outpost as around three-thousand-five-hundred years old. Isn't that *fascinating*? The Rider Wars were roughly two thousand years ago. That means Iskandia had a presence on this continent much earlier than originally thought. Actually, I don't recall the textbooks mentioning a presence here at all. Though I wouldn't have been surprised to learn we were here during the Rider Wars. I wonder how long we maintained troops and dragons here after that."

I guess that answers my question, Jaxi thought. *It's a shame Sardelle isn't with us. I know she would have enjoyed exploring an old outpost, especially if some distant relatives might have manned it.*

Trip was more interested in not-so-distant relatives.

"What's fascinating is this blood." Kaika had moved about a dozen paces down the hallway and now crouched by a dark spot on the floor. "Very fresh blood."

"You and I have very different ideas of what constitutes fascinating, ma'am," Rysha said.

"I've noticed. How many people did you say you shot, Lieutenant?"

Blazer landed next to Trip, with Duck's boots visible in the shaft above.

"Two, I think," Rysha said.

"You *think*?"

"I only saw two together at one time, but they wore identical clothing, those white robes I showed you."

In addition to the man who had died at Trip's feet, Rysha had pointed out another body near the cliff and the trail. Trip had stopped to open the robe enough to see a brand identical in design and placement to that of the first. The man had died as soon as he'd been shot, a bullet to his brain.

"It's possible there was another person in the same clothing that got away before I reached the top." Rysha grimaced, looking miserable at the thought of some perceived failing on her part.

Trip thought about brushing her hand to reassure her, but the whole team was down there now, and he needed to worry about appearing—and being—professional. They were both soldiers. They could have a relationship off-duty, but not while they were in the middle of a mission. The day outside the hangar when they'd almost kissed... had been a mistake.

"You did good to shoot two from where you were," Kaika said. "Not your fault if you didn't see them all, but we better hurry. If there was a third that got away, he could make trouble." She gazed down the tunnel, her hand on her pistol.

Neither she nor Rysha reached for the *chapaharii* swords. Despite glowing earlier, they didn't appear to be on high alert now. Interesting, since Trip sensed residual magic emanating from the walls, from all around them. Maybe the weapons had figured out that whoever or whatever had imbued the outpost with power had moved on long ago.

"You think we should stick together or split up?" Blazer pointed her thumb down the hallway in the opposite direction and raised her eyebrows at Kaika. Now that they had landed, she must have been willing to take advice from the more experienced ground officer.

"Better stay together." Kaika drew her pistol and headed in the direction she'd found the blood. "Trip's probably only got one special glowy lightbulb."

Blazer grunted. "I've got a lantern in my pack."

"But is it special?"

"It doesn't float." Blazer eyed the conjured light as she passed it. "Not sure that makes it less desirable."

ORIGINS

The group headed down the hallway, soon coming to a large stairwell that spiraled downward in circles, appearing to descend fifteen or twenty levels. In addition, their hallway split, offering right and left options.

Rysha trotted past the stairs to an empty pedestal. Whatever it had once held was gone, but she slid her hand over the surface, then lovingly touched tiles on its base, smaller tiles than the ones on the walls. These were green and blue and featured different patterns.

"So beautiful," she breathed. "Especially given their age."

"Let's stay focused on what we're looking for," Blazer said.

"Uhm, what *are* we looking for?" Duck asked.

"Clues." Blazer waved at Trip, as if that would explain everything.

"What kind of clues?" Duck asked.

"I'll know them when I see them." Rysha stepped back from the pedestal and looked at another one farther down one of the hallways, but she kept herself from running to inspect it. There were also doors in that direction, the wood remarkably preserved if it was original. "I believe we need to go down to find the dragon area," she added, pointing down the stairwell.

"The people I sense are down there," Trip said.

"In the dragon area?"

"I don't know. What would the dragon area look like?"

"Probably some large, interconnected open spaces. They would lead to that ledge we saw from the outside."

That's where the people are, Jaxi thought. *In one of the large chambers down below. They're all gathered there for some reason. I have no idea what they're doing.*

Indeed, Azarwrath said. *The magic continues to make it difficult to read minds and fully sense our surroundings. Some of the people seem to be agitated.*

They might have been warned about us—about me—*by now,* Trip replied.

I find the interest in you confusing.

Tell me about it.

"More blood on the stairs." Kaika pointed down a few steps, then trotted down to investigate it. "Fresh. *More* than fresh. It's still warm. Same person, I'm sure."

"I think we're going to run into trouble if we go down there," Trip said. "That's where the larger chambers are, and it's also where a bunch of people are."

"How many is a bunch?" Kaika rubbed her thumb on the side of her pistol. "Close to a hundred."

"Well, one of my bombs could put an end to that if they're all in one chamber, but I suppose it's not polite to invade a random continent and start blowing people up."

"Don't the Cofah do that on a regular basis?" Duck asked, though he sounded appalled by the idea of bombing strangers.

"Everyone here, and in the city, is descended from criminals that were put here for a good reason," Blazer grumbled, sounding less appalled.

"There were natives here before our ancestors and Dreyak's ancestors started using the continent for penal colonies," Rysha said. "Also, just because someone's ancestors were criminals doesn't mean *they're* criminals."

"I agree that it would be unfair to judge someone on the basis of his ancestors," Trip said, thinking how Agarrenon Shivar sounded less and less savory every time he heard something about him. A part of him wouldn't mind turning around and forgetting this mission.

Blazer lifted a hand. "I'm just grumpy because we were attacked on sight. I'm not truly suggesting we blow anyone up, at least not until we get to know them. Ravenwood, do you want to look around up here instead of riling up those people down there and getting us all shot at again?"

Rysha hesitated.

"They already *know* we're here. Or they will soon. Unless we catch up to this fellow bleeding all over the place before he reaches the others." Kaika raised her eyebrows.

"That sounds like something you're qualified to do," Blazer told her. "Take Trip with you. The rest of us will look for clues up here. When you catch the person leaking blood, *question* him. These people might have more clues in their heads than there are lying around this place. Especially since everything except the doors and wall tiles has been looted. If you get discovered, try to lead your pursuers out of here. Then Ravenwood's archaeologist brain can peruse the place while everyone is distracted."

Trip thought Kaika might object to being the bait, but she merely jerked two fingers toward Trip and started down, not just jogging but running. Startled, he pushed past Blazer and raced after Kaika. His sword belt jangled, and the scabbards slapped against his legs.

ORIGINS

Kaika threw an exasperated glance back at him. He had no idea how to silence himself, but he willed the rattling to stop and for the scabbards to cease banging. To his surprise, it worked.

It must be nice to be so gifted, Azarwrath thought as Trip raced down the spiral staircase, descending countless levels and struggling to keep his lightbulb following them while he remained silent.

Indeed, Jaxi thought. *Fire came easily to me, but little else. I started my studies at age five, and was still horrible at healing and the mental arts ten years later.*

I suppose that explains why you didn't become a healer.

That and because I had no interest. I am fairly talented at cauterizing wounds.

Trip couldn't believe they were chattering in his mind while he focused on two types of magic and sprinted to keep up with Kaika. He would have asked them to be quiet, but that would have required yet another shred of concentration.

Kaika slowed down. She had passed several landings with doors they could have tried, but it wasn't until she reached the bottom of the stairwell that she stopped. Trip didn't know if she'd seen more bloodstains along the way.

"Light off," she whispered as Trip caught up.

The vast chamber they had dropped into was lit, albeit dimly, with lanterns on the distant walls. Trip did not sense any magic about them. The chamber spread hundreds of feet in all directions, stretching away from the staircase in the center. The floor was tiled except in places where the large tiles had been pried up, revealing stone underneath. Old scratches in the remaining tiles caught Trip's gaze. Claw marks? The distant walls held a few wide doorways, large enough that a dragon with its wings folded against its body may have strode through them.

Kaika ran toward one of the doorways, seemingly choosing it at random. The sound of rushing water came from that direction.

Kaika lowered to a crouch as she stepped through the doorway. Trip stretched out with his senses as he emulated her. Now that he didn't have to concentrate on the light, he could do so more easily. His step faltered as he sensed all the people ahead of and below them.

He and Kaika had come out on a balcony that overlooked another large chamber. Still crouched low, Kaika eased to a railing and peered over. The murmur of dozens of voices drifted up, along with the source of the rushing water. An underground river. The water flowed from the distant mountains, tumbled down through the outpost, then rushed out into the sea, escaping via the waterfall the group had seen on the way in.

Though his senses had already given him the gist of the area, Trip crouched next to Kaika and peered over an ancient railing carved from stone, a few of the spindles missing.

The people he'd been sensing for hours stood on the banks of the river, lush green moss—or maybe that was mold—lining the rock under their feet. Trip wondered if that was the "intriguing mold" from his mother's letter. The people weren't paying attention to it. Their gazes were turned upward toward a massive dragon carved into the far wall. It had been painted long ago, and though the paint had faded and peeled over the centuries—millennia—Trip thought the remaining spots were gold.

The men and women below, all wearing the loose white clothing, something between a wrap and a robe, had their hoods back as they looked upon the statue. They swayed, as if some music were playing, and they chanted. In prayer? Trip didn't understand the chant, not a single word. It definitely wasn't any variation of the Iskandian/Cofah language. Was this some cult? Maybe that was what the Brotherhood of the Dragon was. Did cults have their own languages?

A scream from the far side of the river and beyond the mass of people almost made Trip jump.

"Let me go!" someone yelled in words he had no trouble deciphering. The accent sounded Iskandian.

The lighting was dim in that direction, so he reached out with his mind, trying to see what his eyes wouldn't show him. He sensed five, no six people in a cage. Five women and one man. One of the women, the one who'd screamed, was being pulled out by two robed figures. The chanting grew louder and faster, as if these people might drown out her screams with the intensity of their passion.

"What hell is this?" Kaika whispered, her fingers tightening around the grip of her pistol.

Trip couldn't yet see the woman with his eyes, but he did spot a flat table carved into the rock under the dragon. The way it was placed made it seem like the stone creature's front talons would sink into anything placed atop it. Or anyone.

"A sacrifice?" Trip guessed.

"Shit, maybe bombing them isn't a bad idea."

The crowd parted, and the people dragging the woman came into sight. They headed straight for that platform. Another robed figure sprang to the top of the table, a wicked black knife in his hand. The blade was over a foot long. His hood was up, but Trip could tell it was a man.

"Dragons have finally returned to our world!" he shouted, arms lifting. This time, Trip understood the words, but they were accented, similar to those of the man who'd died at his feet up above.

The blade he waved in his hands glowed with a dark violet light. Trip would have sensed its magic even without the eerie glow.

The people in the crowd cheered and threw up their arms. Trip lost sight of the captive being dragged toward the platform.

He drummed his fingers on the stone balcony railing, debating what he could do to stop this without putting his team at risk.

"The one we've awaited for generations and generations shall now return to us. The god who blessed our ancestors, who promised he would come back one day and make us powerful wizards, powerful enough to send the brotherhood all over the world, to claim what has been denied us, to leave this barren place and capture a lush and rich land for our own."

More cheers erupted. The two "brothers" dragging the woman reached the table and hoisted her up toward the man with the knife. Her blonde hair grew visible, tumbling down her back, as she tried to kick and bite her captors. With her hands bound behind her, she struggled to effectively hurt them.

Trip grimaced, more certain than ever that she was Iskandian. A young Iskandian. Fifteen? Sixteen?

Kaika gripped Trip's wrist. "Use your power to do something, or I will," she growled, her eyes intent as they locked with his.

Her pistol now lay at her feet, and she'd pulled out a grenade.

"I will," he promised, horrified at the idea of her hurling the explosive and taking out the prisoners as well as the cult members. "I'll—"

"Enemies!" came a shout from directly under the balcony.

A man in white ran into view, gripping his shoulder, blood leaking through his fingers.

"Oh hells," Kaika muttered. "I wondered where he went."

"There must have been more stairs that we didn't see," Trip whispered, drawing back from the balcony, hoping they wouldn't be seen. He could work his magic—or more likely, the soulblades' magic—without needing to see.

But he was too late.

"Up there!" someone shouted, and the mass of people turned toward them.

CHAPTER 9

EVERY PEDESTAL WAS EMPTY, AND every room they checked was devoid of furnishings. Only the tiles remained, and many of them had been pried free. After they'd checked more than a dozen rooms on two different levels, Rysha began to suspect they should have stuck with Trip and Kaika instead of splitting up the group. Hadn't that been Kaika's suggestion?

Duck and Blazer shuffled along behind Rysha, impatiently tapping their weapons, and she tried not to take too long examining anything. With so little left inside the outpost, that wasn't a hard task, though she hadn't seen some of the tile designs before and wished she had one of the university's field cameras so she could take photographs of them. She supposed she could join in with the looters and pry some free, but that seemed sinful. Her archaeology professors would have chastised her soundly for not leaving them in situ.

"I think we need to go down to the larger chambers," Rysha said, joining Blazer and Duck in yet another doorway, the flickering flames of their lanterns casting shadow and light on their restless faces.

"Let's do it," Blazer said, and they headed for the stairwell. It seemed to represent the center of the multilevel outpost.

Rysha regretted that she hadn't found much on the upper levels, and also that they'd been driven away from the city. It would have been ideal to start her research there, especially if something like a library existed. Reluctantly, she admitted that coming here with so little information to guide them had been optimistic, at best.

She led the way down the staircase, sliding her hand along the granite railing that spiraled down the inside of the steps. It was worn smooth by the passage of thousands of people doing the same thing, but her thumb brushed against something slightly rough, and she paused to squint at the bottom of the railing. A carving that looked like a snake followed the bottom, undulating between the spindles.

Crouching and descending the stairs at the same time, she followed it along, trying to get a good look as she held the lantern close. The carving was so worn that it was hard to make out. Also, it was incomplete. It appeared to have once wrapped around the entire railing until hands had worn away the top portion. The snake widened, and she realized it had been a dragon tail, not a snake.

"She's either about to make a great discovery," Blazer said from a few stairs above her, "or she's lost her mind."

"Her mind looks fine," Duck said. "Her legs look like they might cramp up."

"There's a dragon carving and some text here," Rysha said, shrugging her pack off. "I can't read it like this. I'm going to see if I can make a rubbing."

"Text underneath a railing and between the spindles?" Blazer asked. "Was it expected to be read?"

"I think it was all over the railing at one time, but has worn off on the top." Rysha fished in her pack, glad she'd thought to throw the rubbing paper and charcoal in at the last minute.

A thunk sounded somewhere below them, a few levels down. On the stairs? Rysha couldn't tell. She also couldn't tell if Kaika and Trip were returning, or if that was someone else.

"Rub away," Blazer said, stepping past her.

They fell silent, aside from the rasp of her charcoal against the paper and stone. A faint rustle rose up to them, like fabric brushing against fabric.

Rysha leaned as far away from the railing as she could so she wouldn't be visible to someone below peering up through the center of the stairwell, but she kept working, grabbing what appeared to be portions of Old Iskandian letters, and as many segments of the pattern as possible. In addition to the dragon itself that stretched along the rail, weaving in and out between the spindles, numerous flowery vines were carved into the stone. They were probably ornamental and nothing more, but she wanted a sample.

Two male voices drifted up from below, both whispering. That definitely wasn't Kaika and Trip. Rysha couldn't tell what the men were saying, but had a feeling they knew her team was up here.

Blazer calmly drew her pistol. The noise of a firearm going off in here would echo throughout the entire outpost and likely down to the people the others were trying to sneak up on.

Rysha tapped Blazer on the leg, pointed to it, touched her ear, and shook her head. Blazer's lips pressed together. She pointed at the rubbing and at Rysha's pack, then made a finish-up motion. Duck had also drawn his pistol, and he pressed his back to the wall so he could fire past them if need be.

Rysha quietly returned her paper and charcoal to her pack. As she stood up, two white-clad people burst into view, running around the bend and toward them. One carried a pistol, the other a long scimitar.

Blazer threw something at the face of the firearm wielder, and he flinched, his weapon wavering. Blazer charged down at him.

Afraid his buddy would attack her from the side, Rysha also raced down, opting to draw Dorfindral rather than her pistol.

The scimitar man started to turn toward Blazer, but he spotted Rysha and raised his blade toward her.

With her heart slamming in her chest, Rysha jumped down to engage him. Unfortunately, Dorfindral neither lit up with its green glow nor cried its eagerness to hunt into her mind. That meant her opponents did not possess any dragon blood, and it also meant she wouldn't get any magical help in battling them.

Trying not to think about how little sword training she'd had, Rysha took the offensive immediately. She had the upper ground. Hopefully, that meant something.

She swung first for his head and then, not surprised when he parried, tried to sweep Dorfindral down toward his thigh. He jerked his leg away too quickly. Her blade clanked against the railing, deflecting uselessly and sending a jolt up her arm.

Her opponent snorted, but he had the same problem. Not enough room to fight. Blazer and his buddy had disarmed each other and now punched and grappled on the stairs next to Rysha's opponent. The railing hemmed him in on the other side. He lifted his scimitar high enough to clear the railing and swept it in from the side, angled toward Rysha's head.

She ducked, then sprang toward him right after it whizzed past. His attack left his side open. She stabbed instead of slashing, the *chapaharii* blade having a point as well as double edges. He leaped back, but not before Dorfindral's tip sank several inches into his flesh.

His foot came down between steps, and he cried out, flailing for balance. Rysha knocked his scimitar out of his hand and kicked out. She didn't want to kill the man, but definitely wanted him out of the fight.

Something slammed into her from behind—an elbow? She lost *her* balance and almost tumbled down the stairs. She jerked her sword up, lest she land on it, and the blade cut into her foe's flesh again, this time his arm.

"I yield," he cried, lifting both hands over his head.

Rysha jumped close and pressed the tip of her sword against his throat as she looked back up the stairs, afraid Blazer's opponent had gotten the best of her. But Blazer had gotten behind her man, one arm locked around his throat. He was down on his knees, straddling two stairs, and from the awkward position, he couldn't break her grip. But he was trying. He grabbed her forearm, his nails digging in as he tried to tear it away from his throat.

Jaw set with determination, Blazer tightened her hold and kneed him in the back. The man, his face turning red, jerked, trying to find the leverage to throw her over his shoulder.

It didn't work, but he was likely stronger than Blazer, so Rysha wasn't sure he would continue to fail. She wanted to help but didn't want to risk removing the sword from her foe's throat. It would be ideal if they could question someone.

Duck stepped into view on the step beside Blazer. He leaned in, showed the man his pistol, then pressed it to his temple.

"Nice of you to decide to help," Blazer grumbled at him between her clenched teeth, her face still taut with the effort of holding the struggling man.

"Well, I didn't have a sword. And it seemed like we were trying to be quiet."

Blazer grunted. "Ravenwood's sword is about as quiet as a bell in a clock tower."

Remembering the way she'd clunked the railing, Rysha couldn't refute that. Since the face of Blazer's opponent was turning purple and he wouldn't be conscious much longer, Rysha focused on her man, capturing his gaze with her own.

"Who are you people, and what are you doing here in this outpost?" she asked.

Deep furrows formed between the man's eyebrows.

"I think that was the question he wanted to ask us," Duck pointed out.

"Well, I already know why *we're* here." Rysha lightly pressed the sword tip into her prisoner's throat, trying not to feel like a bully as she did so. The deaths of the two men she'd shot, having never exchanged words with them or even known who they were, disturbed her. "Who are you people? The Brotherhood of the Dragon?"

She couldn't see under his tunic, so didn't know if a brand marked his chest, but he wore the same clothing as the other two men had.

"He shall rise again," the man whispered.

"Of course he will," Blazer muttered, then stepped back from her own prisoner. He'd lost consciousness, and he slumped down on the stairs when she released him.

"He shall bless us and make us powerful. And grant us a better place in this world. A rich and fertile land. And in the next world, he shall watch over us."

As accented as the man's words were, Rysha struggled to understand them. With the way he was babbling, she wasn't sure he would have made a lot of sense under any circumstance.

"Who?" she asked. "Who is *he*?"

"The great dragon god, he who swore to return to us. He whose time has come."

"A lot of dragons have returned lately," Blazer said. "It's the trendy thing to do."

"Dragons are not gods. Only our savior has divine power and immortality. Only he will pass it on to us, those who have been patient through the centuries, those who have served him and haven't forgotten him. We shall be rewarded."

"He talks a lot for a man with sword holes in his chest," Duck observed.

Rysha wanted him to talk. The more he spoke, the more she might learn, though it was hard to pick useful information out of the zealous babble.

"Maybe his faith keeps him from feeling the pain," Blazer said.

"You will be defeated. The over father will smite you down for invading our temple to Him. He knows you are here, even now. He will find you."

A sonorous clang rang up from below. Others immediately followed.

"Speaking of bells in clock towers..." Duck muttered.

"The over father knows you are here," the man said again, his eyes burning with some inner fervor. "And the dragon god shall rise and slay all the infidels."

"Would it be evil to throw him over the railing?" Blazer asked.

"From this height, I believe so," Rysha said.

"What if we went down a couple of levels?"

The man's eyes rolled up into his head, and he pitched backward, away from Rysha's sword. Startled, she didn't grab him in time to keep his head from cracking against the wall.

"Loss of blood catches up with you, no matter who your god is," Blazer said.

Shouts drifted up from below, interspersed with the clangs.

"Do we go down after the others or just get out of here and trust them to escape?" Rysha peered over the railing and frowned at the levels above and below them.

"Kaika and Trip are providing a distraction so *you* can explore," Blazer said. "You've got to want to rub more things."

Rysha glanced at the railing. "You're right. I do."

"Good. Trip will be glad to hear that." Blazer waved for them to follow her down the stairs, as if she wasn't worried at all by the clamor coming up from below.

"That's *disgusting*, Major." Duck ran down the stairs behind her.

Rysha ignored the joke and kept pace with them.

"What if someone was rubbing your things?" Blazer asked over her shoulder. "Would it be less disgusting then?"

"Maybe. That wasn't an offer, was it?"

"Sorry, Duck. You've got nothing I want to rub."

"That's disappointing, ma'am."

As they continued downward, Rysha glimpsed arms and shoulders on the stairs several levels below. All covered in white clothing. They were only three or four floors down and coming up rapidly.

At the next landing, Blazer veered through a doorway without a door on it. She sprinted down a long, tiled hallway and turned left at the first intersection. If Rysha hadn't known better, she would have guessed Blazer had a map of the place memorized. But she was probably just trying to get as far from the mob as possible, the mob that might be chasing Kaika and Trip even as Rysha and the others ran in another direction.

Rysha winced at the idea of abandoning them, using them for a "distraction." But Blazer was right. Rysha hadn't had time to decipher the pieces of words she'd gotten yet, but she doubted a rubbing of a stairway railing would contain ground-shattering information.

The clamor faded from Rysha's hearing as they raced down another hall. This one ended at a window slit allowing the fading daylight from outside to enter. Blazer ran up, peered through it with one eye, and backed up.

"We're not going that way," she said.

Rysha peeked through and saw the ocean far below. They were still hundreds of feet above the water.

Blazer pushed on one of two wooden doors on either side of the corridor. It didn't open. The hinges were rusted into almost unrecognizable brownish lumps. Rysha tried the other door. Its hinges were in a similar state, but it creaked and opened an inch under her shoulder. Duck and Blazer joined her, and they shoved it open a foot, enough to slip inside.

Dust assaulted Rysha's nostrils as soon as she stepped inside. The urge to cough competed with the urge to sneeze.

"You brought us to a bedroom, Major?" Duck whispered, peering around, his nose also twitching. Another slit in the wall allowed in light. "Are you sure you don't have rubbing in mind?"

"Well, Ravenwood is cute when her nose wrinkles like that."

Rysha brought her sleeve over her nostrils to stave off the dust. And to hide her wrinkling nose as she considered their surroundings.

Rat droppings covered the floor, and the straw mattress that likely once sat on the chunky wooden bed frame must have been eaten or otherwise decomposed over the centuries. Not much of the frame remained, either, the wood rotten and chewed.

Rysha doubted it was original to the dragon-rider era, so she didn't bother investigating it. She wandered around the room, poking her lantern into the dim corners, including what must have been a closet carved into the stone. Though she doubted this had been anything more than some guest bedroom, she hoped she might find more carvings.

"This dragon the broken cogs here worship," Blazer said, "it isn't Trip's papa, is it?"

"I don't know." The thought had crossed Rysha's mind, but there wasn't any evidence yet to support it.

A lot of dragons would have come and gone in the heyday of this outpost, and others may have lived on the continent, magic dead zone notwithstanding.

"So far, the only thing that led us here was a letter Trip's mother sent back home," Rysha said. "She wasn't even looking for dragons. At least, she didn't mention it in any of the letters to her parents. She was an herbalist, and she was seeking out exotic ingredients to try in her tinctures. She was interested in investigating some mold here."

"We're here, dealing with a bunch of lunatic cultists, because of a dead woman's obsession with mold?"

"Her obsession was medicine. Mold was just an ingredient."

"Mold medicine. Sounds appealing."

"Actually, mold and bacteria are natural enemies, and in the last decade, numerous medical researchers at Northern Pinoth University have started experimenting with harnessing strands of mold to kill bacteria that infect and can even kill humans. The research is very promising, I understand. Trip's mother may have been ahead of her time. Did you know—"

"Is this a laundry chute?" Blazer asked, peering into a large square hole on a tile-filled wall.

"I'm finding it extremely difficult to educate that woman," Rysha told Duck.

He was standing guard by the door while they investigated.

He shrugged. "At least she likes your nose."

"I'm not sure that's a positive development." Rysha pointed toward the hallway. "Has it quieted down out there?"

"I can still hear the alarm bell sounding, but not the shouts. I don't know if that means they all ran outside or if we got far enough from the stairwell so we can't hear them."

"It *is* a laundry chute," Blazer said, her voice muffled. Her head and shoulders had disappeared into the hole, and her toes dangled above the floor. "Duck might have to tape his ears to the sides of his head, but I think we could all fit into it."

"To what end?" Rysha asked as Duck touched one of his largish ears.

"Alternative stairwell. It's tight enough that we wouldn't need a rope. We can just walk ourselves down it. It must go somewhere, probably to the lower levels."

"What if it's a garbage chute that drops us into the ocean?" Rysha asked.

"We'd see some light coming up if it did that, right?"

"It could bend. There could be a flap."

"Stay here, then. I'll check it out. Here." Blazer pulled herself out, tossed something at Duck, then turned to enter the chute feet first. "Update Leftie on our status. If you don't hear me cry out in pain or alarm, follow me down. If it takes me to the lower level, I'm not climbing back up to get you two."

Duck opened his palm, revealing the softly glowing communication crystal Trip had removed from his flier. "Update him on our status?" Duck shrugged and thumbed the crystal. "Leftie, you there?"

Several seconds passed before he answered. "Yes, Captain. Dreyak and I are throwing rocks at seagulls to keep them from pooping on the fliers."

"Is that as exciting as it sounds?"

"More so. What are you doing?"

"Blazer is in a laundry chute, and Ravenwood and I are in a bedroom."

"Unless you and Ravenwood are doing something horizontal in that bedroom, it sounds boring. I guess I didn't need to be jealous about not being invited along."

"Have you seen Kaika or Trip?" Duck asked. "We separated, and there's an alarm going off in here and people are running all around."

"Did Trip cause it?"

"We don't know."

"Ten nucros says he did."

"Keep an eye out," Duck said. "If you see a mob running down to the beach with Kaika and Trip sprinting in front of it… Well, let me know. We'll try to get out there as soon as possible so we can all take off. You might have to buy time by taking off and flying over the mob, pretending like you're going to shoot."

"*Pretending?* If mobs are chasing my friends, I don't *pretend* to shoot."

"Just keep me updated, and be ready for action."

"Yes, sir."

Rysha poked her head into the laundry chute. She didn't hear anything.

"Major Blazer?" she called down softly. "Are you making good progress?" Seconds passed without an answer, not so much as a scuff. "Did you fall into the ocean?"

Duck leaned out into the hallway, but only for a moment. He lifted his hands, as if to shut the door, but probably remembered how hard it had been to open it. Instead, he jogged to Rysha's side.

"Two people are heading down the hall toward us," he whispered. "They're looking in all the rooms along the way."

"I hope that means they haven't found Kaika and Trip."

"It *means* they're going to find us."

"Not if we're not here." Rysha nodded to the chute. "Do you want to go first, or shall I?"

Duck grimaced and looked toward the closet alcove, but it didn't have a door or curtain. "Is there an Option C?"

"…check in there," came someone's order from the hallway, only a room or two away.

"I don't think so," Rysha whispered.

"Damn."

CHAPTER 10

TRIP WATCHED IN HORROR AS Kaika's grenade lofted into the air and out over the gathering of people. That gathering was charging toward the doorway under their balcony—or maybe they would climb straight up *onto* the balcony—but he didn't want to hurt dozens of people.

Kaika grabbed his arm, pulling him back into the chamber behind the balcony. The grenade exploded in the air high above the heads of the white-clad cult members. The boom reverberated from the walls, and light flashed as the explosive unleashed its power. As she tugged him away, Trip realized she'd held it for a few seconds after pulling the pin, long enough to make sure it would explode before landing. Smoke filled the room, and bits of rubble struck people, but his senses told him nobody had been dismembered or killed.

"Nowhere to hide?" Kaika looked around the huge chamber they'd crossed through minutes before. The spiral staircase leading up was the only thing in there besides them.

"Here." Trip pulled her to the wall and pressed his back to it. "The soulblades will keep them from seeing us."

"I don't think—"

People swarmed in from an open doorway near them, and Kaika clamped her mouth shut. She froze next to Trip, her fingers clenched around her pistol.

You can camouflage us, right? Trip silently asked the soulblades.

Already done, Azarwrath said as more people streamed in. Dozens of them. Some women, but mostly men, some dark-skinned, like the ones Rysha had shot up top, but others pale-skinned, like Iskandians. They were all armed, some with swords and cudgels, others with old flintlock pistols, others with modern pistols from Cofahre or Iskandia. *Be careful not to speak or move. That makes it easier for people to see through the illusion. Also, those with dragon blood can often detect something awry, but I've only noticed one person like that so far, the man who was standing on top of the table.*

The cult leader? Wonderful.

The first two-dozen men raced for the stairs and charged up, not hesitating or even looking around. Some of the others followed more slowly, peering left and right toward open doorways as they followed the leaders.

Can you make a noise or something upstairs so they'll believe we went that way? Trip asked.

We could, Jaxi replied. *But the rest of your team is up there. They just had a battle on the stairs.*

Rysha did? Do they need help? Trip stepped away from the wall before thinking better of it.

Kaika must have heard Azarwrath's instructions because she grabbed his arm, her grip like a vice as it held him in place.

A big, sunburned man with a long black dagger strode out of a doorway. His hood was back, and Trip recognized him even before his senses told him he had dragon blood. It was the cult leader. The man who'd stood on the table, intending to sacrifice—to *kill*—that young woman.

There are only a few people left in the river chamber, Jaxi said. *If he runs up the stairs, we should be able to get down there and free the prisoners.*

Good news, but the leader did *not* run up the stairs. He halted halfway to them, his head coming up as if he were a dog that had caught a scent.

Kaika fingered her pistol, but the man wasn't alone in the chamber. Several of his people were jogging past and heading for the stairs. Others ran through as they checked connected chambers.

Trip's first thought was to add his meager efforts to strengthening the camouflage the soulblades were providing, but he realized this man might have the answers he sought. This cult might have nothing to do with Trip and his sire, but one of his hunches plucked at his senses, and he strongly felt that it wasn't unrelated.

He unlocked his bank vault and mentally strode out, opening his mind for whatever the man might be projecting. But unlike the other people racing about, from whom Trip sensed outrage and a determination to get the invaders spying on their secret meeting, the leader kept his thoughts locked down, protected by a bank vault of his own.

Trip tried to break through it as the cultist continued to peer around the chamber, as if he was certain the intruders were here with him. Trip imagined having an auger, such as one used to cut through ice for winter fishing, and he envisioned applying it to the man's vault door. But that wouldn't do against steel. He swapped out the simple ice auger for a massive steam-powered tunnel-boring machine. As soon as the drill bit got up to speed, he rammed it against the cultist's mental defenses.

Not truly expecting it to work, Trip twitched in surprise when the figure dropped to one knee, gasping and grabbing his temple. He hadn't meant to hurt his foe, but reminded himself what this man had been about to do. Glaring, he sent his thoughts into the hole in the cultist's defenses and searched for information, for everything the man was thinking about and had been thinking about recently.

Memories of dozens of recent sacrifices blasted into Trip's mind, of young female virgins and also of any of the leader's own people who had dared question him, dared doubt that this was the way to call back the dragon god, the god who'd founded this religion in the desert mountains ages ago, who'd spread his seed among his human subjects, blessing them with vitality and great power. The descendants of those subjects longed for the kind of power their ancestors had once possessed. The leader had promised it would be theirs, if only they followed and believed, and prayed and chanted to the dragon, pleading for his return. Back when the dragon god had lived among them, he'd enjoyed being attended by his followers, and he'd approved of the sacrifices of all those who weren't believers. He'd reveled in the blood of the dead bathing him, just as the blood of the young woman would have bathed his statue today. And the cult leader—Xarishtar—would have bathed in it, too, knowing it was what his god wanted, feeling ecstasy at that knowledge.

Kaika shook Trip's arm, and he stumbled back, his shoulder blades thudding against the wall. He'd lost himself in the vividness of the man's visions—his memories—and hadn't noticed when Xarishtar regained his feet. Trip sensed the soulblades' camouflage still wrapped around them, but the cultist was staring right at him.

What is your god's name? Trip asked, throwing all the power he could muster into the question, urging the man to blurt the answer without hesitating.

Xarishtar again dropped to his knees, grabbing his head with both hands. His face contorted with pain, but also with defiance. *It is blasphemy to speak the name of a god!*

What is his name? Trip roared into the man's mind.

Blood dripped from the man's nostrils. *Agarrenon Shivar!*

Still on his knees, Xarishtar hefted his knife to throw it at Trip.

Kaika fired. Her bullet slammed into the man's forehead.

The cultist tipped backward, dead before he hit the floor.

Trip braced himself against the wall, his hands trembling. His whole body trembling.

He'd had a hunch, hadn't he? And all along, there had been hints that the dragon who'd fathered him was... a complete asshole. This shouldn't have come as a surprise.

"Shit, Trip. You look worse than he does." Kaika waved to the dead man while squinting at him.

She didn't hold that squint for long. As Trip drew in shaky breaths to steady himself, she reloaded her pistol and watched the exits and the stairs. The chamber had emptied while Trip had been scraping through the cultist's mind, but that gunshot would bring people back again. Even though a clanging alarm continued to sound, that noise would have risen above it.

"We should get out of here." Kaika gripped Trip's arm again, looking like she would sling him over her shoulder if he didn't move quickly enough. She was probably strong enough to do so.

Trip nodded and pushed away from the wall. "We have to free the prisoners first. Oh, wait." He halted, remembering what Jaxi had said about Rysha and the others being engaged in a battle up the stairs, in the direction the mob had gone.

Jaxi? Are they all right? As he asked, Trip sent his own senses upward, trying to find familiar auras among those of the cultists, men and women who'd branched out to search all over the place.

ORIGINS

He found Rysha close to Duck at the outer edge of the outpost. He sensed they were near the cliffs overlooking the ocean, but not outside. Some kind of vertical shaft? Blazer was several levels below them.

You're getting better at that, Jaxi remarked. *Though I'm certain imagining launching a tunnel borer at someone's mental defenses is an exercise that would only work for you.*

Are they stuck? Trip asked, ignoring the rest of her words. Kaika kept dragging him toward a doorway, and he let her, but barely paid attention to their movement. He sensed concern from Rysha and was tempted to try to speak telepathically to her, something he'd mostly done by accident so far. But he didn't want to alarm her by appearing in her mind.

I suspect she's figured out by now that you can do that, Jaxi said. *She believes you'll be able to shape-shift and fly and all manner of things she's only read about soon. It's clear she hasn't seen you struggling with the first page in that workbook.*

Trip couldn't tell if the narrow shaft Rysha and Duck were descending led to an exit. It seemed to parallel the central stairwell, and numerous other shafts fed into it, but they appeared too small for humans to climb through.

"The prisoners, Trip?" Kaika shook his arm. She'd led him down the set of stairs the cultists had all rushed up, the ones that led into the dragon statue chamber and the river. "Are you with me? There are guards we're going to have to deal with."

"Sorry, just checking on the others. They—"

An ominous crack thundered through the outpost, like rock snapping under pressure. A *lot* of rock.

You may want to retrieve the prisoners before worrying about the rest of your team, Jaxi said. *It looks like Kaika's grenade did some structural damage to the chamber out there. Some rocks are giving way, and it's allowing water to flow in more quickly than usual. The prisoners are on the opposite side of the river and might be trapped as the water rises.*

As she spoke, the sound of rushing water had grown louder.

Also, you may find one of those prisoners particularly valuable to rescue.

The girl? Trip wasn't sure valuable was the term he would use for a teenager, but he certainly didn't want to see harm come to anyone that young.

A self-made archaeologist and treasure hunter that goes by Rock Cheetah, actually. He's trapped in the cage with the others.

Rock Cheetah?

He gave himself that sobriquet.

"Looks like seven guards in sight," Kaika said, peering into the chamber, past the rising river and to the white-clad men on the other side. "Two holding the girl, four by the cage, and another one standing by the statue and that table."

His real name is Moe Zirkander, Jaxi said, and judging by the way Kaika glanced at the soulblade, she also shared the information with her. *General Zirkander's father.*

Even though it was cool inside the outpost and the laundry chute—or garbage shaft—sweat dripped down Rysha's face. She was descending with her back against one side and her boots against the other side as she carefully walked herself ever downward. She'd shifted her pack around to hang in front of her chest with her rifle and Dorfindral's scabbard strapped to it. There was no other logical way to descend, but it was awkward, the long weapons bumping and scraping no matter how hard she attempted to lower herself quietly. She could brush her hands to the other two sides, but was careful not to rely on them, both because her palms had grown sweaty and slick, and because her legs were stronger and could more easily support her.

In theory. After climbing down seven or eight levels—there were no markers, so she could only guess—her thighs were trembling. She had no idea how many levels down that central staircase went, nor did she know if this shaft went as far down as it did. It could go *farther*. She well remembered how high those cliffs had been when the squadron had flown past them.

"This is torture," Duck whispered from above her.

Normally, Rysha would have been glad his thighs were trembling as much as hers, since misery loved company, but if his legs gave way, he would crash into her and take her down with him.

"It's a good thing you're so strong," she told him, opting for encouragement rather than commiseration. "And have great stamina."

"Uhm, you're thinking of elite troops, not pilots. We pilots try to weasel our way out of physical training whenever possible."

"Is that true? General Zirkander looks fitter than most generals I've seen."

"Only because he's twenty years younger than most generals. And doesn't like to be shown up by his lieutenants. I, on the other hand, don't mind lieutenants showing me up. As long as I can fly, I'm happy."

"This shaft *is* torturous," Rysha admitted. "I'd suggest that Kaika have something similar added to the elite troops obstacle course, but I don't particularly want to experience this again."

A faint scrape sounded below them.

Rysha paused, taking a second to rub her lower back. "Major Blazer?"

Thus far, they hadn't caught up with her, but maybe they were getting close to the bottom. They had passed numerous holes in the sides where other chutes angled into theirs, but they hadn't yet come to a spot where they could have easily climbed out.

A hiss drifted up from below.

"That doesn't *sound* like Blazer," Duck whispered. "Not unless she's in a crankier mood than usual."

The hiss came again. Whatever was making it was in the shaft with them. Great.

"Would there be a snake in a three-thousand-year-old laundry chute?" she wondered.

"*You're* the one with the archaeology degree."

"I don't remember that question being covered in any of my study guides." Rysha patted her rucksack, hunting for the lantern she'd tied to the outside. She'd turned the flame down but not completely out, and was glad for that now.

Another hiss floated up to them. It sounded closer than it had before.

Rysha shifted uneasily, aware that her butt would be an easy target for something coming up from below. A faint scraping sound accompanied the hiss.

"What are we doing about it?" Duck asked.

"I'm going to turn up my lantern."

"Are we sure we want to look at whatever it is?"

"Need to see it to fight it."

"Are we sure we want to *fight* whatever it is?"

"My legs are shaking," Rysha said, "so there's no way I'm climbing back up to that bedroom. Whatever is down here, we're going to deal with it."

"Uh, all right. I'm right behind you. Er, above you."

How comforting. "Just don't fall on me."

Ignoring the persistent tremble to her legs, Rysha turned up the lantern and unhooked it. She wondered if she ought to be unhooking Dorfindral instead. Right now, there wasn't room to draw it. Not that she could envision a sword fight from her current position.

The flame came up, shining on smooth rock walls the same tan as the rest of the landscape. As she lowered her lantern, something glinted ten feet below her. *Two* somethings. Eyes.

Another hiss floated up to them, this one more irritated than before. Rysha had the sense of numerous legs, a furry, bulbous body, and fangs. Then the creature launched itself upward and became a blur, taking up half the space of the shaft as it drew close.

She shrieked and dropped her lantern. It clunked off the giant spider or whatever it was and went out.

"Damn it." Rysha yanked her pistol free and fired four times, but it was pitch black, and she could only guess at her target's location. But the creature filled half the shaft. Surely, she had to hit it.

Something sharp stung the back of her thigh, and she dropped her pistol. Roaring in pain and alarm, she almost lost her footing altogether as she tried to scramble upward. She slipped, falling two feet before catching herself again. Another hiss sounded right under her, and her thigh burned as if a branding iron had been pressed against it.

Swearing to punch Blazer when she found her, Rysha shifted around so she could draw the sword. Why wouldn't it *glow* when she needed it? She couldn't see a thing. But she stabbed downward, swiping and poking furiously.

The blade struck something—the spider—and sank into flesh.

It hissed, and she felt it attack the sword, trying to bite down on the blade.

Rysha whipped Dorfindral back and forth to free it or maybe slice open the creature's jaw. Then she stabbed again and scooted herself down in the shaft, pressing the offensive.

Numbness was spreading up and down her leg, but fear mingled with her rage and determination. Over and over again, she struck the creature. Finally, it disappeared, leaving her stabbing empty air.

Had the spider fallen? Or simply retreated?

Rysha lowered herself slowly, swiping the route below with the sword. The blade clanged off the sides of the shaft, and she didn't encounter anything with flesh and bone.

A distant thump floated up from below.

She stopped her wild slashing, and only the sound of her ragged panting filled the shaft. A light appeared above her.

"Found my lantern," Duck said.

Rysha let her head clunk back against the wall. "You're my hero."

"That didn't sound very sincere."

She squinted her eyes shut as the back of her thigh throbbed with pain. Though she wanted to take a minute to rest, her entire leg was going numb, and the other one wasn't much better. She feared that some spider venom coursed through her veins, perhaps enough to kill her. At the least, it might make her too weak to climb.

"I'm going down," she said, doing her best to propel herself down the shaft rapidly without losing control. That spider had fallen a long time before hitting the bottom.

"You all right? You don't sound all right."

"It bit me," she said shortly, her eyes focused on a crack meandering down the shaft, just visible thanks to Duck's lantern light.

"What was it? A rat?"

"Some kind of giant tarantula, I think."

"Are they venomous?"

"I think that one was, yes." Rysha flinched as the crack opened into a gouge in the wall—she'd almost planted her boot there. Round yellow eggs lay nestled in a sac stuck inside. "There's its nest," she grumbled and continued downward.

Duck made a mournful sound as he passed the spot. "We killed a mama?"

Rysha resolved to punch Blazer when they caught up to her. How had she made it past that spot without having to fight the tarantula? Had it been elsewhere and then come running when it heard its home being invaded? Or—her gut lurched—had Blazer fought it and *lost*?

Rysha imagined Blazer's body crumpled at the bottom underneath the dead tarantula. But surely, they would have heard Blazer battling some oversized spider.

Distant clangs reached her ears as she labored down the shaft. *Now* what?

"That's coming from below," Duck said. "Blazer?"

Rysha grunted. It was all she could manage. Her entire body shook now, and her injured leg was next to useless. She barely felt her boot touching the side as she maneuvered down the shaft. Would she be able to walk when she reached the bottom?

When her heel squished into something below her, she blurted a startled squawk. She moved her hand down to brace herself but encountered open air instead of the stone wall. Only quick reflexes kept her from pitching to her butt.

Above her, Duck shifted, and more of his light filtered down, enough to see the very large, very dead tarantula splatted on the bottom of the shaft, along with an almost door-sized opening to her left.

Rysha shifted, trying to stand without stepping on spider guts, but the thing must have weighed forty pounds. Its demolished body took up the entire bottom of the shaft.

She clambered out, but sucked in a pained breath as she tried to support herself on the injured leg. It was so numb, she could barely feel it, and she had to brace herself against the wall. For the first time, she had a free hand with which to probe the back of her thigh. Moisture dampened her uniform trousers. Blood? Ichor? She found the fang punctures in her clothing. Underneath, her skin was hot to the touch. The wound itself hurt too much to touch directly.

"Blazer," Duck blurted, coming out beside Rysha and pointing ahead of them.

He raced across a large room—what had once been the laundry room, perhaps—and toward faint light coming through an open doorway. Shadows moved beyond it, and more clangs sounded. Weapons clashing.

"It might not be her," Rysha warned in a low voice, but she followed after him the best she could, hobbling along the wall.

She should have been worried about Blazer and the others, but fear for her own life was creeping into her thoughts again. What if that numbness spread all the way to her heart? What if she died down here without having a chance to say goodbye to her parents? Her sister and brothers? She would leave poor Trip behind to puzzle out the ancient words and carvings by himself.

A firearm fired, and Rysha jerked her focus back to the moment. It had come from beyond the laundry room, outside the door Duck had gone through. The shadows no longer moved out there.

Gasping for breath, Rysha reached the doorway and slumped against the jamb. Duck looked calmly at her, his pistol at his side. Blazer knelt beside a white-garbed man, tearing off strips of his clothing. She yanked his hands behind his back, eliciting a groan, and tied them there.

"You look really bad, Ravenwood." Duck frowned with concern.

"Thanks." Rysha eyed Blazer, still wanting to punch her but feeling too beaten down to try. "How'd you avoid the giant spider, ma'am?"

"Giant spider?" Blazer rose to her feet and looked Rysha up and down.

Rysha turned to show off her blood-stained and punctured trousers.

"I reckon it's like when you go hiking," Duck said, "and the person in front of you pushes aside a branch without a problem, but then it swings back and thwacks you in the face." He came closer and waved for her to sling her arm over his shoulder. "Better lean on me until we can find Trip. Those soulblades can heal people, right? Like they did on the Cofah airship?"

"I hope so," Rysha whispered, wondering how much time she had. And also wondering if a sorcerer could nullify venom. That was different from simply stitching some wound back together. "I also hope he's still down here."

She remembered all those people racing up the stairs. What if Trip and Kaika had left the compound? Rysha groaned at the idea of having to go back up all those steps in search for them.

"He will be," Blazer said firmly, her gaze on Rysha's injury now. "He will be."

"After all this," Duck said, "Trip's daddy better end up being a really good ally."

Blazer came to Rysha's other side to lend her support.

As they stumbled along, Blazer waved to a statue carved into a wall, this one of a woman with a sword standing beside a dragon. "If you need anything rubbed along the way, let me know."

"You're talking to the lieutenant, right, ma'am?" Duck asked.

"Of course." Blazer grinned quickly at him, though she looked more worried than amused. "We already established that I don't want to rub anything of yours."

"That's still disappointing, ma'am."

"That's life."

Rysha couldn't manage a smile as they joked. Nor could she summon any interest in the wall tiles or statues on this level. All she could think about was that she didn't want to die down here.

CHAPTER 11

THE WATER FLOWED OVER THE banks of the river, smothering the green growth that carpeted the rocky ground on either side. Fortunately, the original architects hadn't installed a flat floor and tiled over it as they had in the rest of the outpost. Here, the ground sloped upward from the water, so the rising river didn't immediately flood the whole chamber. Given time, it might.

Trip thought about trying to break open a larger hole where the subterranean river exited and poured into the ocean, but he decided to hold that back for later. The guards, all stranded on the far side, were pacing and eyeing the rising water with agitation. There was a doorway beside the statue, but maybe it only led to a dead end. Trip could have paddled across the river, but maybe the desert dwellers didn't know how to swim.

"That's Moe," Kaika whispered from Trip's side. They were still in the doorway, peering into the chamber. The guards, distracted by the water, hadn't noticed them yet. "The white-haired fellow with the shaggy beard, bare knees, and pocket-filled clothing."

He was the only man in the cage, so she needn't have been so descriptive. "You've met him before?"

"Yes, at a house-warming party a few years ago. He's scarce in the capital, from what I've heard. I think his wife is lucky to see him once a year. Because he spends most of his time in places like this, I imagine." Kaika extended a hand toward the prisoners.

"In cages?"

"In remote ruins. But I wager it's not his first time in a cage. Can you open the door and let them all out? Or create a distraction so I can get close enough to disarm those men?"

"There are seven of them. And there's one of you."

"What's your point?"

Trip snorted. He narrowed his eyes, concentrating on the overflowing river instead of the men. Could he cause it to surge higher quickly and sweep the guards from their feet? If they were poor swimmers, they might struggle to get back in time to keep Trip and Kaika from releasing the prisoners.

You're making more of this than necessary, Azarwrath said.

I don't want to kill them, Trip hurried to say, not wanting the soulblades to throw lightning or fireballs.

A surge of power emanated from Azarwrath and struck one of the guards. It hurled him twenty feet. The man slammed into a wall, his pistol falling from his hands. As the man dropped to the floor, the weapon flew away from him. It splashed into the river and disappeared. Three more men were hurled away from the cage in a similar manner.

One that hadn't been attacked yet knelt and fired wildly, eyes bulging as he peered all around the chamber and its multiple exits. He spotted Trip and Kaika.

Trip formed a barrier in front of them, one of the drills Jaxi hadn't minded helping him refine. Kaika ducked back behind the doorway as the guard fired toward them. Bullets ricocheted off the invisible barrier. Trip hoped one would bounce back and hit the man in the leg.

The next one did exactly that and lodged in the guard's thigh. The man screamed and dropped his weapon.

Did I do that? Trip asked, horrified.

The powerful must be more careful than anyone else with what they wish for, Jaxi said.

Trip was relieved he hadn't imagined the bullet taking his foe in the chest. There had already been enough deaths. As unwholesome and disturbing as this cult was, he couldn't forget that he was the invader here. He did not regret stopping the sacrifice, but he couldn't accept that killing everyone here was the right thing to do. With the leader gone, that might be enough to end this.

Azarwrath swept another man's pistol out of his grip and dumped it in the water as he hurled the rest of the guards against the walls. Some groaned and rose to their feet, but others remained where they were or tried to crawl into dim recesses to hide.

Kaika poked her head back around the doorjamb. "That's disappointing."

"They're all still alive," Trip said, thinking she believed them dead.

"I mean that you didn't leave any for me to fight. Trip, my skills get rusty if I don't get to use them now and then."

"Sorry, you can blame Azarwrath."

"That doesn't sound healthy." Kaika eyed the wall where the last man had struck—twenty feet above the ground.

"Probably not."

Trip strode toward the river and was wondering how cold the water would be when Azarwrath put his wind-manipulation skill to work again. A cushion of air formed under Trip, lifting him from his feet. The girl outside of the cage had already been staring at him with saucer-like eyes, but she dropped to her knees now. Azarwrath had plucked her guards up and hurled them away without harming her, but she seemed to believe she would be the next target.

"We're friends," Trip said, as he walked through the air three feet above the water.

Four more young women stood inside the cage, gripping the bars. The man Kaika had identified as Moe Zirkander watched with his hands in his pockets and his head cocked to the side. He didn't appear terrified of Trip—maybe he recognized the Iskandian uniform—but he did seem puzzled.

"How are you doing, Rock Cheetah?" Kaika asked from behind Trip. She was being floated across too.

The man peered at her. "I believe I remember you."

"Your mind is as sharp as your son's propeller blades."

"I *definitely* remember now. Captain Kaika. Deliverer of kittens."

"Kittens make excellent house-warming gifts. I hear they keep the ravens and turtles away."

Trip had no idea what they were talking about and simply strode to the cage as soon as his feet touched down. An old, half-rusted lock hung from the gate. He glanced toward a couple of the unconscious guards, wondering if one of them had the key.

If you can't open that with your mind, Jaxi said, *you'll never master page one of the workbook.*

Trip blushed, wondering how long it would take him to learn to think like a sorcerer rather than a typical person.

Probably until you embrace your heritage and realize there's nothing wrong with being atypical, Azarwrath said.

Not ready to respond to that, Trip imagined himself seeing through the steel casing to the inner workings. The mechanism was simple, and he saw right away how to push the pins against the springs so he could turn the lock. With a few mental nudges, the shank clunked open.

You could have simply melted the lock, Jaxi said. *Or snapped the metal.*

Is there something wrong with subtlety and finesse?

It's slow and boring.

In other words, Azarwrath said, *no, there is not.*

Jaxi did the sword equivalent of sticking a tongue out and phhhhting into their minds.

"How did you get here, sir?" Kaika asked the senior Zirkander.

Trip opened the gate for the prisoners to walk out and waved toward the other girl, inviting her to join them. He tried to look nonthreatening. Given the circumstances of his arrival, that might not be possible.

"I've been searching for the Forbidden Treasure of Amon Akarth for the last two years, since I located the Lost Treasure of Anksari Prime only to learn it had already been looted. So disappointing. But I made many excellent maps of the underground tunnel system on Echeroh Island. I sold them to the university back home for nearly two thousand nucros, which was enough to fund the supply purchasing for a new mission. Amon Akarth is reputed to have gold and silver, but even better, ancient maps and tablets of a language that predates Old Iskandian and Tvakmar. It's reputed to be here on Rakgorath. Not, however, in an old dragon-rider outpost full of ridiculously gullible cultists." He harrumphed and glared at the fallen guards.

"Is it just me," Kaika asked, "or did he fail to explain how he arrived here with a bunch of nubile virgins?"

"I don't know, but we should get out of here. Eventually, the rest of the cultists are going to come back." Trip looked at the huge dragon statue and the sacrifice table under its talons. Now that they were closer, he could see dried bloodstains on the top of that table. He felt queasy.

Did that statue represent Agarrenon Shivar? And if so, had the dragon condoned all this? That cult leader had thought so. Fervently. As if this was something that had been done thousands of years ago when the dragon had presided over his ancestors. But it wasn't as if the man, someone who hadn't been more than forty or fifty, had been there all those centuries ago. He couldn't *truly* know. These modern-day cultists could have perverted the original message and made a religion out of nothing. Some uneducated, ancient people not familiar with the power of dragons might have seen their magic as godlike and turned Agarrenon Shivar into a divinity without the dragon even knowing it.

"Has anyone seen my notebooks?" Moe peered behind a boulder, then lifted one of the unconscious guard's legs to look under it. "My maps? My *tools*? What did these ignorant troglodytes do with all my *gear*?"

"Trip? Are you ready to go?" Kaika asked. "Or do you need to stare at that statue while you fondle the lock a while longer?"

Trip snorted, glancing at the lock. He hadn't realized he'd kept it. Shrugging, he stuck it in a pocket. He might find a purpose for it.

It clanked softly against a couple of other metal knickknacks he'd picked up along the trail heading here. Mostly litter left by the locals, but he had a notion that he might repurpose the items to create a toy for General Zirkander's new baby.

"Oh, sir." Trip turned toward Moe. "You probably haven't heard the news. Sardelle delivered a new baby boy just a week ago."

He expected the man—the grandfather—to exclaim in delight or thump Trip on the shoulder, but he kept searching behind boulders and said only, "Did she? Huh."

He clambered up on the table and peered behind the slab.

Trip felt dumbfounded by the underwhelming reaction.

"Is it—he—*normal*?" Moe squinted back at him.

"Sir?"

"She's a witch. Didn't you know?" Moe patted around behind the table, pulled out a human arm bone, and tossed it aside. "Can't believe the boy married a witch."

Trip shifted uneasily at the condemnation, abruptly not wanting to draw attention to himself or his abilities. Probably too late since Moe had seen him levitate over a river. Though, if he recognized the soulblades, he might think they had been responsible.

In conflict with his instinct to withdraw and hide his abilities, Trip had the urge to lift his chin and say something in Zirkander's defense. How could Moe think so little of his son's wife and family? Sardelle was nice, too, even when she made students practice things a thousand times. How could a father-in-law not like her?

Then Trip remembered Zirkander's words to him the day they had fished, that fathers didn't always get the children they wanted. And vice versa.

"I saw the kid," Kaika said. "He's bald with a squishy face. Seems pretty normal. No horns."

"Good. It's not good to be a witch. Or a world-renowned treasure hunter." He flung a hand toward the chamber ceiling. "You see the kinds of places it gets you."

"Yes, remind us again how you got here with the women?" Kaika waved toward them.

They'd gathered around her, giving Trip a wide berth. A couple were whispering among themselves, but the others, including the one who'd been seconds away from being sacrificed, watched the goings on numbly, as if they were too shocked to think and react.

"The cultist bastards saw me in town and kidnapped me." Moe stood up atop the table, looking all around from his elevated position. "I don't think my notes are here. We can't leave without them."

"Why did they kidnap you? You don't look like a very succulent sacrifice for a dragon."

Moe huffed. "No kidding. They recognized me—my reputation precedes me even in this benighted place, you understand—and thought I could lead them to their dragon god. They're certain he's alive and in Linora again now that other dragons are about. I can't believe these fools didn't know where their own religion was founded."

"Do you know where Agarrenon Shivar is?" Trip asked.

"I know where he was buried three thousand years ago. Jralk Mountain over there." Moe waved toward a wall. "At the edge of the mountain range over there."

"Uhm, I'm fairly certain he was alive about twenty-five years ago."

"Don't be foolish, boy." Moe frowned at him. "*Captain.* Are you old enough to have that rank?"

"General Zirkander thinks so."

"I suppose it doesn't matter how old and wise you are anymore. As long as you spin upside down in one of those horrific flying contraptions and shoot other people in horrific flying contraptions." Moe hopped down from the table, surprisingly spry for someone who looked to be in his seventies.

"Why didn't you tell the cultists what they wanted to know?" Kaika asked, her determination to question the scatter-brained man admirable.

"Oh, I did. They didn't believe me. As if I don't know what I'm talking about. Do you know how many tombs I've researched over the years? To say nothing of all the temples, ziggurats, pyramids, crypts, and ancient towns buried by volcanos I've visited in person. I'm more knowledgeable than—"

"We could use some help," came a call from across the river.

Trip had been focused on Moe and hadn't had his senses extended to watch for enemies—or friends—heading their way. Blazer and Duck walked through the doorway under the balcony, supporting Rysha between them, her feet dragging along, her chin drooped to her chest. Unconscious? His heart stuttered. *Dead?*

No. As soon as he brushed her with his senses, he felt that she was alive. She wasn't unconscious, either, not completely. She seemed to be floating in and out of awareness, her body flushed with fever.

Trip ran and sprang out over the river, willing himself to sail across it but hardly caring if he failed. He would swim to her if he had to. But his momentum and whatever power he half-heartedly applied carried him more than forty feet to the other side.

Duck's eyes widened as he landed, but Trip only spared him a glance. He sprinted to the trio and slipped his arms around Rysha. Duck and Blazer let go, and Trip lowered her to the ground.

Azarwrath? He narrowed the focus of his senses, seeking and finding her injury. He also found something flowing through her blood, a malevolent presence spreading through her limbs and heading for her heart. *Can you help me?*

Of course. It's venom. We will destroy it, and then lend her some of your energy to help her body recover from the ordeal.

Trip nodded, relieved that Azarwrath didn't sound daunted. He just hoped the soulblade wasn't pretending it was a simple problem to keep Trip from worrying. When he *should* worry. He touched Rysha's fevered cheek, and even though she didn't groan or even react, he could feel pain radiating from her.

Azarwrath had mentioned dealing with the venom first, and he could sense tendrils of the soulblade's power spreading into her body, but Trip willed some of his own energy to flow into her right away. He wanted to make sure her body had the resources it needed to heal. And he longed to take away her pain. Even if it meant drawing it into his own body. Was there a way he could do that?

Since Azarwrath was busy with the venom and Jaxi wasn't a healer, Trip simply tried to make it happen through sheer will. He envisioned all of her pain disappearing, a tingling warmth flowing into her, much as he'd experienced when he'd been healed by Sardelle, and he imagined crushing every tiny mote of venom within her.

Rysha gasped, stirring in his arms. He opened his eyes to check her face, terrified that he'd made it worse.

She stared up at him, her eyes bright. And clear of pain?

Harrumph. Azarwrath buzzed on his hip. *If you didn't need my help, you could have said so.*

What do you mean?

You healed her, genius, Jaxi said. *Leftie would suggest that you give her The Look and collect a kiss.*

Leftie is kind of an ass.

Glad you've noticed.

"Rysha?" he whispered, lifting a thumb to touch her cheek again.

"*Trip.*" Tears appeared in her eyes, but he didn't sense pain from her. "I didn't want to die without helping you. Or without my parents knowing. Or because a stupid spider bit me."

"A spider?"

Had a spider poured that much venom into her? He didn't have a healer's experience, but he would have guessed a giant rattlesnake or something comparable.

"The spider weighed about fifty pounds," Duck said dryly.

"I'm sorry," Rysha said, her eyes locked to Trip's, neither of them paying attention to anyone else. "All I've found so far is a rubbing of a railing."

"I don't know what that is, but I'm sure it's lovely." He pulled her higher off the ground so he could wrap his arms around her.

She slid her arms around him and buried her face in his neck. "Thank you," she mumbled, then repeated it in her mind. *Thank you, Trip.*

I'm glad I was here for you, he thought back before he could consider if she would object to telepathy. *And that I could do something.*

Her grip tightened around him, fingers curling around the back of his neck. This close to her, he sensed her thoughts. He hadn't been trying to wall himself off, so they flooded over him, how she'd been certain she would die and had been devastated it would have meant not being able to help him complete his quest. How she would have left him here in some dingy outpost to figure everything out for himself. She was relieved that wouldn't happen now and thought how nice it would be to kiss him. But she wouldn't, not with the others looking on. If only they would go away. She could truly thank him, wrapping her arms and legs around him and pulling him down to the floor, sliding her tongue across his lips and—

A twinge of discomfort came from Rysha, and he pulled back, afraid he was leaning too much of his weight on her. He mentally drew back, too, abashed that he'd been reading her thoughts, invading her privacy. And more abashed because he hadn't wanted to stop. He'd wanted to urge her to make those thoughts a reality, and who cared who was looking on?

"You're poking me with something, Trip," Rysha said.

"I'll bet," Blazer muttered from a few feet away.

Rysha rolled her eyes and pointed a finger at one of Trip's shirt pockets, the one he'd stuck the lock and his other metal scraps in.

"Oh, those are my finds."

"Finds?" She slipped her fingers into his pocket and drew out a coiled piece of tin, the lid from a fish container. One of her eyebrows arched. She put it back and pulled out the rusty lock. "You're still a very odd boy, Trip."

"I know. You still like that, right?"

"Yeah, I do." Her gaze dipped to his mouth, and there seemed to be a promise of *later* in her considering look. He hoped so.

"Shit, where did our treasure hunter go?" Kaika asked, peering over the heads of the young women gathered around her.

What were they supposed to *do* with these women? Trip hadn't considered that when he'd been determined to rescue everybody. Could they get back to the city by themselves? Showing up there didn't seem like a good idea for the team. But at least one of those girls had an Iskandian accent, so she probably wasn't a native. Where had these thugs gotten their sacrifice victims?

"Who?" Blazer asked.

"We found Moe Zirkander in a cage with all these girls."

"Zirkander? Is that—"

"The general's papa, yes," Kaika said. "I think you met him at one of the barbecues a couple of years back."

"He's *here*?"

"Well, not at the moment."

Trip turned, reaching out with his senses as well as looking with his eyes. Moe had left the chamber, but Trip located him nearby. "I believe he's looking for the notebooks the zealots took from him."

"Notebooks? Yes, I should take some notes too." Rysha peered around, seeing her new surroundings for the first time. "And more rubbings. Is that a pre-Arkrovian dragon statue?" Her thoughts had clearly turned from kisses as she rolled to the side to push herself to her feet.

"I think you'll need to rest a while first." Trip held his hands out, wanting to stop her from rising, but settling for staying close enough to catch her if she fell.

"This is hardly an infirmary. Those people are still searching the— erg." Rysha wobbled before she made it higher than her knees. She lifted a hand to her head, and Trip caught her as she swayed.

"Dizzy?" He tried to help with that, but her body simply needed more time to recover. "Do you want some water?"

"I want some rubbings." Rysha squinted toward the giant dragon statue and that sacrifice table.

Remembering the dried blood on it, Trip hated the thought of her going anywhere close to it. He also hated the thought of her confirming what he'd read in the leader's mind, that all this, the entire sacrificing cult, had come into existence because of his sire.

"Demanding patient, isn't she?" Kaika handed her a canteen.

Rysha frowned but accepted it and reluctantly allowed herself to be lowered down.

"I'll get whatever you need," Trip said. "What's a rubbing?"

"Something neither Major Blazer nor Lieutenant Ravenwood was interested in doing to me while we were alone in a bedroom," Duck said.

"That could be a lot of things," Trip said.

Rysha dug into her pack and pulled out pieces of paper and charcoal. "Here. I only need them if you see carvings of writing, hieroglyphs, or interesting artwork. I'm not particularly interested in contributions from the cultists, as I believe they're all much more recent. I get the sense that the outpost has been used off and on for various purposes by the locals from Lagresh." Her lips thinned in disapproval, and she handed paper and charcoal to Trip. She handed identical items to Kaika and Duck.

"We're rubbing things too?" Duck asked.

"Anything interesting. The faster you finish…"

Blazer sighed. "Do it. I'll stand guard, but I'm already hearing some clangs from up above. I don't think it'll be long before they circle back down to check."

We have a few minutes, Jaxi said. *I'm prying tiles off the walls near the search groups and dropping them with a clatter. They're convinced the party is hiding up there.*

Prying tiles and breaking them? Trip asked. *I better not mention that to Rysha. She'll call you a delinquent for defacing an ancient ruins site.*

I hardly think she has room to judge when she viciously slew one of the inhabitants. Jaxi shared the image of a giant tarantula, before and after death.

I don't think spiders count as significant archaeological finds.

"Trip?" Rysha asked.

"Yes?" He stretched a hand toward her. "Do you need something else?" He worried some of her pain had come back.

"My rubbings." She quirked her eyebrows in the direction Duck and Kaika had gone.

He snorted. "Yes, ma'am," he said and trailed after them.

"Oh, and get me a sample of that mold, will you? Now that the water is receding, you can see that it truly is rather lush and interesting. I wonder if your mother found a use for it in one of her compounds."

"Lush and interesting?" He made a face at the spongy stuff as he walked over to it.

"It's surviving down here, despite dozens of feet walking over it however often. It acts more like moss than mold, but it's definitely from the fungi kingdom. How intriguing that it's growing on the rock like mold would usually grow on a piece of bread. Do you think it derives sustenance from the rock? And look at the variety. It's like a whole garden of mold."

"I think there's a reason you don't mind me being odd," Trip said.

"You're not going to call *me* odd, are you?" Rysha waved at the mold—implying that he should get to work collecting her sample.

"How about quirky?"

"I might accept that."

CHAPTER 12

RYSHA MANAGED TO BE GOOD and rest for five entire minutes before curiosity drove her toward a doorway in the wall behind the dragon statue. A crudely improvised curtain hung on a metal rod, covering up the entrance, and clanks and clatters came from behind it. Trip had said the man they'd freed, Moe, was searching in there. Since the water level had fallen, she decided to ford the river to see what was keeping his attention occupied for so long. Another chamber?

More like an office, a voice spoke into her mind. Jaxi.

Had Rysha not been so exhausted, she might have jumped with surprise. The soulblade had spoken to her before, but not often.

An office full of garish things, Jaxi amended.

Like archaeologically significant artifacts?

I'd call it junk.

Do you have an archaeologist's training?

You mean do I have the capacity to consider dusty old gross stuff anything other than junk? No.

Rysha felt certain Jaxi meant to deter her for some reason, but that only piqued her curiosity more.

She pushed aside the curtain and spotted the white-haired man on his knees, poking through a crate under one of many stone slab tables pushed against the walls of a room the size of her father's study back home. The carpet of mold continued in here, and his knees were planted in it as he searched.

An office might have been a reasonable term for the stone room, but there weren't any papers or pens that Rysha could see, and only a handful of books, the pages yellowed, the covers worn and faded. She might have headed straight for them, but all the ceramic cups on the tables made her pause, as did the bas-relief images carved into walls that appeared to be made from a softer stone than those in the majority of the outpost. Based on the style, Rysha suspected the artwork had been done by the cult rather than the dragon riders. Though dragons did feature prominently. They dominated the images, or maybe it was the same dragon repeated over and over. It posed often with its wings spread as it peered down at human beings chained on the floor before it.

Rysha realized these images were similar to what the cultists must have intended to recreate with the women they'd captured. How many times had these sacrifices happened over the years?

Steeling her heart, she walked in and examined the carvings more closely. "I don't think these were original to the outpost. It's hard to date them by simply looking, but they don't even vaguely illustrate what dragon-rider outposts embodied, nor was the style favored by Iskandians of the time." She thought of the dragon curving along the staircase railing. That had been much more in line with what she would have expected from the place.

"Absolutely not," Moe said, pulling back from the crate and rising to his feet. He wore pocket-filled cut-off trousers that revealed knobby knees and wiry leg muscles that hadn't lost much of their tone with age. "Those brotherhood fools perverted this whole outpost. As if the looting wasn't bad enough. That dragon out there was originally Samar Shola, a gold who, along with his rider, deposited the first criminals on this continent, a rogue sorcerer and his equally rogue dragon. They'd schemed to steal the independence from the free clans of Iskandia through deceit and treachery. After depositing the criminals, Samar Shola and his rider led others to build an outpost here. The Rider Wars hadn't begun yet and wouldn't for many more centuries. They just believed someone had to keep an eye on those early, dangerous criminals."

Rysha gazed at him. "Did something here tell you that, sir, or have you—"

"Of course, I've studied this area extensively. You can't find the Forbidden Treasure of Amon Akarth without knowing something of the continent." He made a disgusted noise, glared at the cups, and stalked toward the door. "My belongings are not here. Tell me those fools didn't simply cast them into the ocean. My notebooks held years and years' worth of work." Groaning, he stalked out without a glance toward Rysha.

She shivered as she looked around the room again. Normally, she could study long-past civilizations and cultures without passing judgment on practices that had ranged from murder to ritual suicide to cannibalism, but this wasn't the long past. This was now.

With Moe gone and his human presence, albeit an indifferent one, no longer in the room, she found the space more chilling. She was about to turn and leave, but noticed a lidded ceramic bowl on a table, colorful bones and skulls painted on the side in purples, greens, and reds. Had the subject of the artwork not been so macabre, it would have looked like a soup tureen in someone's kitchen set.

Rysha crossed the room, lifted the lid, and peeked inside. She immediately regretted it. The smell of butchered meat left out too long oozed out, and dark, thick blood pooled inside, several liters of it. A few meaty chunks floated around in the bowl.

She dropped the lid back down and hustled away. There was nothing to prove it was human blood, but she couldn't imagine it being anything else, given the prisoners and the sacrifice table in the cavern outside.

As she backed toward the door, she bumped into something and gasped, spinning.

Trip lifted his hands, rolled paper and her charcoal in them.

"This place is horrible," she blurted, not sure if he'd seen her looking in the bowl, or if he'd seen what was in it.

Judging from the sad cast to his eyes, he knew.

"I've come to the same conclusion," he said quietly. "It's appalling to think that all this might have evolved because of my… because of him." His jaw tightened.

Rysha grimaced. She hadn't meant to remind him that his sire, whether inadvertently or purposefully, might be at the center of this. "It could be some other dragon," she said. "I haven't had a chance to spend time looking at the rubbings yet. The name was only partially visible."

"It's not."

"You're sure?"

"We ran into the cult leader, and I saw into his mind." Trip closed his eyes. "He named Agarrenon Shivar."

"That doesn't mean the dragon was *responsible* though. He may have no idea what the humans here were doing. There were a lot of old religions built up by primitive cultures that deified dragons. I'm sure it didn't help that dragons like Bhrava Saruth were flying around, proclaiming themselves gods." Rysha smiled.

Trip's dark expression did not lighten. He handed her the rubbings he'd made and said, "If what that cult leader believed was even vaguely true, then Agarrenon Shivar was there at the inception. If it wasn't his idea to begin with, he seemed content to go along with it."

"People will think all sorts of odds things are the truth in order to validate their beliefs."

Trip looked at the tureen of blood, shook his head slowly, and walked out.

Rysha wanted to protest his certainty that Agarrenon Shivar had been at the root of all this, but until she went over her findings more carefully, she wouldn't know if she should. Still, whatever Agarrenon Shivar had been—or done—it didn't mean Trip was to blame.

She headed for the doorway, but paused, eyeing the books. Though she ought to have learned by now not to poke her nose into things in here, she veered over to take a look. To leave a book unopened seemed a sin.

They were all handwritten, even the ones that appeared to be from the post-printing-press era. Two were full of notes scribbled in a brown ink that had faded over the years. She thought it might be blood, or blood-based, but decided not to dwell on that. One was a handbook with instructions for the cult leader, and she had the urge to drop it in a fire somewhere so nobody could find it and carry on. The others appeared to be logs of the ceremonies over the years. Judging by the dates, they held one of their sacrificial rites every full moon. She shuddered to think of all the blood spilled on that table over the years.

In the last book she opened, the pages were made from parchment rather than paper, but they were still brittle and frail. They'd all fallen out of the binding and were simply stored inside the cover. She recognized the writing inside as being in the trade language of the ancient world, one usually more concerned with economics and bookkeeping than recording history, but who knew what the book might contain? With time, she could decipher the contents. Maybe it was the original handbook for the cult. Or something else altogether.

Since she couldn't take rubbings of written pages, Rysha borrowed the book to examine it more thoroughly later. She wasn't sure how she would manage to return it, but she wanted to peruse it to see if it contained any useful clues.

She didn't know if it would be possible, but she would love to exonerate Agarrenon Shivar from the taint Trip now associated with him. At the least, she wanted to know more about the dragon and whether it would truly be useful to find him. If he had condoned and fostered evil among humans, then perhaps he would be best left unfound.

Rysha had recovered some of her energy by the time the group headed up the stairs, but she noticed the weight of her pack far more than she had earlier in the day. She trailed after Blazer and Trip, with Duck and Kaika, and the rescued women following after them. She was surprised none of the cultists had found their group, especially after she'd seen the leader's body sprawled on the floor near the base of the stairs, but Trip paused now and then, his head tilting as his eyes grew distant, and she suspected he and the soulblades were continuing to lead searchers astray on the floors above.

"Got it," came an exuberant call from below them. Moe appeared at the bottom of the stairs, waving a leather journal with a lock on it and a pack bristling with climbing gear and numerous digging tools. "My belongings were cast in a pile with refuse to be thrown into the sea. Can you believe it?"

"You're lucky these people don't throw the trash out very often," Kaika said.

Moe threw her an aggrieved look and joined in at the end of the group.

Would he want to come with them on their journey? There was an empty seat in one of the fliers, and he seemed to know a lot about the area. Rysha had no idea what they would do with the women. Would they be safe if Blazer simply pointed them down the path that led back to Lagresh? They might not be *from* the city. The one with the Iskandian accent had said she was the daughter of a merchant captain and had been kidnapped from their ship in the harbor.

As the group climbed higher and higher up the spiral staircase, Rysha caught her hand straying often to the rubbings the others had made for her and a couple she had done herself with the last of that paper. She had that book to examine too.

"Where will we go after this, ma'am?" she asked Blazer, hoping the answer would be that they would find a quiet place to make camp and contemplate their options. That would give Rysha time to study her finds.

Blazer shrugged without looking back. "Moe mentioned a mountain. Jralk Mountain."

"Perhaps we should find some place to camp, and you could find it on a map while I study the various clues I've found." Rysha called them clues in the hope that Blazer would be more likely to approve a clue-studying session. In truth, she had no idea if anything would help them find Trip's sire.

"It'll only take me two minutes to find a mountain on a map. It'll take you two months to look at your clues."

"I can restrain myself to a brief look. Say two hours? Doesn't the group need to find a place to camp for the night?"

"We can't camp on the beach or anywhere near the city," Blazer said. "I checked in with Leftie earlier. He said a boat motored past, so the Lagresh authorities, such as they are, likely know our fliers are on the beach. They probably also know that we're the reason their other boats never returned."

"So, we can move the fliers ten miles inland and—"

"Let's just get out of here and figure it out up there." Blazer waved up the never-ending staircase.

Trip looked back and smiled at Rysha. He seemed preoccupied by dark thoughts, so she appreciated the gesture.

Realizing Moe might be as good a resource as her rubbings, Rysha dropped back until she was climbing next to the man. He didn't seem to notice. He had his journal open and his pencil out, and he was putting checkmarks next to items on a list.

"Blazer said you think Agarrenon Shivar can be found at Jralk Mountain, sir?" she prompted.

"What?" He squinted at her.

Rysha didn't know if he hadn't fully heard the question or if she'd misinterpreted Blazer's comment and confused him.

"We're looking for Agarrenon Shivar, sir. That's our mission."

He glanced at the nametag on her uniform.

"I'm Lieutenant Ravenwood," she said, realizing she should introduce herself. "Artillery officer training to be elite troops."

"You're not related to Jyvona Ravenwood, are you?"

"That's my mother," Rysha said, pleased at the recognition. She should have led with that. An archaeologist—or treasure hunter—would be more interested in the history scholars in her family than in her nascent military career.

"I've read her papers on infrastructures of the ancient world, and they're moderately accurate, but it's clear she hasn't gone out into the field to look for herself very often."

"She's a full-time professor at the university," Rysha said, her pleasure being replaced by a twinge of irritation at the dismissal from this… treasure hunter. He was probably the type of person to disturb ancient sites and think nothing of looting from them. Of course, since she had taken that book, she wasn't in a position to judge.

"Teaching." He sniffed. "What did you ask?"

"About Agarrenon Shivar. An elder gold dragon. We're looking for him."

"So I heard. I don't imagine that will go well since he's been dead for millennia."

Rysha looked up the stairs toward Trip's back. "We have evidence to suggest otherwise."

Moe shook his head. "I came across a long list of known dragons once when I was looking for the lost treasure hoards of two elder golds that were known to collect valuables and squirrel them away. Agarrenon Shivar was on the list. Not as a hoarder, but as one of dozens of dragons that died from a virus that some early human scientists stumbled across. With the assistance of a bronze dragon that was tired of his lowly place in the pecking order, they found a way to encapsulate and disseminate the virus to key dragon leaders. Golds and silvers, predominantly."

"Are you referring to the Kantiot Virus, sir?" Rysha had read about the illness that had caused the deaths of many dragons long ago, but she hadn't heard anything about it being man- or dragon-made.

"Yes, that's what they call it in the history books, I believe. Many of the elders and scholars among the dragons were purposely infected. But the group of scientists—they were more ignorant potion makers back then—didn't realize the disease they'd created would be infectious across species. Most of the scientists themselves died as a result, and other dragons that were in the vicinity of the sick also contracted the virus and died. Those who survived attempted to quarantine the ill, but most ended up scattering and holing up in deep caves for years while they waited to make sure all those who had been infected died out. It was a quiet era for humanity, and they flourished for a time."

"The Golden Age?" Rysha had read about that, a lull in dragon activity more than three thousand years earlier.

Moe nodded.

"I've never seen a list of the dragons that died during that time of illness," she said.

Moe sniffed derisively. "Because, like your mother, you probably never go out in the field."

"Only as a soldier. I studied dragon history in school, but then joined the army."

"That sounds like a waste."

"Isn't your son in the army?" Rysha tried to decide if she could see any of General Zirkander in the wiry white-haired man. Maybe in the face and lean build. Moe did still possess some of the family looks too.

"Also a waste."

"Even though he's a national hero?"

"Nationalism, such a ridiculous sentiment."

"No worse than imperialism, I should think."

"Humanity was better off when tribes were splintered and independent, and people formed solid bonds with everyone they knew."

Rysha shook her head, not wanting to argue with him about this. "Agarrenon Shivar, sir. We're positive he's not dead. And we need to find him."

"Why?"

"We believe he may be a good ally for Iskandia." The words came out before Rysha had more time to consider them. Given what she now knew, did she believe that?

Moe threw his head back and laughed so hard he almost fell down the stairs.

"We're in an enemy stronghold here," Blazer growled back in a low voice. Moe winked at her.

"Agarrenon Shivar was an utter ass, even by dragon standards," Moe told Rysha. "That's stated in numerous different accounts. Seek his burial chamber if you wish, but you won't find an ally. Nor do I believe you'll find him alive. As none of those who were infected ever appeared in the world again. Until that silver dragon my son dug up. Phelistoth."

"But you have reason to believe Agarrenon Shivar was entombed in those mountains?" Rysha asked, refusing to be deterred.

Just because a dragon hadn't been seen again didn't mean he couldn't still live. Perhaps it had taken him a long time to recover from the disease, and he'd hibernated for countless years.

He could be in a stasis chamber, Jaxi spoke into her mind.

This time, Rysha wasn't as surprised by the contact.

I've been listening to your conversation in between my efforts to help Trip convince the cultists that they find the bedrooms at the far ends of the hallways incredibly fascinating. One man is rubbing a dust ball between his fingers in deep contemplation.

He's manipulating people's minds? Rysha understood that such abilities were within sorcerers' repertoires, but somehow, she always found the notion more disturbing than that of hurling fireballs.

Azarwrath is mostly handling that, though he's making sure Trip is watching so he'll learn how to do it too. Whether he wants to learn or not. It's a useful skill to have in one's repertoire.

Not wanting to debate the pros and cons of mind-manipulation just then, Rysha focused on the more pertinent part of the discussion. *Stasis chamber, you said?*

A hint of sea air wafted into the stairwell from somewhere, and she hoped that meant they were almost out. Her legs burned, and everyone was breathing heavily except for Kaika, who probably thought climbing fifty stories was a refreshing warmup and nothing more.

Yes, such as the one we found Phelistoth in on Owanu Owanus, Jaxi said. *That's a long story, but he was dying from that disease when we found him. Actually, the Cofah found him first, and they'd opened the chamber—which included a barrier that had been keeping him and his diseased air inside—to extract his blood and use it for weapons. We had to figure out how to slay the bugs infecting him in order to save his life.*

I was instrumental in doing so. He's not nearly as grateful about it as you would expect. Dragons are so arrogant and uppity.

So they seem. Are you telling me this because you believe Trip's sire might also have been kept in a stasis chamber all this time?

It's a possible explanation of how he could be alive today.

If so, how did Trip's mother find him and, uh, impregnate herself with him while he was in it? Presumably he would have had to have been let out, at least for a while, right? Rysha tried to imagine some deathly sick dragon being interested in shape-shifting and having sex. And then what? She put him back in? Would a dragon have allowed that? And if she was there, and they had physical contact, how did she avoid getting the disease?

I can't solve your entire mystery for you, Lieutenant. How boring would it be if I simply gave you all the answers?

Is that your way of saying you don't have all the answers?

You're a clever lieutenant, aren't you? It's no wonder Trip dreams of snoffling with you.

Are you this lippy to Sardelle? Rysha decided not to ask for clarification on what snoffling was.

We have a deep and personal bond of more than twenty years. We're like sisters.

Was that a yes?

Rysha had the sense of the soulblade grinning into her mind.

Up ahead, Blazer stopped. They were only a level from the top of the staircase and the hallway they'd entered the outpost through. Rysha grimaced, remembering they would still have to climb that rope to get out.

Trip and Blazer conferred quietly, Kaika on the step below them. Curious. Rysha eased past Duck so she could hear them.

"...about thirty," Trip was saying.

"All under the hole?" Blazer whispered. "What are they doing? Guarding it? Or enjoying the sun and fresh air?"

"It's gotten dark outside."

"So guarding is more likely?"

Trip shrugged.

"You have a magical solution?" Blazer asked. "Because after what I've seen of this place, I'm inclined to just run into the hallway shooting. Or have Kaika hurl a couple of grenades to clear the area for us."

"That might bring the ceiling down on everyone, us included."

"Given time, I can create more controlled detonations," Kaika said. "But magic is probably the ideal solution. Damn, I never thought I'd hear myself say that."

"Because you don't trust witches and never will?" Duck asked.

"Because I prefer it when explosives *are* the ideal solution. They're delightful to set off. You get a feeling of euphoria, the same as after bed-shaking sex."

"Trip?" Blazer prompted. "Thoughts?"

"On bed-shaking sex, ma'am?"

"On magical solutions." She squinted at him. "Are you being deliberately obtuse because you don't want to use magic?"

Trip sighed, and Rysha suspected Blazer had guessed right. Trip wasn't the most intuitive person that Rysha had met—mostly, because he didn't want to know what people were thinking, since it might involve unpleasant thoughts about him—but he wasn't a dummy.

"Azarwrath suggests we attempt to simply order them to leave the area. He believes I have the power to do so and has promised his guidance."

"Good, do it. I'd order them to leave the area myself, but I don't think they'd listen to me unless firearms were involved."

Trip looked down at his feet. When he'd worried if he would be accepted in the flier squadron as a magic-user, he probably hadn't worried if he'd be accepted to the extent that superior officers started ordering him to use his powers. Rysha didn't have any advice to offer. She could understand why he might hesitate to develop such powers, but if, as Jaxi had implied, the mind manipulation could keep people from being hurt, maybe it was for the best.

"Stand on the landing." Trip waved everyone off the stairs and onto the tiled floor.

"I hear someone," a man blurted from above them.

One of the girls rushed over and gripped Kaika's arm. "Don't let them take us back," she whispered. "Please, please."

"Nah," Kaika said, drawing her onto the landing along with the others. "We won't let that happen." With her free hand, she pulled a grenade out of her pocket. "If Trip's plan doesn't work, we have backup options. And I wouldn't mind ridding the world of some crazy cultists."

"It's possible the cult will disperse now that the leader is dead," Trip murmured, his eyes toward the upper level, even though nobody had come into view yet.

"Possible but not likely," Kaika said. "You know these things always have a second in command. There's probably a whole scheme where you can work your way to the top if you're loyal enough and bring in enough virgins to sacrifice."

"You seem oddly experienced with cults," Blazer said, though her gaze was also locked to the floor of the landing above.

"If you have a reputation for handling ordnance, you get approached by nut jobs now and then."

It grew quiet on the level above, so Rysha started in surprise when the first person stepped into view, white-clad and hooded as everyone else in the outpost had been. The figure walked down the stairs calmly and normally as far as she could tell, but he never looked left or right. His eyes remained focused on the steps below him.

More people came behind him, filing down the stairs in an orderly line. They, too, looked neither left nor right.

Rysha remained still—her entire team did—certain that the people would look at them, that the spell would break. But the people continued past the landing, one after the other. She caught one mumbling under his breath.

"The dragon god is gone. Pack your belongings, and go back to your normal life." He repeated the words as he continued past their railing, as if reciting an order over and over.

Most of the men and women passed in silence, but a few more mumbled those same words as they passed.

Would Trip's mental suggestion work? From what Rysha had read about mind-control magic, it wasn't something that generally lasted more than a few minutes. One couldn't completely take over another's mind without constantly being near that person. The soulblade had probably told Trip that, but she couldn't blame him for trying.

She thought of that bowl of blood, and, as much as the science and archaeology student within her found the idea of destroying a culture abhorrent, no matter how malevolent, she couldn't help but wonder if they should have let Kaika loose with explosives to destroy the entire outpost. Had the place been built by the cultists, she might have suggested it, but they'd simply expropriated it from its long-dead previous owners.

And if the cultists didn't meet here, they would find another spot for their foul congregations. Given the reputation that Lagresh had, she figured they could do their sacrifices in people's basements without anyone noticing.

By the time the end of the line came into sight—more than fifty people had walked past them, never noticing the intruders on the landing—Rysha looked at Trip, wondering how he was doing. Even with the soulblades assisting him, he had to be using a lot of energy to control so many at once.

He stood at the edge of the landing, one hand on the hilt of Azarwrath's blade, the other curled around the railing, and Rysha's breath caught because he was radiating power, his aura blazing in such a way that even she, a mundane human woman with no sense for the magical, could feel it. More than that, she had a hard time looking away from it. From *him*.

She found herself moving across the landing toward him, drawn to him, wanting to touch him. To be touched by him. A tingle of heat surged through her body, and when his gaze turned toward her, his dark green eyes fiery with inner power, the tingle turned to a blaze, and she flushed with the desire to be with him in every sense of the word.

Someone bumped her shoulder, and she realized she wasn't the only one who'd been drawn over to him. But he only looked at her, his gaze locked with hers. Triumph filled her with a sense of smug superiority, the knowledge that she would be his.

Trip closed his eyes and looked away, and disappointment replaced the triumph. He'd rejected her.

Trip lowered his head and stepped away from her—away from them. Their whole little group had swarmed to him, moths to a flame. Only Moe had seemed oblivious, perhaps because he'd been peering at the people and scribbling notes in his book.

Blazer frowned and stepped back, confusion furrowing her brow. Duck too appeared utterly puzzled. Apparently, dragonly allure—*scylori*—worked regardless of sex. Kaika eyed Trip up and down, not bothering to hide an interest she'd never shown in him before. The girls were all staring at him, too, their mouths parted, their expressions more disappointed than confused.

Rysha shifted uneasily, knowing she'd worn a similar expression seconds before. She grew aware of an irritated buzz coming from her hip, from the *chapaharii* sword sheathed there. Had it been buzzing the whole time? And she'd failed to notice it because she'd been too wrapped up in gazing at Trip's power?

Even though he wasn't looking at any of them now, and seemed to be doing his best to dampen down his aura, it took a minute for her body to forget the way his eyes had blazed as they stared into hers. It made her uneasy to think that she, with her years of education and her rational mind, could be drawn in as easily as the next person to a sorcerer with mind-control powers. How scary to realize he hadn't even been *trying* to control them. That had simply been a result of his aura slipping out while he worked his magic toward another goal.

Another goal. Rysha lurched around to look at the stairs, realizing she'd forgotten all about the cultists when she'd been busy ogling Trip.

But they had descended all the way to the bottom, apparently still following Trip's urging. A few soft mutters drifted up, the same words the cultists had spoken as they passed, a chant of the orders he'd instilled in their minds.

It chilled Rysha to think that Trip had the power to control people now. More than that, it chilled her to think she might cross paths with some dragon or other sorcerer who had the power to control *her*. Would Dorfindral be enough to fight that? And if so, what if that potential enemy knew the control words, as Kiadarsa had? As Trip did. Granted, she'd given both of them the control words, however inadvertently it had happened with the Cofah sorceress. But the commands had been in those books forever. Many people out there could know them.

When Trip had first made the suggestion of reprogramming Dorfindral to obey words of her choosing, she hadn't put much thought into the idea, but now she decided it would be a good thing if it could be done. When this mission was completed, she would hunt for more ancient texts that discussed the *chapaharii* weapons. With some references, maybe Trip would have the power to do the job himself.

"We can get out now," Trip said quietly, not looking at any of them.

"Good," Blazer said. "I've had enough of this place."

CHAPTER 13

THE SALTY NIGHT BREEZE RUFFLED Trip's uniform jacket, and he inhaled deeply, willing the fresh air to clear his mind of the disturbing thoughts lurking there. Everything he learned about Agarrenon Shivar was making him want to kill the dragon rather than strike a deal with him. And he couldn't manage to quash the tendril of doubt that had spawned within him about *himself*. If his sire had been a sick and depraved being who relished the pain and deaths of others, was that something that was in his *blood*? Something that could manifest as he learned how to access and use more of his power?

The fact that he'd been able to convince those cult people to walk past their group en masse made him more uncomfortable than anything else he'd done. It didn't help that it had been far easier than he'd expected—Azarwrath had shown him how to touch multiple minds at once and then to use their fears and motivations to his advantage. Because he'd already been in the head of the now-dead leader, he'd had a good idea about what those people wanted and what they feared. He'd attempted to keep himself detached as he injected his ideas into their minds, to see it as nothing more than a way to get his team out without hurting anyone else. But a part of him had marveled at how easy it had all been.

He'd spent so much of his life trying to fit in, trying not to be discovered as atypical. Could he have adjusted the thinking of those people who'd judged him unfairly? Perhaps made their derogatory thoughts turn into thoughts of regard?

Trip remembered the surreal experience of turning toward his teammates on the landing and finding them all staring at him as if he were some divine being they were drawn to touch. No, he admitted with a derisive snort. There'd been nothing holy about their looks. They'd all had a sexual hunger to them, all directed toward him. It had been startling, but for a moment, it had also made him feel powerful and desirable, as if he were the alpha wolf in the forest, the one all others wanted to follow and to mate with. He'd been ashamed of the thought as soon as he'd had it and hadn't ever intended to act on it, but then Rysha had walked toward him with that same hungry look in her eyes, and temptation had flirted much more seriously with him.

He still thought often of the kiss they'd shared that night on the airship, the intoxicating taste of her mouth, her appealing womanly scent filling his awareness, the lush feel of her body pressed against his.

Trip lifted his eyes to the stars, willing the thoughts to wash away along with the tide washing out far below. He wanted to be with her, but he wanted it to be because she liked *him*—not half-dragon him but pilot and person him—not because he was turning on some stupid magical allure. Still, he suspected he would have lurid dreams that night that centered around what might have happened had he not broken eye contact on that landing.

Maybe it would be better if he didn't sleep. He had a number of scrap parts in his pocket. He could start working on that toy. Yes, crafting something simple and wholesome like a child's toy would be a good way to focus his mind.

"You girls know how to get to your homes?" Blazer asked when the group reached the crossroads, the stone cairn that marked the spot visible even in the starlight. "Or to your families? Whatever you have waiting for you back in the city?"

A couple of women said yes. A couple more made less certain sounds. Trip was tired and wasn't keeping his bank vault around his mind, so he sensed a few of their surface thoughts and got the feeling that at least one wasn't a native and had been blindfolded for the trip here.

"I must return to the city," Moe said, shuffling to the front of the group. "I can guide them."

"I thought you might come with us, sir," Blazer said.

"Why would I want to do that?"

"To help us finish our mission to aid Iskandia."

"By finding a dead dragon? You're fools if you believe Agarrenon Shivar is alive and that he would help you even if he was. You'd be better served going home now and finding saner ways to defend the country. Besides, I know very well what those winged pins on your uniforms mean." Moe pointed at Blazer's chest even though he couldn't have seen her pin in the dark. "You've got some of those awful flying deathtraps nearby, I'm sure of it. I don't go anywhere with pilots. Damnation, those contraptions will be the death of you all."

"Perhaps he would not be the most suitable guide for a handful of girls," Trip murmured to Blazer. He wouldn't think Moe a particularly suitable guide for *anyone*. "Dreyak wants to go to the city. He'd be a good deterrent to highwaymen along the way."

"He's a weird thug who's full of himself," Blazer said.

"I fail to see how that makes him an inappropriate chaperone, ma'am," Trip said.

"I don't trust him."

"A good reason not to insist he stay with us on our mission."

Blazer started to respond, but a tinny voice came from her pocket. She dug out the communication crystal.

"Blazer, here."

"It's Leftie, ma'am. There are two of those boats now. I can see their running lights out there when the waves are just right. They're watching the beach."

"Is Dreyak still with you?"

"Of course I am here, Major Blazer," the aloof Cofah-accented voice came over the crystal. "Did I not give you my word that I would guard your fliers until you returned?"

"You did, and we appreciate you doing it with such good cheer. Captain Trip has volunteered you for another assignment."

"Assignment?" Dreyak asked coolly.

"*Major*," Trip protested. "I just said—"

"He thinks you're the perfect person to chaperone a bunch of teenage girls to the city."

"*Major*," Trip said again.

Even though he had more or less said that, he hadn't meant her to give it to Dreyak as a command. The Cofah warrior irked him, and Trip didn't trust him, but he also didn't want to make an enemy of him. Even if Dreyak hadn't admitted it, Trip had read between the lines that he was close to Prince Varlok and perhaps Emperor Salatak. He had no desire to rekindle a war between Iskandia and Cofahre by being rude.

"What, did you want to use your witchy ways to coerce him to obey?" Blazer held the crystal toward him. "Because I wouldn't mind, given that he manipulated *me*."

"Witchy ways?" Trip had a feeling she was irked because she'd been drawn to his aura along with the others. He made a note to figure out how to dampen that down even when he was drawing upon his power. "Surely, they were manly and magely ways."

That is not a word, Telryn, Azarwrath said.

It's a better word than witchy.

Is there no chance that we could visit the city, as well? I long for more cuisine comparable to what your grandmother cooked. It has been ages since we dined well.

That was the day before yesterday.

Ages.

Trip held a hand up toward Blazer, waving away the crystal. "Even if I wished to do such a thing, I don't think I could do it over that."

"Remote witching doesn't work?"

A drawn-out sigh came from the crystal. "I'm coming. Where are you?"

"Take the path up the cliff," Blazer said. "Then we're a little over a mile to the south."

"The path up the cliff," Dreyak repeated. "That sounds like something fun to navigate in the dark."

"I'll go get him." Trip tapped Azarwrath's hilt. Either he could work on his magical illumination or the soulblades could light the way.

Powerful soulblades love it when their handlers use them as night lights, Jaxi informed him.

Trip headed down the path. Nobody followed him. He hadn't asked for company, but he wondered if the others had realized he'd inadvertently affected them and felt similarly to Blazer. Did *Rysha* feel that way? That he'd manipulated her?

ORIGINS

He knew he shouldn't pester her and certainly shouldn't try to read her thoughts, but he reached back, trying to get a sense of her emotional state. That wasn't intrusive, was it? Had it been light out, he might have guessed that state by looking at her face.

When he brushed her thoughts, he got more than he intended. Rysha was thinking strongly about something, and a twinge of irritation from her almost made him jerk back, certain she had sensed his intrusion. But she was irritated with Blazer for not letting her strike a light while they were waiting so she could study a book she'd taken from the outpost. And she longed to take a good look at the rubbings, especially those that others had done. She hadn't seen the original carvings for those.

He smiled and drew back, leaving her to her thoughts. By the time he returned, she would probably have found a way to sneak off to study her finds.

Trip decided to jog to meet Dreyak, both so he would spend less time by himself and with his thoughts, and to warm his body. The temperature had dropped significantly since the sun went down, leaving no hint of the scorching heat that had blasted the dry earth earlier in the day.

When he reached the top of the cliff, he spotted a torch on the path below and sensed Dreyak holding it. Out in the water, the boats Leftie had mentioned bobbed beyond the whitecaps. Four of them now. They were either massing for another attack, or they had been sent out to search for their missing comrades and had congregated here. On the beach below, the fliers hunkered in darkness, invisible to the naked eye. But the boat captains had to know they were there. Maybe they had some plan to sneak onto the beach after dark.

Trip considered the boats and tried to send his senses out toward them, searching for the crews and captains. The vessels bobbed at least a mile away, and he hadn't spent much time testing his range yet. He'd sensed dragons that had been much farther away before, but dragons had much more powerful auras than humans.

Still, he soon located people aboard the boats, two on each one. The vessels were identical to the ones his team had battled earlier, sleek and fast with motors powered by... ah, interesting. Before, he'd been busy fighting and hadn't noticed the energy crystals built into the boats, integrated with their engines. They weren't exactly like the power crystals—the Referatu light fixtures—his people used in their fliers, but they were similar. He remembered the missing lamps in the dragonrider outpost. Perhaps these people had heard of Iskandian fliers and figured out a similar system for their watercraft.

While he waited for Dreyak, Trip tried to read the thoughts of the closest of the captains, a stern older woman who kept glaring at the dark beach. His heart sank. They *were* planning to attack after dark, but they knew they had to be wary because their comrades hadn't returned. They believed the Iskandians had found a way to destroy them. Right now, she was planning to, once two more boats arrived, to pretend to head north on patrol. Then, after a couple of hours, they would return with their lights off and attempt to sneak up to the beach and capture the Iskandian craft. The fliers, and their power crystals, would go for a good price at the junk market, and she could pay back the oppressive loan that someone called The Torpedo had against her family.

Trip suspected his team would be ready to depart before the boats sneaked to the shore, so maybe there was no need to do anything. But if he could convince them to leave, wouldn't that be safer?

He chewed on the inside of his cheek while debating whether that was true or if he was looking for an excuse to use his powers again. Had he *liked* that? More than he should have?

What do you two think? Trip asked.

About what? Jaxi asked, as Azarwrath gave a mental shrug.

Should I try to convince the captains to go back to port for the night?

You could, Azarwrath said. *They are scheming against us.*

I know. Were you not monitoring my thoughts?

I've been having more trouble with that lately, Jaxi told him. *You're getting better at your bank vault.*

I concur, Azarwrath said. *If we were to truly join through the old ceremony where handler and soulblade are officially bonded, I would likely sense your thoughts even through your defenses, as you would sense mine, but we have not done this.*

I didn't realize there was a ceremony. And that we hadn't—weren't bonded. It still seemed so odd to him that he, a pilot in the Iskandian army, would be bonded to a magical soulblade.

Yes. Both parties must wish it. You have not made it clear yet that you do. Azarwrath sounded oddly deferential, as if he was worried about presuming.

If anything, Trip wouldn't want to be the one to foolishly presume something about a fifteen-hundred-year-old sorcerer's soul.

You should probably make him master the fish page in the workbook before bonding with him, Jaxi said.

Azarwrath snorted.

Would Sardelle be able to perform the ceremony? Trip asked.

Likely so, Azarwrath said.

Then we should do it when we get back, if you're willing.

Excellent. I am.

An image filled Trip's mind of him standing atop some mountain, Azarwrath in his hand and glowing fiercely as they looked down upon armies that they commanded, all eyes turned up toward them. Had the men in those armies been clad in modern uniforms, Trip might have thought it a vision, but this seemed some fantasy coming from Azarwrath, perhaps based on his memories of the past. He remembered how the soulblade hadn't wanted to bond with Kiadarsa, that he'd wished to be linked with someone more powerful. It continued to boggle Trip's mind that he could be that person.

Order them to go, Azarwrath told him. *Convince them that they won't survive an encounter with Iskandian soldiers.*

Trip hesitated, wondering if he wasn't the only one who'd secretly liked the feeling of having power over people.

My megalomaniacal days are over. I will also inform you if you grow arrogant and full of yourself, as I've seen that happen often with sorcerers, usually to their own detriment. Even if there is nobody around as powerful as you are right now, there are others who could keep you in check. Don't forget the chapaharii *blades that you're surrounded by.*

I haven't. I'll attempt to rein in my budding arrogance. Trip remembered his thoughts of reprogramming Rysha's sword and decided that he would definitely look into it. He liked the idea of there being checks to keep anyone from growing too powerful. Perhaps he could change the control words on all the swords so that only their handlers knew them.

Even if you are powerful among humans, you, too, could be easily turned into a kebab by a dragon.

Trip snorted. *There's that.*

But do convince the captains to leave. You need the practice, and as I've been telling you, being able to manipulate people on these small levels can result in less bloodshed overall.

I understand.

Trip took a deep breath and focused on the vessels again, on the female captain. He shared images of the Iskandian fliers bearing down on her, machine guns firing, bullets finding a way into her cockpit and striking her.

He sensed her alarm, but her hand tightened on the wheel, and she tried to push the images away.

Go, he spoke into her mind. *You will not best soldiers in the Iskandian army, especially those who travel with a sorcerer.*

Speaking of arrogance, he felt like an utter fraud for calling himself that after a few evenings of training, but she licked her lips, growing even more nervous and worried. He presented an alternative to her, a comfortable bed and the safety of her home, if she simply left.

It worked. She turned the boat away. Trip repeated his efforts on the other captains. Perhaps because she'd already turned around, they were more easily swayed. Who wanted to be left out alone on a dark night with a sorcerer about?

"I see you've come into your powers," Dreyak said, looking up at Trip as he climbed the last few steps to the top of the cliff. The torchlight showed wariness on his face.

Trip shrugged and did his best to dampen down his aura, suspecting Dreyak had sensed him using his power. "Just doing my best to convince those people they don't want a fight. Especially since you left Leftie down there all by himself."

"At your request, I understand."

"You wanted to go to the city. I thought I'd suggest it so you would have your excuse. Blazer wasn't planning to let you out of her sight. She doesn't trust you."

"You don't trust me, either."

"No, but I've seen enough of your thoughts to think that perhaps you were telling me the truth." Trip narrowed his eyes at Dreyak. "I do hope you won't make me regret that."

Dreyak gazed toward the dark desert, the black shapes of the mountains visible against the starry backdrop. "I've told you no lies about my mission—you know what brought me here."

Dreyak might not have lied, but Trip had no idea what he would do if he found Emperor Salatak. What if Dreyak had been wrong and the emperor was alive and healthy, not dead? Would he feel compelled to rescue him?

"I wish you luck with finding what you need to ensure your brother is officially appointed emperor," Trip said honestly.

"Good."

Trip snorted. Not exactly a thank-you. He did sense, however, that Dreyak believed Trip was telling the truth and didn't intend to double-cross him.

Dreyak headed down the trail, holding the torch aloft, and Trip followed him.

Is there a way to perform magic without oozing power all over the place? he asked the soulblades, wondering if he would have to continue to worry about people sensing him drawing upon his power. And being oddly drawn to him because of it. After being the kid last picked for things his entire life, he didn't think he would ever grow comfortable with people gazing raptly at him.

Oozing? Jaxi asked. *It's not a pus-filled pimple.*

Indeed, Azarwrath said. *You are radiating the magnificence of your soul.*

Uh, right. How can I not do that?

Eventually, you should get to the point where you can quash your aura at the same time as you're concentrating on magic, Azarwrath said. *Until then, just make sure there aren't any dragons around to sense you. Some of them find half-breeds an abomination and like to strike them down.*

Lovely.

Dreyak stubbed his toe on a rock, then grunted. "Did you know you walked here in the dark?"

"I didn't think about it."

"Maybe you're half wolf instead of half dragon."

"Do dragons not see in the dark?"

"They probably do, but I'm joking. I've known other sorcerers with preternatural senses."

"Joking?" Trip asked. "I didn't know you knew how to do that."

"I'm suave and entertaining when I wish it. I have no reason to be scintillating for Iskandians."

Trip hadn't noticed him being suave or entertaining with those Cofah in the Antarctic, but all he asked was, "You don't have any preternatural senses?"

"No. As I'm sure you can tell, I've scarcely enough dragon blood to light a match with my mind."

He's being modest, right? Trip could now tell when he met people with dragon blood, but he didn't think he could detect how much they had, having only encountered a few since he'd learned to sense people.

Somewhat, Jaxi said. *But he is a lot of generations removed from his dragon ancestor. He's actually been trained well to use what he has. It's surprising that he can keep me from reading his thoughts.*

"Fortunately, I have the supreme athletic prowess of a thousand generations of great Cofah warriors in my blood," Dreyak said, his nose in the air.

For the first time, Trip sensed that some of that arrogance was a show, that Dreyak had grown up training with other future sorcerers and had felt lacking next to those with more potential. He'd worked hard to master swordsmanship, marksmanship, and unarmed combat skills, knowing he would have to stand out that way.

"I'd be more likely to believe that if you hadn't stubbed your toe on a rock," Trip said.

Dreyak glared back at him. "If you doubt my ability, I will gladly fight with you any time you wish. No swords, no magic."

"As fun as that sounds, I've got something even more enjoyable for you to do tonight."

"The chaperone mission?"

"Indeed. Five defenseless young women and an easily distracted seventy-year-old archaeologist need your help to safely return to the city. It's a daunting mission, one few could accomplish, but I'm certain someone with a thousand generations of warriors in his blood can do it."

"You should have used your magical power when you said that, if you'd actually wanted me to be swayed by your bullshit."

"Does that mean you won't do it?"

"I *will* do it, because neither young women nor old men should be left to navigate this desert or that city alone."

"Then I didn't really need to use magic, did I?"

"You are an odd Iskandian."

"It's amazing how many people tell me that."

CHAPTER 14

"DON'T FORGET THE MAGIC DEAD zone," Rysha said for the fifth time as the fliers cruised low over the dark desert, the mountain range up ahead appearing black against the starry sky.

"We haven't," Blazer said. "That's why we're flying low. Still."

Rysha bit her lip to keep from saying more. She'd already shared everything Bhrava Saruth had told her, along with her opinion that flying through a strange land at night was a bad idea, especially if there was a zone where the fliers' power crystals could stop working. True, Bhrava Saruth hadn't said anything about magical devices being affected, but it seemed a logical assumption to make.

"It's been twenty miles, and no troubles yet," Leftie said, sounding chipper. Glad to be back with the group, Rysha guessed. "Maybe Bhrava Saruth was just passing along rumors he'd heard."

"Maybe," Rysha said, "but we're far enough from the city and the coast now that we could risk stopping for the night and camping."

"There are some large predators down there," Trip said. "I've sensed them from time to time."

"We've fought dragons," Leftie said. "What could be considered difficult to deal with after dragons?"

"Giant tarantulas come to mind," Rysha said, shivering at the memory.

Part of her desire to camp and rest might stem from her weariness from that event. Even though Trip's magical power had coursed through her and healed her in an amazingly short period of time, she still felt more tired than usual.

"We'll land at the base of Jralk Mountain," Blazer said. "It'll be hard to find a cave or whatever we're looking for in the middle of the—"

"I sense something," Trip said sharply.

"What? A dragon?" Blazer asked.

"No, a—actually, wait. It's gone now. I thought there was some flying predator ahead of us."

Silence followed the words. It was too dark to tell, but Rysha imagined everyone looking in all directions around their fliers.

"There it is again," Trip said.

"Where?"

"No… it's gone again. Hm, maybe this is what Bhrava Saruth spoke of. An area where—"

"Shit!" Leftie blurted.

"What now?" Blazer demanded.

"My power crystal just went dark." Thumps sounded from his cockpit, and then halted abruptly.

"Leftie?" Blazer asked. "Report."

Rysha leaned forward in her seat and touched Duck's shoulder. "You should take us down, Captain. Better a controlled landing than a forced one, right?"

Duck didn't acknowledge her—he was staring ahead and toward the right, toward Leftie's flier. Rysha couldn't see much in the dark. All their craft had been flying with the hoods down over the power crystals, so they wouldn't emit light, but before, if one of the craft had been close enough, she'd detected a faint glow from the communication crystal. She couldn't see that now, not from Leftie's flier.

Not from *anybody's* flier. Nothing had come over Duck's communication crystal since Blazer spoke. Rysha found the silence unnerving, and she tried to tell if the buzz of the squadron's propellers had changed tone, if their blades were slowing down.

Rysha resisted the urge to dig her nails into Duck's shoulder and repeat her suggestion. Her pilot wouldn't appreciate backseat navigation, and she didn't want to distract him.

Fortunately, Duck shifted his attention forward again. "Major, I'm taking us down."

Blazer didn't answer. Nobody did.

Duck swore as he tilted the nose toward the dark ground below. "You're right," he called over his shoulder. "We'll want to get down before the power goes out; otherwise, the wheels are all we'll have for landing. That's not a sane way to land in a dark desert at night. I—" He cursed and lifted the hood protecting his power crystal.

From behind him, Rysha couldn't see the crystal itself, but she could tell it wasn't glowing. The cockpit had gone dark, including the communication crystal. They were on their own.

"Make sure you're harnessed in tight," Duck yelled, not taking his eyes from the route ahead. "I'm disengaging the propeller from the drive shaft. Will do my best to take us down easy."

This time, Rysha definitely heard the shift in the sound of the propeller, the buzz fading as all the power to it disappeared. Her stomach sank into her boots as the feel of the craft altered, and they dropped toward the ground. Rapidly.

When she peered over the side, the wind whipping at her cheek, she couldn't tell how far away it was. Everything was just *dark*. How in the hells would Duck be able to gauge a landing? And what if they struck something? There weren't any trees down there, but washes, boulders, cactuses? Absolutely.

"Hang on," Duck yelled.

Rysha gripped the sides of the seat well and sank low.

The wheels of the flier slammed down instead of touching down lightly. Rysha bounced upward, her harness straps gouging into her shoulders. If not for those straps, she would have been thrown out.

The flier rose up, slammed down again, and once more, they bounced up. Rysha couldn't brace herself enough to keep her body still. Her head whipped back and forth with the bounces, and she felt as helpless as a rag doll.

Finally, the wheels stayed down, but the flier lurched and wobbled as it sped over the rough terrain. Washes, rocks, and holes made the ride no less torturous than before. Cracks and thuds came from underneath the frame. Some desert foliage scraping at the belly and tearing into the wings. One wheel must have gone over a rock, because Rysha pitched sideways, the harness again the only thing keeping her from being thrown free.

Despite it all, or *because* of it all, the flier slowed down. Just as Rysha thought they might survive the unorthodox landing, the wheels splashed into water. Droplets sprayed up, spattering her cheeks.

For a bewildered moment, she thought they'd somehow gotten turned around and were landing in the ocean. The flier rolled deeper into water as Duck cursed, but their momentum finally slowed, and they came to a halt.

Rysha couldn't hear the roar of the sea. All she heard was disturbed water lapping at their sides. Whatever body of water this was, it wasn't an ocean.

"Thought this was the desert," Duck said. "What's a lake doing in the middle of the desert?"

"Some natural spring, maybe. Be glad for it. If we're stuck here for a while, having a water source around will be useful."

"Stuck?" Duck asked. In the now-silent night, she heard the click of him unbuckling his harness. "We're not going to be stuck. We'll find a way to fix this. Trip's an engineer, and Blazer's got some mechanical know-how."

"I don't think you can fix your power crystals without magic, and that may be in short supply now." Rysha kept herself from pointing out that she'd warned everybody about this. It wasn't as if Duck was in charge of the mission. Besides, what had the alternative been? To leave the magic-dependent fliers somewhere in the desert, hoping nobody chanced upon them and stole the crystals, while the team hiked across some invisible dead zone with boundaries none of them knew?

"Trip can fix magic things. We just need…" Duck stood up, peering across the dark desert. "I'm not sure where everybody went down."

Rysha could barely see *Duck* in the dark. There was no way she knew where the other fliers were. The crystals had seemed to go out in a staggered manner, so the squadron could be stretched across ten miles of desert.

She didn't point out there was no guarantee that everybody had survived. As rough as their landing had been, they had been lucky the ground had been relatively flat.

"Guess we'll have to wait for morning to round everybody up," Duck said. "You all right back there? Sorry about the bumps."

As if they had been his fault. Rysha was glad the squadron had heeded her warning enough that they'd been flying low to the ground. She was also glad that, for whatever reason, as the flier design had evolved over the years, the thrusters being added for takeoffs and landings, nobody had considered the wheels obsolete and removed them.

"I'll live." Rysha rubbed the back of her sore neck, wondering if Trip would object to healing her twice in the same night. And would his magic work here?

Of course, by the time they gathered and walked out of the dead zone, it wouldn't be the same night. She just hoped… She refused to believe he hadn't survived the landing. He had uncanny ability in the sky. Surely, he would have found a way to bring his flier down safely.

"I reckon we should start a signal fire," Duck said. "So the others can find us if they don't want to wait until morning. I'll hop down and see if there's anything flammable here. I suppose finding wood is right out."

"Some of the brush we ran over sounded solid."

A splash sounded as Duck jumped down. "It's not too deep. About three feet. Going to be a pain getting the flier out, though, especially if we don't have power."

"Something to worry about in the morning," Rysha suggested.

A roar floated across the dark desert. Rysha thought of Trip's warning about large predators. It had seemed far less alarming when she'd been flying a thousand feet above them.

She found her rifle in its mount, unfastened it, and also assured herself that Dorfindral remained secure at her hip. The scabbard had wedged itself further than usual into the small gap between seat and hull, and it took some tugging and grunting to extract it.

"You *sure* you're all right, Lieutenant?" Duck asked, his voice coming from the tail of the flier now.

"There are times when being attached to a sword is inconvenient."

"I've heard that, ma'am." Duck's voice was dry, but he didn't make a lewd or anatomical comment, as Kaika might have.

As Rysha lowered herself over the side, splashing into the cool water, the roar came again. Closer this time.

"If we have to fight wildlife again," she said, "I expect you to stand in front this time, Captain."

"I would have been happy to stand in front last time, though my butt's on the scrawny side, and might not have taken well to spider venom."

"I assure you mine didn't, either." As Rysha slogged through the water to shore, she scraped through her mind, trying to remember if she'd ever read about the local flora and fauna. She knew her country's offerings well enough, but few Iskandian texts mentioned Rakgorath in more than passing.

A third roar drifted across the night. It sounded like a lion. Iskandia's southeastern steppes were home to the species. As a girl, Rysha had gone with her family on a safari down there and had seen the animals lounging in the sun on rocks.

Answering cries came from the opposite direction, not roars but the hair-raising yips and screeches of coyotes or something similar. A higher-pitched roar came from yet another direction, toward the mountains.

"Is it just me, or are we in the middle of a lot of animal activity?" Once she stood on dry land, Rysha slung her pack to the ground so she could poke through it and find her lantern.

"We might have landed in the only watering hole for dozens of miles in any direction."

"So, they're only heading this way because they're thirsty?"

"Well, they might not mind it if they found some steaks by their watering hole." Duck's voice was farther away now.

Only because he was finding wood, not because he'd abandoned her, Rysha reassured herself. She also reassured herself that she could handle some animals. She'd battled men that day and won, and she'd helped battle dragons and survived that. She was training for the elite troops. That meant she was *definitely* a match for lions.

Assuming she could find her stupid lantern and make some light. It hadn't flown off her pack during that wild landing, had it?

The thwacks of Duck cutting wood with the flier's small emergency axe rang out in the night. Rysha thought the noise might make the animals stop their own racket, if only while they listened to figure out what was making it, but if anything, the roars and yowls and yips grew louder and more agitated.

"Ouch," Duck blurted. "Everything here has thorns or prickly leaves. Wish I had some gloves."

"I think I lost my lantern," Rysha reluctantly admitted, kneeling back from her pack. It had been attached to the outside before. She was sure of it. It must have flown off.

Duck grunted as he dragged something toward her. A pile of wood? "I'll look for mine. We'll need a flame to light the fire."

"Think the fire will keep the animals away?"

Duck hesitated. "It might help. Just shoot at anything you hear moving around out here. They've got firearms on this continent. The animals should know to be afraid of humans with guns."

"Think I should fire a couple of warning shots into the air?" Rysha squinted into the gloom across the spring. She thought she'd heard a rustle over there.

"It's up to you." Duck splashed to the flier. Retrieving his pack?

Rysha readied her rifle, putting her back to the tail of the craft. She drew Dorfindral a few inches and whispered the command for it to stand ready, hoping the blade would flare to life and provide magical light. But it remained dormant.

More rustling came from the brush around them. The animals weren't roaring or yowling as much now, probably because they'd had a nice chat and were ready to take action.

Rysha pointed her rifle in the air and fired twice. Even if it didn't scare the animals, it would let the others know where they were.

The rustling paused for a few seconds. Unfortunately, she didn't hear the sounds of any terrified animals taking off at top speed.

Two answering shots rang out to one side, perhaps a mile away, and Rysha smiled.

"At least one other flier landed successfully," she said.

"I reckon so." Duck splashed down again and pushed through the water toward her. "Unless someone else of the rifle-owning persuasion is out here. Or the critters have thumbs. I heard a story of flash apes in the Dakrovian jungles that stole some firearms, then started appearing and disappearing outside of a village, only sticking around long enough to shoot banana trees."

"*Just* banana trees?" Rysha assumed he was trying to ease her tension, but she didn't know if that was a good idea. Her instincts told her they were in danger, that the animals out there hadn't been that scared by the gunshots.

"That's what the story says. Apparently, it was a drought year, and the trees weren't producing well. The apes must have figured the trees were just being stingy and that a few bullets would help things along. Eventually, the apes ran out of bullets and didn't seem to know how to find and load more, so peace returned to the jungle. And the banana trees recovered from being brutalized."

"Who told you this story? The wolves that you claim raised you?"

"Nah, wolves live in a different climate from apes, so they don't tell stories about each other. Don't you city folk know anything?" Duck clucked with disapproval. "It was a macaw that told me the story."

"Naturally."

Rysha glimpsed a flame in the distance at the same time as a familiar voice called, "Whose flier is that in the pond?"

"That's mine, Major," Duck called back.

"Should've known only you could find water in the desert to crash into." Blazer came into sight, the small glow of her lantern lighting up the front of her uniform and not much more. "Living up to your name."

"Didn't crash, ma'am. This was a real fine landing, and the water helped slow us down at the end."

"A fine landing?" Kaika asked, crunching through brush behind Blazer. "We'll check that in the morning when we look at the bottom of your flier. If it's like Blazer's, there are cactus guts spattered all over it."

"Cactuses don't have guts, ma'am."

"You can call that pulpy green stuff whatever you like, but it makes a mess."

Rysha, feeling better with reinforcements—and light—coming, lowered her rifle. But the soft crunch of a twig sounded behind her, and she whirled, instincts shouting a warning in her ear.

A dark shape sprang toward her, a black blur blocking out the stars for an instant.

She fired, cried, "Look out!" and dove to the side. Shouts erupted behind her as she rolled away, dust caking her nostrils and tongue. As she jumped up, more rifles fired. Something landed in the dust a few feet in front of Rysha. She aimed her rifle, finger tense on the trigger. But whatever that dark shape was, it only twitched a few times before growing still.

Nothing else did—the foliage around the spring erupted with yips, yowls, roars, and even hoots.

Blazer and Kaika jogged up, pistols in their hands. Blazer held her lantern over the dark figure, the dim light showing a scaled tan animal that looked like a cross between a lizard and a mountain lion. A *large* mountain lion. It had died on its side, its snout open, displaying very sharp fangs.

Rysha shuddered to think how close the animal had come to sinking those fangs into the back of her neck.

"Is there a reason animals are targeting me today?" she asked. "Do I smell particularly tasty?"

Duck stood the closest to her and leaned over for a sniff. "I'm not sure about tastiness, but you're a touch aromatic."

Kaika ambled up and slapped him in the chest. "You're smelling yourself."

"Am I? You sure?"

"Positive." Kaika looked Rysha up and down. "Still, a bath in the spring in the morning might be wise for all of us. Especially those of us who've recently been slathered in spider innards."

"It wasn't the innards that got me," Rysha grumbled. "That tarantula was medically precise in inserting gallons of its venom without slathering anything on me."

"Anyone seen Trip and Leftie yet?" Blazer lifted her lantern and looked around.

"No, ma'am," Duck said. "I'm gathering some wood for a fire. That might guide them in and convince the critters to stay away."

"Critters." Rysha eyed the desert lion, or whatever it was called. Given its two- or three-hundred-pound mass, "critter" seemed too innocuous a name.

"Wood?" Kaika said. "Not sure much of what we've been tramping through qualifies as wood. Something's been poking me in the foot for the last mile though." She bent over to examine her boot while Duck ambled to the bush he'd been hacking at earlier. He dragged some of the brittle branches over.

Kaika extracted something from the sole of her boot and held it up to Blazer's lantern. "Ouch." The brown thorn was as long and sharp as the lion's fangs. "Good thing I've got thick soles. That would go straight through your foot if you stepped on it in socks."

"This isn't a hospitable land," Blazer said. "Getting the fliers back out of it if the power crystals aren't working isn't going to be easy."

"Easy?" Duck asked. "Will it be possible at all?"

Kaika handed him her thorn. "Firewood."

"Thank you, ma'am." Duck tossed it into the brush pile. "That'll go far."

Something hooted from the other side of the spring. More roars and yowls answered the noise. Rysha imagined the animals speaking to each other, challenging the strong ones to try again to take down these human invaders.

"Getting out might take some creative engineering," Blazer said. "Especially if we have to build a steam engine and boiler to haul our fliers out of here."

"Ma'am," Duck said, "are you joshing? We haven't got the materials to build anything like that. We don't even have any metal."

"Trip has a lock and a sardine tin in his pocket," Rysha said.

"We're saved for sure then."

Blazer shrugged. "I was joking. I hope. Our crystal kept flashing off and on after we landed. Whatever is affecting the magic seems to be intermittent. We might be able to point the fliers in the right direction and fly or drive them forward a ways each time the crystals are on. We need to finish the mission first though. In the morning, we'll get the map out and figure how close we are to that mountain. We'll go on foot if we have to."

Rysha remembered the room behind the statue and everything she'd learned about Agarrenon Shivar so far. And the fact that Trip had implied he'd learned even worse.

Dorfindral buzzed irritatedly into her mind at this thought of Trip. She sent a quelling glare toward the sword's hilt and mentally ordered it to stand down, though it occurred to her to be surprised it was awake. She'd thought it might have gone dormant, along with the fliers' crystals.

"Are we still sure we *want* to complete it?" Rysha asked aloud for the others.

"You think Moe was right and that the dragon's dead?" Blazer asked.

A lion roared from the brush nearby, and Rysha lifted her rifle again.

"Shut up," Kaika yelled toward the noisy animals, "or I'm going to start lobbing grenades out there."

A mocking hoot answered her.

"They're asking for it."

"No, I don't think the dragon is dead," Rysha said, answering Blazer's question, "not unless he passed away in the last twenty-five years. But he's not sounding like a promising ally for Iskandia even if he *is* alive."

"My mission is to find him and point Trip at him," Blazer said. "Majors don't get to randomly decide that they're not going to complete a mission."

"We've come this far." Duck dragged over another gnarled branch and also tossed a few dried cactus pads into his growing pile of possibly flammable fuels. "Might as well see what Trip's papa looks like."

Abruptly, the animals jabbering around the spring fell silent. The entire desert did. Rysha could hear Duck's footfalls as he walked back toward the brush.

"I still want to find him," came Trip's voice from the darkness. "If nothing else, I'd like to find a way to keep that cult from sacrificing more people, and he's the keystone in it, whether by accident or design. If he tells them to knock it off, I'm hoping they will."

The others all jumped in surprise at his silent arrival, even the ever-alert Kaika. Rysha realized Dorfindral had been complaining about Trip's approach rather than her thoughts of him.

"You think he can be convinced to do that?" Kaika asked, recovering quickly.

"I won't know until I try."

Trip came into view, and the sounds of someone walking much more loudly drifted to their ears. Dry foliage rattled, and grunts of pain came from the brush. Leftie?

Trip paused and looked back, frowning with concern. "He wouldn't let me give him a hand," he said quietly.

"That you, Leftie?" Blazer asked.

"Yes, ma'am. Be there soon. Hurt my foot a little."

"You didn't step on one of those thorns, did you?" Kaika asked.

"Pulled *something* out of the bottom of my boot in the dark, yes. It cut deep into my foot in addition to putting a peephole in my boot sole."

"The foliage is more likely to kill you here than the animals," Kaika said.

"Well, maybe not *more* likely." Blazer prodded the dead lion with the tip of her rifle.

"Equally likely?"

"Trip refused to heal me," Leftie said. "I finally worked up the courage to ask for some magicking, and he says his magic isn't reliable right now."

"Maybe you just weren't pretty enough," Duck said, "for him to want to gather you in his arms and spread healing magics all over."

"I *did* offer to carry him," Trip said.

Leftie sniffed. "No man is going to let another man carry him unless both legs and his spleen are blown off."

"The spleen is integral, is it?" Blazer asked. "Just the missing legs wouldn't do?"

"That's right, ma'am."

"Might I borrow the lantern, Major?" Duck waved at his brush pile. "I've got enough gathered to start a fire. That ought to help keep the animals away. I'm not sure about the thorns."

Blazer handed him the lantern. "Status of your fliers, Leftie and Trip?"

"I landed without doing too much damage, I believe," Trip said. "I'll have to take a closer look when it's daylight."

"Yes, I noticed you lost your lanterns too. Or decided trekking around in the dark was a good idea."

Trip's forehead crinkled, as if it hadn't occurred to him to dig out a lantern. Rysha had noticed him tramping around in the dark without needing a light before so she wasn't surprised.

"The critters got real quiet," Duck observed.

"Maybe they realized that an apex predator arrived," Rysha said, looking at Trip.

Leftie lifted his hands. "It's true. I'm a carnivorous beast on the hookball field. If I didn't have a hole in my foot, I'd show them my skills by pegging them with rocks."

Rysha opened her mouth to clarify, but caught Trip frowning again, and closed it. He surely didn't think of himself that way, and he wouldn't want her drawing attention to his otherness.

"Leftie, flier status?" Blazer prompted.

"Mine's probably still flightworthy. If we can get the crystals working."

"And get it out of the ditch?" Trip asked, smiling.

Leftie didn't smile back. "How'd you know about the ditch? I met up with you half a mile from where I landed."

Trip hesitated. "I think you told me."

"No, I didn't. I wasn't real proud of getting it stuck in a damn wash. If you're reading my mind, I sure as hells don't appreciate it."

"I didn't—"

"At least it would be useful if you could heal a man, but nobody wants his privacy invaded. Asshole." Leftie limped toward the opposite side of the gathering, leaving the influence of the light and kicking something into the spring.

A disturbed bird flapped its wings and flew away.

Trip's shoulders slumped, and his chin dropped to his chest.

Rysha scowled after Leftie. She could understand people being disturbed by someone reading their thoughts, but throwing insults around wouldn't help anything. And Trip had enough bugging him right now. Finding out his sire might be some vile cult-inspiring dragon who reveled in bloodshed couldn't be sitting easily with him. Talk about an asshole. Trip wasn't anywhere near that.

She took a step toward him, but he backed away from the group.

"I'll stand watch while you all rest," he told Blazer, then disappeared into the night without meeting Rysha's eyes.

CHAPTER 15

TRIP HADN'T REALIZED HOW MUCH a part of him his magic was. For most of his life, he'd only thought of it as a sixth sense, but it had always been there, his instincts accurately guiding him when his other senses weren't enough.

Oh, his magic hadn't abandoned him completely. He'd still located Leftie, but it had taken him longer than usual, with his certainty that he was going in the right direction faltering often. He'd walked a few steps, then had to stop and wait for his senses to return to him. When he'd attempted to heal Leftie's injury, his concentration had proven elusive. He'd been able to see the wound with his mind but not do anything to fix it. It had been frustrating, especially after his almost effortless success at healing Rysha's injury.

That feeling had yet to fade, frustration mixed with agitation. He'd almost lashed out when Leftie had made that comment as he stalked off, and that scared him. As a boy, he'd occasionally caused nearby vases and plates to break when he'd been having temper tantrums. One had broken close enough to his grandmother that a shard had struck her in the face, drawing blood. That had been about the age he'd realized he was responsible for those items breaking, even if he hadn't understood how, and he'd been horrified that he'd caused her harm. Now that he was training and learning to draw upon more power, he cringed to think of what kind of damage he could do if he had a temper tantrum.

Trip drew in a deep breath as he stared across the spring at the fire burning on the far side. He sat near the water's edge, his knees drawn up, his arms hooked around them. The animals that had been skulking about earlier had slunk away when he'd walked over here. Rysha's comment about him being an apex predator seemed laughable, especially now. What would happen if something sprang at him in one of the periods where his power was gone or unreliable?

From time to time, he sensed the crystals in Duck's flier, but they were just as unreliable as his magic. They went out and came back on again. There was no way it would be safe to fly with them like that, but he hoped the team would be able to drive the fliers out of the desert. Or at least out of the area of this strange magic dead zone. Or whatever it was. That was the term Rysha had given him, apparently given to *her* by Bhrava Saruth. Trip's magic wasn't dead so much as it was intermittent. What could cause that? He could understand why the dragons wanted to avoid it. He itched to get out of the area.

Rysha walked into his view, heading toward the fire, her sleeves pulled down over her hands as she dragged dry, thorny branches to add to the pile. She and Duck had given themselves fire-making duty. They had also dragged that carcass away from the camp so it wouldn't attract scavengers.

Leftie, Blazer, and Kaika had spread bedrolls in a spot between the flier and the fire, but that was it. One of them should have been doing the hard work so Rysha could rest. She'd endured enough that day.

Trip told himself to look away. Since they didn't know he was over here, he was essentially spying on them, a different form of invading their privacy. Seven gods, he didn't even remember poking into Leftie's thoughts to find out what had happened to his flier. He'd just known.

He closed his eyes and rested his forehead on his knees. A part of him wanted to call across the spring to Rysha, to ask her to join him in this secluded spot. But he didn't know if his telepathy would work, and he had no intention of shouting so that everybody could hear it. He'd have to go back over there if he wanted to quietly draw her aside, and that would mean enduring another glare from Leftie. And snickers from the others if he and Rysha went off into the dark together.

Or worse than snickers. Blazer might write them up when they got back for being unprofessional during a mission. She hadn't said anything after walking up on the kiss Trip and Rysha had almost shared outside the Charkolt hangar, but he had no delusions about kissing being acceptable behavior for soldiers on duty. There weren't any rules against officers spending time together or seeing each other off duty, though it was frowned upon if they were in the same chain of command or if there was a great deal of rank separating them, but out on missions, officers were supposed to be professional. Lip-locking wasn't professional.

He sighed, supposing he should return to the group. Stomping off hadn't been professional, either, not when he hadn't asked for permission to stand the first watch.

A rustle came from the shoreline to his right, and he jerked his head up. Instinctively, he tried to stretch out with his senses, but they had no better luck at piercing the darkness than his eyes did. Everything was fuzzy and indistinct. He couldn't tell if some bird tramping around under the brush made the noise, or if a massive predator approached, perhaps a lion like the one that had attacked the camp.

Trip dropped his hand to his pistol—he'd removed the soulblade scabbards, laying them in the dirt beside him, so he could more easily sit down.

A twig snapped, and a branch rattled.

Jaxi? Azarwrath? Can you tell what's out there? Trip asked.

The soulblades had been largely quiet since the power crystals failed. They had managed a few conversations, but the dead zone was affecting them as well as him.

"Trip?" came Rysha's soft voice.

He almost laughed, lowering his hand from his pistol.

"Here," he whispered, just loudly enough for her to hear.

Across the spring, everyone except for Leftie had lain down in the sleeping area. He stood by the fire, alternately watching the darkness and feeding branches into the flames. Blazer must not have been willing to assume Trip would keep an eye on the camp.

That disgruntled him for a moment, but the fog covering his senses lifted for a few seconds, and he grew aware of Rysha's approach. Of her concern for him, her sympathy for all he'd learned about Agarrenon Shivar that day, and her desire to stand beside him, no matter what a jerk his sire ended up being.

He smiled, not sure how she'd known where to look for him, but happy to guide her the rest of the way. "Come here," he whispered.

She patted around, not seeing as well in the darkness as he—apparently, that was some physical attribute rather than magic, because his better-than-average night vision hadn't left him yet—and her hand patted the top of his head. She followed it down to his shoulder, then sat beside him.

"*Leftie* is an asshole," she assured him, "not you."

He chuckled, his mood lightened now that she sat next to him, her shoulder touching his.

"He might be, but he's not wrong," Trip admitted. "I'm doing things without being conscious of it now, and it's scaring me a little." It occurred to him that he might have drawn Rysha over to him without intending to. He swallowed. If true, that disturbed him even more than his reading of Leftie's thoughts. The last thing he wanted was to take away her free will. "How did you find me?" he asked, worried what the answer would be.

"I assumed you wouldn't go far."

He licked his lips. That wasn't an answer.

"I decided to risk walking around the spring, now that it's less animal-infested—I also figured you were still around because of that."

He smiled, some of the tension leaving his shoulders. He wasn't surprised she had used logic to find him.

"And then about a quarter of the way around, Dorfindral started making grumpy thoughts in my mind, so I was sure you were over here."

"Oh? I haven't been able to communicate reliably with the soulblades since we landed. Has Dorfindral's grumpiness been intermittent or consistent?"

"Consistent, I think. But he mostly only gets huffy when I drift close to you, especially now that Dreyak is gone. Not that Dreyak ever irritated him as much as you and the soulblades do."

"Irritating people seems to be my special gift." Trip sighed.

It hadn't been a pitch for sympathy, but the emotion melted off Rysha, and she rested her arm around his shoulders.

He stared at the water. He didn't want her to hug him out of sympathy—or pity. No, he wanted her to be attracted to him because of his handsome masculineness and the way he handled his flier, taking down enemies that threatened Iskandia. Of course, he didn't mind that she seemed to be attracted to some of his quirkier traits, too, his penchant for tinkering with things, even things some would label as garbage. That was a part of his personality and seemed a legitimate thing for someone to be drawn to. But if she had come out mostly because she felt sorry for him…

He dropped his forehead to his knees again. She rubbed his back through his uniform, sending delicious tingles of warmth through him. Even if his pride would have preferred she'd come for another reason, he couldn't imagine pushing her away. Instead, he was barely breathing, afraid she would stop touching him if he moved.

"That feels good," he whispered.

"I'm glad. You deserve to feel good once in a while."

"I don't deserve anything more than anyone else."

"*Everyone* deserves to feel good once in a while," she said dryly. "I haven't observed you looking happy that often. You have a tendency toward moroseness. Is that something you manage sometimes? Happiness?"

He thought about mentioning that he didn't feel morose now, not with her rubbing his back.

"I don't know. I spend too much time in my head, I think. I envy Leftie sometimes. He runs down a field and throws a ball in a net, and he's ecstatic for the rest of the day."

"Maybe you should try that."

"Throwing balls in nets?"

"You might find it fun."

Her fingers drifted from his back to his collar, then touched skin for the first time. She rubbed his neck, and a thrill of heat ran down his spine. For a moment, he forgot the thread of the conversation.

"I, uh—I went to one of his matches once and thought the stationary goal made the game boring and unchallenging. I grabbed a food wrapper and started sketching ideas on the back to create an ambulatory goal powered by a clockwork engine. It would have been able to move along the end line and also raise itself up and down. I was so engrossed in my design that someone had to prod me in the shoulder to let me know the match had ended and people were leaving. I have no idea what the final score was other than that Leftie's team won, as usual."

"So, designing things is fun for you. You should spend more time doing it."

"Yeah, but I'm not sure when. More than ever, I feel my place is in the sky, defending Iskandia, and my evenings are—I feel it would be irresponsible for me not to train with Sardelle when possible. Especially, now that..." He trailed off, not wanting to talk about how he'd seemed to grow stronger in the last couple of weeks. It was as if using his powers instead of shunting them away to some dark recess of his mind was making them greater. Like a muscle getting larger after working out. That wouldn't be so bad, but when he accidentally caused some desire of his to happen, it bothered him, even when it was as innocent as wanting to know if Leftie had landed safely.

"I'm sure you won't have to train forever," Rysha said, her fingers massaging the back of his neck. His chain almost slipped its gears as wonderful sensations rushed through his body. Her fingers pushed up into his hair, nails scraping along his scalp. "And in the meantime, you should still make time for fun now and then."

He groped for something intelligent to say, but most of his blood was rushing *away* from his brain instead of toward it. He leaned closer to her, tempted to drop his head in her lap. The notion that he ought to be offering to massage something of hers came to mind, but he couldn't imagine doing anything that would stop this. He wanted her to keep rubbing his neck, his scalp. Maybe other things too.

Earlier, he'd been reminding himself that they should be professional while on their mission, but would it be so bad if they did what he'd longed to do since they first kissed? No, for longer than that. The memory of her walking onto the airship deck in that revealing pirate attire flashed into his mind. Of how stunning she'd been, how much he'd wanted to brazenly look, to walk up and touch. Even before then, he'd wanted to be with her. Maybe as soon as that first night when she'd stood up for him in that stupid tavern in the capital. And when she'd been poring over maps and studying texts in the corner, preferring that to getting drunk and talking about inane things, the way everyone else there had been doing.

And, he felt certain, she wanted to be with him too. Surely, it hadn't been sympathy alone that brought her out here. All those words about making time for fun. Could she have meant them for herself as well as for him? Maybe she'd been thinking of a private tryst when she came looking for him. And if they had one, who would know? The others had gone to sleep. Only Leftie remained awake, and how much would he hear across the spring and over the crackle of the fire?

Rysha's fingers paused, and Trip sensed her draw back, mentally as well as physically. He also sensed that sword influencing her, warning her about him.

Damn it, they didn't need a duenna. He thought the control words at it, telling it to stand down. He didn't want anything interrupting them, nor making Rysha hesitate to touch him.

His senses were still in and out, and he didn't feel Dorfindral's acquiescence, but the blade must have lessened its warning, because Rysha relaxed. Her fingers returned to his scalp, massaging him and teasing his hair. Her other hand shifted down his back and up under his jacket. She untucked his shirt and slid her fingers up his spine. By the gods, yes. That was exquisite. Now all he needed was her lips against his, hungry and intense.

He tilted his face toward hers, groping for a way to phrase the suggestion, but she anticipated him. Or she'd been thinking of the same thing. Her mouth found his, and he scooted closer, determined that their kiss not be interrupted again, that they have as much time together as they wanted.

She surprised him with her eagerness, her hand rubbing his back as she kissed him hard, hungry, her body pressing against his, full of need. Her desire washed over him, and excitement flooded him as he felt her need. He pulled her into his arms, then into his lap, groaning with pleasure as he started exploring her body, sliding a hand up under *her* shirt. He slid his tongue into her mouth, reveling in her taste, in her scent, in the warm emotions, her desire to be with him, to do whatever he wanted, to make him feel—

A realization slammed into Trip like a bucket of ice water.

He pulled back, horror stealing his desire as it dawned on him that he was influencing her, that he probably had been since she sat down. But especially since he'd told the sword to shut up. Maybe, no matter what she'd said, he'd even affected her decision to walk over here and find him.

"Rysha," he croaked.

She hadn't yet had the same realization. Her hands continued to rub and massage, nails scraping his skin, making it very hard for him to think of pushing her away. It would be so easy to return to what they'd been doing, to pretend he was wrong, or that it didn't matter.

But it did matter.

"Rysha," he said again, and this time, found her wrists, pulling her hands out from under his shirt.

"Mm?" she asked, her lips against his throat, the spot they'd found when he'd pulled his mouth away. She nuzzled him, her kisses painfully delicious.

"We can't. I—I didn't mean to, but I…"

She drew back, looking into his eyes, as if he were a cipher to figure out. He swallowed, groping for words to explain further, but he didn't have to. He could see her expression shut down as understanding grew.

"You used your magic on me," she said, her body freezing, her gaze locked to his. Horror and condemnation filled her eyes now, making him wish he didn't see in the dark as well as he did. "You commanded me to—" Her voice broke off, and he sensed disbelief and then rage welling within her.

"No," he protested. "I promise, I didn't mean to make it a command. I was just thinking about how good it felt and that I wanted you to—"

"You silenced Dorfindral." She pulled away from him, jerking her hands from his when he didn't loosen his grip quickly enough. "I felt his warning, and then suddenly it went away. You used the command words, didn't you? And because you're *you*, the sword listened."

Trip knew he should voice an agreement, to confess, but it was so hard. To admit that he'd been manipulating her and asserting his control over the sword so he could more easily do so. He hadn't even known what he was doing, not truly.

"I should have known." She pushed herself out of his lap. Fast. As if she couldn't get away from him quickly enough. She grabbed Dorfindral's scabbard and stood, towering over him. "I could tell it was complaining about more than your presence, but I couldn't figure out what. I didn't know you were manipulating me. That's what the sword was warning me about."

"Rysha, I'm sorry." He spread his arms and looked up at her, wondering if shifting to his knees to apologize would help at all. "I didn't mean to. But I should have known. I—"

Asshole. She didn't say it, but the thought jumped to the front of her mind so loudly that he heard it.

She spun away and stalked into the brush, heading back around the spring toward camp.

Trip rubbed his face, feeling lower than a slug. If everybody thought he was turning into a jerk, maybe they weren't wrong. Maybe he was destined to be some evil bastard with far too much power to be wholesome. The same as his sire.

Rysha made it back to the camp. Leftie grinned and made some joke about where she'd been. She snapped something that was probably the equivalent of *screw you* at him, then lay down on her bedroll and yanked the blanket over her head. And cried.

Trip dropped his face into his hands, tears of his own forming. But he'd brought this on himself. What right did he have to weep?

"Asshole," he whispered to himself.

CHAPTER 16

"WE'RE ONLY ABOUT FIVE MILES from Jralk Mountain," Blazer said, pointing at the map unrolled on the ground in front of the remains of the campfire.

The sun had just come up, but it already flooded the blue sky with its light, and Rysha had no trouble reading the symbols and words on the paper.

"From the base of this side of it," Blazer added. "The mountain is huge. Who knows where on it a dragon might be found?"

"Somewhere inside it, I imagine," Duck said, yawning.

None of them had slept much that night, Rysha least of all. She'd lain curled up in a ball, tears leaking into the dirt as she replayed those minutes with Trip over and over again. She'd been unable to let it go and get some rest, unable to stop thinking about how far she would have gone last night because he'd wished it.

Had any of *her* truly wanted to be over there, flinging herself all over him like some simpering palace prostitute, trained to exist only to please men? Or had his desires simply been coercing her into action?

No, she knew that wasn't true. She'd wanted to go over there and comfort him. Hells, she'd even been thinking of kissing him if she found him, of making him forget Leftie's dark snarl.

But could she trust those thoughts? What if he'd been subtly manipulating her all along?

No, she doubted that. Dorfindral had known the moment when he'd started using his power on her. She'd wanted to comfort him. And she'd enjoyed touching him, rubbing his warm, muscular body through his clothing. And under it. She just hadn't planned to fling herself at him and fulfill his every sexual desire. She remembered pausing when Dorfindral had warned her that something was awry, but the sensation had disappeared, and she'd been oh so eager to return to what they'd been doing.

Even now, heat flooded her cheeks at the memory of how easily she'd been led, how weak her will had been. How embarrassing. Here, she was so proud of her mind, all the knowledge she'd put into it, and how quickly she could access that knowledge. But along came a sorcerer, and she couldn't manage a coherent thought of her own? She couldn't retain her independence in the face of some green-eyed man who wanted her in his bed?

She vowed to stay away from Trip and certainly not to follow him into any dark nooks in the wilds. Even though she regretted thinking of him as an asshole and understood that he probably hadn't meant to influence her, she wasn't going to surrender her independence, her own will, to a man. To *anyone*. And it would be too easy for those lines to blur with him.

"Lieutenant Ravenwood?" Kaika poked her in the shoulder.

Rysha realized everyone was looking at her. Well, not *everyone*, as Trip had never returned to the camp. But Blazer, Kaika, Duck, and Leftie stood around the map with her, and their eyes were upon her.

"Sorry, what?" she asked, embarrassed anew because she had missed the question.

"We're trying to figure out the best spot to look for a dragon," Kaika said, thankfully not teasing her for her distraction.

Maybe Rysha looked too tired and miserable to tease.

"We're also considering options for the fliers," Blazer said. "The crystals seem to be knocked out a lot more of the time than they're on, and when they're on, they flicker."

Rysha wished Trip's power had been less *on* last night.

"There's this mining town about eight miles that way, at the base of the mountain." Blazer pointed at the map with a stick. "But I've never heard of it, and I don't know if we'd be able to get help there, or if we'd be kicked out because we're obviously Iskandians."

"If we weren't wearing our uniforms, they wouldn't know we were *military* Iskandians," Rysha said. "I've seen people here with similar complexions to ours, even among the cultists. Rakgorath is a melting pot. People from nations all over the world have been dropped off here or came of their own volition." She scratched her head, noticing that half her hair wasn't up in her bun. She'd forgotten to comb it and remake it when she woke up. She *was* a mess. Damn Trip. "I'm not sure what we would find in a mining town. In fact, what makes you think that's what it is? Rakgorath isn't known for its ore or other natural resources."

"It's called Smelterville," Blazer said.

Rysha cleaned her spectacles and crouched to more easily read the labels. "Oh."

"I was joking last night about the steam engine, sort of. But maybe it *would* be possible to create something that could pull our fliers out of the desert. If that's a real mining town, there might be enough raw materials to build something. Maybe they even have a simple boiler and firebox we could buy and convert to meet our needs. If Captain Trip ever deigns to join us again, he's supposed to have that engineering background, and I'm a fair mechanic too. We could jury-rig something if we had appropriate materials."

Rysha eyed the map dubiously. Even though she could verify the name of the town now, she couldn't imagine much of a mining or smelting operation here. They hadn't even seen another human being since leaving the coast. The town might be an abandoned area where people had once set something up for exploratory mining.

"It wouldn't hurt to look. We can walk and be there before it gets too hot." Blazer eyed the rising sun, its warm rays already beating down upon them. "I'd feel more comfortable knowing we have a plan to get the fliers back in the air. We can't *leave* them here." She grimaced, and Rysha imagined how much trouble a mission leader would get into for losing four expensive military aircraft. "Also, we don't yet know where in the mountain to look for the dragon. Maybe there will be some clues in the town. It's not like there are any other towns nestled up to the bottom of the mountain range."

No, with only a handful of exceptions, the entire population, at least as marked by cities and towns, lived along the coast. Rysha didn't know if that was because the inland desert was too inhospitable for too much of the year, or if the magic dead zone had something to do with it. She thought she remembered Bhrava Saruth mentioning that the mountains themselves weren't in the zone—which, if Agarrenon Shivar had his lair there, made sense—but there weren't any towns up there, at least none that were listed on the map.

"Clues?" Duck asked. "Like dragon shrines with virgins being sacrificed on them?" His lips twisted with distaste.

"Spare us any more clues like that," Blazer said, sighing.

"At least we helped those people." Kaika patted Blazer on the shoulder. "Maybe if we tell the general that, he'll be less likely to demote you for losing the fliers."

Blazer glared at her. "The fliers aren't lost."

"As long as nothing decides to eat them while we're gone." Duck eyed a huge vulture flying overhead. "I'm a bit uneasy about leaving them out here."

"So am I," Blazer said. "But the animals here seem more interested in eating people than flier parts."

"You're not supposed to say that like it's a good thing," Kaika told her.

"Ravenwood, you have any clues about the dragon's location? What did all those rubbings and books we helped you find say?"

Once again, heat rushed into Rysha's cheeks. She hadn't *forgotten* about those items exactly—she'd considered trying to examine them while riding out here the night before, but she wouldn't have been able to keep a lantern lit in the flier's open back seat. After they had landed, however, she should have sat beside the fire and examined them instead of going after Trip. Unfortunately, when she'd come back from visiting him, clue hunts had been the farthest thing from her mind.

"There wasn't good enough light to examine them last night, ma'am," Rysha said, trying not to feel like a moon-eyed schoolgirl who'd sneaked out to see a boy instead of doing her homework. "But I'll look things over while we're hiking to that town. I hope to have some suggestions for you by the time we arrive."

"Watch out for the giant thorns if you're going to walk and read at the same time," Kaika advised.

"Very well," Blazer said, her face hard to read.

Rysha hoped she wasn't disappointed. Even if she wasn't, Rysha felt like she'd failed her team. She'd been brought along on these missions, missions that no lieutenant four months out of the academy would typically be invited on, specifically because of her scholarly background. If she wasn't providing scholarly input, what good was she?

Dorfindral, once again belted at her waist, sent a twinge of distaste into her. Without looking, she knew Trip was coming.

A few minutes later, after Blazer rolled up the map, the others noticed his approach.

"Well, well, our engineer has decided to join us," Blazer said.

"Yes, ma'am."

Trip's tone was neutral, and Rysha couldn't interpret his mood from it. She didn't want to look at him, didn't want to acknowledge him at all, but she glanced anyway, curious as to what she would see. Remorse? Indignation? Would he ignore her or avoid making eye contact altogether?

Their gazes met as soon as she looked at him, and she read the anguish in his eyes. It tore at her heart, and feelings of sympathy rose within her all over again. But he had done it to himself, damn it. And to her. She turned her back to him and walked to her blanket. Time to pack up her gear for a hike.

"We're walking to a town called Smelterville to find some materials to build something that will let us drive or haul the fliers out of this desert," Blazer said. "You up for an engineering task?"

"Yes, ma'am." Trip sounded relieved. No doubt, he wanted a distraction.

"Also, our dragon scholar promises she'll have some ideas by the end of the day as to where on that mountain to look for your papa."

The end of the day? Maybe Blazer thought Rysha wouldn't be able to figure out much while walking and reading. Rysha wouldn't object to more time, but she hoped to have some likely starting points before they reached the town.

"Yes, ma'am." Trip's second *yes, ma'am* sounded a lot less enthused.

Once again, Rysha wondered if anything good would come out of finding the dragon.

"Guess we'll find out soon," she muttered.

Trip hiked at the front of their little squadron with Blazer. Leftie ambled along behind, and Kaika walked farther back with Rysha, keeping a watchful eye over her as she perused her documents while they trekked. Trip was impressed that she managed to read as she walked since the ground was uneven and full of brush and dozens of species of cactus, including ones that leaked prickly balls of thorns all over the place. They liked to stick to people's clothes as they passed, and it was hard to pull them out without getting thorns in one's hands. As Trip and the others had all discovered. So far, they hadn't found a road or even a trail, so they were cutting across wild country, country full of snakes and large spiders that hissed at them as they passed.

Rysha glanced up, and their eyes met for a second, but she jerked her gaze back down, as if she were engrossed in her reading.

Trip looked away, sorrow heavy in his heart. He hadn't spoken to her since returning to camp that morning. Both because he hadn't known what to say and because he believed she wouldn't want to hear from him for a long time. If ever. He grimaced, horrified at the idea of a parting that lasted forever. And horrified to know that if it did, it was his fault.

"That look like it?" Blazer pointed toward the base of the mountain towering ahead of them, to an open area that was free of vegetation.

"A town? Not really." Trip didn't see any buildings or smell any smoke or anything else that would have hinted of life. It looked more like they were walking up to the edge of a canyon or other depression.

Earlier in the day, his senses had come to him off and on, enough so he could feel the life around them, animals and lizards and birds, most of them bedded down to avoid the heat of the day. He hadn't seen a single human being during their eight-mile trek. The closer they had walked to the mountain, the fewer moments he'd had where he could rely upon his powers. More often, he'd felt naked and vulnerable, and he'd caught himself jumping at scuttling noises in the dry brush around them.

"Down in that valley or whatever that is?" Blazer pulled out her compass. "We're still heading the right direction."

"How recent is the map?"

"Twenty years old. It was the most recent one I could get from the intel people. It's not Iskandian, so I don't know how reliable it is. It seems our cartographers don't visit often."

"Given the greeting we were given in Lagresh, I can see why."

They walked until they came close enough to the open area to see into it. It wasn't a valley *or* a canyon. As Trip stared down into a huge depression chiseled into the desert floor at the base of the mountain, he realized it was a quarry. A huge quarry with rusty red rock walls. Trip found its presence bewildering, since they hadn't come across a road or even a path leading to it. Maybe the quarry had been dug a long time ago and abandoned.

Blazer cursed. "Is that our town?"

She pointed to a handful of stone buildings squatting at the bottom of a ramp that followed an outer wall down to the bottom of the quarry. None of the structures had roofs. A stone chimney rose up from one, large enough to belong to a smelter, but Trip doubted they would find anything down there that would help them get their fliers out of the desert. Few of the other buildings looked like they had been anything other than living quarters. One exception had a dome shape, though the top half had crumbled inward. Perhaps it had been some religious meeting area. Trip had no interest in exploring it. He felt wary toward this continent's religions at the moment. The last thing he wanted was to stumble across another cult that worshipped Agarrenon Shivar.

For the sake of his teammates, he attempted to use his senses, searching again for human life or anything that might be useful. He got nothing from the quarry or the crumbling buildings hunkered down there. Had his eyes not been open, he wouldn't have even known the quarry was *there*. More than that, he got the strange feeling that those chiseled stone cliffs didn't want him here. As if they were watching him and would take the opportunity to crumble and fall on him if they could. A strange and silly thought, but he couldn't shake it.

"I don't think we're going to find a spare boiler or steam engine down there, ma'am," Leftie pointed out, coming up behind them.

Blazer cursed again. "It's not even going to be worth going down there, is it? Ravenwood?"

"Right here, ma'am." Rysha closed her book as she jogged up, the rubbings from the outpost also clutched in her hand. "Oh, is that a

Referatu Meeting Dome?" she blurted, eyes widening as she looked at the humble collection of buildings. She gripped Blazer's shoulder. "If it is, that is *so* amazing!"

"Uh," Blazer said, eyeing the hand on her shoulder. "Why?"

"Referatu?" Kaika asked. "Like Sardelle's people? Witch people?"

Trip felt as bewildered as Blazer looked, in part because he hadn't known the Referatu had ever existed on this continent, but also because he would have imagined the town of a magical people being more impressive than this. Of course, if those stone buildings had been abandoned centuries ago, he could see why their magical luminosity had faded.

"Yes, they've been around for millennia," Rysha said. "They were one of two early organizations that formed in Iskandia dedicated to studying and teaching magic, and those domes were popular architectural elements for them more than three thousand years ago, possibly as much as four thousand years ago. Even though we saw Iskandian influence in that outpost, I hadn't expected to find sign of early Referatu inhabitation here, deep within Rakgorath. We can go look, right?" Rysha quivered like a hunting dog ready to take to the field. "There's no danger?"

Blazer opened her mouth, but Rysha pulled away from her before she could speak. She jogged down the ramp, waving her rifle over her head.

"I'll go check," she called back.

"Did she just call that pile of rocks an architectural element?" Duck asked.

"It's a *dome*-shaped pile of rocks," Kaika said.

"There's no roof. Everything's collapsed. It's barely circle-shaped."

"You have to use your imagination."

Blazer sighed. "Come on, Trip. Let's go check that chimney down there. I can't imagine there being anything useful left after four thousand years, but maybe we'll get lucky and some archaeologist's steam carriage will have broken down here when they came to study the ruins."

"Based on the month we've had so far," Kaika said, "this group doesn't have that kind of luck."

Since Trip couldn't inspect the ruins with his magical senses, he trailed after Blazer. He would have to look around the old-fashioned way. If not for the order and the fact that Rysha might need assistance, he wouldn't have gone down on his own. Everything about the quarry repulsed him, from the crumbling ruins to the cliffs themselves.

Jaxi? He touched the soulblades' hilts. *Azarwrath?*

They did not respond.

Trip wondered if they were aware of the world around them now or if they were trapped in some strange limbo world. He hoped from the way the power crystals had turned off and on that there was nothing magically or structurally wrong with them and that they would return to normal once the team left this place. And he prayed the same was true for the soulblades, that they were simply unable to use their magic right now but would be normal again when removed from the dead zone.

Trip maneuvered to walk next to Kaika as the team descended the wide ramp. "Is your sword chatting with you at all, ma'am?"

"Chatting? Eryndral and I don't chat."

"But does it seem dead to you or can you sense it now and then?" Trip thought of the way Dorfindral had worked the night before, warning Rysha that he was… making trouble.

"I can sense it right now, complaining that you're cozying up to my side."

"Cozying, ma'am?" Trip shifted farther away from her, but he didn't think he'd been that close.

"He would prefer you find your own ramp and your own pit to walk into." She smirked at him, though it didn't seem that genuine of a gesture.

The sword must have been reminding her that he bore that distasteful dragon blood. Interesting that it wasn't affected by the dead zone.

"Your sword is magical, even if it's designed to destroy those with dragon blood," he mused.

"Yes, I believe we've been over that."

"I can't sense or communicate with *my* magical swords—haven't been able to reliably since right after we crashed. The closer we've come to this mountain, the worse it's gotten."

"Oh? Hm." Kaika tapped her fingers on Eryndral's hilt and surveyed the quarry.

They were more than halfway down the ramp, and the walls towered over their heads. Trip wondered how the miners had gotten their ore out in a pre-steam-age society. Or their ingots, if they had smelted the ore here. On carts pulled by donkeys? Were donkeys native to this continent? He imagined that big, scaled lion eating a donkey for a snack.

"Wait," he muttered as a thought occurred to him. "Are quarries actually used for mining ore? The ones I'm aware of in Iskandia are for pulling out granite, construction aggregate, gravel, and other building materials, not precious ore or gemstones. Though I think those are sometimes found as a byproduct."

"What are you blathering about, Captain?" Blazer looked over her shoulder at him.

Rysha, skipping down the ramp like a kid on her way to meet friends at a playground, had reached the ruins and probably didn't hear their comments.

"I'd assumed, from the chimney and from the name of the place on the map, that this place existed to smelt ore, but…" Trip waved toward the stone walls. "This isn't a typical mining setup. Not for ore."

"If witches were doing it, maybe they could just wave their hands and extract huge chunks of the earth," Kaika said.

Trip grunted an acknowledgment, but he now suspected this place had been used for some of the stone in the outpost. Such as that fancy stone railing that had wound down the levels and levels of that staircase. It could have even been the source for the clay used to create all those tiles. The quarry walls did have a reddish tint.

But if all they had been after were rocks, why was it in the middle of this magic dead zone? Had that existed thousands of years ago? Would the Referatu have chosen to build a quarry in the middle of a place where they couldn't access their power? That seemed an odd choice, especially given the way those towering stone walls were disturbing him. He couldn't imagine spending a prolonged period of time down here.

When they reached the bottom of the ramp, the others headed toward the remnants of the town, Blazer walking straight toward the structure with the chimney. A woman of single-minded purpose. Rysha had better investigate the dome quickly. Trip doubted Blazer would be willing to stay long unless she found something that could help them with the fliers.

Instead of heading for the town, Trip walked to the rock wall rising up behind it. Certain sections of it seemed to repel him even more than others.

Though a headache started behind his eyes and his skin crawled, Trip made himself walk straight toward one of the sources of his discomfort, a portion of rock visibly different from the rest. Instead of being solid sedimentary stone, such as they had passed on the way down the ramp, the rock here was striated. Rusty red bands stretched horizontally, layered through lighter types of stone that he couldn't name.

"Is this iron?" he mused, eyeing the red rock.

ORIGINS

Though he'd read about various types of ores and alloys, and used them in engineering applications, he'd never been out to a quarry or a mine and seen the raw material extracted.

He touched his hand to the stone, thinking of the reputed magical dampening quality of iron, that mages often couldn't sense things through boxes made of the stuff. In the old days, if they'd been captured, they might have been locked up in cells lined with iron.

Trip spotted Rysha crouching outside of the dome, running her hand along something. Though he was reluctant to call her over or even speak to her after the night before, he wanted her opinion on this. Maybe she knew more than he about quarries and why the Referatu might have been mining iron. Or iron in addition to whatever rock material they had drawn out of here.

"Rysha?" he called. "Can you come here for a minute?"

An agonized expression stamped her face when she looked away from the dome. He thought it had more to do with the idea of leaving her find than anything to do with him. But her eyes widened as she looked behind him.

"Is that a banded iron formation?" she asked.

"Possibly?"

Rysha jogged over and touched the red bands. "This is great. Did you know there are numerous hypotheses discussing how banded iron formations were created? They're quite the anomaly in nature, and they only occur in Teroic rocks that range in age from 1.8 to 2.5 billion years old. My mother would love to see this place. There should be some magnificent fossils around, as this would have all been under the ocean once. This should be magnetite." She pointed to a layer of rock above one of the rusty red bands. "Or maybe chert? Do you want to hear some of the hypotheses of how these bands formed?"

She turned her bright eyes toward him as if all the previous night's distress had been forgotten. Trip doubted that was so, but seeing her so interested in something made him smile.

"I'd love to hear about it on the flight back home," he said, "but for now, I'm trying to figure out if *this* is what the Referatu, or whoever lived here way back when, were mining for. And why. It completely and utterly repulses me."

"Repulses?" She laid her hand lovingly on the rock wall, as if she couldn't fathom it.

"Not the science part, but the rock or ore is grating against my senses. Like the very walls themselves hate me and hate anything magical. Maybe they're related to your sword." Trip waved toward Dorfindral's scabbard.

It was a joke, but Rysha gazed thoughtfully down at the hilt. "That's interesting."

"Not very. It's giving me a headache."

"I had assumed that the *chapaharii* swords were made in the traditional manner for that era, iron sand heated together with coal, and that the magic or magic-loathing element was added afterward. Perhaps it was even a part of the smithing process, with a mage working hand in hand with the blacksmith. I hadn't considered that there might be some source of special ore that was used. And if this ore is special, and that's why they were mining it, what made it special?" Rysha stroked the rock as she gazed upward, toward the top of the quarry. "The ore here could be more of a geological oddity than the rare but not unheard of banded-iron formations. Or do *all* banded-iron formations have these anti-magic qualities? I guess we don't have any evidence yet that the iron is oozing an anti-magic quality. Just your headache. But could this quarry, or perhaps all the rock in this general area, be the reason for the magical dead zone?"

She was talking so rapidly, so engrossed in her speculations, with Trip listening intently, that neither of them noticed Blazer striding toward them until she barked orders.

"I don't know what you two are doing over there petting the rocks, but have you forgotten that I want those fliers powered up somehow so they can get out of the desert? And that you, Lieutenant, are supposed to be finding me a dragon lair?"

"We're having an epiphany over here, ma'am," Rysha said, rubbing her jaw as she gazed left and right along the rock wall.

"Lieutenants don't get to have epiphanies. They get to follow orders."

Trip bristled and stood at her shoulder, glaring at Blazer while Rysha contemplated the rock. "I'm the one who called her over here, ma'am. This is about—"

"Captains don't get to have epiphanies, either. There are some scraps in the smelter building over here. Very old, very rusty scraps. I doubt anything will be useful, but come take a look. I'm sure your engineering experience is greater than mine."

Trip wanted to stay where he was and talk Referatu history and *chapaharii* weapons—the possible origin of *chapaharii* weapons?—with Rysha, but Blazer's glare was implacable. A singular focus, indeed.

Well, maybe something in the smelter would shed more light on this mystery for him.

"Yes, ma'am."

Trip passed the dome where Leftie and Duck were discussing the palatability of the lizards scampering among the rocks, and walked into the second-largest structure in the village. He expected to trip over rocks as soon as he entered, but the few that had crumbled over the centuries had done so near the walls. Whatever had once provided the roof for the structure had disappeared. Some biodegradable material, perhaps. Or something valuable enough to loot.

There wasn't much remaining inside, with only the chimney suggesting this had been a smelter. Whatever anvil and smithing tools had once occupied the structure were long gone. Trip spotted a couple of rusty bolts attached to the ragged remains of an aggregate floor in the back. A few more scraps of iron dusted the ground, but Trip didn't think the metal had originally come from the quarry. He was no expert at dating historic materials, but the scraps didn't seem as old as the bolts or the ruins themselves. Nor did they repel him the way the ore in the quarry walls did.

He slipped a few of the scraps into his pocket, thinking he could use his magic to morph them into useful parts for his toy once his abilities returned to him. There wasn't nearly enough iron to be useful in building a steam engine or whatever Blazer fancied they would create to tug the fliers out of the desert.

As Trip moved closer to the chimney, the pounding in his head increased. He was definitely going to suggest that the group go somewhere else for Rysha to do her dragon research. Assuming they could pry her away from the dome and the geological oddities of the quarry.

The chimney and the remains of the smokebox were made from the same stone blocks as the rest of the structure, including a hearth in surprisingly good shape. The granite stones locked together like puzzle pieces with little dirt or broken mortar between them. The hearth was raised about a foot off the floor. He rapped his knuckles against one of the stones. It didn't sound hollow, but the design made him think someone might have created a space below the stones to store valuables. Isolated as they would have been way out here, even Referatu might have worried about thieves or other intruders.

He found himself kneeling and feeling around the area, searching for stones that might move. Even though his magical senses didn't tell him anything, his intuition twanged like an improperly tuned string on a fiddle. Why would his headache have increased as he approached the hearth if there was nothing here but stone?

One of the blocks in the back shifted slightly under his tugging and prodding. He pulled harder, but it was locked in by two others.

"Sorry, Jaxi," he said, drawing one of the swords.

He trusted the magic-imbued blade wouldn't break easily, but he was careful as he slid the point in, trying to find the leverage to pry the block free. Finally, one of the other blocks shifted enough for him to tug out the one he wanted. A dark hollow lay underneath it.

His breath caught. Had he found something that thousands of years of looters hadn't discovered?

"Probably nothing in there," he grumbled, but that didn't keep him from peering into the dark hole.

Something scuttled toward the light, and he jerked back. A scorpion sauntered past, waving its tail, and he scooted farther back. They weren't native to Iskandia, but he'd heard they were venomous. Trip used Jaxi's point to prod into the dark hole. More scorpions scuttled out, and he started to doubt that he'd found anything more interesting than an insect nest.

Then the sword clunked against something that created a hollow ring. His breathing quickened, seeming to echo from the back of the firebox. Using the soulblade again, he pried up more blocks. Finally, he revealed a shallow hiding spot about a foot and a half wide and a foot deep. At the center rested a rusty iron box with hinges and a clasp.

A few unmoving—dead?—scorpions littered the bottom of the nook, making him reluctant to reach in and pick up the box. But it seemed to be the source of whatever magic—or anti-magic—was causing his headache, at least inside the structure. His head had hurt to some extent since he entered the quarry.

He gingerly lifted the box out and set it on the ground. The clasp was locked, but it was an old, clumsy and rusted lock, and he didn't need magic to thwart it. He slid Jaxi's tip into the hole, searching for a spring.

ORIGINS

The inside crumbled under the blade's gentle pressure. He drew it out and started to sheathe the soulblade but rested it in the dust beside him instead. Just in case a squadron of scorpions leaped out.

The lid creaked as he opened it, and one of the hinges broke away.

"This is definitely old," he whispered, wondering if he should have called Rysha in to make the discovery with him. But he couldn't bring himself to leave the spot until he knew what he'd found.

A single dull gray iron ingot rested on the bottom. He clasped his chin and gazed at it thoughtfully. Had it been gold or silver, he could imagine someone squirreling it away, but iron? It was about enough to mold into a single sword.

He touched it, thinking to flip it up to see if anything else was in the box, but a shock of pain ran up his arm and seemed to zap his heart. Gasping, he stumbled back and grabbed his arm. For a bewildered second, he thought a scorpion he hadn't seen had stung him. Then he realized that he'd felt this exact same pain before when he'd touched one of the *chapaharii* blades.

Rubbing numb fingers, he stared at the dull gray bar.

"Trip?" Rysha asked from the doorway. "Are you all right?"

"Yes." He waved her over. She would be able to touch the ingot.

"I heard you cry out in pain."

"I believe that was a gasp of surprise." Realizing he was still rubbing his numb fingers, he shook out his arm and lowered it.

"No, it was a cry. Maybe a squeal."

"It was definitely *not* a squeal. Come look at this, will you? I found this box hidden in the hearth there, and when I touched the bar, it was exactly like touching a *chapaharii* blade."

She looked sharply at him. "Really? Is that why you squealed?"

"I *gasped*. And yes."

"Is Trip all right?" Duck called from outside the smelter. "Leftie and I heard a squeal of pain."

"I told you," Rysha said, though her gaze was now locked on the box.

"I'm fine," Trip called back.

Rysha poked out a finger and touched the ingot with lightning speed, as if she were checking to see if a pan on a cooktop was hot. She didn't react with pain, but Trip hadn't expected her to. She returned her finger to the ingot, held it there, then lifted out the bar. A very old maker's mark was stamped in the bottom, but Trip barely noticed it because his gaze locked on to a folded parchment that had been under the bar.

He wanted to reach in and pull it out, but he was afraid a thousands-of-years-old piece of parchment would crumble under his touch. He also worried it might have absorbed some of the bar's hatred for dragon blood and that it would also zap him.

Rysha saw it and pulled it out after setting down the bar. She paused before unfolding it, her fingers trembling slightly. In anticipation? "If this was the place where the swords were originally made, or the ingots were smelted before being sent across the ocean to be made into swords, this could have instructions, either for the smelting or for the sword-making itself. Do you know what an incredible find this would be?"

"I'm sure King Angulus would be delighted if he learned more *chapaharii* blades could be made without him having to send troops to invade museums around the world."

"I was thinking that it would be a great insight into the process and how it was originally discovered, but I suppose modern-day military applications must be considered too. Wouldn't it be interesting if it was the metal that made the swords possible, rather than some particular ceremony or type of magic that was forgotten?"

"The ingot hates me, and even the raw ore in the cliff over there was giving me a headache. But I imagine instructions would have to have been stamped into the ore. Maybe the paper talks about how that was done. And maybe I, or we, could figure out how to reprogram your sword then."

She looked warily at him, perhaps thinking of the night before, and he shifted uncomfortably. He couldn't regret bringing up the command words, not in light of this new discovery, but he wished he already knew a solution, so he could promise to fix her sword so he'd never have any control over it again.

"Let's find out," she finally said, then carefully unfolded the parchment.

Some kind of sealant had been placed over it, so it wasn't as fragile as Trip had feared it might be. The ink inside wasn't even faded.

"Brilliant," Rysha breathed, laying the parchment out on the ground next to the box.

Unfolded, it was about three feet tall by four feet wide. There was some text up in one corner, but it was mostly a map. One of the surrounding area.

ORIGINS

Trip knelt and touched the location of quarry and the little village. They were about dead center. The desert stretched away to the west, and the mountains rose to the east, including Jralk Mountain right next to the quarry. A red line had been drawn, forming a circle, the edges almost touching the top and bottom of the map.

"Is that our spring?" Trip tapped a spot in the southwest corner of the map, a tiny grey circle. It was just inside the line.

He glanced at Rysha, realizing she might not appreciate it being referred to as *their* spring, but she only nodded and touched the red line next to it. "If it is, maybe this delineates the edge of the magic dead zone."

"That's what I was thinking. If so, it's existed for thousands of years, right? Do you think this box is original to the time period of the village?"

Rysha nodded slowly, her finger shifting to the six or seven lines of text in the upper left corner. "This is Old Iskandian. A very early version of it. I don't recognize a lot of the words, and I can read Old Iskandian." She pointed to a few symbols that barely looked like letters or anything Trip recognized as an alphabet. "I think those are tribal markings. The old clans had languages of their own before the continent-wide language was adopted, originally for trade."

"Does that mean you can't read it?" Trip asked, trying not to feel disappointment. He wanted badly to know if they'd found instructions he could use to alter Dorfindral. Further, this mission might be saved if they could bring back instructions—and ore—that would allow Iskandia to make more *chapaharii* weapons for defense against unfriendly dragons.

"I can mostly read it. This talks about the sacredness of the ore, how it's blessed by the gods, a gift so humans can defend... that may be an old symbol for dragons. Or mages. The Great Storm affected the... uhm, oh, maybe some kind of electrical storm struck the area where this quarry was eventually dug? I can't imagine lightning altering the basic nature of the iron, but perhaps something more significant? I'd have to check the records, see if there were any huge meteorological or geological events recorded around this time period. Oh, it would be interesting to slice up this ingot for study too. Nobody's ever considered doing that to one of the ancient *chapaharii* swords, for obvious reasons, but it would be fascinating to study this iron under a microscope."

"I'm sure." Trip rubbed his aching head, the urge to get away from the ingot much stronger than the urge to study it. "Anything about imbuing the ore with command words?"

"Uhm." Rysha paused, staring at the lines, for such a long moment that Trip believed she would say no.

She bit her lip and looked at him.

"What?" He couldn't decipher that look, and his senses were useless to him right now. "*Is* there something?"

"Sort of. I'm not sure I should tell you."

He frowned at her. "If you don't, I'll take it back to Sardelle and ask her. But why won't you tell me? You want me to be able to reprogram Dorfindral, don't you? Especially now that…" He frowned and looked away, not finishing the thought that came to mind, that she probably regretted ever telling him the words. He hated that she had a reason to regret that.

"All right," she said quietly. "The last line says the ingots shall be stored until such time that the Referatu send a mage of sufficient power and willingness to be sacrificed to instill the commands. I *think* that's what it says. There are some symbols I'm guessing at, but powerful, mage, and sacrifice are Old Iskandian words that I definitely recognize."

"Sacrifice?" Trip mouthed.

He hadn't imagined that reprogramming the blades could be dangerous. Certainly not deadly. He'd thought it would be like sliding in the magical equivalent of a new punch card.

"There's also not anything about *reprogramming* the swords," Rysha said. "Not that Old Iskandian or any of the ancient tribal societies had a word for that. There weren't many steam looms or cleaning automatons at the time." She waved at the lines of text. "I get the impression that the commands were imbued in the metal at the same time the swords were crafted, magically hammered in as the smith hammered the metal into shape."

"They're not canoodling in there, are they?" came Blazer's voice from outside.

"Not sure, ma'am," Leftie said, also still outside. "There was squealing earlier."

"That was a gasp," Trip called out.

"Even more reason to be suspicious of canoodling."

Blazer walked in, a cigar clamped between her teeth.

"What did you find?" she asked, fortunately not bringing up canoodling. Trip didn't want Rysha to have any more reason to think of the night before than he had already given her.

"I believe the original *chapaharii* weapons may have been crafted here." Rysha pointed to the map and the ingot. "Or at least the iron for them could have been mined here. Though this text implies that this is the smithy where it all might have happened. The man who penned it mentioned waiting for a mage to come and imbue the swords."

"Really?" Some of the gruffness Blazer had kept close all day faded from her tone, and she seemed genuinely curious as she walked over. "Does this mean we might be able to make more of those weapons? Damn, the king should love that."

"Maybe. But it also sounds like the mage who did the imbuing was expected to sacrifice himself in order to do it. Or that his death came about as a result of working with the metal."

Trip rubbed his still numb fingers. He could easily imagine someone getting shocked to the point of dying from prolonged contact with the ingots.

"Huh." Blazer eyed him but did not suggest sacrifices might be a part of his duty as an officer. "The metal seems special to you?"

"Oh yes. I've had a headache since we approached the quarry. It was my headache that led me to that box."

Blazer shifted her gaze to the map, perhaps noticing the red line. "Is this related to the power crystals going out, and you losing your ability to perform magic?"

"It seems plausible," Trip said, and Rysha nodded.

"So, we should take that and that with us?" Blazer pointed at the map and the ingot.

Trip grimaced at the idea of the ingot traveling back with them. "Just keep it in that iron box, please." As soon as he said the words, he wondered if that would actually help. He'd been able to touch the box, so presumably it wasn't made from the same tainted metal as the ingot, but he didn't know how much insulation it provided. "And in a flier far away from mine."

"Should we try to mine some more ore while we're here?" Blazer looked through the open roof to the quarry walls.

"We don't have the tools for it," Rysha said. "Better to report back, I should think, and let the king decide if Iskandia should send a team here. This isn't our country, so I imagine some kind of agreement would have to be signed."

Blazer snorted. "Or maybe people could just mine here sneakily. It's not like we've seen other human beings around."

"No, but I'm sure people live out here. The only ones negatively affected are those with dragon blood, and this place is on all the maps." Rysha waved toward Blazer's pack where she kept the map that had led their team here. "If Iskandia tried to sneak in and set up a mining operation, someone would notice."

"Mm." That single syllable didn't seem to connote agreement.

Rysha's nose crinkled in displeasure, but she didn't object further. Instead, some new thought occurred to her, and she blurted, "Oh, dragons."

"Yes?" Blazer prompted.

Rysha gazed down at the map. "If Agarrenon Shivar is like Bhrava Saruth, then—"

"Nobody is like Bhrava Saruth," Blazer grumbled.

Trip agreed—his sire, in particular, did not seem to share the goofy dragon's attitude about anything, except perhaps believing himself a supreme being.

"In dislikes," Rysha clarified. "If Agarrenon Shivar and all dragons loathe this dead zone, or headache-inducing zone…"

"Both," Trip grunted.

"Then it's unlikely Agarrenon Shivar would have built his lair within its influence." Rysha swept her hand across the inside of the circle. "But if we're to believe as Moe said that Agarrenon Shivar lives or lived in Jralk Mountain, then we can narrow down our search area to only the portion of it that's outside the circle." She drew her finger along the northeast side of the mountain, just visible in the corner of the map.

"That would narrow things down by about seven-eighths," Trip said.

"Yes," Rysha said. "We would still have ground to cover, especially considering there are only six of us, and we can't search with the fliers right now, but maybe the soulblades can be of use once we step out of the dead zone."

Trip nodded. "I hope so."

"Your sword and Kaika's sword too," Blazer told her. "Once we get close to the dragon, they should sense its presence, right?"

"If he's there to be sensed, yes."

Trip wondered about that. Given the range that dragon auras could be sensed across, if Agarrenon Shivar was alive, it seemed someone should have known about it. Other dragons, if nobody else. But perhaps if he *was* in a stasis chamber, that would dampen his aura significantly.

"We'll find out soon. I'll take that." Blazer dropped the ingot back in the box and folded the map, also sticking it inside. "Good work finding it, Ravenwood," she said on her way to the exit, the box tucked under her arm.

"Actually, that was Trip, ma'am."

Blazer flicked a couple of fingers toward him on her way out. "Good work finding it, Trip."

"Her praise is so heartfelt and enthusiastic," Rysha said.

"As long as she's carrying the box instead of me." Trip rubbed his head. The ache behind his eyes lessened as the ingot left the structure, but very slightly. He couldn't wait to get out of the circle, even if it meant double-timing it across a mountain.

CHAPTER 17

R YSHA WALKED ALONG THE MOUNTAINSIDE in the middle of their group, which was staggered and stretched out along the slope, searching for caves as the sun dipped toward the western horizon. She licked her chapped lips, wondering why even the copious amounts of water she'd drunk weren't quenching her thirst. The mountain's higher altitude had done little to alleviate the heat and had done nothing to make the air less dry. As with the desert below, there weren't any trees, nothing more than the scrub brush that rose three or four feet high, so shade was scant. She found herself missing the rain and the mud of the capital. She even experienced a few fond thoughts of the obstacle course back at the fort. Nobody had ever died of heat stroke pulling themselves up that wall.

"No dragon caves up here," came a distant call from Duck, the person highest up the slope.

"No caves here," Leftie added, the next highest person. He had been limping all afternoon, but he hid it every time Rysha glanced in his direction.

She looked down to see if she needed to shout her status or if Trip, the next person after her, had heard.

"Nothing," Trip called to Kaika, who said something similar to Blazer, the farthest person down the slope.

Even though they hadn't yet come out of the circled area on the ancient map, Blazer had ordered the staggered formation and for everyone to keep their eyes open. Rysha supposed it was possible that a cave entrance might be within the magic dead zone with a passage leading underground and to an area unaffected by it, but she calculated that they had another three miles to walk before they needed to worry about serious searching. Besides, as soon as Trip had access to his power and he could communicate with the soulblades again, they would have greater resources than six sets of eyes to put into the search.

She was tempted to pick a route closer to Trip so she could ask whether any of his senses had returned. At the edges, the magic dead zone had seemed less extreme, at least according to Trip. It hadn't been until they'd reached the quarry that he'd lost *all* of his power. She was also tempted to say something to squelch his sword reprogramming idea.

More than once, she'd caught him staring thoughtfully down the mountain at Blazer. More specifically, at the box Blazer carried. Did he think he might study that ingot and learn some secret that would help with Dorfindral?

Rugged terrain made Rysha veer downslope to get around it, and she took the opportunity to head toward him. Leftie and Duck disappeared from her sight briefly, but she trusted they wouldn't for long. The terrain of the mountain was an obstacle at times, but there was little foliage to impede their sight.

"Trip?" Rysha jogged down to join him, her pack bouncing on her shoulders.

"Yes?" He waited for her, and then they resumed walking.

"I wanted to make sure—I mean, I want to make my feelings known to you."

"Feelings about… hookball?"

She saw the wariness in his eyes and could tell he didn't want to discuss the previous night. That was fine. She didn't want to discuss it, either, since it made her uncomfortable. If they hadn't been on this mission together, she would have found reasons to avoid talking to him for a few weeks.

"Leftie has already let me know my feelings on that subject," she said. "Apparently, I love it."

"Have you gone to a match?"

"I haven't. And I never played as a kid. It's a team sport, and my brothers and I generally chose games we could play with just the four of us. It was a long walk to the neighbors' houses to round up more kids."

"I've heard living in castles on vast estates is isolating."

"It's a manor." She lifted a hand to swat him, but lowered it again. It was easy to fall back into joking with him, but she didn't want him to think… oh, she didn't know. She wanted to forgive him, but she wasn't about to forget that. Or let it happen again. That made what she'd come to say depressing, but given what she'd read, she couldn't say anything else. "I came to tell you that I think you should give up on the idea of reprogramming the swords."

Trip looked down the slope toward Blazer and that box again. "Because of the mention of a sacrifice?"

"Because it very specifically said the mage that came to imbue the swords would be sacrificing himself."

"But you also said you couldn't read all the words. Isn't it possible you misinterpreted that?"

"I don't think so."

"Maybe—"

"I also don't think you should assume you can figure something out that the mages back then couldn't, like how to do it without killing yourself. Because the people back then were every bit as powerful as you, at least some of them. And if it could have been done… Well, I'm sure they tried not to let their own sorcerers kill themselves. From what I've read, the Referatu were always known as a fair-minded and progressive people. They weren't the types to simply sacrifice their members for some greater good, not typically. With the soulblades, it was always the choice of the mage to go into the blade, usually only when the end was imminent."

"I wasn't thinking that I could do something those mages couldn't," Trip said, "just that it might be possible to do *one* sword without killing myself. There's only one I truly care about reprogramming." He offered her a lopsided smile.

"I appreciate you wanting to do that, but I don't want you to take the risk. In fact, I forbid it."

"You forbid it? Lieutenants aren't supposed to forbid captains. It's against regulations."

"I looked up the *chapaharii* weapons-carrying regulations. Forbidding is allowed between wielders and non-wielders."

"Really?"

Rysha sighed. "No, but I still forbid it."

"I will keep your wishes in mind."

"That's not a search pattern, Ravenwood," Kaika yelled up, making a shooing motion toward her.

Sighing again, Rysha angled back up the slope to her spot between Leftie and Trip. She'd said what she needed to say and hoped it would make a difference to him. She also hoped he couldn't do anything unless she handed the sword over to him while they were standing in front of a forge. Because she vowed never to do that.

Unfortunately, he kept gazing thoughtfully at Blazer's box.

I can't believe you used me as a chisel, Jaxi said, the first words that popped into Trip's head as the group moved out of the magic dead zone. *Me! That's a completely improper use for a soulblade. Besides, you've got that hard-hilted stick on your other hip.*

It wasn't appropriate to use you, but poking Azarwrath into rocks would be acceptable?

Absolutely. Maybe it would help adjust his old-fashioned way of thinking.

Pardon me, Azarwrath said, *but my way of thinking is civilized. Modern notions are appalling.*

What's appalling is that you weren't hanged for your backward ideas decades before you put yourself in that sword.

"We've come out of the dead zone," Trip called down to Kaika. Blazer had paused to peer into a hole in the rocks farther down the slope.

"You've regained your powers?" Kaika yelled back up.

"I'm not sure, but I've regained having soulblades arguing in my head."

"Is that as delightful as it sounds?"

"Maybe even more so."

Azarwrath made a throat-clearing sound in his mind as Kaika turned to relay the message to Blazer.

ORIGINS

Someone got phlegmy during his nap, Jaxi said. *I hear that happens with old, backward men.*

Is that what it seemed like to you two? Trip asked, hoping to stop further arguing. *You seemed to fall asleep?*

Indeed, Azarwrath said. *A most unsettling experience. The last thing I remember is your flier's lamp having energy fluctuations.*

We prefer to call it a power crystal, Trip said.

That doesn't mean it's not still a lamp, Jaxi said. *I lost consciousness a little later. I remember drifting in and out and talking to you once after we landed. And then nothing, except brief, groggy awareness of being used as a chisel, ahem. I'd forgotten what falling asleep felt like. It was weird. I remember being afraid I'd never wake up again. I'm glad you took us out of that dreadful place.*

Did you not also fall asleep, Telryn?

No, but the closer we got to the center of the magic dead zone, the less I was able to use my power or even sense anything around me. Trip wished he hadn't been able to use any of his power the night at the spring. *I hadn't realized how much I'd come to rely on those extra senses.*

What are we doing now? Azarwrath asked. *Still seeking your sire?*

Yes. Remembering that the soulblades didn't seem to be able to read his thoughts anymore, Trip did his best to open his bank vault door and share the day's events with them.

That's interesting, Jaxi thought. *I am Referatu through and through, and I don't remember ever hearing about a mining quarry on this continent or anyone even traveling over here. The origins of the swords—or the ore—must have been forgotten by my time.*

A sorcerer visiting the area would not have wandered in without good reason, Azarwrath said. *Who knows what prolonged exposure does to the brain?*

Trip touched his head, wondering if he'd risked his brain by poking that ingot and soaking up the air of the quarry.

By any chance, does either of you sense any dragons? he asked to distract himself.

No, Jaxi said. *Do you? You've been sensing them before either of us.*

I'm not sure I could sense rust on my own pommel right now, Azarwrath put in. *I feel groggy after that enforced sleep.*

Maybe you're groggy because you're getting senile, Jaxi suggested.

I'm venerable, not senile.
You're fifteen hundred years old.
Are you not also hundreds of years old?
A mere six hundred, Jaxi said. *Young and sprightly in comparison to you.*
Azarwrath sighed.

Trip hadn't sensed any dragons yet, but he stretched out with his mind again, doing a more purposeful search. Not paying much attention to his immediate surroundings, he almost tripped over a hole right in front of him. Alas, it was only a dip in the rocks, not the entrance to a dragon cave.

I sense lizards, birds, and more lizards, Jaxi said. *That's it.*

I also sense larger predators sleeping in dens in the rocks, Azarwrath said, *but they are not deep dens, and the animals are furred rather than scaled.*

Trip sensed those things also. But nothing more. Would he sense a dragon that was hibernating or inside a stasis chamber?

He tried to send his awareness deeper into the mountain, into the stone and the earth far below the surface. The dragon might not be down there, but if he could sense open tunnels or chambers or perhaps some magical artifact or treasure, that could guide him in the right direction. He was certain he'd heard stories of some dragons that hoarded treasures, and of brave, or maybe suicidal, humans that sneaked in to steal them while they slept. But maybe those were just fairy tales.

Do dragons hibernate with artifacts? he asked the soulblades, assuming they knew more about the topic. He could also climb up the slope to ask Rysha. Except Blazer and Kaika might break them up again.

Hibernate with artifacts? Jaxi asked. *Like what, a magical security blanket?*

I'm just hoping that if I can't find Agarrenon Shivar specifically, maybe I can find something that belongs to him. Some sign that he was here. Or is here and is hibernating in a stasis chamber. You said Phelistoth was found in such a chamber, right?

Yes, but Sardelle and I sensed him in it from miles and miles away. Admittedly, the Cofah had breached it, and he was in and out of consciousness. It probably wasn't the same as a dragon fully inside a chamber and in a magical hibernation. Jaxi paused and hummed a thoughtful tune. *When Sardelle was in a Referatu stasis chamber for three hundred years, I was able to sense her, but she was relatively close to me. I might have struggled to sense her from dozens of miles away.*

Her aura was definitely diminished while she hibernated. And she didn't have a magical security blanket to mark the spot.

You are indeed young and sprightly, Azarwrath said, *and foolish. I do not know why Telryn agreed to bring you along on another mission.*

Because he's also young, and he didn't want only a grumpy old man for company. Further, Sardelle told him to bring me after I volunteered to dispose of a dirty diaper by incinerating it. I don't know why. If you had seen the mess, you would know my suggestion wasn't unreasonable.

Were you going to remove the diaper from the baby before incinerating it?

That wouldn't have been necessary. I have pinpoint precision.

I'm beginning to see why Sardelle suggested you come, Trip replied, still searching within the mountain.

Yes, she knew you would need my wisdom on your journey.

Trip halted, his mind brushing against something other than solid rock.

I found a chamber or cavern down there. He closed his eyes, concentrating on the spot. *It's deep down. Can you feel it?*

Not yet, Jaxi said.

Azarwrath didn't respond, but Trip was aware of him also stretching out with his senses. Trip hadn't noticed that he had the ability to sense the soulblades using their magic before, at least such subtle magic. He'd definitely been aware of them hurling lightning bolts and fireballs.

I see now, Azarwrath said. *A large cavern, yes, with several miles of tunnel meandering around and eventually leading to it. A short flight but a long walk. There are smaller caverns along the way, and I also sense an underground lake. The water source may be natural, but I believe the tunnel was hollowed out by magic long ago. Some of it remains. That is what you sensed, Telryn.*

Trip nodded. That seemed right. Now he needed to figure out how to access that tunnel from the mountainside above.

I think there are some artifacts in there too, Jaxi added, her tone growing excited. *I've found the spot, and I sense… I'm not sure, but they aren't blankets.*

The contents are muddled, aren't they? Azarwrath asked.

They are. Even more so than with the dragon-rider outpost. If anyone or anything lives down there, I can't sense it from here. I wonder if the dragon, or whoever hollowed the place out, deliberately camouflaged it so outsiders wouldn't find his lair.

Trip also couldn't sense what was inside the large cavern at the end of the tunnel, but he didn't know if that was because of magical camouflage or simply because of the distance and all the rock between here and there. Even if his group found an entrance that led into the tunnel, it would be, as Azarwrath had said, a long walk to the chamber. No doubt, a dragon could have zipped across the miles in minutes. Too bad Bhrava Saruth and Shulina Arya had objected to this adventure.

You should have told them your papa's cavern was outside of the dead zone, Jaxi said.

I didn't know it was any more than you did.

Yes, but you could have lied.

Lying to dragons seems like a strategy that could backfire. Trip, still examining the inside of the mountain with his senses, spotted something and paused. *Does that tunnel lead to the surface?* He shared the location with the soulblades.

Are you referring to the tunnel behind all that collapsed rubble? Jaxi asked.

Yes.

Maybe. It looks like it would be hard for you to get through.

We'll just have to move some rocks around.

"Yo, Sidetrip, you're falling behind!" came a distant yell from Blazer.

She had finished investigating that hole and caught up with and passed Trip. Everyone had passed him.

"I've found a magical cavern inside the mountain," he yelled back. "And an entrance!"

"Well, get up here and show us. The king isn't paying you to work on your tan."

That woman is tyrannical, Azarwrath observed. *She would have made a poor healer.*

Exactly why women should be allowed to learn battle magic or become soldiers if they want, Jaxi said.

No man wishes to see a woman slain on the battlefield, her eyes dead of life, her body cut open with her entrails exposed. A woman's place is in the home or the healers' tent.

ORIGINS

Or anywhere else she wishes, ideally with her entrails neatly stored on the inside of her body. You're a ghoul, Azzy.

Aware of Blazer waving impatiently, Trip ignored the arguing soulblades and hurried to catch up. The realization that they were getting close to finding out, one way or another, where his sire was made dragonlings flutter around in his stomach.

Would anything good truly come of this quest? It had been *his* idea to go on it. Whatever the outcome was, he would have nobody but himself to blame for it.

CHAPTER 18

"YOU CALL THIS AN ENTRANCE?" Blazer frowned over at Trip and pointed at what might once have been a cave opening but was now filled with rocks from top to bottom. It reminded Rysha of the cliff in front of the outpost, the caved-in tunnel and ledge where dragons and their riders had once taken off. "I think young officers today should receive dictionaries as well as training manuals when they enter the academy. They're not very articulate or educated."

Rysha squinted at her, wondering if she would get in trouble for flicking that cigar out of her mouth. Blazer's mood had improved after Trip found the ingot and map, but only slightly. She didn't seem to be enjoying this mission. Probably because her flier was broken, and she didn't have a plethora of historical and culturally significant finds to take home and study. It was all Rysha could do to keep from caressing her pack full of rubbings.

"It's only blocked for about twenty meters," Trip said. "I can sense a passageway beyond the boulders, one that was hollowed out long ago by magic. Some miles into the mountain and at the end of the tunnel, there's a cavern, its contents obscured by magic that lingers today. I believe that cavern is what we seek."

"Only blocked for twenty meters. Some *miles* into the mountain." Blazer shifted her cigar from one side of her mouth to the other, the inner end of it noticeably mashed. Weren't cigars supposed to be gently held in the mouth instead of chewed on? "Leave it to a sorcerer to say those things like they're insignificant."

"Aw, stop your grousing," Kaika said, elbowing Blazer before clambering up the rocky slope toward the cave-in. "What's the matter? Nobody has been canoodling with you on this mission?"

"Nobody's supposed to be canoodling at *all* on missions." Blazer glared at Rysha and Trip.

"Are you sure?" Kaika asked. "People might be less grumpy if that happened more."

"I'm game to try," Leftie said, throwing her a wink, though Kaika's back was to him. He and Duck stood farther down the slope behind Rysha and Blazer.

"Me too," Duck said brightly.

"By all means, you two enjoy yourselves," Kaika called back, slinging off her pack as she stopped in front of the cave-in. "I'll be up here setting some explosives."

"You two… What did she mean by that?" Duck asked.

"I think she implied she's not willing to join us," Leftie said. "Which is unfortunate, because I'm not nearly as excited about getting naked without a woman being involved."

"Not nearly?" Blazer asked. "But there is some interest?"

"Uh." Leftie eyed Duck and took a large step to the side. "No, ma'am. I misspoke."

"I'm getting rejected a lot on this mission," Duck observed. "Is it because I didn't bathe in the spring when we had a chance?"

"Don't worry," Kaika called back. "I'll take you with me to the Sensual Sage when we get back. We'll find some women willing to bathe you."

"I'd have to pay them, wouldn't I?"

"Yes, but that's only fair. Paying for services rendered."

Duck's nose wrinkled. "I can bathe myself, ma'am. For free."

"Usually, other things happen after the bathing. Stimulating things."

"Like what?"

"Use your imagination."

Duck scratched his rather grimy and stubbled jaw and looked at Leftie.

"If you can't imagine post-bathing activities to do with a woman," Leftie said, "I'm not helping you."

Duck wasn't any younger than Rysha was, so she could only assume he didn't visit a lot of brothels. Maybe the wolves that had raised him hadn't instructed him in such things. Admittedly, she hadn't ever visited a brothel, and she couldn't claim the most personal experience when it came to stimulating naked activities, especially since it had been almost two years since she and Srekan had broken up. Her parents had *loved* him, a handsome, polite noble-born scholar. But he'd stood alongside her father when it came to lectures on how much of a waste of talent it would be if she joined the military. No wonder she hadn't seriously dated anyone since then. She'd gotten tired of the men in her life telling her what she should and shouldn't do.

"This is fantastic." Kaika rubbed her hands together as she walked around, studying the cave-in from several angles. "I'm going to need my TE-84s. Yes, those will be perfect. Probably have to set up multiple detonations if the boulders go back twenty meters."

"The soulblades and I could help, ma'am," Trip offered from the side. "Actually, we could probably—"

"No way." Kaika made a shooing motion at him. "I've waited this entire mission to be useful. *I'll* handle this."

Blazer snorted. "She just wants an excuse to blow things up."

"That seems likely, ma'am." Rysha picked her way up the slope to stand behind Kaika, who had extracted fuses and a couple of different types of explosives from cases in her pack and was setting them up. "May I help, ma'am? You once mentioned that you would be willing to instruct me on bombs."

"I'm happy to share my knowledge on a wide variety of topics," Kaika drawled and patted the rocks beside her. "Have a seat. Do you have some paper? Since you're new, I'm going to want you to go through the calculations."

"There are *calculations?* Ma'am, you're getting me excited."

"Save that for the Sensual Sage. You and Duck can broaden your horizons together."

"Me and Duck? Uhm."

"I mean in adjacent rooms. I know you're saving your excitement for another. You can bring him along too. He could definitely stand to blow off some tension. Hand me that fuse, will you? And that explosive there. The army TE-84s are waterproof, flexible, *and* easy to light. I've got some timers in my pack, but we'll save those for when we need delayed explosions."

Rysha passed the indicated fuse, bemused by Kaika's ability to talk about sex and bombs in the same breath.

She looked over at Trip, wondering if he'd heard her comments.

But he was gazing at the mountainside, as if he were looking *through* it, and wore a concerned expression.

Rysha worried that the tons of rock and the miles of tunnels inside might be the least of their problems.

The third explosion took out the last of the caved-in boulders. Somehow, Kaika had laid her bombs so that most of the rocks flew outward instead of inward. Trip wasn't sure how that was possible, but he was glad. Even though he felt much better since they'd left the magic dead zone, his intuition itched, telling him something unappealing waited for him ahead. A part of him wanted to walk away without ever confronting it. Another part wanted to get this over with as soon as possible.

"That was a good one," Rysha said, grinning, soot coating the side of her face. She pushed her spectacles higher on her nose. She'd managed to get soot all over their frame too.

Trip smiled fondly at her even though she wasn't looking. He loved that she was so enthusiastic about so many things.

Kaika slapped her on the back. "Yup, you set them well."

Jaxi sniffed in Trip's mind. *Azzy and I could have cleared those boulders out faster. And without alerting everyone for twenty miles around that we were coming.*

Fortunately, there's nothing but lizards and animals around.

I wouldn't be so sure about that.

What do you mean? Trip asked warily, though he worried he knew exactly what Jaxi meant. Earlier, he'd thought he'd sensed something alive down there, something aware of and waiting for them. He'd told himself that was silly, especially since it hadn't felt like a dragon, and since, a moment later, he hadn't detected it when he'd tried again to sense it.

Jaxi shrugged. *The magic is obscuring more than the chamber down there, but I believe something's alive inside the mountain.*

Perhaps the very dragon that we seek is what you sensed, Telryn, Azarwrath said.

I don't think so. I know a dragon when I sense one. This was something different, something... odd.

Kaika walked toward Trip while waving to Blazer and the others, indicating that it was safe for them to come up to the entrance.

"Before we head in," she said when they'd all gathered, "I thought you should know that those rocks weren't caved in thousands of years ago."

"It didn't look like it," Blazer said. "Was it recent?"

"I don't think so. There were a few cactuses growing in nooks here and there. But I do think it happened in the last twenty or thirty years. None of the cactuses were as large as the full-grown ones we passed elsewhere on the mountainside."

"How do you know if a cactus is full-grown?" Leftie looked at Duck.

Duck shrugged. "We don't have a lot of cactuses in Iskandia, so they're out of my realm of expertise. I do know the flowers are edible. And the tall ones with the arms can live two hundred years. Oh, and the pads of those prickly low ones over there are edible. You just have to remove the thorns. There's a lot more to eat in the desert than people think."

"Is anyone else puzzled that more women aren't interested in him?" Blazer asked.

"No," Leftie said.

Trip barely heard them talking. His breath had caught at the words *twenty or thirty years*, and he had to remind himself to inhale and exhale again. "My mother," he said quietly, meeting Rysha's gaze. "She would have been here a little more than twenty-five years ago."

"Why would your mother have blown up the cave on the way out?" Blazer asked.

"Because something was following her?" Trip thought of the life he'd sensed deep down there. "Or *someone*?" he added, his thoughts shifting. "My grandmother said—uhm, I got the sense that my mom had been worried that someone might want me for nefarious purposes."

"That's almost as puzzling as someone wanting Duck for bathing purposes," Leftie said, grinning at his own humor.

"No, it's not," Blazer said. "A half-dragon sorcerer? I could see how anyone from a king to an emperor to some street tough looking to profit would want to raise a kid with the potential to have great power."

"I'm not sure who it was," Trip said, "only that my mother was worried about it when she got home."

"She might have wanted to keep people from finding the dragon too," Duck suggested. "If he's sleeping down there somewhere."

"Well, the way is open now," Kaika said. "Let's go take a look, eh?" She stretched out an arm and bent in a semblance of a noble gentleman's bow. "Mages first."

Trip snorted, but didn't object. Now that he had his power back, he was the logical choice to lead.

As he started into the mostly cleared passage, he wondered if he should even let the others go with him. This was his mission, after all, even if he wasn't the commander. Did he have the right to risk the others when it could be dangerous?

But as Rysha jogged to catch up with and fall in beside him, he couldn't imagine telling her that she couldn't come. Especially when she patted Dorfindral's scabbard and gave him a firm nod, as if to say she was ready to battle dragons or whatever else they encountered. And if Trip came face to face with his sire and his sire decided to kill Trip for his impudence, he would need Rysha and Dorfindral. And probably Kaika and Eryndral too. It wasn't as if he had the power to defeat a dragon by himself. Even if he was learning a few things and growing stronger, he would never be a match for a dragon, especially a strong gold who had been a force of nature thousands of years ago, when humans had been mastering bronze weapons and pushing stone blocks together to build huts.

He snorted, admitting that a lot of the structures in the capital today were little more than bricks stacked atop each other. Was that less primitive? Because the stone blocks were smaller? And technically, bricks were made from clay and shale.

"What?" Rysha asked.

"I'm being amused by my thoughts on how little basic building practices have advanced over the millennia."

She cocked an eyebrow at him.

"Are you going to call me an odd boy?"

"Do I need to? It's been established." Rysha smiled, but didn't swat his arm or do anything playful, as she might have the day before. She was walking at his side, but farther away than she would have before.

His return smile was sad at this reminder that he'd destroyed something between them.

"You two paying attention up there?" Kaika asked, veering to the side. They had moved past the previously caved-in area and into a wide tunnel with smooth walls and a high ceiling. She plucked up a lid from a small cracker tin. "More proof that this isn't a pristine and unexplored place. This is an Iskandian brand. Winged Eats. I remember seeing this style of tin when I was a kid. More to suggest that whoever last walked these tunnels did so twenty or thirty years ago."

"Twenty-five," Trip said again, taking the lid from her hand and turning it over in the light of a lantern that Rysha had lit. He ran a thumb over the faded paint on the top. A silly thing to get emotional about, perhaps, but he couldn't help but think that his mother might have held it all those years ago, sitting and having a snack before venturing into the dragon's lair.

He still had no idea what had prompted her to come out here. Had it been the existence of the dragon? Maybe she had found some clue in the outpost that had eluded his team.

Surely, Moe Zirkander hadn't been there back then to offer the name of the mountain. But if those cultists hadn't been in the outpost—he assumed their sacrifices were infrequent events and that they didn't live there—she would have had more time to explore. Maybe the dragon had never been what interested her. Maybe someone had pointed her to more intriguing mold out here. Or some other underground growth she had heard had medicinal properties. Would she have traveled all the way out here by herself to look?

"If Trip's going to stand and fondle every piece of trash we come across, it's going to take us a month to find the dragon," Blazer said.

The lid was too large for his collection of pocket scraps, so Trip slung off his pack and made room for it inside. Out of the corner of his eye, he glimpsed Kaika elbowing Blazer.

"This is a personal mission for him," she said.

"So? He can fondle things later."

With his lid tucked away, Trip turned to face them, all of them. "You're right, ma'am. It is a personal mission. You all may already know, but I'm the one who suggested it to General Zirkander."

None of them appeared surprised. Blazer merely arched her eyebrows, as if to ask if he had a point.

"I don't know if he ordered you all to come along—" Trip looked at Leftie and Duck as well Blazer, Kaika, and finally Rysha, "—or asked if you were interested, but either way, I appreciate you being here. I hope…" He stopped before saying the words that came to mind, that he hoped he didn't get them all killed, and switched to, "I hope we find the dragon and can convince him to come help Iskandia, so that this won't have been a waste of all our time."

"I'm sure he ordered the pilots to come along," Kaika said, propping an elbow on Blazer's shoulder, "but he *asked* me, since I'm far superior and more valuable than a pilot."

Blazer glared at her and gave the elbow a pointed look.

"I said to him," Kaika went on, smirking at Blazer but not moving her elbow, "'I'm willing to go if you can promise me some fun. Will it be fun?' He said, 'A hunt for a dragon? How can that not be fun?' Well, I have to admit I haven't been overly entertained thus far, but now that I got to blow up fifty tons of rock, I'm having more fun."

"I'm glad to hear that, ma'am," Trip said, though he wasn't quite sure what to make of this response.

"If you can find me a few more things to blow up, I'll go home happy. And so will Lieutenant Ravenwood."

Now, Rysha's eyebrows twitched upward.

"She was extremely excited when she was handling those explosives," Kaika assured Trip. "She's not one to jump up and down or whoop, but I could tell. I know my young protégé."

"It might have been a little fun, ma'am," Rysha said.

"A little. Please. Blowing things up is as good as sex. Or in your case—" Kaika eyed Trip, "—probably better."

Trip rubbed his head, now regretting his impromptu decision to share his gratitude with his teammates. Even if Leftie looked highly amused. No, *because* Leftie looked highly amused.

Rysha blushed, glanced at Trip without making eye contact, then studied the ground.

Trip had no idea if he should protest and proclaim that he was indeed good, or keep his mouth shut. After all, his brief sexual experiences thus far had all involved inadvertently breaking things with his mind and scaring the women he was with—if not scarring them for life. All Rysha knew about was his kissing, and he reluctantly admitted that she'd taken the lead on most of that. All he'd done was telepathically tell her sword to leave them alone. Gods, he needed to be more... *more*. If she gave him a chance again, he vowed he would think more about her than about how good things felt for him.

"Any chance of us finding this dragon before it dies of old age?" Blazer asked into the silent tunnel.

"Not according to Moe," Duck said.

"Let's try anyway."

"I'm ready, ma'am," Trip said and strode into the passage. He'd never been so glad for Blazer's relentless determination to complete missions. Maybe he would buy her a sewing magazine when he got home. One that covered practical things. Like boxing clothes. And boxing gloves. Gloves that could be used to punch Kaika in the nose.

"I'll bet he is." Kaika snickered.

Maybe Trip would forego the sewing magazine and simply have a new set of boxing gloves delivered to Blazer's door. With a card containing suggested uses for them. Such as nose-punching.

In my time, a powerful sorcerer did not allow a woman to say embarrassing things about him to his face, Azarwrath said as Trip walked deeper into the tunnel, keeping his back to Kaika.

Oh? Jaxi asked. *The powerful sorcerer made sure the woman waited until his back was turned to say embarrassing things?*

No. He acted in such a manner that a woman was forced to treat him with respect.

Forced, sure. What happened when the woman was the more powerful mage in the duo?

If she was a healer, then it did not matter. The man still wielded greater real power.

Because healing, that's not real, right? It's just saving lives. Not important at all.

That is not what I said. To answer your question, when the woman was more powerful, such relationships were often fraught.

I'll bet, Jaxi said.

But that is not what is happening here. Telryn is allowing these mundane women to mock him. This is totally unacceptable. I do not believe this military organization is a good thing for a sorcerer. It gives others a false sense of power over him. *Azarwrath, in his indignation, seemed to be doing the telepathic equivalent of sputtering.*

Relax, Pointy and Curmudgeony. The spittle you're spraying is going to rust your blade. Besides, if you had any brain cells left alive, you'd know Kaika is simply trying to give our young handler an incentive to treat her protégé well. Trip, if you don't know how to do that, I'm sure she would be available to advise you.

Trip wasn't as outraged as Azarwrath by all this. He simply felt mortified. And he'd already vowed to treat Rysha well, so he didn't want to discuss it further. *I'm positive I can figure it out.*

Based on events so far, I'm not. You better take any advice you can get.

Trip closed his mouth—and his mind—not wanting to invite more comments. He was already walking like a dog with its tail clenched between its legs. He forced himself to straighten his spine and look like the capable leader of a mission into a dragon's lair. As well as a competent lover.

Jaxi snorted into his mind. Apparently, he'd left his bank vault door ajar.

The smooth cave floor grew uneven as the group progressed into the mountain, the rough terrain giving Trip something else to concentrate on. Sometimes, it slanted downward like a ramp, and other times, it descended in oversized stair steps. Either way, the route was usually half blocked by rubble.

A creature flying through it wouldn't have been bothered by the footing, and Trip, after hearing a few bats flap their wings and take off, admitted a certain envy of them. Even if his flier had been working, he couldn't have sailed it into a mountain without worrying about coming to a spot too tight for it. Though this tunnel was broad so far, there wouldn't have been room for him to turn a flier around.

Rysha had mentioned once that someone with half-dragon blood might be able to shape-shift. He wondered what would be involved. Was there a workbook one could study?

He glanced at the soulblades on his hips. It was quiet inside his mind without their commentary. He cracked his vault door open and tried to let out his curious imaginings of bats and the likelihood of shape-shifting into one. Would that be enough to prompt commentary?

You want to turn into a bat? Jaxi asked immediately, and Trip smiled. What an ugly little creature. Have you seen one up close? They're all squat-faced and flat-nosed with needle-like fangs.

What would you consider an attractive winged creature? he asked.

A dragon. Admittedly, you'd be a very small dragon. A dragonling.

Can you not alter your mass when you shape-shift? Trip thought of the gold dragons that turned into ferrets at General Zirkander's house.

Mass must be conserved, Azarwrath said. *When humans shifted shape in my time, it was generally into a creature of similar size, an extremely large wolf or panther or the like.*

Then how do dragons…

Through magic, Jaxi said. *Mages in the First Dragon Era hypothesized that dragons have the ability to access a parallel dimension that exists alongside our own. They can store some of their mass there.*

Yes, and if you see a human or a dragon taking the shape of something much larger than they are, it's likely part illusion, Azarwrath said. *Or they've drawn upon the mass of something else nearby. In my time, there was a dragon that disguised himself as a part of the emperor's palace. It had so many spires, you see, that people rarely noticed an extra one.*

Why would he do that? Trip couldn't imagine wanting to be an inanimate object, unless it were to spy on some meeting.

For precisely that reason. He was an Iskandian dragon, and he listened in on the meetings going on in the throne room below.

Kaika, who had taken the lead, presumably because Trip wasn't spending enough time watching the ground for clues, veered to the side and stared at something in front of her feet.

"What is it?" Rysha joined her.

"Something new for Trip to fondle?" Leftie asked from behind Blazer.

"Feces," Kaika said.

"Never mind," Leftie said.

"I don't reckon anyone wants to fondle that," Duck said.

"I've seen bat guano all over the place." Blazer waved her hand as if to usher them past.

"Bat guano the size of cow pies?" Kaika pointed down at the black substance.

Blazer frowned at it. "No."

"And relatively fresh." Kaika knelt, prodded it with a knife, then brought the tip up to sniff.

Rysha wrinkled her nose. "It would be immature of me to say that's disgusting, right?"

"Yes. If you make it through the elite troops training and get assigned to a unit, you'll end up being sent to extra schools, like the wilderness tracking and survival one." Kaika flicked the stuff off her knife, wiped the blade, and sheathed it. "You, too, will get to sniff spoor one day."

"You make the job sound so exciting, ma'am."

"*Is* it bat guano?" Blazer eyed the dark route ahead of them.

"Looks like it and smells like it. But it had to come from a giant bat butt." Kaika shrugged and started walking again, but she kept her hand on her sword hilt as she advanced. The other held a lantern, the light barely piercing the gloom.

"Let's hope we don't see that."

"I didn't enjoy my experience with a giant tarantula," Rysha said.

"I'm not fond of giant anything," Blazer said. "And I'm starting to appreciate all the normal-sized animals in Iskandia."

Trip, realizing the others couldn't see very far ahead, concentrated on forming the illusionary—but bright—lightbulb he'd conjured in the outpost. It appeared in the air ahead of Kaika, making her start and glance back at him. Trip sent it drifting ahead of their group, illuminating the passage.

"Did we ever figure out if things are giant here naturally?" Duck asked, stopping to take his own look at the guano pile as the group moved on. "Or is it like Dakrovia and Owanu Owanus where there are a lot of weird things that are descendants of dragon-animal or, uh, dragon-octopus pairings?"

Blazer glanced at Duck as he jogged to catch up. "I'd forgotten you were on that mission Zirkander gave himself to find Phelistoth."

"Yes, ma'am. I saw some very strange critters there."

"I guess Trip would be the one to tell us." Blazer nodded toward him. "Or Jaxi. Or the other one."

The other *one?* Azarwrath asked. *Is she referring to* me*? Telryn, why do these people not know my name?*

You haven't chatted with them much, have you? Trip asked. He'd carried the soulblade for quite a while before Azarwrath had deigned to talk to him. To Blazer, he said, "If I met an animal with dragon blood, I think I would know it. Or the soulblades—Jaxi and *Azarwrath*—definitely would."

I've found that mundane humans are alarmed by telepathic contact from sentient swords.

Hard to believe, isn't it? Jaxi asked.

"But you can't tell just from the trace they left behind?" Blazer asked.

"Uh, no."

"Maybe you should ask General Zirkander to send you to the wilderness tracking class too," Rysha said, grinning at him.

"Just let us know if you sense anything dangerous up ahead," Blazer said. "Kaika, you said that spoor was fresh, right?"

"Less than twenty-four hours."

"Wonderful."

Trip hoped the animals here ran toward the large side naturally. He had a hard time imagining a dragon wanting to shape-shift into a bat and mate with it, but he definitely didn't want to fight the descendant of that mating.

We don't always get what we want, Jaxi said.

Do you know something I don't know?

I know billions of things you don't know. You're quite the neophyte.

Thanks.

Just step lightly, Telryn, Azarwrath said. *We'll warn you as soon as we're aware of danger. The way ahead is obscured to my eye, but I do sense life.*

Dangerous life? Trip asked.

Is there any other kind?

Well, the mold in the outpost was fairly innocuous.

Are you sure? Alchemists have long used mold spores in concoctions designed to alter the brain.

Does that explain the craziness of the cultists? Jaxi asked.

It could play a role in it, if they're down there often, inhaling the spore-filled air.

Trip sniffed tentatively, now worried about the group breathing in the musty cave scents. *In that case, I'm going to hope it wasn't intriguing mold that drew my mother to these caves.*

A wise hope. There are other things to worry about down here.

As they passed another giant pile of guano, Trip couldn't disagree.

CHAPTER 19

THE RUBBLE SHIFTED UNDER RYSHA'S boots, and she cursed as a huge rock slipped away. She leaned down, gripping boulders to either side to catch her balance, but the one she'd dislodged clunked and clattered down the steep slope. She winced with each bang, certain the noise would be audible all the way back to the dragon-rider outpost.

Blazer sighed from above her, most of the group still on a ledge at the top of the slope.

So much for Azarwrath's admonition to step lightly, Jaxi spoke dryly into her mind.

Rysha grimaced, not in the mood for soulblade sarcasm.

"Sorry, ma'am," she called back to Blazer after the rock finally clattered to the bottom of the cavern they'd entered, a vast place larger than a hookball field.

The tunnel they'd been walking through earlier had brought them out more than halfway up a rock wall, the ledge looking out over stalagmites and stalactites, some the size of buildings. The crumbled slope of boulders and jagged chunks of rock Rysha was navigating down was the only way to the bottom. She doubted the others would have more success, but since she was leading, she got a chance to make noise first. Lucky her.

I merely wish to inform you that I detect creatures heading toward this cavern from the opposite direction, Jaxi said.

Creatures? Rysha peered into the gloom beyond Trip's floating lightbulb, but the stalactites and columns sprinkled throughout the cavern made it impossible to see to the far end.

They're large, and they're flying. Creatures seemed as likely a descriptor as any.

"Can you levitate the group down?" Blazer asked Trip. "You and the swords? The way you did in that ice canyon?"

"Yes." Trip's gaze was toward the opposite end of the cavern. No doubt, he "saw" more than Rysha did. "If you toss down the *chapaharii* blades. And your ingot." His eyes narrowed. "But we have company coming. It may be better if everyone simply gets down of their own accord as quickly as possible."

Without waiting for Blazer's opinion, Trip jumped off the ledge. Either he or the soulblades floated him into the air, and his momentum took him sailing over Rysha's head on his way down to the cavern floor.

"Show off," she said, not daring to call the words loudly, not if *creatures* were coming. Though it probably didn't matter now. Those creatures must have heard her and already knew the group was there.

If it makes you feel less inept, I believe they were coming before you kicked the rock free.

Not really, Rysha grumbled in her mind.

As she navigated down the rest of the slope, Dorfindral buzzed in her mind. Rysha hoped that was a response to Jaxi speaking telepathically to her, but she doubted it was.

"I think whatever's coming is magical," she said, raising her voice to be heard over the clatter of the others descending behind her.

Pebbles and rocks bounced down to either side of her as her teammates had no more luck than she at navigating soundlessly down the uneven slope.

"Of course it is," Blazer muttered.

"Are we sure we wouldn't have been better off staying on the ledge?" Duck glanced toward the shadowy cavern, the leering stalactites. "I feel vulnerable here."

"Get to the bottom quickly," Blazer said. "If our enemies are flying, they'll have a hard time maneuvering between the rock formations. We can more easily duck and shoot from behind them."

"Doing my best, ma'am. I—awwwk!"

Rysha glanced up in time to see Duck float past overhead, his arms flailing.

"Don't even think about it," Leftie growled down. He must have seen Trip looking up at him.

Trip turned his back to the group still on the slope. Duck landed beside him, and Trip pointed into the darkness and then toward a rock mound. Duck ran to it as he pulled his rifle off his pack.

Dorfindral's irritated buzz grew more insistent. *Hunt!* it seemed to order Rysha.

"I'll be happy to do so as soon as I reach the ground," she muttered, eyeing the deep shadows of the cavern. "Can you make more light, Trip?"

Trip drew Jaxi and Azarwrath, a sword in each hand. The soulblades flared, blue for Jaxi and red for Azarwrath, and their combined light drove back the shadows for dozens of meters in front of Trip. Rysha didn't know how he could see anything with suns blazing in each hand, but maybe he wasn't relying on eyesight.

Rysha was almost to the bottom when a dark winged shape appeared at the edge of the light. It looked like a giant bat. An *extremely* giant bat. Its wingspan had to be fifteen feet, but it swooped around the columns and stalactites as if it had been made for such obstacle courses. It drew in its wings when necessary, then flapped them to gain momentum, and drew them in again to arrow through a tight spot. The bat came into a clear area and flew straight toward Trip.

Red lightning shot forth from Azarwrath, branching to go around a stalactite without hitting it. It should have struck the bat in the head, but between one wingbeat and the next, the creature disappeared. Duck fired at where it should have been, but the bullet clanged off the distant ceiling. Azarwrath's red lightning crackled through empty air.

"What the hells?" Duck spun around, squinting into the gloom above them.

"Was it an illusion?" Blazer asked.

"No." Trip turned, like he was tracking something, then barked, "Look out!"

He was staring at Rysha.

She flattened herself to the rocks as he lifted his soulblades. The giant bat appeared in the air right above her, clawed limbs only two feet from her head.

A fireball formed and streaked toward the creature. Rysha swore and did her best to roll out of the way on the boulder-strewn terrain. She only made it a couple of feet before the fireball flew over her head, its heat almost searing her eyebrows off. It slammed into the bat, taking it dead on.

That should have killed it—should have killed *anything*—but Dorfindral threw a warning into her mind.

Rysha scrambled back up the slope as the fireball dissipated. The bat sprang off the rocks toward her, claws slashing toward her face.

Though terrified, she whipped Dorfindral across her body in time to parry the attack. The blade eagerly sliced off two of the creature's clawed toes.

She brought the sword back up, hoping to lunge up the slope and plunge it into the bat's body. Its *huge* body. This close, she had no trouble gauging its size, the fact that it was twice as large as she.

Just before her blade would have plunged into its chest, huge wings slapped inward. She saw them out of the corners of her eyes and sprang back. She slashed at them instead of the bat's chest, beating them away and drawing some satisfaction when the blade cut into leathery flesh.

The rocks shifted under her feet as she landed, and she flailed for a second, but caught her balance, landing in a sword-fighting crouch, the blade ready again. Instead of chasing after her, the bat screeched.

This was not some simple cry of pain. The tremendous volume pierced her eardrums like daggers, and it took all Rysha's will not to crumple to her knees, drop her sword, and fling her hands over her ears. Rifles rang out from the sides and behind her, but their reports were tiny and insignificant compared to that ongoing screech.

"No!" someone yelled from behind her. Trip?

Rysha lifted her head and jerked her sword up as a leathery brown wingtip whipped toward her face. That wing had a claw on it. She lunged with Dorfindral, meeting the attack out in front of her.

Just before the wing struck her blade, some invisible power slammed into the bat. It flew away from her, wings flapping erratically as its butt end tumbled over its head. It might have been hurled dozens of meters, but the slope got in the way, and it struck the rocks with bone-crunching force.

Rysha ran after it. The horrible screeching had stopped for the moment. This was her chance to finish off the bat.

She glanced over her shoulder as she raced up the shifting rocks, the footing treacherous. Belatedly, she worried that she might be putting herself in Trip's way.

But a second giant bat was swooping all around him. On the cavern floor, he spun and leaped like a trained sword fighter, alternating between defending and attacking with the two soulblades, sometimes doing both at once.

A roar from above and to Rysha's right jerked her attention back to her own fight. Kaika leaped in from the side, landing on the bat as it was pushing itself upright. Eryndral blazed green in her hands as she hacked down, slamming the blade into her foe. It slashed through wings and pierced flesh.

The bat screeched again, and Rysha faltered, gritting her teeth against the pain that noise brought. More than sheer volume hurt her ears. There seemed to be magical power in those screeches.

Something warm trickled inside of her ear. Blood?

Rysha pushed forward. She reached the bat as the creature, furling its wings tight, tried to roll away from Kaika. Rysha jumped in, hacking at it, hoping to kill it before it could rise. And hoping to halt that cursed noise.

The screech stopped, and Rysha thought they'd succeeded in killing the bat, but those wings flexed open, unfurling like whips. One of them clubbed Kaika. She stumbled back, her heel catching, and she swore as she dropped to one knee.

The other wing almost caught Rysha, but she was fast enough to bring her blade up first. Dorfindral seemed to sing in her mind as she pierced the wing. She drove the sword through it, then yanked it down, as if she were slicing a curtain all the way to the floor.

The bat rolled and tried to batter her with its free wing, but Kaika sprang back into the fight. She drove Eryndral into the creature's back.

Finally, the bat's movements slowed as it grew weaker. A few more times, it attempted to pull its wing free from Rysha's sword, but it did not succeed. Kaika drew her blade out, stepped closer, and drove it point first into the creature's chest. The bat slumped, the life seeping from its body.

As it died, its head lolled to the side. Its face was definitely bat-like, but the eyes that turned toward Rysha startled her. They weren't beady and brown, as she would have suspected, but dark green. A disturbingly familiar dark green that made her draw back, gaping as a strange sensation of dread filled the pit of her stomach.

Rifle fire came from the cavern floor.

Kaika slapped Rysha on the shoulder. "We're not done yet."

Rysha tore her gaze from the dead bat's eyes. She raced down the slope after Kaika as quickly as she could on the treacherous rock. She sucked in an alarmed breath at the sight below.

Trip knelt on one knee, his head bowed, Jaxi's point pressed into the ground beside him as he leaned on her. Azarwrath had fallen from his grasp.

Duck, Leftie, and Blazer were all over to one side, crouching behind rock formations as they fired over Trip's head at a bat arrowing out of the stalactites toward him. It was even larger than the one Rysha and Kaika had killed.

Cursing, she willed her legs to move faster. The team fired again, but the bat disappeared, just as the first one had done. Their bullets bounced uselessly off the stalactites. No, *dangerously*. One ricocheted back, hitting the rocky floor only a few feet from Trip.

"Where'd it go now?" Leftie blurted.

"Stop shooting," Kaika yelled, springing off the slope and over a lumpy, scorched corpse.

Rysha hadn't noticed it before. Was that the bat that Trip had been fighting earlier? That meant there had been three, damn it.

The giant bat reappeared right behind Trip, claws slashing toward his back.

"Trip!" Rysha shrieked.

Only a few meters away, Kaika raised her sword and sprinted toward them.

But Trip jumped up, whirling in the air, Jaxi coming across to slice into the clawed limbs only inches away from him. The bat's momentum carried it into him, but Trip braced himself, and the creature bounced off him.

He held his hand out to the side, and Azarwrath flew through the air to land in his grip. Trip sprang at the bat before it recovered from its failed attack, driving both soulblades toward it. Lightning and fire poured into the creature as the swords sank through its wings and into its chest.

A high-pitched screech erupted from the bat's mouth as their eyes met. Rysha couldn't read the expression on Trip's face, but couldn't help but wonder if he noticed the similarity there.

As more lightning and flames assailed the bat, it struggled to pull back, to batter Trip and somehow escape, but he strode into it. Somehow, the flailing wings never touched his body. The smell of scorched meat filled the cavern. Finally, the bat stopped moving.

Trip pushed it away with his boot so he could pull the swords free. The flames and lightning faded, though a few remnant sparks danced along their blades.

Trip turned toward Rysha and Kaika. Kaika still had her sword raised, poised to spring in, and Dorfindral hummed against Rysha's palm, as if to say it was ready for another fight, ready to slay this other magical being in front of them.

"*Meyusha*," Kaika said, eyeing her raised blade with a determined expression.

Rysha murmured the same command to Dorfindral while meeting Trip's eyes. He could have spoken the words to both swords and quelled their eagerness for dragon blood right away, but he neither spoke the command aloud nor silently. It took Rysha a few more utterings before Dorfindral allowed her to lower it.

She drew a kerchief and willed her breathing to slow to normal as she cleaned the blade. The bat blood, a dark ichor that seemed as unnatural as the creature had been, did not come off easily.

Duck, Leftie, and Blazer walked over, eyeing the two corpses near Trip.

"Any more around?" Blazer asked.

"Not in this cavern," Trip said.

"But elsewhere in these tunnels?"

He sighed, his eyes holding an expression Rysha couldn't read. Regret? Unease? "Probably. The soulblades and I can sense more life down here. It's difficult to tell exactly what or where it is."

Kaika finished cleaning her sword and sheathed it, then looked frankly at Trip. "Those bats had your eyes."

Rysha grimaced at the bluntness. Though she had made the same observation, she wouldn't have shared it in front of the whole group. Trip didn't look surprised by the comment, nor did there seem to be any lack of understanding in his gaze.

Leftie's lip curled as he looked back and forth from Kaika to Trip. "What are you saying, Major?"

Blazer frowned as if she hadn't caught on yet. Probably because she hadn't seen those bats' eyes close up.

"That I bet family gatherings at Trip's papa's place are very interesting," Kaika said.

Trip's jaw clenched. He didn't look pleased by the comment or the situation in general.

Rysha stepped toward him and laid a hand on his sleeve. She wanted to say something light, something to make him and the others forget the uncomfortable possibilities, but he turned his gaze—his green-eyed gaze—toward her, and her tongue tied. He had human eyes instead of bat eyes, but the color… it was exactly the same.

"Can't be much crazier than gatherings at General Zirkander's house," Blazer said.

"Possibly true," Kaika said. "One of those ferrets has green eyes. Bhrava Saruth isn't a relative, is he, Trip?"

"Not that I'm aware of. He didn't mention it when he sniffed me."

Rysha snorted, remembering that moment in the ice caves.

Trip lifted a hand to the side of her face. She thought it some gesture of endearment, but then her eardrum tingled. She remembered that it had been bleeding earlier. Now that her awareness of it returned, she noticed that both ears ached deep inside.

But almost as soon as Trip touched her, the ache faded. Every ache in her entire body seemed to fade, and a warm surge of energy flowed to her limbs. She suddenly felt that she could sprint ten miles with her rucksack on and a rifle in hand.

When Trip lowered his hand, the sensation didn't fade, but she did feel disappointed at the cool air that replaced the warmth of his touch.

"You're getting better at that," she whispered.

"Good." He was still holding her gaze, his eyes narrowing thoughtfully. Was he looking into her eyes? Or at her spectacles?

She almost asked what else was on his mind, but Duck spoke first.

"Are you getting your ears healed? Because those hollering screeches hurt like bees stinging your drums." Duck stuck a finger in his ear, drew it out, and grimaced at the blood on the tip.

"Yes." Trip waved for them all to come closer.

Leftie hesitated. He touched his ear, then grimaced when his fingers came away bloody, but he looked like he might cross his arms and stay mulishly away from Trip's healing touch.

"I'll heal your infected foot, too," Trip said quietly, meeting his eyes.

Leftie flinched. "It's not infected."

"There's pus all over your sock."

"I like it that way."

"If you get gangrene, you could lose your foot."

"Damn it, Trip. Stop knowing so much about what's in my head and what's in my foot." Leftie dropped his chin and rubbed the back of his neck, the gesture tense and frustrated.

Rysha wanted to punch him for being difficult. She understood him not being willing to forget—or forgive—that Trip had read his mind, but if his foot truly was infected, he was foolish not to get help from a healer.

Leftie must have reached the same conclusion because he limped over after Duck left Trip's side.

"I'm sorry," Trip said, resting a hand on his shoulder.

"For spying on the status of my foot?" Leftie asked.

"For poking into your head. I'm not used to having the ability to do so, and sometimes, I do it without realizing. I'm trying to get better at not invading people's privacy. I don't *want* to see what they're thinking."

"Good."

Rysha thought that would be the end of the conversation, especially since that "good" had sounded sullen, but Leftie surprised her by speaking again, in a lower tone of voice, one she probably wasn't supposed to.overhear.

"It scares me when you do things that aren't human," Leftie said.

"I know," Trip said. "It scares me too."

"It's only going to get worse, isn't it? You're going to get more—less human."

Rysha wanted to come to Trip's defense, but the men were speaking quietly, their words for each other, not for her. Maybe she shouldn't have been eavesdropping.

"I don't know," Trip said, "but I'd appreciate it if you point that out if you see it happening. I don't want to be... inhuman. Or inhumane. You probably don't believe this, but I didn't want any of this."

Leftie raised skeptical eyebrows.

"I still just want to fly and shoot," Trip said wistfully. "But I feel it would be irresponsible of me not to learn how to use the power inside of me. To learn to *control* it."

"Yeah."

Trip lowered his hand. "How's your foot?"

"Can't you tell?"

"I'm choosing not to invade your privacy to check."

"Hells, what's it matter *now*? You magicked my ear and did weird things to the inside of my foot. What secrets could be left?"

"I'm going to assume that means you're feeling better. You're welcome."

Leftie grunted. Such a grateful patient.

"Once everybody's bandaged up or healed up—whatever—we're pressing on. This place is creepy." Blazer nudged one of the dead bats with the tip of her boot. "I don't want to spend the night in here."

Trip opened his mouth, but he shut it again and turned toward Duck to heal him.

Rysha had a feeling he'd been about to point out that the odds of them getting to the dragon lair and out again before needing to sleep were slim. She suspected the sun had already set outside. Not that they would ever know, here in the depths of the mountain. She didn't like the way Trip kept glancing toward the far end of the cavern, as if he was certain there would be more trouble.

CHAPTER 20

DESPITE BLAZER STATING HER DESIRE not to spend the night in the cave system, after a few more hours of travel, she'd called a stop in a cavern with a large pool in the middle, water trickling down damp walls and stalactites to feed it. Thanks to the uneven terrain, it had taken the group a long time to progress only a couple of miles.

Trip believed it was another couple of miles to the large central cavern he'd been directing them toward, the cavern that he'd thought would grow easier to sense as they traveled closer. But it remained opaque to him, and he had only a vague sense that there was life and magic inside.

Blazer had assigned Trip, Jaxi, and Azarwrath to the first shift of guard duty, so he sat on a rock formation overlooking the pool and the team's spread blankets. The water was serene, with the group's lanterns providing enough light to show the reflections of the stalactites hanging above it. The small drops of water dribbling from the rocks made tiny ripples in the otherwise still pool. Despite the serene spot, everyone rested with their boots on and their weapons close at hand.

Trip looked down at the pieces of metal spread in his lap, the lock from the outpost, the cracker lid from the entrance, and the other scraps he'd gathered along the way. He was shaping them, using his mind as both melting furnace and forge to manipulate the metal. The cheerful cracker picture painted on the lid pleased him, a splash of color among all the gray, and he was trying to keep it intact.

The tinkering took some of the tension from his body, but he couldn't keep his thoughts from wandering, from dwelling on dragons. And the things around this one that didn't add up. Was Agarrenon Shivar truly down here? Trip still couldn't sense him. The same questions continued to haunt him. If the dragon was in a stasis chamber, how had his mother gotten him out? And why, if Agarrenon Shivar had been freed, had he gone back in? And what of that disease Moe had spoken of? Was the dragon even now dying a slow death inside the stasis chamber?

If the dragon was sick and locked in stasis, where in all of Linora had his batty offspring come from? Seven gods, it had been creepy running into animals—beings—that shared his blood—and his eyes.

Trip had known they did right away, even if Jaxi and Azarwrath had been less certain. The strangest mixture of familiarity and repulsion had come over him. He hadn't wanted to lift the soulblades or use his magic against them, but they had clearly not felt the same way. Still, when he'd killed that first one, his blood or who knew what dark reptilian part of him, had cried out, the emotion driving him to his knees. It had felt as if he'd committed some crime against all dragon-kind. All of *his* kind.

He blinked at moisture gathering in his eyes. He didn't know if he was mourning for the deaths of his alien brothers or for his own lost innocence. Every day, something new happened, and he felt more and more of a freak. Less human.

He longed for the days when he'd simply flown with his squadron mates, the wind sweeping his cares away as he soared up the coast, the waves breaking below, fluffy white clouds drifting in the sky over the calm sea.

His hands kept working as his mind ran sprints in a thousand directions, wrestling over and over with the same issues. After hundreds of drops had fallen into the pool and his comrades had drifted off to sleep, Trip looked down and found the toy he'd barely been paying attention to now complete.

For the first time in days, he felt a twinge of satisfaction at something he'd done. Maybe even pleasure. Though he sat in the dark, outside the influence of the camp's lanterns, he could see his creation well enough.

Inspired by that workbook he still hadn't mastered, he'd shaped all the various scraps of metal into interlocking pieces that formed a three-dimensional puzzle, one that happened to be shaped like a fish. The cracker logo had ended up on the side, the tin creating one of the larger pieces. Most of the pieces were big enough for a toddler with unrefined motor skills to manipulate, and they all attached to a central spindle that had been made from the shank of the lock. The pieces connected to it so they couldn't be taken out, merely moved to various spots around it.

The toy shouldn't be a danger to a baby, even though a newborn would be more likely to suck on it than do the puzzle. Trip would clean it thoroughly and maybe find some tongue-safe paint to color the rest of the pieces. In the meantime, maybe the toddler, Marinka, would be old enough to tinker with it. Would any of General Zirkander and Sardelle's children have an interest in tinkering? The general had clearly wanted to instill the love of flying in his little girl, but Trip imagined Sardelle being a more neutral encourager, letting the kids try all manner of things to see what they liked.

Trip tucked the toy into his cargo pocket, barely able to button the flap with it in there. Maybe he would take it and stick it in his pack.

He shifted and looked at the camp, spotting his ruck and his blanket next to Duck's. Before heading over, he stretched his senses out to make sure nothing inimical was sneaking up—or flying up—on their group. As before, he sensed life deeper in the complex, but nothing approached. Outside, the sun had long ago set. Maybe the cave dwelling creatures somehow knew and lived by its influence, even down here.

He supposed if *he* knew, then weird animals that shared his blood could also know.

Trip shook his head, not wanting to contemplate the bats again. But perhaps his thoughts leaked out of his bank vault, because Jaxi spoke up, as she had occasionally done while he'd been standing guard. Azarwrath seemed more inclined to leave Trip alone with his thoughts.

We've been arguing about those bats, she thought.

About what possessed a dragon to get frisky with their mother? Trip wondered if, from a dragon's point of view, a human was little different from any other animal.

No, I've ceased wondering about things like that. Dragons are odd beings. An image of Bhrava Saruth accompanied her words, the big gold dragon lying on his back in the sun, his legs crooked in the air, while he convinced Sardelle to rub his belly.

From what Trip had seen of him and the young female, he would gladly spend time with them over Agarrenon Shivar. He recalled Bhrava Saruth's green eyes, and that he had a reputation for being promiscuous. It was a shame that, as Kaika had suggested, *he* couldn't have been Trip's sire.

What we were debating, Jaxi went on, *is how old those bats were.*

Trip hitched a shoulder. He had no idea how long normal bats lived or if dragon blood could extend an animal's life. He would have believed anything from a few years old to thousands of years old.

Neither of us is certain how long typical bats live, Jaxi said, *but we don't think those were some strange timeless creatures that have been alive for millennia.*

Agreed, Azarwrath commented. *Even though dragon magic keeps* dragons *alive for an impossibly long time, I never observed or heard that the offspring of human-dragon pairings lived inordinately long lives. They were typically known for having good health and living to a hundred or a little more, but certainly not many centuries. Any animals we encounter that share your blood are likely to have been born after you, or around the same time as you. Not earlier, unless they're sea turtles or parrots or some notoriously long-lived creature.*

It doesn't really matter, does it? Trip asked, not wanting to think about being related to any more animals. Sea turtles, hells.

Doesn't it? I find it quite fascinating, since your archaeologist acquaintance seemed to believe it a given that Agarrenon Shivar was dead.

Moe is a treasure hunter and occasional mapmaker, Jaxi said. *I have a feeling that real archaeologists would be insulted by the idea of him being labeled as one of them.*

That matters little in this conversation, Azarwrath said.

Trip hoped they weren't going to start arguing in his head again. His gaze shifted from his rucksack, where he'd been thinking of putting the toy, past Duck and to where Rysha slept curled on her side, using the book she'd taken from the outpost as a pillow. Her sword was in its scabbard next to her, acting as a paperweight for the rubbings she'd been looking over before going to sleep.

It had been good that Dorfindral and Kaika's blade had allowed them to defeat one of the bats, since the rest of the team's rifles had done little. Trip had managed to defeat one without too much trouble, with the soulblades' assistance, but the backlash he'd experienced after killing it had almost made him an easy target for the next one. Since he didn't know what else they would face, or if Agarrenon Shivar himself would prove anything but an enemy, he was glad he had allies along who could fight magic.

He just wished he could give Rysha what he had suggested in regard to that sword. The power to fully control it without forever having to worry that some enemy sorceress or dragon would know the command words and have the ability to turn it against her—or her allies.

He well remembered her turning on *him* in that ice chamber. Had he known the command words then, he could have stopped the battle without breaking her spectacles, but if there had been a dragon in the room that knew them and uttered them, his words would have been ignored. He feared that a new dragon era had come and that there would always be a dragon in the room—or in the sky—for future battles.

Even though they hadn't found instructions in the iron box with the ingot and the map, Trip believed he could figure out how to reprogram the sword if he had some time to examine it up close. Unfortunately, he suspected he couldn't do that without physical contact with it. And that would involve a great deal of pain. Simply touching that ingot for a split second had nearly put him on the floor.

Maybe that was why the mages that had come to imbue the commands in the swords had ended up dying. Extended contact with the *chapaharii* blades. But had it been a one-for-one tradeoff? A mage had to die each time one was forged? Or had a mage been able to program the terms—and had they instilled some of the weapons' personalities too?—in multiple blades before dying? If so, why hadn't they simply programmed one less than was required to kill them?

Trip still wondered if maybe Rysha had misinterpreted those ancient words. Maybe they'd spoken of self-sacrifice but not true sacrifice of one's life.

Are you listening to us, Telryn? Azarwrath asked sternly.

Sorry, no. I'm thinking about trying to reprogram Rysha's sword.

Now? The alarm in Jaxi's single word surprised him.

Maybe she actually cared if he lived or died.

I don't know if I can do it right now, in a single night, but it would be better if it could be done before we face Agarrenon Shivar. In case… just in case.

I won't argue that, but you don't know how to do it. You could be risking your life for no reason.

I don't know how to make toys, either, but… it's a mechanical thing. I have an aptitude for such things.

A sword is a metal stick, not a mechanical construct, Jaxi said.

I would have expected you to think of your physical self in more flattering terms. Trip's comments were distracted, as he was still gazing thoughtfully at Dorfindral, debating how he might pick it up and carry it off to study and perhaps experiment on. It wouldn't let him touch it with his bare hands. But what if he could insulate himself somehow?

Oh, I'm a magnificent metal stick, but I'm still a stick.

Would a glove do? Trip didn't have one, but perhaps one of the others did.

He could wake up Rysha and ask her to carry it off to a quiet spot for him, but she might not be willing to help, out of fear that he would hurt himself. Might he ask Kaika? Or one of the others?

Perhaps, but he found himself reluctant to ask for help. In part because they might deny it. In part because he didn't want witnesses as he possibly did something stupid.

Trip looked toward Blazer's sleeping spot. She dozed by her rucksack, the flap open. She must have needed to take something out, because that iron ingot case rested next to her pack instead of being tucked inside. Iron that dampened the effect of magic, including the anti-magic of the swords.

Before he'd fully decided what he would do, Trip rose to his feet and headed for the box. He stepped lightly, not wishing to wake anyone up and have to explain.

Are you about to do something stupid? Jaxi asked suspiciously.

I'm going to try to help Rysha.

Ugh, you are *going to do something stupid.*

Trip didn't reply. He needed to concentrate if he was going to pick up the sword without killing himself. Or even get the ingot out of that box without waking up Blazer.

He crouched near her head, wondering what he would say if she woke up.

Jaxi sighed. *I can make sure they stay asleep while you do… whatever foolish thing you're going to do.*

Your eternal and enthusiastic support is surely why Sardelle values you so.

I sense sarcasm. Do you want a metal stick up your butt?

Not at this moment. Trip stuck out a finger to make sure he was right and that he could touch the iron box.

He could. As he'd suspected before, the box, no doubt designed to insulate the tainted ingots inside, ingots that would give any mages in the vicinity extreme headaches, was made from normal iron.

He opened the lid and immediately felt the power of the ingot inside, the way it repulsed him and made his head throb.

Though he wanted nothing more than to shut the lid on it again, he instead tipped the box on its side, carefully dumping the ingot onto the corner of Blazer's blanket. He marveled that none of the others felt anything from the ingot and that they'd strolled through that quarry without a reaction to the strange iron within.

The ingot landed with a soft thud, and Trip glanced at Blazer's eyes. Her lids remained shut, her breathing steady. As Jaxi had promised.

Thank you for your help, he thought without sarcasm as he lifted the box and stepped back.

This is because you were kind enough to make a toy for my handler's children, not because I think it's a good idea.

So noted. He gazed down at the box, willing the iron to bend and morph in his hands.

Uh, you shouldn't be able to do that. Not to iron.

Rysha keeps telling me I'm a special boy.

No, she says you're an odd boy, and I agree wholeheartedly.

She doesn't seem to mind.

Because she's an odd girl. Clearly, you should keep her.

Trip wished he could, but he feared he'd screwed up and lost that possibility forever. At the least, he could give her more power to control her destiny, to retain her independence as she went into battle. That, he sensed, was the most important thing to her.

The metal warmed in his hands as he willed it to stretch into a new shape. After a minute, he held a long set of tongs.

Again walking as quietly as possible, he moved to Rysha's blanket. Would the sword scream some warning into her mind as he tried to take it?

Jaxi? Can you make sure she stays asleep for a few minutes too?

Another sigh. *I'll try. I don't think I can override Dorfy's warnings.*

Moving quickly, Trip clasped the ends of the tongs around the scabbard. He tensed, waiting for sparks of energy to lance up his arms and through his body like lightning. But they didn't.

He lifted the scabbard and carried it at tongs' length like a blacksmith moving a near-molten bar of iron straight from the forge. He headed along the pool, up over the ledge where he'd sat earlier, and past stalagmites and mounds of damp lumpy rocks.

Trip tried not to feel like a thief as he looked for a spot to work on it, but he wanted to be far enough away that they wouldn't hear him if he whimpered while handling the blade.

"Or scream out in agonizing pain," he muttered.

You may need to take it out of the mountain if you're hoping to avoid people hearing you caterwauling.

"No, this is far enough." Trip climbed down into a wide depression between two lumpy rock formations, a quiet nook looking out over the pool. The rocks rose high enough to block his view of the camp—and the camp's view of him. "I'll bite down on a stick if I need to."

Good luck finding a stick in here. I haven't seen a tree yet on this continent, and all those desert bushes are more thorns than wood.

I have a metal stick if I get desperate. Trip placed the *chapaharii* sword down on the rocks, let go of the tongs, and sat cross-legged next to it.

We're going to have cross words if you bite down on me. Also, that could be extremely unhealthy for your lips.

Unhealthy? Azarwrath asked. *Are you suggesting that you carry some disease he might contract?*

No, I'm suggesting I'm sharp. Unlike your fifteen-hundred-year-old dullness.

I assure you, my sharpness has only grown over the centuries.

Trip used the tongs to shake Dorfindral out of its scabbard, and angry images flooded his mind, images of the sword slashing his throat, stabbing him through the heart, and hacking him into tiny pieces.

"It's good to be loved," Trip murmured, pushing aside the scabbard, then setting down the tongs again.

He rested his elbows on his knees, his chin on his intertwined fingers, and focused on the length of steel, a bluish gray that glowed with pale green light. The dual edges were sharp even after more centuries than Azarwrath had existed. Odd that iron interfered with magic and hindered mages, but that steel could become a powerful conduit and container for magic. Why did the addition of carbon change its properties so? Was there anything in that he could use? He imagined extracting the carbon in the sword for long enough to handle it, then placing it back in, but he feared he would destroy the weapon if he attempted that. In truth, he hadn't the foggiest idea how it might be done.

He opened his thoughts to the soulblades in case they had any insights, hoping they weren't still arguing. For the moment, silence filled his mind. Were they, too, studying the blade?

Minutes passed as Trip gazed at it, and he began to see more than a single slab of steel. He saw individual molecules combined together to create something larger. Most of those molecules appeared homogeneous, sort of a dark blue to his senses, but intertwined with them were molecules with a green tint. They had been altered somehow to have a different appearance and a different function from the rest.

Almost like cancer cells, Azarwrath mused. *Though presumably not malevolent. Just different in goal and function from the majority of those in the body of the sword.*

With his healing knowledge and experience still rudimentary, Trip didn't think the analogy helped him. But he did realize that the magic was in those altered molecules. He would need to interact with them and not the rest of the sword. He realized as he nudged one with his mind and the atoms inside seemed to vibrate that maybe he could. He nudged a couple of them, checking to see what altering their structure would do, but as soon as he stopped focusing, they returned to their original state.

Further, a warning growl sounded in his mind. Dorfindral. The sword seemed to be telling him it would fight him, not willingly allowing him to alter it.

Trip drew his focus outward, away from the microscopic level he'd somehow been seeing with his senses. He tried to see the magic as a whole, the pattern it wove as it threaded through the mass of the blade. And it *was* a pattern, he realized. Not unlike the loom punch cards he'd been likening it to. The commands were stored in the pattern of molecules a long-dead mage had altered.

The longer he studied it, the more Trip believed he could change the pattern. Though he feared that he would have to touch the blade with more than his mind in order to do it. Maybe that was how mages in the past had inserted their programming. They'd touched the swords, causing the blades to react by attacking them, and then used the weapons' distraction to work their magic. So, if he distracted Dorfindral, he might be able to slip past its defenses and change the pattern.

"Only one way to test the theory," he murmured.

He reached for the blade but paused, his hand in the air above it. Even a foot away, he felt Dorfindral's displeasure, that antagonistic force it sent out toward him.

But that wasn't what made Trip pause. He was wondering what new words he should program into the sword. They should be words or terms that meant something to Rysha but that would be hard for others to guess. Ideally, he shouldn't be able to guess them either, but he had no idea how he could program the sword without knowing the words himself. Besides, even if that were somehow possible, the first time she thought them at the sword, he would likely hear it. Unless he got better at staying out of other people's heads. That was certainly something he *should* work on.

"Let's just see if I can actually alter anything," he whispered. He could worry about specific commands later.

Trip took a deep breath and touched his hand to the naked blade.

Agony ricocheted up his arm, as if a bullet had been fired into his body and was trapped inside, tearing through all his muscle and flesh as it bounced around. He panted, fighting the pain and also the intense urge to yank his hand away. He pressed his hand harder to the blade, snarled, and tried to once again see the molecules. But what had been easy before was elusive now with his mind so distracted.

"Focus," he growled. "Focus."

Blackness encroached on the edge of his vision, and he realized he might have been an arrogant fool to believe he could change anything, to even believe he could survive when others far more experienced than he had died trying to do this.

CHAPTER 21

*W*AKE UP!

Rysha sat bolt upright, clutching a hand to her chest. She didn't think she had been sleeping hard, but it took her a moment to remember where she was. She looked around for what had woken her. Some danger? No, she'd heard someone speaking, hadn't she?

Yes, you heard me, Jaxi spoke into her mind. *Get up. Trip needs your help.*

Where? Remembering the bats, she shifted to the side, reaching for Dorfindral. But the sword wasn't there.

Confused, she looked on her other side and then up by her rucksack.

He's got it. That's the problem.

What? He can't even touch it. Rysha hadn't taken off her boots or any of her clothing, not in this monster-infested cave system, so she surged to her feet quickly and grabbed her rifle.

He got creative. He's trying to reprogram it for you, but... come on. Hurry. I can't break the lock he's got on it. I'm hoping you can. This way.

Even though Jaxi didn't give further directions via words, Rysha felt an otherwise inexplicable pull in one direction. It guided her past the others, Blazer, Kaika, Leftie, and Duck all sleeping still, and then along the pool. The team had left a couple of lanterns burning low, and as soon as she headed up a rock formation and into pitch blackness, she realized she would need one.

Before she could turn back, a blue light appeared up ahead, hovering over the shoreline a third of the way along the pool. It showed up in the reflection of the water and drove shadows away all around it. The light was enough, Rysha decided, for her to make her way to it. Assuming that was Jaxi.

It's not the dragon. Hurry up.

Yes, ma'am.

Rysha ran over the uneven rocks the best she could, but she had to climb and jump often. Once, her toes slid off a dubious foothold, and her knee slammed down on the rock, all her weight behind it. She kept from crying out, not wanting to wake up the whole camp, but she swore vehemently under her breath. Only worry for Trip propelled her back into motion without stopping to investigate what was sure to become an epic bruise on her kneecap.

"Worry about it later," she ordered herself, scrambling over the next rock mound.

When she reached the blue light, it faded so she could look at it—under it—without squinting. She sucked in an alarmed breath.

Trip sat cross-legged but flopped forward, his chest and head on the ground, his hand pressed to the flat of Dorfindral's green-glowing blade. He appeared unconscious, or worse.

It would be better if he was *unconscious,* Jaxi said. *He's in a lot of pain. Go yank his hand away. Please.*

Rysha leaped down into the hollow he'd chosen and dropped to her knees, ignoring the pain in her right one. She gripped his arm to pull it back, but his fingers tightened around the sword. Blood dripped onto the stone floor as the edges bit into his hand.

"Trip," she whispered. "Stop. Let go."

Rysha rested her palm on his back, wincing at the spasms of pain that coursed through his body, as if he were some prisoner being flogged over and over with a whip. With her other hand, she gripped Dorfindral's hilt, but she dared not pull the sword away, not with Trip's bare fingers wrapped around the edges.

"*Meyusha,*" she told the sword, speaking the words with the firmness of a drill sergeant barking commands. "He's a friend. Ease off. *Meyusha.*"

Green light flashed from Dorfindral, as if an explosion had gone off, and she squeezed her eyes shut. Some alien, intangible energy surrounded her, something she couldn't identify, but the air around her crackled with power. That power also crackled around the sword and around Trip.

The chapaharii *blade is prepared,* Trip's voice rang in her mind. *Your arrival is timely.*

His body wasn't moving, and she still sensed the pain flogging him over and over, but the words came out calmly, as if another Trip who was completely detached from his body spoke them.

What do I do? she yelled back in her mind.

Choose new command words, words that will mean something to you but that won't be easily guessed by others. Especially by me.

How can I—you're right here with me. How can I tell them to you without letting you know them?

Trip hesitated. *Direct your thoughts at the sword. I will try not to listen. Also, I believe I can key the sword to your blood to give you and your descendants the highest preference in the sword's eyes. But please hurry. I—the heart in my body is close to failing.*

Shit, Trip! Tears sprang to her eyes, and she was tempted to yank the sword out of his grip, and the hells with his hand. He could magic his fingers back on later if they fell off.

Just hurry and choose. It will not take long to finish this.

You could have warned me so I would have something prepared. Rysha groped for appropriate words, knowing she would never ask him to do this again. She hadn't asked him to do it *once*. She'd been afraid it would be like this.

Doubting that she would be able to hide the words from him in the future, she thought of terms that named the different categories of ancient Dakrovian potsherds. Based on dead tribal languages from the continent, they had unwieldy names with unseemly numbers of vowels tangled together. They would be hard for other people to remember and even harder for them to pronounce.

I'm done, she told Trip.

Nothing happened. She shook his shoulder and spoke aloud. "Trip? I'm done. Let go, or I'll—"

He gasped, and his bloody fingers opened. He rolled away from the blade, jerking his hand to his chest and curling into a ball on his side.

Tremors shook his body, and blood trickled from his mouth. He looked like a man in his death throes.

"Jaxi? No, Azarwrath. You're the healer, aren't you?" Rysha looked for the soulblades, assuming they were nearby. Yes, he'd removed their scabbards from his belt and stacked them to the side.

Yes, an older male voice spoke into her mind. *This is not a typical wound, and my healing methods may be inadequate, but I shall try.*

Rysha crawled to Trip, again resting her hand on him, on his shoulder this time. His eyes were clamped shut, his face contorted in pain, and the tears that had formed in her eyes earlier rushed down her cheeks. She wanted to gather him into her arms and soothe the pain, but she worried about interfering with whatever the soulblade could do.

She knelt as close as she could to him, dropping her head to his shoulder and finding the hand he hadn't cut with hers. She gripped it, willing her fingers to somehow lend him support and comfort. Also, she vowed that she would smack him if he survived this. Why had he risked so much just to alter something that wasn't that important?

No, she admitted. That wasn't true. It was important. She knew he'd been disappointed in himself after the night at the spring, and hadn't she also been disappointed in him? Frustrated that he could, even accidentally, take her free will from her? This was his answer, his attempt at fixing the problem. Making it so he couldn't tell her sword to back down, making it so all their interactions had to be on even terms, that if she was to stand at his side, it would be by her choice.

She kissed the side of his neck. "You're a good man, Trip," she whispered. "Even if this was really stupid."

Are you supposed to call a dying man stupid? Trip's words sounded weakly in her mind, a whisper.

No, but you're not dying. I won't allow it.

You won't? I thought Azarwrath was the one healing me.

Yes, but I'm nuzzling your neck. You're more likely to come back for that than for him.

This is very true.

Some of the tension eased from his body, and she lay down on her side next to him, her face to the back of his neck and her arm around him. The rocks were about as comfortable as a bed of nails, but she wouldn't move until he was well enough to get up and go back to the camp. Or someone came looking for them and made jokes about canoodling.

I always imagined canoodling being more vigorous, Trip murmured into her mind.

When you get better, we can get vigorous if you want. But these rocks aren't very conducive to it. I imagine a lot of bruising would happen. She kept herself from thinking of the giant one she would have on her knee in the morning. If it hadn't already turned purple.

Bruises sound delightfully benign right now.

I'll bet. Do yourself a favor, and don't touch any chapaharii *swords again.*

That seems wise, at least until I have more time to study and find methods that would be less dangerous to—

Your heart almost stopped three times, Telryn, the male voice said firmly, ringing in Rysha's mind as well as Trip's. *Do listen to this woman and follow her advice.*

Rysha's arm tightened around Trip at this confirmation of how close he'd come to dying.

Trip didn't argue with the soulblade, and a sense of sheepishness emanated from him. He shifted to lie on his back and look up at Rysha.

She pulled off her spectacles so she could wipe a sleeve across her eyes, though she knew she couldn't hide the moisture gleaming there. When she lowered her hand, she also did her best to wipe the blood from the side of Trip's face.

His expression grew wry. "I guess that means you're not holding me because of the ruggedly appealing and masculine way I'm lying here." His voice sounded rough, like speaking hurt.

"You can use your telepathy on me. As to your appeal, it's quite nice, blood and all."

She'd propped herself up for the wiping, but she lay down again on her side, facing him and resting her hand on his chest. She shifted to rest her forehead against his temple.

I'm relieved to hear that. About my appeal. Trip closed his eyes, but he found her hand again, threading his fingers between hers. *I suppose I'd have to crawl down to the pool and wash my face in order to have a chance at getting a kiss.*

It would be a little weird kissing dried blood.

That's what I feared. With his eyes still closed, he looked like he was more likely to fall asleep than go clean up.

Such things could wait until he'd rested.

Or so Rysha thought. Movement drew her eye, and she gaped as something that looked like a giant raindrop a couple of feet in height floated away from the pool and toward them.

"Uh, Trip? Is that you?"

"What?" He opened his eyes as the mutant raindrop stopped to hover over his face. Those eyes widened with alarm.

Guessing what was coming, Rysha rolled to the side. She immediately wished she'd stayed there to endure it, since she cracked her knee on the rocks again.

A splash sounded as the equivalent of a bucket of water fell on Trip's face.

He groaned and wiped his eyes. "Thank you so much, Jaxi."

Just doing my part to ensure smooches aren't withheld tonight, Jaxi said cheerfully into their minds.

Rysha brought her fingers to her mouth to hide the giggle that wanted to escape. Aunt Tadelay would say this was an inappropriate time for an unladylike giggle, but with Trip propped up on his elbows, his hair stuck to his head, his face dripping water, and the top half of his uniform jacket soaked, he looked quite bedraggled. And cute.

Rysha thought about crawling back over to his side, but eyed the puddle of water on the rocks around him.

Allow me, Jaxi said.

A gust of warm air came from nowhere, blowing over Rysha, but blowing even harder around Trip. The water under him evaporated as his hair was pushed back from his eyes, fluffed by the wind. When it died down, his usually tidy hair stuck up in a hundred different directions.

This time, Rysha's giggle did escape. She couldn't help it.

He shook his head and flopped back down on the rocks. "I'm glad I don't have a mirror. If my appeal just took a dive off a cliff, I don't want to know."

A real woman doesn't mind a man with mussed hair, Jaxi informed them. *And now that you don't have dried blood spattering your chin, you look far less pitiful overall. If Lieutenant Ravenwood won't kiss you, I'll find a nice female who will.*

Rysha blinked at the threat.

Trip snorted. *In this place? What will it be? A bat?*

No, you're related to the mutated creatures in this cave. I'd have to convince Kaika or Blazer to do it.

I think my odds would be better with a bat.

This is possibly true.

Since the ground was dry, and Trip was mostly dry, if somewhat bedraggled, Rysha returned to him, once again lying down by his side. This must have satisfied Jaxi because she made no more comments about kissing. Rysha wondered if she could convince the soulblade to float her blanket over to cover them up. The cave system wasn't that warm. And Trip was damp. She supposed there were other ways she could warm him up, if he was up for them. He probably wasn't, not after nearly dying.

A man is always up for being warmed by a woman, Jaxi shared.

Azarwrath said his heart almost stopped three times, Rysha replied.

I fail to see your point.

Rysha snorted.

Trip lifted an eyebrow and met her eyes.

"Sardelle's sword is surprisingly invested in you getting attention from a woman," she said, though she couldn't contemplate offering *too* much attention. Her career would not be well served by a surprise pregnancy.

Jaxi sighed dramatically into her mind. *Don't your Iskandian first-aid kits come with those lambskin devices designed to prevent that from happening? I'm positive I've seen soldiers using them.*

I didn't bring a first-aid kit over here.

Extremely short-sighted. If your attention *grows vigorous, I will arrange for one to arrive in a timely manner.*

"I think she likes the idea of romance in general," Trip said, apparently unaware of Jaxi's latest words. "I understand she used to read novels about dragons and humans falling in love."

"Given the dragons I've met, love seems an unlikely emotion to associate with them."

"I'm sure they were fictionalized stories." Trip smiled.

He did look tired, but not… exhausted. Content, actually. Maybe because she was resting her chin on his shoulder and her hand on his chest? He might be able to tell that she'd forgiven him for something that was only nominally his fault. He needn't have nearly gotten himself killed to earn her forgiveness, as she doubted she could have stayed upset with him for long, but she appreciated what he'd tried to do. What he'd maybe *done*. They would have to test the sword later. But now, she preferred to stay like this, the warmth of his body contrasting nicely with the cold stones underneath them. The warmth of Trip's eyes as he gazed at her through his lashes, his lids drooping.

She couldn't tell if he was thinking bedroom thoughts or falling asleep. Even though this wasn't exactly the ideal place for expressions of romantic interest, a twinge of disappointment went through her at the idea of him dozing off. She would understand if he did, but she was wide awake now, her thumb brushing a button of his jacket. It would be easy to unfasten that button. And a few more.

"You hurt your knee," he murmured.

"Just a benign bruise."

"Mm." His gaze never strayed from her face, but a warm tingle started under her kneecap and spread all around the joint.

A hint of his power emanated from him as he healed her, the aura she'd noticed around him before when he called upon his magic. As it had before, it sparked something within her, a warm tingle that was nowhere near her knee, and thoughts of getting closer entered her mind, of pressing her chest to his and—

Trip closed his eyes and looked away. "Sorry," he whispered, and she could almost feel him trying to dampen down that aura.

The warmth disappeared from her knee, but she could tell without moving it that it was better than ever.

"Sorry for healing me?" She rested her hand on his cheek, wanting him to turn his face back toward her.

"For being... I don't know. Dragonly. On you."

"It's called *scylori*," she said dryly.

"Yeah." He kept his eyes closed as if he worried it would seep out of him. "I know it makes you uncomfortable."

She bit her lip. Had she said that? Maybe she'd thought it. It was true that she was more comfortable with Trip the pilot and socially awkward engineer, perhaps because that part of him attracted her intellectual side, and she'd always put so much more stock in rational thinking than in emotions. But she had to admit that her body, and maybe her soul, had been drawn to his dragon side almost from the beginning. Seeing him use his magic attracted her. She couldn't help it. She found the power of the attraction alarming and feared she might lose herself—her independence—in it, the way she had the other night, but at the same time, it wasn't fair for him to have to be something less than he was because it made her uncomfortable. Besides, was she truly afraid that something bad would happen if she gave in to her emotional side? She trusted Trip. Maybe she didn't fully trust herself and that was why she feared the idea of losing control. But that was her issue to work through, not his.

"Trip," she whispered. "Telryn—do you prefer that?"

"Not really." He smiled. "Sidetrip always seemed to kind of fit me."

"Your superiors seem to agree." She stroked the side of his face. "I care about you, and I don't want you to have to hide a part of yourself because of me. You should be… all of you. Always. I can get used to it. I like odd boys, remember?"

He met her eyes again. "Odd *boys*? Are there a lot of them? Do I have competition?"

"Not a lot. And those other boys don't have a huge bulge in their pocket that's getting me excited."

His smile turned into a smirk. "That's a fish."

"You don't have a better nickname for it than that? Most men do."

His smirk deepened. "Do you want to see it?"

"Absolutely."

She could have shifted away to give him more room to unbutton the flap of his cargo pocket, but admitted to getting a zing of pleasure when his arm brushed her chest. She wanted to get closer instead of farther away.

Trip drew out the finished toy which did indeed look like a fish. A fish in multiple pieces that fit together. Curious, she took it from him, experimentally moving a couple of the pieces.

"It's a puzzle?" she asked, realizing that if she shifted a few more of them around, she would have trouble getting it back into the shape of a fish.

"Yes. The kids may have to grow into it, but it's the kind of thing I would have liked as a boy."

"As a boy? Or now?"

"Both."

His eyes gleamed, and she found it hard to look away. She didn't want to look away. She wanted to be closer, to spend the night with him.

He lifted his fingers to her lips, tracing them gently, and a warm zing went through her body again. It was different from when he'd healed her knee, but it also felt good. More than good. It curled through her, tingling in all her sensitive places, and she realized this was more than a response from her own body.

"Are you using magic on me, Trip?" she murmured, lowering her lips to his, wondering why it had taken so long.

"Yeah," he murmured against her lips, then fell to speaking telepathically, which had the benefit of not interrupting kissing. *I want to be better for you than playing with explosives.*

Remembering the way Kaika had mocked Trip, Rysha quelled the teasing response that came to mind. Besides, another little zing went through her, touching her from the inside out as his arms came around her, pulling her against his chest, and she couldn't have managed anything that wouldn't be a lie.

I look forward to it, she thought, then placed her spectacles on a nearby rock as they deepened the kiss. She looked forward to the rest of the night.

CHAPTER 22

TRIP WOKE UP WITH A grin on his face and Rysha snuggled in his arms, a *bare* Rysha in his *bare* arms. He wasn't sure where the blanket they were wrapped in had come from, but it took the edge off the coldness that seeped up from the rocks.

You're welcome, Jaxi spoke into his mind. *And I woke you because Duck woke up, and he's looking around, wondering why nobody's on guard. I've informed him that Azarwrath and I have been standing guard—again, you're welcome—but the others are probably going to wake up soon, so you and your lieutenant may want to put clothes on and mosey back to camp.*

Thank you, Trip said, though he didn't want to talk to Jaxi or mosey anywhere. *And her name is Rysha, not my lieutenant.*

Yes, yes, I'm sure it will also be honey, dear, love, and snoffle partner soon.

Trip kissed Rysha's shoulder, wanting to simply enjoy having her in his arms. Even if a rock was gouging him in the hip. He wondered if she was still interested in taking him for a weekend in that cottage at the back of her family's estate. It probably had a *bed.* But once they returned to the real world—and she returned to the influence of her family—would she be embarrassed to be seen with someone like him?

Someone who oozed dragonness—*scylori*, whatever—and had animal half-siblings roaming the world and trying to kill people?

No, he didn't think she would turn away from him because of embarrassment, but having a relationship might be less simple back in the capital. He would enjoy this now, as he'd enjoyed their night together. He smiled and, sensing her wakening, moved his lips to her mouth. He hoped Jaxi wasn't waking her up with sarcasm, like some pre-dawn bugle call. With a thought toward soothing away any intrusions, he slid his hand over her hip under the blanket, caressing her gently with his fingers and his mind.

"Mm, Trip," she murmured against his lips, then slid her tongue out to taste him. "You're amazing."

"Amazingly odd?" he said lightly, though her groggy honesty filled his throat with a lump of emotion and almost made it hard to get the words out.

"Yeah, but I can hardly judge after the unpronounceable commands I assigned to a millennia-old magical sword." Her eyes opened, and a smirk quirked her lips. "I may be as odd as you."

He returned the smirk. He had done his best not to listen as she'd assigned the words, but he'd had the vague impression of ancient pots categorized by age, shape, and whether they had male or female reproductive organs painted on them. He would most definitely not intrude into her thoughts to hunt for the specific command words.

"Can we have sex again or do we have to go?" Rysha asked.

He blinked at her honesty. "You are indeed Major Kaika's protégé, aren't you?"

"Apparently so, but I have no need to go to that Sage place with her, not now."

"I'm glad to hear that." He kissed her, his hand drifting along her thigh again, and he was thinking that they had time to enjoy each other's company before returning to the camp, but a bang and an alarmed shout floated across the pool.

Sighing, Trip released Rysha. She took a little longer releasing him, her leg hooked possessively over his under the blanket, and he vowed that he would find a way to stay with her when they got back. To make a relationship work. He would go to her parents in his dress uniform and recite for them a list of reasons why he was an excellent choice for their daughter, even if it included a pedigree that was unlike any other. Or maybe he would offer to repair something for them. Did Rysha have any young nieces or nephews in need of clockwork toys? He could branch out from fish. Perhaps submarines or fliers?

"I don't think you're contemplating sex," Rysha said, her eyes narrowed. "You've got the same look on your face you had when you were plucking up scraps of metal from beside the trail."

"In fact, I was contemplating what I could do to convince your family that we should have sex. Often."

"Oh? Let me know if you come up with something genius. As a rule, my father doesn't approve of me getting horizontal unless it's to dive for a ball or to tackle someone."

"You can tackle me."

"Now?" Her eyes crinkled.

Another bang and barked order came from the camp. Trip swept his senses in that direction to make sure giant bats weren't eating anyone. He didn't detect any strange creatures—or un-strange ones, either—but the group did seem agitated.

"Soon," he said, rising to his feet and picking up his clothing, which wasn't in the usual tidy stack he made when he disrobed.

His jacket was crumpled next to their blanket. His shirt was draped artfully over a stalagmite—Rysha's panties dangled from the same rock. His socks were wadded up, only inches from having met with calamity at the pool's edge. His trousers... ah, there they were. That was an impressive height.

"It was kind of Jaxi to bring a blanket," Rysha said, grinning as she dressed and watched him retrieve his clothing. Somehow, most of hers, aside from the panties, had found a closer berth.

"Did you suggest that?" Trip spotted the tongs he had created from the iron box. He grabbed them, realizing he would have to change them back so Blazer could carry the ingot without him getting a headache any time he was close.

"I might have."

"We'll have to get her a gift for her thoughtfulness." Trip would happily get both of the soulblades gifts since they had kept their swordly mouths closed while he and Rysha had been having their passionate moments.

"Indeed so. What does one buy for a sword? I can't imagine she would be interested in a massage."

I do enjoy getting my blade oiled by a handsome young man, Jaxi said as Rysha and Trip headed back across the rocks toward the camp, their respective scabbards in hand. Trip still sensed Dorfindral sending him dark thoughts. Apparently, their night of bonding hadn't meant much to the sword. *I'm certain Azarwrath does too,* Jaxi added.

Azarwrath made a noise in their minds akin to throat clearing. *Young men need not be involved.*

Old men? Jaxi suggested.

Women who know their proper place in a man's life.

Such as standing in front of the man and being supported by him?

Trip had more trouble deciphering Azarwrath's next sound. Maybe that was for the best.

"*Shoot* them," came Blazer's voice across the rocks.

A faint splash reached Trip's ears as he finished his work of turning the tongs back into a box.

Frowning, he swept his senses out again, certain some creature must have invaded the camp. But once again, he didn't detect any life in the cavern besides that of his teammates.

"Ma'am," Duck said, "are you sure? I think they're just—"

"That one's *looking* at me," Blazer said. "And it spat something. Right there. It's on the ground, *smoking.*"

"Should we… uhm, shoot?" Leftie asked.

As Trip climbed over the rock formation where he'd been sitting watch the night before, the camp came into view, along with what had everyone concerned. Out in the water, some only a few yards from the bank, grayish-green bulbous heads on one- to two-foot high stalks waved back and forth. Not animal heads, but… flower heads? They reminded him of giant tulips, but their petals flexed and tightened, their strange heads turned toward the camp. They definitely acted like they were alive.

"They're *flowers*," Duck said.

"I don't think so." Leftie had his rifle butt pressed to his shoulder.

Kaika, who stood right at the shoreline with Eryndral in one hand and her opposite fist propped on her hip, frowned at Leftie. "Just be careful where you aim if you shoot. And remember that bullets *ricochet.*"

Kaika pointed her sword toward the hanging stalactites and the stone wall on the opposite side of the pool. She also pointed her sword at a flower bobbing and waving its head at her from eight or ten feet away. She looked like she wanted to slice Eryndral through its inch-thick stem to see if that put an end to the plant's agitation.

Leftie scowled but held his fire.

"Rysha?" Trip whispered as they slid down the rock formation to join the others, barely noticed as their comrades focused on the eight or nine flower heads waving at them. "It's not possible for *plants* to have dragon blood, is it?"

Trip couldn't fathom the scenario in which a dragon could reproduce with a plant, but he also had a hard time imagining a dragon and a bat getting together.

"I haven't heard of it," Rysha said.

Kaika waved her sword. "Maybe we should just—"

The petals on the flower head closest to her opened wide. Kaika jumped to the side as some kind of thick liquid spat out. If she hadn't been watching and moved quickly enough, it would have struck her. Instead, it spattered to the ground, hitting the corner of someone's blanket. The material promptly smoked as corrosive goo ate through it.

"—pack up and get out of here," Kaika finished, turning a sour eye on the plant.

"They're not magical," Trip said, noticing that her *chapaharii* blade wasn't glowing.

Now that he could see the flowers, his senses confirmed there was something there, and he could tell they had large lily-pad-shaped bases attached to the rock bed under the water, but they didn't register as anything more interesting than foliage. He didn't feel anything more from them than he had from the cactuses they had passed in the desert.

"Nice of you two to join us," Blazer said, glaring at them. "And so good to know that someone was faithfully standing watch over the camp all night."

Trip grimaced, belatedly realizing he should have woken someone else up to take his place on watch when he left. But he had wanted to work with the sword without anyone knowing about it. And Jaxi had said she would keep an eye on things.

I was on watch, Jaxi said, and from the way several people twitched, Trip knew she shared the words with everybody. *Until I sensed that several people were awake. I believe Leftie was looking right at the water when the plants first appeared, so you were not taken unaware. In addition, I convinced several large badger-like creatures to leave the camp alone during the middle of the night, so you are welcome.*

Jaxi did an impressive job of sounding indignant. Trip mostly felt embarrassed. The night before, he might have left with noble intentions, but he'd forgotten about the sword as soon as Rysha had lain down beside him. And then she'd told him he should be himself, *all* of himself around her, and he'd wanted nothing more than to show her everything.

Yes, yes, she was impressed by your amazing dragonness. Now, can we focus on these odd plants? They don't seem to like your friends much.

Trip's cheeks warmed, and he walked forward to stand next to the others, tossing the iron box toward Blazer's blanket while he created a barrier to protect them from further plant spittle. After warning them not to shoot while they were behind it, he silently said, *I thought you couldn't read my thoughts as easily now, Jaxi.*

It doesn't take a genius to guess what you're thinking about when you're gazing at your lieutenant with gooey eyes. Also, your bank vault door was flapping open in the breeze.

Ah.

Another plant spat its corrosive ichor, and Duck jumped to the side. But the brownish gunk spattered against Trip's invisible barrier. It appeared to hang in the air for a few seconds before slowly dripping down.

"That's disgusting," Leftie said.

"It's actually quite fascinating," Rysha said. "I wouldn't have expected to find plants down here. Plants need the light from the sun to engage in photosynthesis."

"What about the mold in the other place?" Leftie's lip curl suggested he didn't find the plants fascinating.

"Mold requires oxygen to grow, but not light. It's also not a plant. Molds are eukaryotic micro-organisms that live by decomposing dead organic material."

Trip almost asked what kind of dead organic material had been in that chamber at the outpost, but then he remembered the sacrificing table and imagined blood dripping from it and onto the stone floor. Less grimly, he supposed organic matter could have come downstream in that river.

"There's not a lecture coming, is there?" Blazer asked. "Because I think it should wait until we get out of here. Everyone, pack your gear up while our wayward captain protects us."

"That wasn't the start of a lecture," Rysha whispered to Trip. "I was simply answering a question."

"It was an interesting answer," he said. "If you want to expand on it, I believe Major Blazer just invited you to offer a lecture as soon as the group moves from this area."

"What?" Blazer shook out her blanket. "I didn't say that."

"I heard it that way, ma'am," Duck said, winking at Rysha.

"I didn't," Leftie grumbled, glowering at the plants.

A couple more of them had popped up, and Trip sensed even more stirring on the bottom of the pool. Many of the attached pads that seemed to be the plants' bases were gathered around vents in the rock floor down there. He sensed air bubbles trickling from those vents and also that the air was warm. Maybe the strange plants were able to live by utilizing some geothermal energy leaking up from within the earth.

"I suppose taking a sample of one wouldn't be wise," Rysha said, gazing sadly at the flower heads. "Since they're clearly agitated with us and seem far more like animals than plants. I have friends at the university who might be interested in studying them. My sister might like samples too. She studies botany."

Trip recalled that Rysha had collected some of the "intriguing mold" specimens from the outpost. Would her sister get those too?

It was too bad his mother hadn't lived to meet Rysha. Trip was certain she would have appreciated her academic tendencies—and respect for interesting plants.

"Oh!" he blurted, a thought jolting him. "Could these *plants* be what brought my mother here?"

"They certainly are unique," Rysha said. "I have no idea if they have medicinal properties, but I'm sure an herbalist would be fascinated by them. And they do seem like the kind of quirky thing that might be mentioned in journals by travelers who found these caves."

A flower spat its corrosive goo in Kaika's direction. It splashed against Trip's barrier, but she glared balefully at the plant.

"By travelers who *survived* finding these caves," Rysha amended dryly.

"You want a sample?" Kaika hefted her sword over her shoulder. "I can get you a sample. Trip, lower that barrier."

"We sure that's wise, ma'am?" Duck asked. "We got a saying back home about how it's safest for the fly to go *over* the forest dotted with carnivorous Provarian flytraps rather than through it."

Trip looked at Rysha. He was inclined to leave the plants alone and pack up and leave, but if she wanted a sample…

"Trip, if a superior officer gives you an order," Blazer said, looking up from packing Kaika's ruck as well as her own, "you don't look at your girlfriend for permission before following it."

Trip rubbed his face. He didn't regret spending the night with Rysha, not for a damn minute, but he had to admit that if they'd been behaving responsibly, they would have waited until they finished their mission to engage in extracurricular activities. He couldn't blame Blazer for being sarcastic—and a little corrective. She was right.

"Yes, ma'am." Trip waved a hand to let Kaika know he'd lowered the barrier in front of her.

Kaika strode into the water, eyes intent as she approached the plant. Several of the heads rotated toward her. She shifted her angle of approach so she could keep them in her line of sight.

Trip, worried they had some sort of collective intelligence, or at least awareness, reconstructed his barrier so that only the plant she approached would be able to shoot her. Unfortunately, he couldn't place a barrier in front of *it* or she wouldn't be able to get her sample.

Kaika swung her sword like an executioner lopping off someone's head. Belatedly, it occurred to Trip that he could have done that with magic. She needn't have strode out waist-deep in the water.

But her sword cut easily through the plant's stem, severing the head. The flower flopped into the water right beside her.

"I'll take a sample of the stem, too, please," Rysha said.

As Kaika grabbed the flower head and stuffed it in her pocket, the nearby ones fired their ichor at her with eerie precision. She anticipated the attack and ducked. Trip thought she would have been all right even if his barrier hadn't been there, but he was satisfied when the ichor spattered against it well away from Kaika.

"Thanks," Kaika said, and sliced off part of the stem that still stuck upright. "I—gaaawk!"

She jerked her foot up, her gaze lurching down toward the water. She tried to leap back, but something had her leg.

Trip swore and strode to the water's edge. He'd forgotten about all the plant pads there that hadn't deployed their flowers. Several of the dormant ones had come to life. Instead of simply shooting their flowers up above the surface, the flowers and stems were stretching toward Kaika. One already wrapped around her ankle.

Before Trip could form a magical attack, Kaika drove Eryndral's point down into the water. Even without being able to see through to the dark bottom of the pool, she managed to skewer the pad and slice off the stem. That killed the plant, but other tendrils reached toward her, some under water and some above.

Trip kept the barrier up because the original threats he'd walled off were shooting more of their goo. The entire pool had come alive with the plants, and they were all focused on Kaika now.

She wielded the sword as if she were in the middle of a battlefield, not simply flailing but striking with impressive accuracy, especially given the barrage of enemies that had appeared. Including more stems that proved to have the flexibility of vines as they snapped out and wrapped around her legs.

Kaika tried to back to the water's edge as she fought, lopping off flower heads left and right, but the plants fought valiantly to keep her in the pool. From the way they tugged at her, they seemed to want to drag her under the surface.

In addition, a keening sound started up. Was that coming from the plants? Or had they triggered some magical alarm?

Splashes sounded as someone else charged into the water to help Kaika. Rysha. She raced in with Dorfindral in her hand. It glowed a faint green, but Trip suspected that was because of him and his magical barrier rather than the plants. Whatever these crazy things were, they weren't magical.

That keening is coming from the plants, Azarwrath observed. *The ones with their petals spread. They're acting like trumpets. Shall we destroy them? It would be a simple matter to incinerate them, even in the water.*

I do love incineration, Jaxi put in.

Trip manipulated his barrier, trying to protect the women. He was tempted to try to attack the ones near them at the same time, but he didn't want to accidentally hurt Rysha or Kaika.

Do not think so small, Telryn, Azarwrath warned. *Remember the tidal wave you created? You have the power to end simple confrontations such as this.*

I remember that the people in those boats all died in that tidal wave, Trip thought grimly. Though he worried about Rysha and Kaika, they weren't hurt yet, and Kaika was proving rather amazing with that sword. Also, she was grinning as she spun about, slicing off the flower heads leering in from all sides. With Rysha's help, they were making their way back up toward the shoreline. *For all I know, these could be the only plants like this in the entire world. I don't want to be responsible for making a species extinct.*

I understand, Azarwrath said. *It is a worthwhile consideration. This place does appear to be isolated and unique.*

A little incineration wouldn't hurt, Jaxi said, sounding less understanding.

But Kaika and Rysha had made it out of the water, hacked-up gore sticking to their wet uniforms. The plants did not—could not—follow them onto dry land, but they continued to wave menacingly from the water. Many of the stems had lost their flowers, but that didn't keep them from posturing like apes beating their chests.

Rysha glanced down at her ankle where a vine was wrapped three times around it, its severed end dragging on the rocks. Grimacing, she used Dorfindral's tip to pry it free.

Kaika picked up a flower head floating near the water's edge and grinned at Rysha. "How *many* samples did you want?"

"With all due respect, ma'am, you're a maniac."

"Yes, I am." Kaika's grin widened. "Do you have something to put this in, or does it just go in my soggy pocket?"

Trip could barely hear their conversation over the keening that continued to come from the water. Every single pad on the bottom had sent its flower above the surface. Even though Kaika and Rysha had severed dozens of them, many more remained, their petals unfurled and making noise.

Trip kept his barrier raised, but the plants weren't shooting anymore. They were all too busy adding their voices to that unearthly keening. The torturous song echoed from the walls, and he wouldn't have been surprised to learn it was audible all the way back at the entrance to the cave system.

"Come on." Blazer shoved Kaika's pack at her—her own was already on her back. "I don't like the way that sounds like an alarm. We're getting out of here."

Trip shifted uneasily. If the noise was floating back to the entrance, it might be floating deeper into the cave system too. Was it possible that was intentional? That the plants functioned as some kind of natural alarm system? Or was their existence here merely a coincidence?

Leftie had packed Trip's gear, and he tossed the bedroll and rucksack to him.

"Thank you," Trip said, keeping the barrier up while he shrugged on his belongings.

While the rest of the team shouldered their own gear, he eyed the plants again, wondering if he could coerce them somehow to fall silent. Without killing them. Dragons and sorcerers had the power to manipulate human beings and animals. Couldn't that extend to the plant kingdom?

But they had no minds to manipulate, no thoughts with which he could tinker. Still, he gazed toward the swaying flowers and imagined them furling their petals and sinking back below the water. As agitated as they were, he had the sense that they were running low on energy, that they couldn't keep up the display indefinitely.

Rest, he told them. *Return to your warm watery sanctuary and rest.*

Are you talking to the plants? Jaxi asked.

I'm trying to, yes.

That's odd.

Odder than talking to a sword?

Definitely.

Weren't there ever any sorcerers that specialized in magic related to plants? Trip sent his silent suggestion to the plants again because it had seemed to help. Their keening wasn't quite as loud, and a couple in the back slipped below the surface.

Yes, and they were odd. One of my handlers was like that. He thought plants were superior lifeforms, and he only ate meat and fish because he didn't want to harm the divinely blessed trees, bushes, and flowers providing oxygen for humans to breathe.

You're lucky Sardelle came along.

This is true. Even if she doesn't let me incinerate things as often as I'd wish. I do hope she'll return to adventuring once the children are old enough to support themselves.

Considering her newest child was only a few days old—and more might come along—Trip couldn't imagine that being any time soon. *In twenty years?*

Twenty? I was thinking more like five.

I don't think children can support themselves at age five.

Marinka is learning how to make cookies. What more do humans need to know?

"Trip, are you coming?" Rysha called, waving a pouch in the air. Her samples?

Blazer, Leftie, Kaika, and Duck had already disappeared into the passage leading deeper into the cave system.

"Yes," he said and strode toward her.

As he walked out of the cavern, the keening stopped and the rest of the plants disappeared beneath the surface. He didn't know if he had been responsible or if they were simply done fighting now that the intruders had left their place. He also didn't know if they had silenced the alarm soon enough or if every creature that made the system its home was now alert and ready for Trip's team.

CHAPTER 23

AFTER MORE THAN AN HOUR of walking, Rysha began to believe that they might have escaped the plant pool without repercussions. She'd been feeling like a fool for giving Kaika the idea that she wanted a sample. She should have known that nothing good would come from cutting down plants with that much awareness.

"We're getting close," Trip said quietly, his eyes toward the dark passage ahead, a passage that had grown surprisingly wide, straight, and clear of debris shortly after they'd left the pool. The remains of old rusty ore cart tracks ran down the center of the tunnel. In spots, they disappeared, then started up again with no apparent reason for the gaps.

Rysha couldn't see anything in the darkness ahead, but was sure Trip was looking with more than his eyes.

"To the dragon?" Blazer asked.

She walked at the front with Trip and Rysha. Kaika, Leftie, and Duck walked behind, glancing backward often. Kaika, in particular, seemed to believe some pursuit would find them in the aftermath of the plant incident. Rysha also glanced back often, for the same reason. She wondered if Jaxi's words about badger creatures had been true, or if the soulblade had been trying to cover for Trip and Rysha and their unexplained absence. Technically, Rysha hadn't been on watch, and Trip's watch period should have ended by the time she went out looking for him, so their only error had been in not waking up the next person. Though she supposed wandering off to have sex wasn't typically approved of on military missions.

"Perhaps," Trip replied to Blazer.

"*Perhaps?* I thought you sorcerers could *feel* dragons from a dozen miles away."

"From forty or fifty miles away, typically. But the place we're getting close to is shrouded by some kind of protective magic that makes it hard for Jaxi, Azarwrath, and me to detect what exactly is inside. If Agarrenon Shivar is in there, he may be in a stasis chamber." He summed up some more thoughts on that, perhaps from discussions he'd had with the soulblades.

"If he's sick and in a stasis chamber, how did he impregnate a bunch of bats?" Blazer asked.

Trip shrugged a shoulder. "A great mystery of the universe."

"Technically, he may have only impregnated one bat," Rysha said, "though now that I think about it, I seem to remember that bats aren't particularly fecund and usually only have a single pup at a time."

"So, he impregnated *multiple* bats. And a woman. While sick and dying. Trip, your story doesn't make sense."

"It's not my story."

Blazer removed her latest cigar and arched her eyebrows at him.

"I mean, it *is*, but I don't know any more than you do."

"Not any more at *all*? That's alarming."

"Yes, ma'am." Trip looked glum.

Rysha wanted to hug him, but not with Blazer looking on.

To her surprise, Blazer offered her cigar to Trip. "You look like you could use something bracing. And it'll sharpen your mind if we're about to go into battle."

Trip's mouth dropped open.

"Don't fall for it, Trip," Rysha said, though she believed it was a peace offering or something similar rather than a trick. "Kaika gave me one to try in the Antarctic, and I left half a lung on the railing of the airship."

"You inhaled, didn't you?" Blazer asked.

"Not intentionally."

"Just take a puff, hold it in your mouth, and let it trickle up into your sinuses. You can try blowing the smoke out through your nose."

"And this will be bracing?" Trip asked dubiously, though he accepted the cigar.

Like Rysha, he probably felt it was the kind of thing comrades did, sharing cigars, and that Blazer's offering meant something. It amused Rysha to know Trip probably felt even more of an outsider than she did and wanted his superior officers to think well of him.

"Not for your lungs," Rysha said. "Or your nostrils. Or your mouth. It may clear your sinuses of odd alien plant pollen."

"Only pollen?" Kaika asked from behind them. "I think I inhaled a flower petal and got it stuck up there."

Blazer thumped Trip on the chest with the back of her hand. "Pass it back to Kaika after you take a puff. Clearly, she has an even greater need."

Trip snorted and lifted the cigar to his lips. He barely seemed to inhale, but he did exhale a small amount of smoke through his nostrils. Rysha was a little disappointed that he didn't cough and gag, but maybe his magic protected him.

Or he followed instructions better than you did, Jaxi spoke into her mind as he passed the cigar back to Kaika.

Are you sure? I know Trip pretty well now, and that seems unlikely.

This is true.

A hum reverberated from Dorfindral's scabbard. Rysha thought it had to do with Jaxi's contact, but the soulblade fell silent, and the hum intensified as the group continued down the passage. Ahead, it bent slightly and a faint light grew discernible.

"That's it," Trip breathed, gripping Azarwrath's hilt.

He didn't warn them to get ready or brace themselves, but Rysha could see his tension in the set of his jaw and the way he carried his shoulders.

"What do you sense?" she whispered.

He shook his head. She couldn't tell if it was because he had no words to articulate what he sensed or because he didn't think there was time to talk.

On her other side, Blazer checked her rifle, making sure it was fully loaded. Kaika moved up to walk beside them, Eryndral drawn and glowing green in her hand. Wordlessly, she returned the cigar.

Blazer put it out and tucked it away.

"We're going to try talking first, right?" Rysha whispered. "If he's awake? Our whole mission is to get his assistance."

"*If* he's awake," Trip said. "Yes. But I think that will have to wait."

"Wait for what?"

Another tense head shake.

Rysha would have tried to draw more out of him, but a faint sound reached her ears, something between a scrape and a rumble. It reminded her of a train rolling along tracks, and she glanced at the twin iron rails they walked along. They were so rusty, the metal bulbous with the brownish stuff, that she couldn't imagine wheels rolling along it without getting stuck.

The light ahead of them grew brighter. Rysha drew Dorfindral, and its light also grew brighter. Soon it and Eryndral glowed so intensely that she thought Blazer might complain. But the grating-rumbling had increased in volume, and Blazer didn't look away from the route ahead.

They rounded a final bend, and a quarter mile ahead, the passage opened into another cavern. It was bright enough to see the wall of a stone structure on the far side. A pyramid? Distance and a few dangling stalactites made it hard to see details.

Rysha thought she glimpsed light glinting off water in there, too, but she spotted something on the floor inside their tunnel and focused on it instead. A mound of clothing or some other fabric lay crumpled on the ground near the tunnel wall.

"I think there's more of that tainted iron up there in the cavern." Trip grimaced, his gaze toward the opening. He didn't seem to have noticed the mound, or he'd already dismissed it. "I sense something that repulses me."

"There's a lot here that repulses me," Leftie muttered.

Trip glanced at Dorfindral and Eryndral, but didn't say whatever was on his mind.

Rysha veered to the wall to look at the mound and played her sword's bright green light over what turned out to be shredded clothing, bones, and the remains of a blanket and pack. Most of the bones were gone, and those that remained had been chewed bare of flesh, so the sight wasn't gory, but it was disturbing. It looked like someone had tried to escape. And hadn't made it.

ORIGINS

The pack and blanket were almost as chewed as the bones, but she could tell they were fairly modern, years old rather than centuries old. Twenty-five years old, perhaps?

She poked at the hole-riddled pack with her sword, wondering if clues remained within it. Who had the person been? A man? The clothes suggested that. But what had brought him here? Tales of the dragon?

"Think this might be someone who came with your mother?" Rysha asked, but neither Trip nor Blazer nor Kaika had stopped advancing.

Leftie and Duck had paused to look with her, or to keep an eye on her, but they only shrugged.

"Something in the pack," Duck said, pointing.

Rysha crouched and pulled out a metal canteen that hadn't yet succumbed to rust. There were also a couple of tin packages of salted and chopped meat, the labels worn off, and a leather-bound book. She gasped and clutched that to her chest. It looked like a journal. If the pages hadn't faded too much, maybe she could find some answers inside.

"Hells," came Blazer's voice from up ahead. "What are *those*?"

Duck and Leftie ran to join her. Blazer, Kaika, and Trip had reached the end of the tunnel and all stared at something inside the cavern and to their right.

As much as Rysha wanted to flip through the journal, she stuffed it into a pocket in her trousers and raced to catch up with the others.

Trip stepped out into the cavern, raising Jaxi and Azarwrath. The blades glowed with red and blue light.

Rysha cursed. Had they already found some enemy to battle?

Lightning shot out of Azarwrath's blade, and a fireball sprang from Jaxi's tip. Kaika ran out into the cavern, Eryndral raised. Blazer leaped to the side of the tunnel and raised her rifle.

Hunt! Dorfindral seemed to cry in Rysha's mind.

"They're immune to my attacks," Trip said, as Rysha reached the mouth of the tunnel. He lowered the soulblades as she stepped out, raising Dorfindral.

She didn't have to search to find a target—*two* targets. Twin giant dark-gray metal constructs rolled around in front of a tunnel that led into a stone pyramid at the back of the cavern. The lower portions of their bodies were metal versions of the pyramid, the bottom half of it, but instead of being stationary, they rolled around on dozens of small wheels, wheels similar to those found on ore carts. Rysha had no idea how to describe the top portions of the constructs. The pyramids seemed to have been sawn off to create platforms, and a body rose up from the center of each one. They had human-like heads and torsos—from her position on the ground, she couldn't tell if they had legs—but they had eight arms instead of two, like some ghastly blend of a person and a spider.

The bodies also appeared to be made from metal, but they were lifelike with those arms moving around and the eyes in those heads shifting to track those below. Those arms all had hands that held weapons: axes, spears, shields, and swords. Half of those weapons glowed a very familiar pale green.

"*Chapaharii*," Rysha gasped in recognition.

Eight of them. Damn.

"Yeah, and they're coming this way," Blazer growled.

Yes, the constructs rolled toward them with deadly intent. The ground had been carved into a flat floor between the pyramid and their tunnel. That made it easy for the wheeled creations to maneuver. Further, the stalactites that had once stretched down across the entire ceiling of the cavern had been shaved away in the middle and would not interfere with the towering constructs.

Rysha spotted heaps of abandoned ore carts in a pile to the right side of the cavern. Their wheels were all gone, and she imagined some ancient engineer making those constructs, some peer of Trip's with a love for machines. *Magical* machines. The water she had glimpsed earlier formed a pool along the left side of the cavern, with yet more stalactites leering down over it. Rysha also spotted a few of those plants waving from the shadows.

"*Meyusha!*" Trip called as the constructs approached the tunnel. "*Meyusha!*"

His voice rang with power. Rysha glanced at Dorfindral, then realized he was directing the command for "stand down" at the *chapaharii* blades the figures atop the pyramids carried.

"Shit, Trip," Kaika growled. "You turned Eryndral off." She shook the sword, but its green glow had been extinguished.

Dorfindral continued to blaze brightly, as if it hadn't heard the command. Because it responded to *new* commands now.

Later, Rysha would be delighted at this proof that Trip's pain hadn't been for naught, but for now, her gaze lurched toward the closest construct. Had the command worked on the four *chapaharii* weapons it carried?

"*Meyusha!*" Trip yelled one more time, but he was already shaking his head.

None of the green-glowing blades that the figures wielded had gone dim like Eryndral.

"It's not working?" Blazer looked at Rysha. "Why not?"

"A dragon or powerful sorcerer might have given them the attack command, which would supersede Trip's order," Rysha guessed, but Trip kept shaking his head.

"I don't sense an enemy like that around."

"Then maybe someone else had the reprogramming idea. Or those weapons could have been created before or after the period during which the Iskandian ones were made and the instructions printed in books. Maybe they're prototypes."

"Trip," Kaika said in exasperation, shaking Eryndral again.

He waved at the blade and gave the command for it to stand ready. It flared back to life, glowing green again.

"Stay in the tunnel, everyone," Blazer ordered. "They're too big to get in here."

She fired as she backed into the tunnel mouth. Duck and Leftie also fired, the reports deafening so close to Rysha's head. Their bullets struck the torsos and heads of the constructs, but bounced off the metal without doing damage.

"I'm getting tired of that," Blazer growled.

"Ancient guardians," Trip spoke, his voice again ringing with power as he stepped in front of the group, both soulblades raised once more. "I am not an intruder. I share the blood of Agarrenon Shivar. Stand aside and let my group pass."

One of the automatons pumped its arm and hurled an axe at him. Trip sprang to the side so swiftly that Rysha was sure some power, either his or the soulblades', assisted him. The glowing green axe whistled past, embedding in the stone wall of the tunnel behind him.

Blazer stepped toward it, as if to claim the weapon for herself. But the axe shook itself free, then flew back toward the construct, landing again in the hand that had thrown it.

"What the hells are these things?" Blazer asked for the second time. "Magic or not magic? If they're magical, how can they be using *chapaharii* weapons?"

Trip shook his head as he climbed to his feet. "Some of the metal from the quarry is embedded in them, and then some regular iron, and then… I'm not sure. Magic was definitely used to create the bodies, and I can sense that it plays a part in ambulating them, but it may be compartmentalized somehow. I'm surprised the *chapaharii* weapons are allowing something even partially magical to use them, but if a dragon played a role in creating these constructs, who knows what was possible?" Trip spread his hands, the soulblades still in them. "I just know I can't affect them with my power. And neither can Azarwrath and Jaxi."

Kaika looked at Rysha, then pointedly at their glowing swords. "This is going to be our battle."

"I don't object to fighting, ma'am," Rysha said, her gaze transfixed by the inexorable approach of the massive constructs, and the unsettlingly human-like automatons built atop them. "But they've each got four *chapaharii* weapons. We've got two between us."

"Is it necessary to fight them if they can't follow us into the tunnel?" Leftie asked.

"If we just leave, we came all this way for nothing," Blazer said. "At the least, I'd like to take those dragon-slaying weapons back to Angulus."

"I have to see what's in the temple," Trip said.

Temple, not pyramid. Did he know something that Rysha didn't yet?

The group withdrew fully into the tunnel, and the constructs rolled back and forth in front of it, as if they were pacing. From wheels to humanoid figures on the top, they towered over thirty feet high, so only the pyramid-like metal bases were visible now.

Trip didn't seem to be looking at the constructs. He gazed through them, with his mind if not his eyes, and toward the tunnel leading into that pyramid.

"My blood calls to me," he added.

"That's as creepy as ghosts walking, Trip," Leftie said.

"I don't disagree," Trip said.

Rysha looked at the back of his head. If he could get into the pyramid, maybe he could do something. Wake up the dragon. Or find the switch that turned off the constructs. If he couldn't hurt them with his magic, there was little point in him staying here.

"All right," Rysha said, nodding to Kaika, who looked like she was ready to leap out, run up the sides of those ambulatory pyramids, and challenge the automatons and all eight of their arms waiting at the top. "Trip needs to get inside the pyramid. That means we get to distract the guards."

She gripped Dorfindral tightly, feeling its hunger burning in her veins. Whatever those constructs were, there was a lot of magic in them. And perhaps also in the stone pyramid on the far side. Dorfindral wanted to destroy it all.

"No." Trip looked back, locking gazes with her. "It's too dangerous. You're outnumbered four weapons to one. Give me some time to figure out a way to attack those things." His gaze was drawn back toward the pyramid as he spoke.

Rysha was no telepath, but she could tell he ached to see what was inside, not stay out and deal with the constructs.

"They've been here thousands of years," Trip said firmly, nodding to himself. "As has the temple. There's no reason to hurry."

"Look, neither of you two are making the decisions around here," Blazer said.

"Ma'am," Trip said. "The best thing to do is—"

A glowing axe spun toward them, aiming right for his chest.

"Trip!" Rysha lunged toward him, but Kaika was the one to step out as Trip scrambled to the side. She whipped Eryndral into the air in front of him, deflecting the axe with her own blade. It struck the wall and fell to the stone floor.

"Gods," Rysha breathed, her heart in her throat. Trip's magical barriers wouldn't do anything to stop the *chapaharii* weapons, and those constructs were targeting him specifically.

"You're mine," Kaika blurted, lunging after the axe.

She landed on it like a cat pouncing on a mouse. Rysha would have laughed if those constructs hadn't been maneuvering around right in front of the tunnel, one probably looking for the angle to hurl another attack.

As soon as Kaika's hand wrapped around the axe hilt, she toppled to the side, blurting a startled squawk. Rysha froze in confusion for a second. Something pulled Kaika down the tunnel, like she was a fish being reeled in on a line. The *axe* was pulling her. Back to its handler.

Cursing, Rysha raced after her. Duck ran at her shoulder. They sprang after Kaika together, gripping her ankles, trying to keep the thing from pulling her out into the cavern.

"I can't let go," Kaika shouted in alarm.

Not willing to release Dorfindral, Rysha could only wrap one hand around Kaika's ankle, but she held on tight and tried to sink her weight into the floor. Duck had both of his hands around her other ankle. He snarled, also fighting the force. But the axe pulled all three of them out of the tunnel.

Light blazed down from the ceiling, though Rysha couldn't see any lamps, and the hulking body of a construct towered above her, silhouetted by that light. Arms moved, and steel glinted.

Acting more on instinct than understanding, Rysha released Kaika and rolled to the side. A split second later, something slammed into the floor where she'd been, a thunderous crack echoing through the cavern. The wood shaft of a spear quivered, its green tip glowing where it was now embedded in the floor.

"Damn it, I *hate* magic!" Kaika yelled from several paces away. A clang sounded. Had she gotten away from the axe? Was she striking one of the metal bodies while still attached to it?

Rysha couldn't tell. All she knew as she sprang to her feet was that one of the hulking constructs had turned toward her. The spear flew back up into the air, landing in its handler's grip again, and the massive pyramid rolled forward. *Toward* her. Its bulk blocked her from returning to the tunnel.

"I'm cut off," Rysha yelled.

She wanted to flee. Every instinct screamed for her to do so, but she ran toward the construct instead. She searched for a target, a weakness in the pyramid base, even as she kept glancing at the armed figure on top, worried it would throw a weapon.

Another clang came from the other side of the construct. Kaika. It had to be.

But hitting the hard metal exterior would be useless. Rysha crouched as the construct rolled close, and swung at one of the wheels under the massive gray skirt.

Her blade sank in, as if she were striking butter instead of solid metal. But she had to yank it free and leap back right away to avoid being run over.

"Watch out, Rysha!" came Trip's cry from somewhere.

The tunnel? She couldn't see it anymore. Another spear plunged down from above.

She dodged and swept Dorfindral out in a block at the same time, afraid she would be too slow in jumping away. Under normal circumstances, she never could have knocked a spear out of the air, but the *chapaharii* blade's power flowed into her, guiding her movements as it had in previous battles. The spear clanged aside, clattering to the floor.

Rysha lunged in to attack that corner wheel again. She thought she had damaged it last time.

She struck it again, but she got a good glimpse under the pyramid as she struck and saw dozens—no, *hundreds*—of wheels under there, all rotating and spinning, somehow aligning perfectly to allow the hulking machine to maneuver in all directions. Even if she could destroy a few of them, she doubted it would impact the overall construct.

As she jumped back to once again avoid being run over, her heel splashed into water. The edge of the pool.

She'd forgotten about it—and those plants. She risked a backward glance, afraid the flowers might be readying their acid compound to hurl at her back.

But they had disappeared beneath the surface. Maybe they wanted nothing to do with this battle.

Rysha ran along the edge of the pool, knowing she would be slower if she had to slog through water, but then an idea came to her. What if she could draw the construct into the pool? Would its wheels work underwater?

She knew they wouldn't rust quickly enough for it to matter, but maybe the water would interfere with its mechanical innards. At the least, it might get bogged down in the pool as it drove deeper into it. Maybe she could maneuver it into some of those stalactites and get it trapped.

"I'm trying to keep this one out of the way, Trip," Rysha yelled, though she had no idea where he was now.

Another clang echoed through the chamber. She could only guess that Kaika and maybe the rest of the team were battling the second one.

"Now's your chance," she added as she turned into the water, slogging toward the forest of stalactites in the back and hoping she didn't step on any of those plants. "Get inside the pyramid and see if you can find a way to turn these off."

When Trip didn't answer immediately, Rysha feared something had already happened to him. But it must have only been his reluctance to leave the battle—to leave *them*—that made him pause.

"All right," he finally called. "I'm going in. I *will* find a way to stop this."

As Rysha pushed deeper into the water, the construct driving in behind her, the automaton on top readying its spear again, she could only pray that his promise bore out.

CHAPTER 24

TRIP RAN ACROSS THE SMOOTH floor of the cavern, Rysha drawing one of the constructs into the water on one side, and Blazer, Leftie, and Duck on the other side, shooting to distract the second one so Kaika could dart in and do damage with her sword.

The way ahead of him was completely clear. He felt like a coward, running while his friends battled for their lives. But he hoped Rysha was right, that there was some switch inside he could flip to stop the huge constructs. So far, he hadn't been able to do anything to them. All the attacks he'd tried had bounced off, their entire bodies protected by the *chapaharii* blades they wielded.

When he reached the open tunnel at the base of the pyramid, he made himself slow down. He would be surprised if there weren't more dangers inside.

We're watching for them, Jaxi told him. *But there's a lot of power in here muddling our senses. A lot of your damn blood.*

I know. I feel it. Trip still didn't sense a dragon, but he sensed magic and blood, blood that called to him, almost achingly so, with its familiarity.

Until he'd stepped into the cavern, he hadn't sensed the blood, but he did now. Mostly, it seemed centered in the back of the pyramid, but he was also aware of a few more of those bats hiding on the ceiling near the stalactites out there. He hoped they wouldn't come out and trouble the team, but he sensed fear from them. Whether it was from the battle or from something else—from *him*?—he didn't know.

It's confusing, Jaxi said. *I don't know what to make of it. Azarwrath agrees.*

Azarwrath snorted. *For once, I do.*

The light faded as Trip moved farther and farther from the entrance, but he could still hear the clangs and shouts of the battle, punctuated by rifle shots. Jaxi and Azarwrath increased their glow, lighting his way. Trip sensed an opening before he reached it. The center of the pyramid. The place wasn't as massive as he'd feared. He'd imagined a maze of tunnels that would take him hours to navigate.

It's not laid out anything like the giant pyramid we found Phelistoth in, Jaxi said, *but whoever built it had a lot less room to fit it into. For obvious reasons, caves aren't the ideal place to erect pyramids.*

That didn't stop them.

Whoever *them* had been. Trip eyed the stone walls, heavy blocks that appeared to have been placed by human hands long ago. He hoped to spot some large switch that would turn off the constructs, but he saw only paintings. Though old and faded, they were discernible. Unfortunately. Pictures of young women being sacrificed. Of people slitting their own wrists as they gazed heavenward. Of others prostrating themselves to a dragon, their foreheads pressed to the ground.

Trip was no archaeology expert, but he immediately suspected the same cult that had redecorated the outpost had decorated this place.

The Brotherhood of the Dragon, Azarwrath said.

More like the Bloodthirsty Cult of Agarrenon Shivar, Jaxi said.

Trip didn't want to believe that, but he couldn't come up with a plausible counter argument.

He reached a couple of desiccated bodies in the middle of the passage, dried and sunken skin still draped over skeletal frames. They were in far better shape than the bones in the other tunnel, but he suspected these people had died at the same time. Maybe the constructs had kept would-be scavengers from getting inside the pyramid.

As with the other body, these men had fallen in such a way to give the impression that they had been running from something. They didn't have packs, only the faded clothing on their backs, but they had both fallen with pistols in hand. They weren't Iskandian weapons, so Trip couldn't guess the year of manufacture, but they were cartridge weapons rather than black powder firearms, so they were less than fifty years old.

I have a feeling we've been running across people from my mother's mold-collection party, Trip thought.

Gunshots back in the main chamber propelled him forward. He could figure out the mystery after he'd made sure the others were out of danger.

I suspect your mother was the only one here for mold and weird plants, Jaxi replied.

The others may have wished to harness the power of Agarrenon Shivar, Azarwrath suggested. *Perhaps she ended up with them because she needed their help to find this place. Or maybe they needed* her *help to find it.*

I'm glad she got out alive. Trip shuddered to think of how close he might have come to never existing at all.

He reached the end of the tunnel, and a soft glow started up ahead of him, gradually increasing in intensity to illuminate the pyramid's inner chamber. His skin crawled as he sensed the magic in use, and his hands tightened on the soulblade hilts even though no enemy sprang out to face him.

A huge block of clear glass, or something like it, stood in the center of the chamber, the top stretching up to where the pyramid stone-stepped inward toward its peak. Like some giant square terrarium, it was large enough to hold a dragon, but it appeared to be empty. Unless a large part of it was sunken into the ground?

Stone tables and platforms spread across the floor all around the glass enclosure. Here and there, artifacts sat, magic emanating from them. A glowing sphere rested on a pedestal in front of the glass. A long dagger thrust up from between two stone pavers, blood drops etched into the flat of the ancient blade. A large ceramic bowl on a table reminded Trip uncomfortably and unwholesomely of the one in the outpost that had contained blood.

All over, giant slabs of stone had fallen to the floor, many of the pavers shattered from their weight. A couple of the tables had been crushed. Trip spotted the places in the ceiling and the tapered walls where they had tumbled free. He had no idea if it had happened all at once, during some earthquake, or one at a time over the centuries.

He walked around a few of the slabs, heading toward the glass enclosure. He could see more furnishings behind it and sensed more magic coming from that area, but he had to see the dragon first. He had to know... he wasn't sure what. But he needed answers.

Trip still didn't know whether Agarrenon Shivar had started this cult or if it had arisen after some people had found him here, locked in his stasis chamber. No matter how it had happened, he had a hard time believing the dragon had an innocent soul. This entire place had a creepy, unholy feel to it.

His pace quickened as the call of his blood drew him toward the enclosure. Maybe the dragon was in there, down below the level of the floor. Something was definitely pulling him.

Trip climbed a couple of steps to a platform that surrounded the enclosure. He eyed the glowing sphere on the pedestal, wondering if it was some kind of control orb. It was one of two such spheres, both on identical stone pedestals a few feet apart, but the other sphere was dark. As he drew closer, he could make out a hairline fracture running along its circumference. One of the massive blocks, its end sheared off, rested on the floor nearby, and he imagined it falling from the ceiling and landing on the orb at some point in history. Though if that had happened, surely, the sphere would have been pulverized, not merely cracked.

Magic makes artifacts powerful, Jaxi said. *But not powerful enough in this case.*

No, Azarwrath agreed. *I believe this all happened long, long ago. Perhaps even before the time of my birth.*

Their conversation confused Trip, as they seemed to be talking about more than some cracked sphere, until he stepped closer and could see fully into the glass enclosure. He gaped at the perfectly arranged pile of... bones. Dragon bones.

The creature—Agarrenon Shivar?—had died curled on its side. His side. As if in sleep.

There's a crack in the glass at the top too, Jaxi thought. *Enough that some bacteria, or perhaps Rysha's decomposing molds, got in to munch on his remains. He's been dead for a long, long time.*

Trip pressed his palm to the cool glass. "I don't understand."

Some enemy may have attacked the pyramid or deliberately weakened the stasis chamber to make it vulnerable, Azarwrath suggested. *If the dragon was weakened from a disease, perhaps he was unaware of it or couldn't fight back.*

"No, I mean... where did I come from if..."

Trip shook his head and stepped back. The dragon bones startled him, since it was so different from the scenario he had expected, but he would have to contemplate it later. He had to find a way to help the others.

The glowing sphere on the pedestal drew his eye again. It was the strongest artifact in the chamber, the one with the greatest aura, the greatest magic. If it had controlled the stasis chamber, perhaps that made sense, but he wondered if it might do more. Such as turn off those constructs.

Trip rested his palm on it, and swirls of light inside captivated him, drawing his mind downward.

Have you investigated the rest of the chamber with your senses? Jaxi's voice sounded oddly far off. *I believe you'll find the answer to your question.*

Her words intrigued him, but he couldn't look away from the swirling lights inside the orb. A vision started to form, not within the sphere but inside his mind.

It expanded, stampeding through his brain and driving out all other thoughts. All other awareness. He heard distant gunshots, but he couldn't remember what they meant. The image of a gold dragon filled his mind. It turned toward him, its neck long and sinewy, its head reptilian, its maw full of sharp unfriendly fangs. Its eyes opened, a deep dark green, and Trip knew he looked upon his sire's face.

The gargantuan stalactite snapped and splashed down, cracking against the bottom of the pool and hurling a great wave over Rysha's head. She wanted to duck and hide, but she couldn't.

The construct continued forward, knocking stalactites down like an elephant crashing through a bamboo forest. Water lapped around the bottom of the metal pyramid, the wheels propelling it not visible, but Rysha's idea that the pool would slow down or break the construct now seemed delusional.

With the water lapping just under her breasts, Rysha scooted back farther, half walking and half swimming. She was deep within the shadows, in a nook between the side of the stone pyramid and the cavern walls, and she worried she would get herself trapped. But she thought she still had room to circle around and swim out. She hoped.

When she'd volunteered to distract one of these things so Trip could run in, she'd imagined him taking a minute or two to find a switch to turn them off. After that, her role would have been done. But he had been gone far longer than two minutes.

An explosion ripped through the air on the far side of the cavern, echoing off the stone walls. The bottom of the pool trembled, and Rysha pitched sideways, her shoulder banging into a stalactite. Water sloshed against the walls and the construct. Unfortunately, the hulking pyramid did not slow down. It snapped another stalactite free of the ceiling as it continued toward Rysha.

She glimpsed the back wall of the cavern behind her. She didn't have much space left to hide in. It was time to work her away around the construct and back out of the water. She would have to try something else.

"Explosives hurt them!" Kaika yelled from the far side of the cavern.

"You'll bring down thousands of tons of rock on us," Blazer yelled from the same direction as Kaika.

"There's way more rock up there than that, but—" Clangs of steel interrupted Kaika, and Rysha imagined her in a sword fight with the humanoid figure atop the construct, her one blade against its four. "I've got plenty of control," Kaika finished, still yelling. She sounded exulted rather than worried.

As Rysha worked her way to the side wall, trying to keep numerous stalactites between her and the construct, her hulking foe adjusted its route. It knew exactly where she was, and it shifted, trying to cut her off.

Rysha's boots slipped on the slick bottom of the pool. More stalactites snapped off, close enough to her that shards of rock pelted the side of her face. Water sloshed up to her shoulders. If she hadn't carried Dorfindral, she would have given up on running and swum. That would have been faster.

One of the falling stalactites tumbled toward her. She shrieked and flung herself back to avoid it. The top, sheared clean from the roof, slammed against the wall just ahead of her and stuck there. If it hadn't caught, it might have slammed onto the top of her head.

"Ravenwood, explosives work!" Kaika called.

"Great news! I don't have any!"

Though she wanted to curse and yell at the construct and the situation, Rysha took a breath so she could swim under the stalactite blocking her way. Her shoulder bumped against the wall, as did her boots as she kicked to propel herself forward. Dorfindral clacked against rocks, the sound tinny under water.

Rysha came up with a gasp, stroking and kicking, but she wasn't fast enough. The construct was scant feet from her, about to ram her against the wall. She saw the corner of it and the light of the cavern beyond it, but it seemed so far away.

Rysha dropped down, pushed off the bottom, and arched over the surface like a dolphin as she scrambled to reach that corner before she ran out of space. She repeated the movement, taking hope from the bright light of the cavern now visible beyond the construct.

The base of the pyramid rolled into the wall, and Rysha feared she wouldn't escape in time, but it created a wave as it shoved against the rock. That wave propelled her out of the gap with a split second to spare.

Knowing the construct would only shift directions to follow her again, Rysha kept swimming and running, angling for shallower water.

Another boom sounded. This time, Rysha could see out of the pool and toward the other construct. Smoke wafted out from under its body on all sides, and then it smashed down to the ground, its wheels broken or smothered.

"That's it," Duck yelled. "Do another one, ma'am!"

But Kaika was too busy to answer. She stood atop the pyramid, fighting with the eight-armed automaton, her glowing blade clashing against the axe, sword, shield, and spear her foe wielded. She defended well, dancing away from the barrage of attacks that came from all sides, but even from across the chamber, Rysha could see that it was only a matter of time before Kaika misstepped or missed a crucial slash. In addition to the threat from all those arms and blades, there wasn't that much room to maneuver atop that platform.

Duck and Blazer were climbing the pyramid toward the platform, as if to help Kaika, but Rysha was the only other one with a *chapaharii* blade. She was the only one who could truly help.

Rysha snorted. An arrogant thought, that. She hadn't put more than a dent or two in the one pursuing her. As she made it to knee-deep water, then sprinted out of the pool, her construct followed her.

She ran across the cavern toward the other one, thinking that maybe if she joined the others in climbing up to battle the automaton, the construct pursuing her would hesitate. Maybe it was programmed not to get in the way of its fellow magical guard.

"One can hope," she panted, short of breath after her frantic efforts in the pool.

Rysha glanced into the tunnel in the pyramid as she ran past it, but she didn't see any sign of Trip. She glanced the other way, toward the passage through which they'd entered, wondering if it was too late or if they could all flee that way. But she remembered the dead man, someone who had once thought he, too, could flee. And he'd failed to make it.

"Give some of those to Ravenwood," Kaika yelled.

Rysha had no idea who she was talking to. Blazer, Leftie, and Duck were all on the construct now, hanging from the flat ledge at the top of the pyramid. The men shot at the eight-armed figure whenever they got a chance.

Rysha wanted to yell at them for risking themselves and wasting ammunition, but one of Duck's shots knocked a spear out of the automaton's hand. It bounced off the platform, skidded down the side of the pyramid, and struck the stone floor.

"I'm going to shove them all into the innards of this thing," Blazer yelled. She held Kaika's bag, Kaika's *explosives*.

"Not all of them. You can't just—shit!" Kaika ducked as three arms ganged up on her at once.

A sword swept over her head, and she somehow dodged aside an axe aimed at her gut, but the shield butted her in the shoulder. It knocked her off the ledge, and she slid down the pyramid, cursing and scraping Eryndral down its outside as she fell. The spear Duck had shot floated back upward at the same time, once again landing in the figure's hand. One of its *eight* hands. The odds were too ridiculous.

Rysha ran to Kaika to help her up. "Ma'am, this is impossible."

"No, it's not. Look, we broke the bottom half. It can't move anymore."

"If that's true, then can't we just get out of its range?" Rysha glanced toward the construct now trundling out of the water, another eight-armed automaton, hands full of weapons, waving them menacingly as it approached.

"Uh. Maybe." Kaika jumped to her feet. "Get down, you three."

The words had barely come out when Leftie was knocked from the platform. He tumbled down, landing ungracefully on the hard floor. He groaned, but pushed himself to his feet.

"The other one's coming," Rysha warned, and they ran around the corner of the stationary one to use it for cover. The figure atop it continued to wave its weapons as Blazer and Duck slid down the pyramid. It didn't—couldn't—move to give chase. "How did you break that one?" she asked Kaika.

But Kaika was watching the automaton atop the closest construct. "Axe, look out!"

As soon as Duck and Blazer touched down, they sprang to the sides. But an axe hurtled down, and it caught Blazer in the back of the head.

It looked like the flat had struck her rather than the edge, but Rysha wasn't sure. She cried out something useless, horror filling her heart as Blazer pitched forward. Seven gods, what if that had been a killing blow?

Kaika roared and ran toward Blazer as Duck hefted her over his shoulder, staggered, and ran toward the tunnel. Kaika whirled, anticipating another attack. A spear zipped down, but Eryndral flared, and she knocked it aside.

"To the tunnel," Duck yelled. "Everyone."

"My rifle," Leftie blurted, looking around.

"Get it later," Duck barked. "It doesn't do anything anyway."

Leftie scowled, but ran after him. Kaika didn't look like she wanted to retreat, but the other construct was advancing to cut them off.

Rysha started after them, but she spotted a rucksack nearby, the flap open. Kaika's. While the construct that remained ambulatory rolled toward the tunnel, hurling weapons at her comrades, Rysha sprinted for the pack. She crouched, digging through components and rolls of wire while being careful not to get anything wet. Her clothing dripped water onto the floor all around her.

There were so many kinds of bombs she hadn't seen before, much less used. But she remembered how to assemble the type they had employed on those boulders. Would that work to blow the wheels off that other construct?

"It better," she muttered, pulling out the components. It was all she knew how to make.

The construct chased the others into the tunnel, then rolled back and forth in front of it. Rysha grimaced, realizing she was trapped once again.

More than that, the automaton at the top of the stationary construct had turned its attention on her. She was about to find out if she could assemble explosives while dodging spears hurled at her.

CHAPTER 25

THE GREAT GOLD DRAGON SHIFTED into human form to lounge on one of the many cushioned beds in the temple his servants had built for him. A female attended him, rubbing his body and delivering morsels of food. Other humans enjoyed each other's company in the aftermath of the ceremony. They had given him a worthy sacrifice this time, though it was more the sexual enjoyments that brought him to this remote mountain lair where he deigned to grant favors to his minions. He shape-shifted into human form to mate with the females, and he occasionally intrigued himself by rutting with females of different species that his devotees brought to him. The pleasure was different in each form, and he enjoyed experiencing it all. He'd known many females of his own kind over the centuries, but they always believed themselves the dominant and superior being in the pairing, and that galled him. As if he, a great gold dragon, should be subservient to anyone else.

Agarrenon Shivar? a tentative voice spoke into his mind. It belonged to the bronze dragon researching the pesky virus that had been irritating him all year, weakening his strong and virile body.

What do you want, bronze?

I am here with several of the elders.

Yes, Agarrenon Shivar sensed that, sensed unwelcome guests descending upon his secluded domicile. Invading his privacy. Why would other dragons have come here to this inhospitable continent and risked the *slvenomorsh*?

Leave my home, Agarrenon Shivar growled into their minds.

You requested I do this research for you, the bronze said. *I have. But there is no known cure. You will only grow weaker.*

Lies! You seek to claim my domain, my minions. All that I have built and claimed for myself. You bronzes have always been known for your treachery.

I am a doctor and a scientist. That is all. With time, I will find a cure for you, but you may not have time. Unless... You are aware of our stasis magic?

You think you will put me to sleep? So I am weak and you can kill me? I refuse! Better to die in the sky.

You haven't a choice, another voice growled into Agarrenon Shivar's mind. Who was that? Yorlinorash from the Circle of Elders? *The last time you came to a meeting, you infected others with your disease. Others who are weaker than you and are already dying.*

It's possible you could infect our entire race and cause our extinction, the bronze added.

You did this! he bellowed at the bronze. In his anger, Agarrenon Shivar hurled power around the temple, sending some of his minions flying. They cried out in pain and fear. He didn't care. This was intolerable. *Some conniving bronze dragon. I refuse—*

You have no choice, Yorlinorash repeated. *We've brought the materials and a human engineer to assist in fitting it all into this... place. This place made for you by your human slaves.* A sneer accompanied Yorlinorash's words. As if there was anything wrong with being attended by servants, by ruling over them instead of living alone on some drafty mountaintop. *We will handle the preparation of your stasis chamber. Our engineer has made devices to protect your lair from intruders while you sleep, and we have brought additional chambers to hold your unholy offspring to care for you when you wake, in case time weakens you. Perhaps this will be an appropriate use for the proliferation of half-breed monstrosities you've thrust upon the world.*

Weakens! Nothing shall weaken the great Agarrenon Shivar.

You have no choice, Yorlinorash repeated.

ORIGINS

Power swept down the tunnels with his words, invading Agarrenon Shivar's home. It was not just the power of one, but the power of a half-dozen dragons, all golds. They were too many to fight, and he found himself helpless and pinned as they brought in the materials for one large stasis chamber and many smaller ones. His human minions fled, having no idea what was happening to their great dragon leader.

The engineer, a human woman Agarrenon Shivar remembered claiming for himself, guided the work. She whispered and bowed often to Yorlinorash, and Agarrenon Shivar realized she must now be his. No wonder the dragon was spearheading this. It was jealousy. No, *revenge*. And the sniveling bronze was standing close by, helping now and then, but mostly looking pleased at seeing a great gold dragon laid so low.

There was nothing Agarrenon Shivar could do. Yorlinorash had gathered too many to help in this, and in the end, Agarrenon Shivar was forced against his will to step into the chamber they created.

The human engineer stood next to the bronze dragon, the two working together to seal the chamber and activate the control spheres. She rested her palm on one, then gazed backward, her expression sad as she watched crying babies and whimpering animals being brought into the temple. A wave of sorrow flowed from her, but she had no choice but to do this, no choice but to give her own baby and all the other mothers' offspring to the future. One day, she hoped, there would be a cure for them.

Go, the bronze dragon told her. *I will finish the rest.*

Deceit lurked in his thoughts, but the human could not know. She bowed her head and walked away as the bronze slid his claws over the second control orb, planting a weakness in it, sabotaging the main stasis chamber so that it would one day fail.

Agarrenon Shivar tried to spread his wings and break out, to attack, but it was too late. A deep weariness came over him, and awareness slipped from his thoughts. The bronze dragon looked smugly back at the stasis chamber, flicking his tail in dismissal as he flew away.

Trip gasped as his mind returned to him and he grew aware of his surroundings again, aware of his hands locked to the warm orb, of the temple all around him, and of the battle that still raged outside. A thunderous boom sounded, the noise and a cloud of dust rolling down the tunnel and into the pyramid.

Telryn! Azarwrath's shout was frustrated, as if he'd repeated it many times. *Your comrades will fall to the automatons. We are unable to affect them as long as they carry those* chapaharii *weapons, and your team's attempts to knock them aside aren't working.*

In other words, now would be a good time for you to find a switch to turn them off, Jaxi said.

Trip didn't know if the soulblades had seen the vision, or if it had only been for him, but he shook it and all its ramifications aside and focused again on the sphere. The control orb. It had to do more than man the stasis chamber. He hoped.

The device attempted to thrust some other vision on him, but he was prepared this time. He slammed his bank vault door shut to protect his mind, and he delved inside the orb, searching for instructions, controls. Yes, there. He found a map of the pyramid, including a storage area outside where those hulking constructs resided when they were not activated by the approach of living beings. There was a control panel on the wall. He could not read the words embedded in it, but he understood them, nonetheless. He selected the one that meant *return*.

Another boom echoed through the chamber, and Trip worried the others would bring down the entire mountain.

The constructs did not obey, did not roll back to the storage room. Trip swept outward with his senses and saw Kaika and Rysha fighting side by side between the two hulking machines. Machines that no longer moved. He sensed their mangled insides. They attempted to obey the command to return to storage, but the smashed wheels could no longer propel their bases forward.

The automatons that had been mounted atop them, the eight-armed humanoid fighters, had come free somehow. They had leaped from their immobile platforms and now faced Kaika and Rysha while Duck and Leftie waited in the mouth of the tunnel, each gripping grenades, waiting for opportunities to throw them.

Where was Blazer? Trip didn't see her.

As the automatons maneuvered, trying to surround Kaika and Rysha, Trip abruptly realized why those who'd run from the cavern hadn't made it. The metal figures must have leaped free of the constructs and chased them down. Most of them. Somehow, his mother had run far enough and fast enough while the others fell to those wicked blades.

What can I do? Trip manipulated the control panel again, hoping another lever might tell the automatons to return, but the commands seemed only to apply to the pyramid bases.

Do something, Jaxi ordered, frustration seeping into her words.

Trip sensed that she'd been trying, hurling magical attacks uselessly at the figures, figures protected by those swords. Kaika and Rysha were fighting well, but their weariness was obvious, and they each bled from a dozen wounds. Rysha's spectacles were fogged from the steam her own heated body produced. Seven gods, could she even see?

The chaparahii *swords will protect the constructs from magic but not from physical attacks, remember,* Azarwrath said.

Of course. Trip should have remembered that earlier.

He released the orb, closed his eyes, and clenched his fists at his sides. *Help me,* he ordered the soulblades as he gathered his power.

His first thought was to bring down the ceiling atop the automatons, but that would endanger them all.

Get ready to turn and sprint for the tunnel, Trip said, speaking into Rysha's and Kaika's minds. He had to trust they heard him because they were too busy fighting for their lives to acknowledge the words.

He spotted all the broken stalactites, huge megaton chunks of rock, that had crashed down into the pool. He willed them to lift into the air all at once, refusing to feel daunted by their incredible weight. If he failed at this, Rysha might die.

The soulblades poured their energy into him, helping him lift all the broken rock formations at once, then pushing them together into one huge mass of rock. He floated it up as high as the ceiling allowed, then over toward the fight.

Kaika glanced up, spotting them. "Now!" she yelled.

She and Rysha flung final blows at the two automatons, trying to drive them back, then turned and sprinted for the tunnel. Leftie and Duck stepped out and threw grenades at their foes. The automatons did not pause. They started to run after the women.

Trip released the broken stalactites. More than that, he hurled them downward with all the force he could muster. The grenades exploded just before the rocks landed, but the noise was abruptly muffled as tons and tons of rock slammed down atop the two figures.

Trip trembled in the aftermath of drawing upon so much power and leaned against the orb's pedestal for support. He searched through the rubble with his mind. Had it been enough to destroy the automatons? To bury them?

Long seconds passed, and he didn't sense any movement underneath the rocks.

Finally, he allowed himself to slump to his knees, his head against the cool stone pedestal. He was exhausted from his efforts. Exhausted from everything.

Though Rysha's entire body ached, and warm blood made her clothes stick uncomfortably to her skin, she forced herself to walk back into the cavern. Around the massive pile of rocks that had smashed the two automatons, destroying them forever, she hoped.

As she continued past them, toward the tunnel of the pyramid, she decided there was some justice in knowing the stalactites the construct chasing her had broken had been used against it in the end.

"Those dead too?" Kaika asked warily, limping behind her and looking at the pyramid bases.

They had stopped moving. Rysha hoped that meant Trip had done something, and she also hoped nothing had happened to him inside the stone pyramid. That he was all right. He must be. He'd surely been the one to bring those rocks down. She remembered his warning in her mind.

"I hope so," Rysha whispered.

"Is Trip still inside there? We need his help with Blazer."

"I know. Have the others carry her into the pyramid, in case he's been injured too."

It felt wrong to give orders to a superior officer, but Kaika nodded and dropped back without complaint.

Dorfindral continued to glow as Rysha strode into the tunnel, and she wondered what she would find inside. A dragon? Tons of magical booby traps? So long as Trip was in there, she could deal with the rest.

After passing numerous disturbing wall paintings, Rysha entered a light-filled chamber. She noted stone tables and artifacts, places where the ceiling had broken away, huge chunks of rock having slammed down atop the furnishings. She ignored it all for now, though perhaps later there would be time for a better look.

"Trip?" she asked warily, not seeing him in the front half of the chamber.

She ran up to a platform overlooking a glass enclosure. The giant bones inside made her pause. Not just bones. An entire skeleton. Was this the dragon they'd come for?

"Back here," came Trip's soft voice from the other side of the enclosure.

Rysha could see him through the glass, his back to her as he looked down at something. She squeezed between the wall and the side of the giant glass enclosure to reach the cramped spot where he stood, the back half of the platform.

"Are you all right?" Rysha asked, easing around the back corner of the enclosure.

Trip still had his back to her as he stood, his chin propped on his fist, gazing down at what looked like a bunch of metal wine barrels sawed in half. Several of the lids were open, nothing but dust inside. Other lids remained down, but they were semi-opaque. She was able to make out indistinct shapes inside, but couldn't identify them from where she stood. A soft hum came from the barrels as a whole, as if they generated electricity. Some kind of bronze-plated wiring that appeared very old linked them all together.

"Me?" Trip finally looked over, his gaze traveling over her from head to toe. He winced, his expression sympathetic, as he spread an inviting arm. "I'm not the one who fought the battle of her life. I can heal you if you set Dorfindral aside."

More worried about him than about being healed, Rysha hurried forward as quickly as her aching body would permit, wanting the hug he offered, wanting to collapse against him for support.

He shifted to wrap both arms around her as she leaned into his chest. His hand came up, resting on the back of her head, and she pressed her face into his shoulder. Tears threatened, even though there was no logical reason for them. They had won. But then she thought of the dragon bones and realized they hadn't succeeded in their mission. They had at least *survived*. Maybe her tears simply denoted exhaustion.

"What's in the barrels?" she asked, her mind curious even if her body wanted to do nothing but slump against his.

"Babies."

She leaned back to look in his eyes, suspecting him of a joke or inadvertently giving some creative interpretation of the word.

"And pups," he added, his expression without humor. "And kits. And whatever baby lizard… things are called. I don't think any of them are dragons, not *full* dragons. They're all his offspring, but from matings with other creatures. And humans. Some of the stasis chambers in the front were opened—that's where those bats came from, I think. Some of the other chambers failed over the years, and their occupants withered and died. How horrific if they woke for any part of that and were aware of being trapped inside." Trip closed his eyes, then added, in a softer tone, "The human babies are in the last row. One of the stasis chambers back there was opened, not broken. It's empty."

His lids lifted, and he gazed into Rysha's eyes. She had the feeling he expected her to twig to something.

Maybe her brain was too tired after that battle, but she found this whole situation confusing. She pulled away from him to walk to the edge of the platform and peer into the barrels herself.

The voices of Kaika, Duck, and Leftie drifted to them from the other side of the chamber. Rysha needed to ask Trip to check on Blazer, but she couldn't pull her gaze from the barrels. The stasis chambers, she realized. And the babies inside. As Trip had said. The young of several species, frozen there in time—and in a gelatinous-looking substance exactly like what had held the dragons they'd found imprisoned in the Antarctic. Each individual half-barrel had a small plaque on the side. They reminded her of the plaques that had been beside the alcoves in the dragon prison, the controls for letting the occupants out of their cells. Would Trip's hand be able to open these? As he had opened those? If it could, what then?

Rysha's gaze was drawn to the row that held the human babies. There were eight of them, ranging in age from a couple of months to roughly a year.

"But why would babies have been imprisoned?" she whispered.

Trip's eyes were closed again, and he did not answer.

Rysha looked to the wall behind the collection of barrels—miniature stasis chambers. Words had been carved into the ancient stones, so precise and even that she felt certain that magic had done it rather than a human hand. Which made sense since the words were Middle Dragon

ORIGINS

Script. Dragons, with their genetic memories, hadn't written much down, but as she read, she realized this message had been meant for the future, an uncertain future. The person—or dragon—who'd left the words there hadn't known who would read them.

"I see," she said slowly.

"Do you?" Trip's eyes opened, and he also gazed at the words. "I got a vision from the orb that somewhat explained this, but I can't read that."

"It basically says that Agarrenon Shivar was afflicted with a disease that the dragons didn't understand or know how to cure. He'd been infecting other dragons he came in contact with, so the elders decided to lock him in this stasis chamber until, they hoped, some dragon or human would know how to cure him. They could heal Agarrenon Shivar and remove him from stasis."

"That much I know," Trip said.

"Since they weren't sure what the world would be like when Agarrenon Shivar woke again, they left his offspring here to renew his cult and attend to his needs." Rysha's lip curled at the suggestion that the dragon had started the cult rather than it having been something that developed after his passing—his disappearance into hibernation.

"I got the feeling that the other dragons might have wanted an excuse to get rid of Agarrenon Shivar's offspring," Trip said. "And that this was a way to do it without murdering them. Agarrenon Shivar was apparently fecund, but rarely with other dragons."

"That's horrible." Rysha's gaze shifted to the empty barrel in the back, the one in the human row, and she rocked back on her heels as understanding struck her. "Seven gods," she whispered, meeting his eyes. "This means…"

"The woman I always believed was my mother wasn't, not by blood. And I was born thousands of years ago and slept in a box until she unlocked it." His voice was flat, devoid of emotion.

Rysha couldn't believe he didn't care and wasn't dumbfounded. Maybe that wasn't it. Maybe he was in shock. She couldn't imagine how she would feel if she found out her parents weren't truly her parents. And the rest… If she hadn't been standing here, looking at the proof, she never would have believed this story.

"I don't know what to do," Trip whispered, some of his flat facade cracking. "I can't leave them here. They're my kin. Even the animals." He winced. "What do I do, Rysha?"

He was asking *her*? She couldn't begin to grasp all this, and she didn't know a thing about motherhood and raising children. But she agreed with Trip that they couldn't simply leave them here for the next set of treasure hunters to discover, especially now that she and Kaika had cleared the way into the cave system.

"I believe someone pursued my mother at one point," Trip said, "because he or she or they wanted me for their own purposes. My grandmother believes that, I should say, based on the circumstances of my mother's arrival at home. That was twenty-five years ago. I don't know if that person is still out there, but there are many people who, if they found out about these... half-dragon babies, might want to use them for their power. Power that they *will* have. If someone started teaching them to use it at a young age..."

Rysha nodded. "They could be very powerful before they're even full adults. I understand. I guess taking them back to Iskandia and asking Sardelle would be the way to go. She's the only one around from a culture that understood magic and was surrounded by it. I'm sure she'll be as daunted by this as I feel right now, but I think she'd be the one to ask."

"Yes, I agree."

"But wait. Can we? The dragon was afflicted with some disease. Is there a way to tell if the young are?" She frowned at the barrels and then at Trip again. "You clearly didn't die as a baby."

"Jaxi says they aren't. She ran into the disease when dealing with Phelistoth so she would recognize it. She was surprised, because she figured they would have been infected if they were in proximity to Agarrenon Shivar, but maybe they weren't brought close to him until after he was already locked up. Though I wonder what the parents—the mothers—were told. I think I saw one of the mothers in the vision, maybe even mine." Trip lifted a shoulder and smiled faintly. "She was an engineer. She seemed to believe her baby had been infected. If she didn't have dragon blood of her own, then she wouldn't have had a way to know, I suppose. I don't know. I find this all..." He closed his eyes again.

Yes, he looked shocked. Rysha returned to his side and slipped her arm around his waist. They leaned against each other, both of them needing support this time.

"You two back here?" came Kaika's voice as she walked between the wall and the glass enclosure. "This place is even creepier than the outpost. Did you see those rusty torture tools? And those paintings? If these people weren't having orgies—nothing wrong with orgies, mind you—they were sacrificing people and doing weird rituals with—damn, I don't even know what those wall paintings over on that side represent." She waved past the enclosure.

Trip didn't move or seem like he wanted to answer. Maybe Rysha wouldn't either. They would just stand there until they regained some energy and figured out what to do.

"Uh, this isn't the dragon we came to recruit, is it?" came Blazer's voice, also from the side of the enclosure. "Because he doesn't look like he's in a position to be real helpful right now."

Rysha turned and stared at her, surprised she had walked in of her own accord. And also surprised she didn't sound hurt.

"I could heal you too," Trip murmured to her, "if you would take your sword off."

"Oh," she said, understanding dawning on her. He'd healed Blazer without even touching her? "You're getting much better at that."

"She was lucky she left her pack with that ingot in it outside, or I wouldn't have been able to help her so quickly."

Rysha unfastened Dorfindral's scabbard, set it down, and found Trip's hand and squeezed it. Some of his healing warmth flowed into her, easing the aches that plagued her.

"We wouldn't want that dragon," Kaika told Blazer. "He was a sick freak. And the humans who followed him were sick freaks. Trip, if that was your papa, you better look into adoption. Maybe we can find you a new papa."

Rysha leaned against Trip's chest again and looked at his face, worried the words would upset him. Upset him *further*.

But Trip only snorted. "General Zirkander let me go fishing with him."

"There you go." Kaika pointed at him. "You can adopt Zirkander. Or vice versa. I bet he'd like that. You're probably one of the more normal beings to come visit his house lately."

"Did you just call me normal, ma'am?"

"In comparison to Zirkander's other house guests, you're a paragon of normalness."

Trip smiled, appearing pleased by this encomium.

"Compared to other people, you're odd," Kaika said.

The addendum didn't dent Trip's smile.

"Lieutenant Ravenwood likes odd boys," he said, smiling shyly at her.

Rysha thought his flier might have lost a few screws after the battering of revelations he'd endured, but she patted his chest and smiled back.

"Yes, because she's odd too," Kaika said.

"Should we be insulted that someone whose hobby is fondling bombs is calling us odd?" Rysha asked Trip.

Very insulted, Jaxi spoke into their minds. Strangely, the interruption no longer startled Rysha. *You should punish her with your dragonly powers, Trip.*

Punish her? Trip asked, speaking telepathically.

By doing something dire. Like giving her a rash on her nether regions. It would be good practice for when you encounter enemies that you want to incapacitate without killing.

It sounds like an unkind thing to do to a superior officer, Trip thought.

It may also be against regulations, Rysha thought, trusting these magical beings would hear her response.

There can't possibly be an army regulation covering nether-region rashes, Jaxi informed them.

"Are you two talking to each other telepathically?" Kaika squinted at them.

"Jaxi is suggesting someone give you a rash, ma'am," Trip said politely.

"*Jaxi.*" Kaika frowned at the scabbard hanging from his hip. "I was *joking* when I said I'd throw you into a volcano if you didn't help with the crazy pyramid machines."

Rysha arched her eyebrows. She hadn't heard that threat. It had either been a silent one or it had occurred while she'd been dodging through the pool.

"I don't think there are any volcanoes on this continent," Kaika added.

Leftie and Duck, who had been pointing at and discussing the dragon bones, joined the group.

Leftie walked over and thumped Trip on the shoulder. "Glad you could help with those weird magic things." He waved toward the front of the pyramid and the jumble of rocks outside.

Trip nodded.

Rysha hoped that had been a thump of acceptance, maybe even an apology for his earlier blowup. She didn't think Leftie was the kind of person to actually voice apologies.

"Uh," Duck said, peering over the edge of the platform. "Where did all these babies come from?"

Trip sighed. "It's a long story."

CHAPTER 26

BLAZER FOLDED HER ARMS AND watched as the steam-powered locomotive Trip had made rolled away from the pool. Since there was no magic about it, it operated in the magic dead zone. The team had just attached the last flier, the one Duck had landed in the pool, to its little train of fliers. The machine tugged it out of the water.

The locomotive had oversized metal wheels that clunked and ground noisily over the rough terrain, but thus far, it had handled the task of gathering the fliers. It looked somewhat ludicrous trundling across the dirt with the winged craft rolling behind it, attached by tow chains, but all that mattered was that it got the fliers back to the coast where the power crystals should once again work.

Trip had used almost every scrap of metal in Agarrenon Shivar's lair, including pieces torn from the constructs that had attacked them, to create the locomotive, chains, and tow hooks. He'd reserved some to create the wagon now loaded with two dozen miniature stasis chambers. A blanket tied across the top protected them from the sun. Trip was hauling the wagon himself, carefully. He had no idea how well magical devices that hadn't moved for over three thousand years would deal with travel.

Thousands of years. Trip's mind still boggled at the idea that he'd come out of one of the stasis chambers, that his mother hadn't been his true mother, and that he wasn't related to his grandparents at all, not by blood. How would he explain that to them? Or *should* he explain it to them? And what about all the babies?

He hoped Sardelle would know what to do. There were eight half-human babies, with the rest being animals of various types. Animals and *lizards*. Trip couldn't drop half-dragon animals off at the zoo.

His brain hurt. For so many reasons. He couldn't articulate them all.

The only good thing to come out of this last week—this last *several* weeks—was that Rysha now came over to stand beside him and supportively touch his hand while sneaking shy glances at him that suggested she had bedroom thoughts in mind. Even if they'd only shared a cave thus far, not a bedroom. He hoped the next time they enjoyed each other's company, it would involve more cushioning. Pillows, perhaps.

"I keep waiting for that thing to blow up," Blazer grumbled, smoke wafting from her cigar as she watched the locomotive.

"Your faith in my engineering skills isn't heartening," Trip said.

"It's the fact that you didn't use any *tools* to make it."

"I did too." Trip pulled out his pocket toolkit, complete with a tiny hammer, pliers, screwdriver, and foldable ruler. Admittedly, he had only used the ruler for measuring. For the rest, he'd relied upon the same magic he'd employed on the fish toy to shape and meld the scraps of bronze and iron into these creations. Other magic might not come so easily to him, but with anything that had to do with repairing or building something, it was almost as if the metal wished to comply with him, that it was eager to bend into the shapes he wanted. And he found it peaceful and relaxing to work with it. If only people were so simple to work with and understand.

"I'm so reassured," Blazer said.

"Trip can do amazing things without any tools at all." Rysha patted him on the back.

"Yes," Kaika said, "the warm flush to your cheeks every time you look at him lets us all know that."

Blazer snorted and nodded. Leftie and Duck looked at each other, appearing more confused than knowing.

Rysha's cheeks turned a scorching red. Trip felt his own cheeks heat, mostly because he'd thought they'd been discreet, aside from their late arrival to battle the pond flowers that one morning. Since then, he and

Rysha had stolen away for a few kisses, but Trip and the soulblades had been too busy carting metal scraps out of the mountain and building their temporary vehicles for him to contemplate doing more. Further, Duck, Leftie, and Blazer had been right beside him most of the time, hauling metal and assisting with the construction in any way they could.

Blazer, in particular, had made it clear that she wanted to get out of "this freak-infested place" and back home to her normal life of shooting things from the comfort of her flier. She also wanted to hurry back with the *chapaharii* blades Trip had helped recover from under the rubble. King Angulus wouldn't get the assistance of a dragon out of this mission, but at least he was getting more anti-magic weapons, along with that ingot of tainted iron to experiment on. Perhaps the scientist, Deathmaker, would find it useful.

Kaika thumped Rysha on the back. "I am pleased to know our dragonling is a better lover than we expected. Though I suppose you don't have much of a basis for comparison. Perhaps we should all take that trip to the Sensual Sage when we get back. To broaden your horizons." She waved her hand to include Rysha, Trip, Leftie, Blazer, and Duck.

"Pass," Blazer said.

"What do you mean *all*?" Duck asked, his expression somewhere between intrigued and mortified.

"There are group rooms," Kaika said. "With private heated pools. The Captivating Cavern has a bed big enough for six. I've heard."

"Nobody's going to any more caverns," Blazer said. "Captivating or otherwise. We're splitting up as soon as we get out of this magic dead zone."

"Splitting up, ma'am?" Rysha asked.

"Unless Trip wants to build us an airship from driftwood, we don't have any way to get those baby boxes—" she waved at the wagon, "—back to the capital. They're not going to fit in our fliers, even if Dreyak isn't waiting and expecting a ride back. There are way too many to stow in the spare seats. So, while Wolf Squadron flies back to report in—and let's hope the capital isn't in trouble dealing with all those portal dragons at this very moment—someone's going to have to take the babies to the city here and find a boat that'll take them back to Iskandia. A boat or an airship, if any of them are allowed to land here without being blown out of the sky. After that, hells, I don't know what the king will want to do with them. That's above my pay grade."

Trip bristled at the thought of something being *done* with them or their fate being up to a king he barely knew. He had no idea what the right thing was to do with his unorthodox siblings, but he vowed they wouldn't be stuck in some orphanage. Or worse.

The king won't try to hide them away somewhere, will he, Jaxi? Trip asked.

I'd be more concerned about him wanting them to be raised so they become assets to Iskandia.

Better that than a detriment to your country, Azarwrath said.

Indeed, we wouldn't want them to randomly decide people from Cofahre are appealing, Jaxi said.

Azarwrath sighed dramatically into Trip's mind. *Telryn, I do look forward to you returning this female soulblade to her owner. Though it does seem that would be a punishment to her handler.*

Sardelle finds me a delightful, wise, and irreplaceable partner.

I have not heard her say these things.

You've barely met her.

Trip cleared his mental throat. *Wouldn't it be possible for the babies to be raised to just be people? Not assets? Maybe they'll want to be flier pilots. Or hookball athletes. Or dancers or engineers or painters or plumbers.* Not for the first time, he wondered if he should be the one to raise them, but the idea of suddenly being a father to eight children, none more than a year old, terrified him. He couldn't be a soldier and raise eight children at the same time, not by himself. And it was far too soon to think of asking Rysha to be a wife and mother. Besides, she wanted her own military career.

A half-dragon plumber? Jaxi asked. *You definitely shouldn't be allowed to raise children.*

Better a plumber than some ambitious megalomaniac with the power to conquer nations, Azarwrath put in.

That was what truly terrified Trip. That if he did have a hand in raising them, he would screw up, and his siblings would grow up to cause trouble for Iskandia, maybe for the entire world.

If it makes you feel better, Jaxi said, *judging by the way Bhrava Saruth has been seducing nubile young women all across Iskandia, little dragonlings are going to be all over before long. Your future plumbers may be insignificant in the grand scheme of things.*

That did not make Trip feel better.

Welcome to the Second Dragon Era, Azarwrath murmured.

You mean dragonling era, don't you? Jaxi asked.

Both, I suppose.

"*Could* you make an airship?" Rysha asked Trip curiously, oblivious to the conversation going on inside his head. She waved at the locomotive. "Maybe you could disassemble that for the basic parts."

"I could make the compartment and the frame, but there's nothing around here that could be used to create an envelope, and I don't know how to simply magic fabric into existence. Also, I'm not sure how to make helium. Hydrogen would be easier, I suppose. But, uh, Sardelle's workbook doesn't cover how to cleave atoms."

"Were her ten-year-old students not interested in that?" Kaika asked.

"I guess not."

"Trip looks daunted at the airship idea," Blazer said, "so we're going with my plan. Trip, due to your blood connection, you're the nanny. You get to see those whelps home. If anyone has the power to deal with any trouble that might arise along the way, that's you. That leaves me without a pilot for a flier, but I can't imagine you not going with the babies. Agreed?"

"Yes, ma'am. I have an obligation to them. I doubt our sire cared about any of us, but I'm sure their mothers would have wanted them to be raised well and want for nothing." He wondered if there was any way, millennia later, to find out who the mothers had been. One day, the children would grow old enough to ask.

"Wolf Squadron will stop in Charkolt first, grab an extra pilot from their base, and go back across the ocean to pick up your flier. After that, we'll report in to the king and General Zirkander. Let them know you're coming and what to expect." Blazer waved a hand at the wagon again. "I won't send you to be the nanny and handle the transportation by yourself. You can have anyone who's not a pilot to take with you." Blazer extended her hand toward Rysha and Kaika.

Kaika grunted. "With such equally appealing options, however will he choose one of us?"

"Actually, I thought he might choose both of you. Someone has to keep an eye on the babies while he's dancing horizontally with his new partner."

Trip's mouth dangled open. He wasn't sure how his relationship with Rysha had become an open topic for discussion, but it was horrifying him. Rysha merely lifted her gaze skyward, as if she expected nothing less in this group.

Fortunately, Blazer smirked after she spoke the words. A few days earlier, she'd seemed irked with Rysha and Trip for their impropriety. She had been less crabby with him since he'd healed her of that concussion.

"Wait, *I'm* the nanny now?" Kaika asked. "I've had this discussion with Ang—my steady fellow. I don't deal with babies."

"They're frozen in those boxes. It's not like you have to nurse them. That joy will go to someone else, assuming the king decides to take them out. I imagine they could go into storage for another thousand years."

Trip found that notion almost as horrifying as them being stuck in some loveless orphanage. Even though he didn't remember any of the years he'd spent in his stasis chamber, it seemed an awful fate for anyone. With their parents long dead, there was nobody left in the world who'd been around when they were born. Nobody who'd even known they existed until his mother stumbled upon the temple. Trip still had questions about how she had found her way there and who she had been traveling with, but he didn't know if he would ever find those answers.

"Lieutenant Ravenwood and I can handle it," Trip said. "We can contain our libidinous tendencies long enough to see them safely home."

"Doubtful," Blazer said. "No, I've decided. You need a higher-ranking officer to help out. If you end up in some random port without a flier base, Kaika should know someone in the local intel unit who can help get you home. Especially since it's possible you won't be able to find a ship or a flight directly to Iskandia from here."

Trip hitched his shoulder. "It's fine with me, ma'am."

"Good, because I wasn't asking for your consent." Blazer waved at the train of fliers behind the locomotive, then gave W-08, her craft, a loving pat. "Let's get these babies home."

"It's somewhat alarming that she's more interested in those babies—" Rysha pointed to the fliers, "—than these." She waved at the stasis chambers.

"Alarming, but not surprising." Kaika smirked.

"So says the person who feels the same way," Rysha said.

"I don't have any fond feelings toward the fliers. I save my loving pats and terms of endearment for my bombs."

"I share terms of endearment with my machine guns," Blazer said.

"Oh, everybody does that," Duck said, looking at Leftie.

Leftie nodded. "They're more likely to jam if you don't speak nicely to them."

"Is it odd that I'm going to miss flying back with these people?" Rysha asked Trip quietly.

"Extremely odd."

"I guess I'm lucky that you're as drawn to odd people as I am."

"Definitely." He hesitated, then draped an arm around her shoulder. It wasn't as if there were secrets out here anymore.

Rysha smiled and leaned into him.

Even though Rysha, Trip, and Kaika had removed as much of their Iskandian uniforms as they could without drawing attention to exposed bits, Rysha felt vulnerable walking into a town full of people who had proven themselves insular at best, and hostile and murderous on occasion. There was no hiding the military rucksacks they carried, nor their Iskandian-issue rifles. The soulblades and *chapaharii* blades didn't mark them as Iskandians necessarily, but they certainly marked them as strangers. And possibly as strange.

And then there was the wagon Kaika was currently pulling, a blanket tucked over the contents. In the busy harbor city, it was surely only a matter of time before someone attempted to sneak close and look under it to see if there was anything worth stealing.

Or perhaps not. Even though the city was crowded, with people in loose clothing and sandals filling the streets and dodging delivery bicycles, nobody came close to their little group. Because of all their weapons? Some might find the rifles and swords intimidating, but Rysha, Trip, and Kaika passed numerous other people with firearms and swords. Weapons seemed more common here than not. Rysha gaped when they passed a pregnant woman carrying a baby in a sling and balancing a huge scimitar on her shoulder as she stalked down the street with a grocery sack.

When Rysha glanced at Trip to ask his thoughts on going straight to the docks or looking for Dreyak, she realized why people were giving them space. Even though he was walking normally in his black trousers and short-sleeved shirt, the uniform jacket removed, he exuded his dragonly aura, at least to some extent. It wasn't as noticeable as when he actively used his magic, but he definitely radiated power, something intangible but nonetheless obvious to those who looked at him. She was no longer surprised when their eyes met and she felt that charge of attraction, that hum as her body grew hyperaware of his. She caught herself staring at him, forgetting their mission and wondering where the nearest hotel was. But she kicked her libidinous side in the butt and reminded herself this wasn't the time for that. A thrum of agreement came from Dorfindral. She snorted, tempted to kick the sword in the butt too.

Trip must have noticed her gaze because he touched her hand and smiled, but he soon turned his attention back toward the route ahead, watching the busy street for danger.

"Do you want to go right down and try to find a ride off this continent?" Rysha asked, remembering her question. "Or should we look for Dreyak and Moe to see if those women from the outpost were taken back to their families or some other safe place?"

"I would be curious about that, but Kaika is in charge." Trip tilted his head back toward her.

"Something that wouldn't be apparent to outsiders since I'm carrying your baggage," Kaika said, not missing any of their conversation, though she was also watching their surroundings and the route ahead intently. Always alert, she didn't miss much.

"I refuse to feel bad about that since I have blisters from my turn pulling the wagon." Rysha lifted her hand to display them.

Trip had dragged the heavy wagon for even longer than she had, not able to apply his magic to make the task easier until they'd gotten out of the dead zone, something that hadn't happened until a mile away from the city. Kaika, who hadn't taken her turn at pulling until they reached the dirt and cobblestone streets, both easier to navigate than the cactus-filled desert terrain, had only been at it for ten minutes.

"Dreyak left us," Kaika said. "We're under no obligation to check up on him. Besides, thanks to all the things we had to build before leaving that cavern, it's been a week since we parted ways. I bet he found whatever he was searching for and is gone."

Rysha looked at Trip, wondering if he agreed. He hadn't said anything to confirm it, but she suspected he knew more about Dreyak's mission than anyone else did. Maybe even King Angulus.

"Likely," was all Trip said.

"And Moe Zirkander," Kaika said, "has a knack for getting out of tricky situations and maneuvering himself all over the world, even though he hates flying. I'm sure he's moved on too. Either that, or he's in some nearby cave, absorbed in whatever he was originally searching for. I do hope those girls all made it to safety, but unless we stumble across Moe or Dreyak, there's probably no way to confirm that. Let's just head down to the harbor and see if either of those two ships docked down there are heading our way." She waved toward the water, visible now and then between buildings, the calm surface reddened by the setting sun.

When the docks came into view, Rysha slowed down. They weren't crowded, and only a few people ambled through the area, so it should be easy to walk straight out to the ships, but an unsettling sight made her stop.

Two large posts rose up to either side of the walkway leading onto the metal docks. The posts were made from wood, some of the only wood she'd seen here, and a muscular man was tied—or staked—to one of them. She could only see the person from the side, but knew he wasn't moving, and probably hadn't moved for some time.

The odds suggested it wasn't anyone they knew, but a feeling of dread crept into Rysha's stomach.

Trip stopped. "Hells," he whispered.

Rysha glanced at him.

"Dreyak," he said.

"Is he...?"

"Dead."

"Keep walking," Kaika said quietly, coming up behind them. "There are eyes out here. A few people have noted our passing with more interest than it should have deserved."

Trip turned onto the waterfront street leading to the docks—and the posts. Rysha didn't want to look as more of Dreyak's body came into view, but she couldn't help but notice his chest was bare and someone had carved words into the flesh.

"What's that say, Ravenwood?" Kaika asked. "It's not the king's tongue."

Rysha would have preferred not to use her linguistics background for deciphering languages carved into people's bodies, but she made herself look long enough to read the two words. "Spy. And witch."

"Guess that answers what I was wondering earlier," Trip muttered.

"Dreyak's location?"

"How commonplace magic is here and if sorcerers are shunned." Trip stopped a few feet onto the docks and looked out toward the water. "I did also wonder if Dreyak had completed his mission."

"It looks like he was killed recently, doesn't it?" Rysha wasn't an expert on how long it took bodies to decompose, but no scavenger birds had been by to peck at the flesh yet—thank the gods. She wagered he'd been killed the night before or even that morning and strung up that day.

"Keep walking," Kaika repeated. "We shouldn't be seen staring at the body. I don't know *what* his mission was, but we don't need the locals thinking we were a part of it."

Trip didn't move. He gazed out at the calm water, as if he sought answers in it.

"Let's check with the captains of those ships to see if they're taking passengers." Kaika moved to pull the wagon past Trip if she needed to, but she frowned at him as she did, and added, "*Captain*," as if to remind him of his rank and that he was supposed to obey orders.

"Go see if they're sailing tomorrow, ma'am," Trip said. "I need to—I'm staying here for the night so I can sneak out here after dark. I'm not going to leave his body strung up for the seagulls to peck away at."

"And do *what* with it?" Kaika asked, sounding exasperated as she surveyed the area around them again, squinting at anyone watching them with too much interest.

"Have a funeral, put his body to rest. And then find out…" Trip opened his hand, then closed it in a fist. "Why and how he was caught and killed. He was too good to simply chance upon criminals or police officers and be shot. And, if I can, I'll find out for him what he came to learn."

Rysha started to ask what that was, but Kaika gripped Trip's shoulder.

"Listen, it's not wrong that you want to help a fallen comrade, even if he was an ass of a comrade most of the time, but you *have* a mission." She tilted her head toward the wagon.

"Yes. Now I have two."

When Trip turned his determined gaze on Kaika, Rysha saw the sorcerer, not the humble and obedient lower-ranking officer. He wasn't exuding power or attempting to manipulate Kaika, at least Rysha didn't think so, but he *was* letting them know he wouldn't be swayed in this.

"I'll stay with you and help," Rysha said, not that there had been a question. She just hoped Kaika wouldn't be stubborn about this and insist on going back on her own, on reporting that they'd deliberately disobeyed orders and gone AWOL.

"Fine," Kaika growled. "*One* night. I doubt anyone is sailing out this late in the day, anyway. This doesn't look like the kind of city where captains take besotted couples out on sunset cruises."

Rysha smiled, vaguely aware that there were outfits in the capital that did that.

"Watch the wagon," Kaika told Rysha, then headed down the docks.

"Yes, ma'am," Rysha said.

Kaika gave her a flat look over her shoulder, probably finding the polite obedience hypocritical after Rysha had implied she would stay with Trip, no matter what orders she was given.

"We might get in trouble when we get back," she murmured to Trip.

Rysha wasn't sure what Kaika would report. Blazer would definitely have written them up for insubordination. Rysha liked to think she had a closer relationship with Kaika and that she would be more lenient. But she wouldn't place money on that. For all her silly talk about sex and having fun, Kaika always did her job, and she did it well.

"I know." Trip shrugged. "But even if we didn't owe anything to Dreyak for helping us with the portal and the pirates, it would be good to investigate this. We—Iskandia—might stand to get in a different kind of trouble if the word gets out that we were the ones to fly Dreyak over here, that he was last seen in our company, and now he's dead."

"Trouble with whom?"

"Prince Varlok and his family."

"The current ruler of Cofahre? What is—was—Dreyak to him?"

"Unless I miss my guess, a little brother."

Rysha stared at him. "I know the names of all of Emperor Salatak's legitimate heirs. There are eight males, including Varlok, the oldest."

Trip nodded. "None of whom are known to have dragon blood, right?"

"Right," she said, wondering how he'd known. The names of the imperial family were common knowledge to those who paid attention, but dragon-blood status wasn't something newspapers printed.

"Dreyak did have some dragon blood, so I assume he had a different mother. That would make him a half-brother then. But someone who worked for the throne and was trained to protect its interests. He was here because of those interests and the role Iskandia played in them."

Rysha removed her spectacles to clean some of the travel grit off them and to contemplate this new information. "Something to do with the exile of Salatak?"

Trip nodded.

"So, in staying to investigate, to help Cofahre, do we risk betraying our own people?" This wasn't why she had agreed to stay with Trip.

"I just want to find out what happened to him. It may matter someday."

Rysha looked at the covered wagon again and couldn't help but worry what might happen if they stayed here, but she leaned against his arm to show her support. Or maybe she wanted his support. She wasn't sure.

Kaika walked back toward them, scowling.

"Nobody leaving in the morning?" Rysha asked when she was close enough.

"Nobody going toward Iskandia *or* willing to take us. I could have worked on the latter problem—" Kaika pounded a fist into her open palm, "—but there wasn't much point when the ships weren't bound for anywhere convenient to home."

"We'll find a way back," Trip said. "Once we've dealt with this." He didn't look back at Dreyak's poor dead body, but he tilted his head in that direction.

"You're building an airship if nobody wants to give us a ride, right?" Kaika asked.

"It *is* likely I could find the necessary materials here." A smile ghosted across Trip's somber face as he looked toward one ship's sails.

Rysha couldn't imagine the city's authorities standing by as a sorcerer magicked an airship together at their docks, but she kept the thought to herself. If they had to build their own transportation, that would give them time to investigate Dreyak's death. Even though she worried about all the babies they now had the obligation to care for, she supposed that if they had stayed in those stasis chambers for thousands of years, they could survive another week.

THE END

Made in the USA
Monee, IL
28 December 2020